Blood Beyond Darkness

USA TODAY BESTSELLING AUTHOR
STACEY MARIE BROWN

Blood Beyond Darkness, Copyright © 2014 Stacey Marie Brown
All rights reserved.
ISBN: 978-1-956600-48-3
Cover Design by Jay Aheer, www.simplydefinedart.com
Layout by www.formatting4U.com
Edited by Chase Nottingham, www.chaseediting.com

This is a work of fiction. Any references to historical events, real people, or real locales are used fictitiously. Other names, characters, places and incidents are the product of the author's imagination and her crazy friends. Any resemblance to actual events, locales or persons, living or dead, is entirely coincidental.

This book is licensed for your personal enjoyment only. It cannot be re-sold, reproduced, scanned or distributed in any manner whatsoever without written permission from the author.

ALSO BY STACEY MARIE BROWN

Paranormal Romance

Darkness Series
Darkness of Light (#1)
Fire in the Darkness (#2)
Beast in the Darkness (An Elighan Dragen Novelette)
Dwellers of Darkness (#3)
Blood Beyond Darkness (#4)
West (#5)

Collector Series
City in Embers (#1)
The Barrier Between (#2)
Across the Divide (#3)
From Burning Ashes (#4)

Lightness Saga
The Crown of Light (#1)
Lightness Falling (#2)
The Fall of the King (#3)
Rise from the Embers (#4)

Savage Lands Series
Savage Lands (#1)
Wild Lands (#2)
Dead Lands (#3)
Bad Lands (#4)
Blood Lands (#5)
Shadow Lands (#6)
Land of Ashes (#7)
Land of Monsters (#8)

A Winterland Tale
Descending into Madness (#1)
Ascending from Madness (#2)
Beauty in Her Madness (#3)
Beast in His Madness (#4)

10 YEAR ANNIVERSARY!

To Eli and Ember for creating a world that has led me on a 10-year-journey, which I only see growing. You two will always be my first muses.

And most of all to the readers, thank you for loving this world, for allowing me to keep telling you stories within this crazy world. If you have just found me or have been with me since the beginning, you are so deeply appreciated.

Happy 10th Birthday DOL…and here's to many more.

CHAPTER ONE

Blood.

Sticky and gooey.

It coated our faces and hands, Eli's and mine, like thick, acrylic paint. Loose strands of my hair stuck to the blood in patches as the light breeze of the Otherworld tickled over my skin, trying to tug my ponytail loose. My mane of jet-black hair with its red streaks hung down the side of my neck, protecting the six-inch pixie who hid there. Walking through the deep greens and glimmering magic of the Otherworld's forest, I felt the enchantment of the world knocking at the edges of my skin, although it could not break past the heavy iron cuffs pinning my arms in front of me.

Even though I had only been here once before, the Otherworld felt strangely like an old friend welcoming me home. In a way it was home. I was born here, where I should have been raised. But nothing in my life had gone according to plan. The fact that Queen Aneira caught me again and was taking me to her dungeon before she killed me bore true testimony of this. Only a few months had passed since she last captured me when I came to save my family and friends. So much had happened since then.

Leaves and gravel crunched underfoot in repetitive cadence while Aneira floated gracefully over the pathway. She gave little heed to the beauty around her. The forest's response to the Queen was to lean away. Branches recoiled and trees shriveled, feeling the twisted and cruel power of the woman who walked several yards in front of me. She should have been nature's champion. Instead, she burned and killed with little thought. If she noticed her effect on the natural world, it did not show.

My boots lurched forward as the guard shoved me. My feet scrambled underneath my body while I tried to stay upright. I cast him a dirty look over my shoulder. The guard's sardonic smile taunted me, and he gave me another push and laughed. I bit hard on my lip, and the coppery taste of blood slithered down my throat. The last time I made a comment he had tripped me, and my face had met a gravely fate.

Being prisoners of the Queen was not how our time in Greece should have ended. We should be back in the small town of Kalambaka, celebrating. After months of searching, we had located the Sword of Light—the only weapon able to kill Aneira, the Seelie Queen, and end her rule. Now this exact sword was in her possession, given to her by Josh, her First Knight, and a former friend of mine I had blindly trusted. Kennedy had been kidnapped by Lorcan, who used the Strighoul to distract us. There was also a good chance Lars was dead. My neck was trying to mend itself from where Drauk, leader of the Strighoul, had ripped into it, before I cut his head off. My bones were bruised from the massive fall Josh and I had in the cavern. And to top it off, Eli, my mom, and I had been captured by the Queen and would most likely be dead soon. Most of all, my heart was still trying to recover from almost losing Eli. All around not a great day. The only positive thing was the rest of my friends were safe and hopefully headed back to the states.

"Hurry up." A guard shoved Eli, who stumbled forward. A growl ripped from Eli's throat, and his eyes flashed red. He quickly checked himself. Normally, he could tear through half these guards before they could pull out a weapon. Not today.

I was still useless. Iron did that to Fairies—our main weakness. I was only half Fay and my Demon and Dark Dweller portions would eventually increase my tolerance to the metal. When I first learned about the Otherworld, Cole had described Fay as a shortened word for Fairy—the elite strain who ruled the Otherworld. Fae was a general term for all Otherworld species. Only Fairies, the Fay, had a weakness to iron although each species of Fae had its own flaw. Today my gradual resistance to the metal wasn't happening fast enough. My body remained too traumatized from all it had gone through back in Greece.

My mother didn't seem to have the strength to fight against Aneira or the soldiers either. And Eli was definitely not at his strongest. Only a half hour earlier, he had been dead—his throat slit by the Queen in front of me. It had been a test from Aneira to see if my powers could push through the iron cuffs. They had, and now she knew I would eventually become resistant to the metal. She wanted the immunity for herself. Aneira wanted anything she didn't possess.

Even though we had not planned on getting captured, we were being taken to the place where my step-dad, Mark, my best-friend, Ryan, and West were being held, along with the Sword of Light, Nuada's Sword. It wasn't completely a bad thing. Right?

Okay, it *was* completely a bad thing, but I had to think a thread of a silver lining hid in this mess somewhere.

Eli's shoulder bumped into me, causing Cal to stir under my hair. I looked at Eli. He wore one of the guard's robes, but I knew underneath it his naked body was coated with blood and wounds matching his face. Blood oozed into the scars lining his head, and his brown hair was streaked with red. He would heal, but he remained weak from the fight with the Strighoul and from bleeding to death. Not *almost* bleeding to death. Fully dead. My powers and resolve were the reason he walked next to me now.

Only a short time ago I had told him I loved him. His response to me was: *"You shouldn't. Don't love me. I'm not worth it."* Not the reply I had been hoping for, especially as I watched him die in front of me.

You okay? his green eyes asked.

Peachy. You? my eyes said back to his. Since the day we met, we possessed this strange way of communicating. I couldn't hear his thoughts. His words appeared in my mind, as though on a computer screen.

Surprised you're not jealous. The guard is riding my ass so close I'm thinking he just made me his bitch.

A choked guffaw came up my throat. Even in this situation, Eli could make me laugh. *Jealous? Hell, I already got you guys t-shirts saying 'Bitch' and 'Master Bitch.'*

Eli paused, shaking his head, and received another violent shove. His eyes flashed as his neck and shoulders tightened.

Breathe, Eli. We will get out of this. Not sure if I believed it, but I wanted to.

Twenty-two years ago, the Queen exiled the Dark Dwellers from the Otherworld, preventing them from using the Otherworld doors. Only the Queen or a Druid possessed the power to break the ban. Eli's recent entry into the Otherworld had not been smooth. Aneira's mind hadn't been on Eli's access, so when the soldier pushed him forward, Eli slammed face-first into the opening. The guard rammed into him, and both ended with bloody noses.

With a simple wave of Aneira's hand and an incantation, Eli fell through the veil. The banishment lifted. His eyes widened as he took in his old homeland. He revealed little emotion through his expression, but because his blood flowed in me after saving his life, I could feel what he felt: excitement, confusion, and trepidation as he took in every detail. He was finally home again, something he had wanted for a long time. Would it live up to what he remembered?

My mother was with us after she "volunteered" for the

journey to the Queen's dungeons. I glanced back at my mom. She walked several yards behind us. Strands of her auburn hair stuck out from the single braid tumbling down her back. She kept her head forward, her chin up. She had yet to look at me, probably knowing she wouldn't get anything but a "what the crap were you thinking" look from me.

To say our relationship had been strained since my mom's reappearance in my life would be a slight understatement. I hated the tension. We used to be so close, but too many things had happened since her "murder." Too much pain. She had kept so many secrets from me. Though, she *had* let Aneira capture her, many years ago, to keep me safe. Her "murder" was arranged to cover up her disappearance. She had not been involved in the details of her demise and had been shocked when I told her I found her body. I could not blame her, but it didn't mean I was all right with it. True or not, her brutal slaughter had tunneled scars deep into my psyche. There were years of medications, therapy, and a stint at a psychotic ward, though her death wasn't the only thing to produce my mental break. The moment she was no longer around, I began to hear voices and see creatures, beasts, and things you only read about in fairytales. My bus drivers and math teachers had dissolved into trolls and goblins.

Doctors convinced Mark I created these worlds to escape my reality. Little did they know the fairytales *were* my reality, *not* my escape.

The guard pushed me onto the bridge bringing me back to the present problems. A gust of wind blew through the strands of my hair, wrapping them in knots around each other. Far below indigo water rushed under foot, sweeping against the rocks as it gushed into the deep water of the lake on the far side of the castle. A rich forest surrounded the fortress, softening the forbidding presence. The deep green of the trees only highlighted the glistening sapphire color of the lake.

We marched across the span to the where the castle stood.

My neck bent back to get a full view. The breathtaking and daunting stone palace reached into the sky. A man in front shouted, and the football field sized gates broke free of their hold, creaking as they spanned their wings open and allowed us to enter.

When I stepped onto the fortress property, my anxiety accelerated higher and higher until it crested, banging against my ribs. Dread of the future sat heavy in my heart. Would I be able to see Mark and Ryan? How could I get West free? Out of the three, he was someone I could possibly help.

An ill-formed and crazy idea shaped in my mind. To be fair, those were usually my only kind of ideas.

I mumbled so low the guard behind us couldn't hear, "Cal, I need you to go to the dungeon. There is a raven there named Grimmel. Tell him *Fire* sent you to help free the *Dark Knight*."

Eli's head quirked to the side. I could feel the question in his movement.

West. I looked directly at Eli. Our group advanced across the cobblestone, nearing the actual entrance of the castle.

Eli gave a slight nod. I had met Grimmel through one of my dreamwalks. Ravens were known dream guides and could see and interact with people who were not actual present. He lived in the dungeon where West was being held captive.

"You want me to go to the dungeon? Again? Shouldn't I wait for you?" Cal's tone sounded apprehensive. "I mean, it's not like you won't be there soon enough."

I flicked my ponytail, the ends of my hair whipping at his face.

"All right. All right." He grabbed onto my hair, pulling himself up. "You are gonna have to distract Tweedle-dickhead and his cronies behind us so I can fly off."

"On it." I let my foot skim the ground catching it on the flagstone. With a stumble, I crashed into Eli. He could have easily taken my weight, but he let himself stagger and fall into an entry side door. With a bang it broke open, and he toppled into the tight space. The soldiers behind me sprang immediately into action. While the guards fussed over getting Eli up and back on the right course, Cal darted for the roof beam unnoticed. I breathed a sigh of relief.

"Get back on your feet." Eli's sentry gripped the stock of his rifle tighter.

"The way you've been shadowing my ass, I thought you'd prefer me down on all fours." Eli winked at the man. My smile only grew wider as the officer floundered and sputtered at Eli's insinuation.

"I-I don't trust Dark Dwellers." The guard huffed. "Now get up." Dark Dwellers made most Fae want to pee their pants.

With a cocky smile, Eli stood and brushed himself off, the robe opening slightly. He took extra care in a certain area. My shackles clinked as I put my hands to my face, shaking my head. Eli was good at unsettling others no matter what tactic he used. He enjoyed playing with people, and most of the time, I also enjoyed it, even when the person was me. He had a way of taunting me which was torturous and euphoric at the same time.

"What is the hold up?" Aneira's silky voice slid along the grand entrance hall.

The guard pushed Eli forward. "I apologize, my lady."

"Is this one giving you trouble?" She slinked through the group and approached Eli, sliding her hand up his cheek. Though Eli noticeably flinched, she drew up on her toes and kissed the corner of his mouth. "He is an unruly one." Her voice sounded like a purr.

Drops of blood slipped down my throat, my teeth digging deep into my bottom lip.

"I think we should celebrate." Aneira took a few steps back. Her gaze glided over Eli's barely covered form. "You and I will have a private party later."

A growl gurgled from the depths of my stomach as I took a step toward her. Her soldiers were on me before I could take another.

"Oh, your dearest doesn't like my idea." The Queen kept her focus on Eli. "I have no doubt you have heard this before, but I am surprised at you, Elighan. A Dae? I expected better. To fall for the precise thing who killed your entire family?"

He kept his face so still he didn't seem to be breathing.

"Well, I do not doubt after tonight both of you will see the error in your choice of lover." She whirled and headed for the doors in front of us. "For now, I feel the need for festivities."

Aneira waved her hand and a gust of wind blew through the corridor, bursting the doors open in front of us. Her main power was controlling air, although this had never been good enough for her. She had been courting my powers of fire, mind, and earth since the day she found out I still lived. She also wanted the added bonus of my Dark Dweller blood, which would eventually make her resistant to iron.

Guards and the Queen's court stood in a line on either side of the doors waiting for their monarch to enter. They stood rigidly as we passed. Not one head stirred, but many eyes followed Eli and me with disgust and fear. I sensed the prickly tendrils of Eli's trepidation, mingled with an oily revulsion in my own stomach. The Queen made sure Fae learned to hate Daes by classifying us as abominations with our half Fay, half Demon parentage. She had killed thousands of Daes at birth and hunted down any who escaped. Her fear of our power, a prophecy, and because we could not be glamoured by her fueled her hate-propaganda toward my kind.

The Queen could only be killed with one weapon, the Sword of Nuada, the Sword of Light. The prophecy stated a Dae would kill her with the sword and become Queen. Everyone was convinced the Dae was me. As much I would love to deny these facts, I believed it, too. I had held a shred of doubt until Kennedy revealed a hidden map on my back—a map showing where the sword was concealed. This discovery blew my last hope out of the water. Now the sword I should use to kill Aneira remained in her hands. And if I used it against her, Eli would die. That had been our deal. She had slashed his throat with a Fae-welded weapon, and the only way I could save him was to make the vow. If I touched the sword, death would reclaim its victim.

Aneira sauntered into the massive throne room, her flaming red hair drifting behind. The fire in the bulbs lining the walls reflected off her gleaming hair in a ripple of gold's, rubies, and crimsons. She stretched out her arms, her presence filling the enormous space.

"We will have a feast," Aneira called, her violet eyes glistening in the fire light. Her servants moved in response and headed for the kitchen area. "And music." Other servants dashed off at her request. I expected some version of Renaissance of music with flutes and guitars made of wood while women in wench outfits served beer. Instead, music filtered from the rafters. I craned my head back and squinted. Lined across the beams were speakers. The music wasn't from Earth, but it wasn't twinkly flute music either. It sounded modern, like a mix of rock, blues, and Celtic.

These were modern Fairies. Nothing like the stereotypes humans knew from years of ancient fairytales. The Fairies blended old and new in beautiful harmony—an old castle fitted with cutting-edge gadgets and modern designs. Even Aneira was not the normal idea of a Queen. Yes, she had long hair usually braided into extremely intricate designs or left hanging down her back, but she dressed sleek, sexy, and contemporary. Today she wore supple black leather pants, but I had also seen her in a backless, sheer dress, which would make any designer in Paris weep at its beauty.

Tables and chairs seemed to pop out of nowhere as servants quickly did her bidding and prepared the room for her pleasure. I had no idea what she was up to, but if she hadn't locked us in the dungeon yet, we were here for a reason. The thought terrified me.

The guards moved the three of us deeper into the Great

Hall. The name of the hall fit perfectly. Great in length, height, and grand in beauty. Windows filled an entire side of the room, overlooking the brilliant blue lake below and snowcapped mountains in the distance. Chandeliers hung along the middle, each draped with millions of raw silk strands. The room blazed with a bewitching glow. At each end of the room, a metal plate floated and held a brilliant fire, which flowed through the chamber, warming the large hall.

Aneira spun to face me, then she looked passed my shoulder. "Oh, good. Josh, my dear, you are here. Why don't you retrieve our other guests? I am sure they would like to join our festivities."

Out of the corner of my eye, I watched Josh bow and retreat through the doors. The pain of his duplicity remained a raw, open wound across my heart. Deep, burning anger thundered through me. *How could I be so stupid? How could I not see it?* I didn't trust most people, but once I considered someone a friend, I went blind. So many people told me my friends and family were my weakness, and Josh proved the theory to be true. After all the lies and deceit, how could I still continue to trust and believe in the ones dearest to me when so many broke off another chunk of my heart? I should have seen his betrayal coming. Deep down, maybe I had. Strangely, there was still a piece of my soul which rejected Josh deceiving me. He had been my friend, but he had turned on me, and I couldn't seem to face it.

Servants carried trays of food, filling the space with the rich smells of bread and roasted meat. My stomach rumbled at the thought of protein. The Dark Dweller part of me preferred raw meat, but I was starving, and it felt like days since I had eaten. Eli fidgeted next to me, his tongue licking at his lips. Dark Dwellers were complicated and basic at the same time. Food and sex were their top primal needs, but nothing in the Fae world was simple. Eli was by far the most complex person I ever met.

A servant brought Aneira a bowl of water and a cloth. She snatched it and marched to Eli, her hips swaying. "We must get you cleaned up for the party, Elighan." She dipped the rag into the water and reached to his face, wiping the dirt and blood off. It was strangely tender, except for a glint in her gaze as she unabashedly looked him over.

Eli hissed through his teeth as she touched an open wound.

"There are some bodily fluids from an imp in here." She wet the fabric again. "Useless things, except when turned into a healing remedy." She didn't have high regard for sub-fae like imps, pixies, or brownies. They still ranked way above Daes, though.

The Queen's hand moved down and opened Eli's robe, displaying his physique. She rubbed at his chest, moving lower with every stroke. Eli's muscles tightened, straining against his skin as he stepped back. Another warning growl burst from my mouth.

"It is so adorable. She thinks her little yap is scaring me." Aneira looked over her shoulder at me. "What are you going to do to stop me, Ember? You think your pathetic growl of possession is going to prevent me from touching him here?" Her hand went to his crotch. Eli grabbed her wrist before her fingers could make contact, and he shoved it away. Aneira peeked through her lashes with a coy pout. "You can get rough with me later."

Fire burned in my gut and boiled out. Glass bulbs broke along the wall, and fire scorched the stone, touching the ceiling. Energy crowded around her as my mind shoved her away from Eli. She staggered, dropping the bowl and cloth, before catching herself. A few servants close to her stumbled to the ground, not prepared for the energy I sent their way.

"Impressive. And to think you can will it through iron. What power you must hold when you are unleashed." Her eyes glittered. "Put another set of irons on her. I feel she might get unruly soon, and I would hate to have to kill her before I get what I want."

A guardsman, already gloved, pulled out another set from a wooden box on the table.

"No-no-no." I chanted, trying to back away. These cuffs were thicker and sturdier than any I had seen before. The blond-haired, blue-eyed Fay snapped the new shackles next to the other set. My knees hit the floor with a thud, pain filled my chest, and an intense groan came out of my mouth.

"My goodness, child. It's like I am ripping your soul from your body." Aneira rubbed at her temple.

I glowered at her. She knew exactly what she was doing. Before these new shackles were placed on me, my powers had been growing stronger, and it wouldn't have been long before I tossed her through the large bay windows to the lake below.

"Get her up." Aneira motioned for the guards to lift me. Several men had to hold my entire weight as I couldn't get my legs to stop shaking long enough to stand.

Josh stepped into the chamber and dipped his head in respect. "Your majesty, I have returned with your guests." He was now dressed as the First Knight. Fitted black leather pants covered his thin legs. The upper half of his body had changed from the boy I met at Silverwood, causing him to appear disproportionate. The black, long-sleeved shirt with the Queen's insignia fit snug on his broadening shoulders and muscular arms. His mop of curly sandy-blond hair was slicked back away from his face.

She turned to him, clasping her hands. "Wonderful. Now we can eat. You all must be famished."

Two people stood behind Josh. My lungs stopped pumping air as I took them in. I now knew what Aneira planned to do. Terror licked through me, like a hot flame.

Oh, please, no...

TWO

"No!" I shouted as I pushed forward, taking my guards with me. They quickly yanked me back, stopping my pursuit, which would lead to all of us planting our faces on the floor.

"Ember?" Mark's blue eyes widened as he took in my disheveled state. Relief and happiness filled his expression.

"Ember!" Ryan called out. Both of them took steps in my direction, but the guards grasped their arms and pulled them back.

I couldn't take my gaze off them. My arms and heart ached to run and hug both men.

"Are you all right?" Mark could have a leg cut off but would still ask if you were okay.

My throat closed, and all I could do was nod.

Aneira stepped around me. "I love family reunions. Let us make it even more extraordinary. I am sure, Mr. Hill, you never thought you would get to see your dead wife again," Aneira declared to Mark as she motioned to the guards holding the person concealed behind me.

Mark's disbelief was tangible. Every emotion rolled over his face like a pinwheel. "Lily?" he whispered harshly.

"Yes. It's me." Mom trembled, tears filling her eyes.

"No! This can't be possible." He shook his head like he was trying to clear his sight and mind of the obvious delusion.

Not too long ago, I had gone through the same thing. She

had allegedly been murdered when I was twelve. Mark had seen the dead body as the coroner took it away. When you are sure something is true and then find out it isn't, it's hard to shift your mindset.

"Catch up, Mr. Hill. I do not have time for your tiny human brain to comprehend the truth. Your wife lied to you from the moment she met you, dragging you into a world you should have never been part of. She even let you love this thing," pointing to me, "making you feel you were the father of a human girl. In fact, she is not human in any way. She's nothing but a Demon, a disgusting, filthy Dae."

Mom rolled her shoulders back. "Don't forget. She is also part Fay, Aneira, you uppity bitch."

Aneira whipped around and struck my mother's face. Automatically, both Mark and I moved toward her. We didn't get far.

"You should learn to silence your mouth, Lily. It always got you into trouble. You were always impulsive and stupid. This time there is no getting out of the mess you created." Aneira grabbed my mother's head, jerking Lily to look at her. Then, like a curtain pulled closed, Aneira's twisted features evened out, a forced smile returning to her mouth. "But I get ahead of myself. Everything in time, and right now I say we eat." Aneira spun to Mark and Ryan. "Guests first." The soldiers pushed Mark and Ryan to the table, forcing them to sit.

"I sense one of you has eaten Fae food." Aneira glided to Ryan, brushing his cheek with her knuckles. "You will be a great servant in my home, or maybe a jester. Your round, chubby body already humors me." She then moved behind Mark. "But you. You will be fun."

Mom looked wildly back and forth between the Queen and Mark, understanding dawning on her. "Aneira, please don't do this."

"Do you not want your husband to finally be truly a part of our world, Lily? If you do not, then you should have let him be.

Left the human to his own kind."

Mom's jaw tightened, as though fighting back the words she really wanted to say to Aneira.

"Your taste in liking these humans doesn't surprise me, with your upbringing. Though I thought your time here in the castle would have instilled some refinement in you." Aneira turned her attention back to the guests at the table. "Now, eat, boys."

Mark sat straight, his face defiant. "No."

Aneira's hands gripped the chair before her head fell back, letting out a hearty laugh. "Your bold disobedience is amusing, Mr. Hill. I think you know by now my asking was only to be well-mannered." She leaned across his chair and rubbed his arm, her tone growing sharp. "Eat."

Mark's eyes glazed over and picked up a piece of bread, placing it on his tongue.

"No!" I bellowed, fighting against the hands holding me back. Mom struggled next to me; a cry erupted from her chest.

Mark robotically chewed and swallowed. My legs went limp. All we had worked for to get him out disappeared with one bite. Now, like Ryan, he could never leave the Otherworld realm.

Aneira's smile lit up the room and then twisted with vengeance. "Now it is time for dessert and fireworks."

Aneira strode across the chamber to a wall covered with antique mirrors. They were set across from the bay of windows and reflected the green mountainous landscape and deep blue lake. The images in the glass transformed the wall into a work of art.

She beckoned her men to draw me forward. My boots dragged across the wood floor as they brought me to her. Trepidation fluttered in my lungs. My anxiety amplified with every step. Even double cuffed I could feel my abilities pushing up, rolling around my chest like a dust cloud.

"I suppose I should wait for the fireworks until after

dessert, but I cannot risk keeping you submissive and controlling your powers." It was a struggle for me to keep my head up, but I latched on to her every nuance. "You were right in thinking I might not be able to handle a blood exchange with you. Fae are not meant to mix with other species. Nevertheless, your very existence shatters this theory. Daes have power no ordinary Fae should have. How does something like you have greater powers than a Queen?"

The Queen was formidable, but there were a lot of Fae who were equal to her if not more powerful. Her real power existed in her ability to control others through glamour and fear. If you didn't submit, she would have her soldiers kill you. Simple and effective. There were many dictators on Earth who had followed the same strategy. And exactly like them, she wanted total control, and I threatened it all.

"My spies have found another way of procuring your powers without transferring blood. And you know who I have to thank for it?" She twisted to face me. "You. I've discovered your magic can transfer abilities."

"What? What are you talking about?" I coerced the words out of my mouth.

"I would rather show you." She nodded, and someone stepped around me, advancing to the Queen. A jolt of terror clenched my heart.

Asim.

Asim was an amplifier. Whatever he touched would heighten to levels able to kill you. He had contributed to my destruction of Seattle and had helped Aneira level other cities afterward. He was a huge reason why thousands died at my hand in Seattle. The ghosts of the dead haunted my soul.

I could not let him touch me. Dread sucked at my lungs, shriveling them down to hollow raisin skins. My shoulders yanked and struggled against the hands which held me. Blood pumped loudly in my ears.

"Your majesty." Asim bowed. He was a beautiful boy with

Blood Beyond Darkness

dark, flawless skin and chocolate brown hair and eyes.

"Asim, you remember what we discussed. I desire it powerful, but we do not want to demolish the castle."

"Yes, your majesty." He bowed again and again, appearing terribly anxious. She did not need to glamour him. Asim's reverence of the Queen was her control over him.

"Two fingers should do it."

What did she plan to do? With one touch from Asim, I would demolish this room and everyone in it.

Asim stepped toward me, his hand outstretched.

I slunk back into the Fay behind me but moaned with the need to reach back out for Asim. Recalling the devastation I had caused was not my only worry. I couldn't deny the exhilaration I felt at the amount of magic he had pumped through me. The necessity and desire to take in more and more till there was nothing left of me brought equal parts euphoria and devastation. I had killed, destroyed, and hurt people. And, sadly, I had desired it because of the elation I received from the power. Sadly, like a junkie I still craved those feelings, the high. Would it be something I would always fight? I had heard the stories of Daes who had destroyed themselves because they couldn't fight the consuming need for more. Magic had killed them. The longing in me remained strong. If I wasn't careful, it would envelop me, killing me and everyone around me.

With every step Asim took, I leaned back further into my captor. When Asim reached my side, the guard let me drop to the floor, the weight of the irons taking me down. With his thick gloves still on, he stooped and unlocked my cuffs.

An instant. That was all the time I had to react after the iron dropped from my arms. My mind was not centered on anything except Aneira.

My magic slammed her back into the mirrors at the same time the room exploded with fire balls. Each flame broke through the glass encasing them and reached for anything in their grasp. Energy blasted from me, fear and anger stirring the flames higher. Aneira's body stayed locked against the wall, unable to move out of my force. My vision was directed on her, but I felt objects moving across the room behind me.

"You think you can *control* me." My voice came out cold and foreign. I felt the shift. I knew my eyes were black, the Demon in me taking charge. All emotion exited, leaving only a need for more power and the desire to control and destroy. It felt amazing to let go of all my fears and worries. It was liberating to not feel or care anymore.

From behind I heard someone call my name. I could not decipher if it were male or female, not that I cared. The only thing I wanted was to kill the thing in front of me. Aneira shouted at her men to seize me, but no one touched me as I moved forward. A chair zipped past my head, colliding with the wall. It splintered into pieces, crumbling to the floor.

"It is me you should fear, Aneira." My mouth moved, but the words did not feel like mine. Somewhere inside a voice begged me to stop before I lost all control. I shoved the tiny, insignificant part of me down deeper. People getting hurt no longer mattered to me.

Another wave of magic rolled out, and the floating fireplace against the far wall rose and burst into a burning rage. A pained scream tore through the room, pulling my focus off Aneira. My gaze snapped onto the person causing the disturbance.

A man lay on the ground, his arm and part of his face singed black. His skin crinkled, melting from the heat of the flame which hit him.

The Demon in me dissolved instantly, emotion filling the space like the sun. My stomach rolled around in bile, ready to be sick.

"Mark!" My legs took steps toward him.

"Grab her," Aneira's voice rung out. Dozens of fingers wrapped around my shoulders and arms, dragging me back.

"Let me go," I wailed. Mark was my only thought now.

I was not the only one fighting to get to Mark. Mom cried out for him, desperately wanting to reach him. Soldiers kneeled around Mark, sitting him up. His face twisted in pain. I did this. *I* hurt him. Whenever I used my power, I only ended up hurting innocent people or those I loved.

Aneira grabbed my face and pointed it straight into hers. "He will be fine. Having Fae food will help him heal. Although, he will always carry the scars of what you did." She gripped my face tighter. "This event only demonstrates you are not capable of handling your powers. For the safety of those around you, I will take them off your hands." Her fingers pulled away from my face, her nails leaving trails down my jaw.

"Now, Asim." Aneira motioned to the boy and stepped out of the way.

Asim placed his two fingers on my arm. Once again my senses tore from me. But it seemed different. Extreme. Probably like going from pot to heroine. The sensation earlier was minuscule compared to this high. I lost most of my sight and hearing, everything blurring into a faraway landscape. I was on a different plane, looking down. Magic boiled out, exuding from my pores. Nothing but absolute power and strength pitched through my core. Giddiness rocked my chest as the bliss took hold. All my sadness and fear lifted, unburdening my heavy soul and letting me fully breathe for the first time in months. No guilt, shame, or regret—only power and strength.

"Another finger," Aneira yelled and slunk behind me. *Hiding Aneira? You pathetic fairy witch.*

Another one of Asim's fingers met my skin.

Power exploded through me and crackled the air. Electricity in the atmosphere sparked, sending a bolt of light out from me. The beam reflected off the mirror, cracking it in a mosaic of pieces. It bounced and headed straight for me and shot through my stomach. Blinding pain shattered through me and expanded to every cell in my body. A scream ripped from my throat. I crashed to the floor. I heard another scream sounding far away, and it bounced off the walls, merging with mine. I was only partially aware of a body falling behind me. The tearing sensation in my body was too much. Pain drilled through me, gutting me.

I swam in and out of consciousness. Voices and people yelling brought me back before I fell into the darkness again. Through thick mud, I clawed my way back. I gasped for breath as my eyes popped open.

"My Queen, are you all right?" A man stood behind me, and several men huddled around the body next to me. Aneira stirred and woke up.

"Majesty?" Josh sat next to her, holding her head in his lap. His gaze darted over to mine, before returning to his lady.

It was brief, but I saw his eyes fill with fear and concern. He had no right to care if I was all right. He chose his side.

"Yes. Yes. I am awake." She stirred with annoyance. "Help me up." Three men fluttered around her, all trying to be the one to assist their monarch.

I sat up and took inventory. Electricity still crackled inside me but was slowly diminishing. That's when I felt it, or rather the absence of it, like someone had eradicated parts of my soul. I felt empty. Vacant. No words could truly describe it, but I knew without a doubt—my powers were gone. A panic descended on me. "What happened?" I looked up at Aneira. "What did you do?"

Aneira swayed a little, and Josh jumped to grab her. "I am fine." She swatted his hand away, then turned to me. "I told you, Ember, I learned how to transfer your powers to me without using blood."

Deep down I hadn't believed she could do it, especially using my own magic. I felt betrayed by my powers, like they had turned against me and willingly chose to go to her. Pushing my feet underneath me, I stood on shaky legs. Our similar heights made it easy to look directly into her violet-blue eyes.

Aneira stretched her arms out. "I now have the powers of a

Dae and a Dark Dweller as well as my own." She turned her hand toward the few lights along the wall, which had survived my wrath, and flicked her arm. At first nothing happened, and relief trickled into my chest. Maybe it didn't work. I didn't have my powers, but maybe she didn't have them either?

My gaze drifted below the lights. Mark leaned against the wall, standing, but the skin on his arm and cheek were red and raw. Our eyes connected, and mine filled instantly with tears. *I am so sorry.* I tried to express my regret to him. He shook his head, his eyes filled with love, his expression telling me he wasn't upset with me. How could he not be? It had been me, my powers, who had burned him. My magic had destroyed and hurt so many.

A sudden burst from the wall drew my attention away from Mark. The flames inside the bulbs surged and shattered the glass. The line of people along the wall ducked, using their arms to shelter themselves from the debris. An exhilarated giggle came from Aneira, and she ruptured every light down the line. "Oh, how enjoyable!"

I felt violated. She took pieces of me, my soul, who I was. Anger pumped into my veins with every heartbeat. "For someone who hates Daes and Dark Dwellers so much, you seem awfully pleased to have their abilities," I said.

The smile fell from her face. "You will be such a pleasure to kill."

A growl came from across the room.

"Tell your pet to behave, or I have a nice thick chain to shackle him with." She sneered, keeping her focus on me. "It is so nice knowing I have absolutely no use for you anymore." A cruel smile again twisted her lips. Energy slammed into me, picking me off my feet, and I bobbled as she tried to control her newfound strengths. With a jolt, I flew back, crashing against the wall. My head snapped with a crack, and I fell limply to the ground.

Eli wrenched from his capture's hold and ran to me.

My head pounded with a sharp ache. I had known fear before, but realizing I no longer had my capabilities sent a new level of terror through me. I felt helpless against her. Naked. Magic was part of who I had always been, even when I wasn't aware of it. My lids lowered; my body wanted to sleep.

"Stay with me, Brycin." Eli cupped my face, turning it to him. *Don't you give up on me.* His eyes said privately.

Aneira's silky laugh filled the hall. "Oh, young love. You guys are so delectable. I could eat you up." She tilted her head and looked at Eli. "We both know, Elighan, if she knew the full truth about you, she would not be so smitten. Shall we see?"

Eli twisted his body, standing to face her. I could not see his expression.

Aneira clasped her hands together and walked to him. "To top off my lovely party, I think it is time to serve the scrumptious dessert I planned for you, Ember." Her tone was patronizing, her smile too wide, too gleeful. Protectively, I pushed my back into the wall, using it and Eli as a brace to stand. Aneira glared at my mom. "It is the least I can do. You should know the full truth about Elighan and about your mother... your *real* mother."

Mom's expression blanched, but she shoved her chin in the air defiantly. "Do your worst Aneira. I am not afraid of you."

Aneira smiled sweetly. "You should be." Her head rounded back to me. "You think Ember will continue to love you after what I tell her?"

THREE

What did she mean by my real mother? My stomach sank, and Mom's flinching expression to the Queen's words sent a wave of cold dread skating around inside me.

Aneira moved toward my mom while watching me. "The person you trusted without question lied to you the most. How much I wish she was your real mother, but this *shifter* is nothing but a fraud."

My gaze went wildly from Aneira to my mom. "What is she talking about?"

"I was going to tell you the truth." Mom gulped, pain set deeply in her eyes. "I am so sorry." She choked, losing her voice.

My heart thumped in my chest. My head shook back and forth. "No..."

"I see Ember is a visual learner. Well, why don't you show her what you've been keeping from her, Lily?" The Queen's hand grabbed my mom's arm. Air rippled around her. Instantly, Mom's body shrank to the floor, her clothes falling off. In my mother's place stood a small red fox.

I gasped. I knew the fox; it was the same one who had come with Torin in our dreamscapes. My mother's orange and brown flecked eyes stared at me through the fox's, wide with worry. No wonder it had felt so familiar to me. Somewhere in me I had made the connection a long time ago: her bond with foxes, her trips north. But denial was stronger than any magic. It could blind you to what happened in front of your face. How many things had I overlooked, too afraid to recognize the truth?

My focus flew to Mark. He stood still, his face and body frozen with shock, confusion, and hurt.

Aneira took her arm away from the back of the fox's head. My mom's naked body slowly formed back, curling around her clothes.

She was a shifter. Not Fay.

I understood now why she had a sense of smell like the Dark Dwellers while it was not a Fay trait. Why iron didn't seem to bother her. It didn't affect shifters. Why she hadn't dreamscaped with me. Because she couldn't. So many incidences I ignored. The intense truth of her not being my mother flooded me, circling the rock forming in my middle.

"Did you never wonder why you looked nothing like her even after you learned Daes take on the qualities of both their parents?" Aneira placed her fingers below my mom's chin, turning it for me to look at her. "Half of your blood is from pure Fay, not from a shifter. You have blood that is not only noble but royal." Aneira ripped her fingers away. A deep-seated anger flushed around her words, but it wasn't her tone catching my attention.

"Royal?" I knew my mother had been noble, which was different from royal. Royal meant only one thing...

"Yes, Ember. You share my blood." She frowned at her declaration. "My baby sister, Aisling, was your true mother."

Aisling.

Oh, God. Once again my name turned out to be a clue to who I was. A cruel, twisted joke.

"So the relationship makes me your auntie. How happy I was to learn my only niece was a Dae." Her mocking laugh pealed through the castle.

My aunt? I was *related* to this bitch?

I looked at the woman on the floor. She was still my mom,

the only solid thing I had for most of my growing years. She had protected and loved me. Now I felt like I stood looking at a stranger. My reflexes wanted to fight against the soldiers who pinned her exposed body. I still wanted to protect her, but her betrayal was a vortex which might never reveal light again.

"Your real mother let herself get seduced by a Demon. Demons are good at that, especially Devlin. He used Aisling. He twisted her mind into believing he cared, but he only wanted to create a weapon against me. And he did. You."

Lars's stories in Greece clicked in my brain. He had been talking about Aisling, my biological mother. Everything he said contradicted Aneira's statement. Lars's version was that Aisling had been in love with Lars and Devlin, and both Demon brothers had loved her. My gut told me Aneira was lying. She knew the truth.

"Are you sure it wasn't *they* who were seduced?"

She got my meaning. Her lids constricted. She marched to me, her hand wrapping around my neck, her lips nearing my ear. "My sister was beautiful, smart, above them in every way, and she was killed because she lowered herself not only to one but two of them. And because she let you live." Now because I knew my mother was a royal Fay, the sister of the Queen, the reasons for Aneira's hatred made more sense. So many things made sense.

Her free hand wrapped around one of the red streaks in my hair. "You look so much like her. However, your yellow eye and your black hair is all a reminder of your true parentage. Every time I look at you, it makes me ill. You are a Demon and a disgusting cross-breed."

My first meeting with Aneira had caused her to step back in shock, like she had seen a ghost. In a way I guess she had. She had seen her dead sister looking back at her.

"Everyone loved her and were like moths to a flame. There wasn't a person who did not fall under her spell. Her magic was unequal. And you are the reason she is no longer here with me.

She chose you instead of me. The fact you are living instead of her is torture. I cannot wait to kill you, slowly and painfully." A crackle from the blazing lights indicated she was losing her temper. Another wave of fury careened through me. She was using *my* power. *My* magic.

She took a breath and stepped away. "Not only will I destroy Earth and everyone you love, I will tell you one more thing before you die." Her eager smile returned. "I want you to know the truth about your lover here." A wicked smile twisted her beautiful face as she pointed at Eli. "He was the one who killed her. He killed your mother."

I collapsed against the wall. "What?"

"Elighan helped murder Aisling. The man you let yourself lie with was there when she was slaughtered." The Queen moved back from me, her eyes hazily scrutinizing me. "I am sure she would have been so proud of your choice in men."

I looked at Eli. He wouldn't look at me.

My knees almost gave out as another truth hit me. The night Lorcan interrupted Eli and me, Lorcan told me they had killed my mother. I had first connected it to Lily's murder. I discovered her torn body. But when I found her alive in the Queen's dungeon, I chalked what he said up to Lorcan trying to annoy me. Now I know he had spoken the truth. It seemed Lorcan always spoke the truth, whether you wanted to believe it or not.

"Em—" Eli's sentence was cut off by one touch of Aneira's hand. His eyes glazed.

"Be quiet," Aneira directed at him. Eli's mouth clamped together, obeying. "You had plenty of time to tell her the truth. I think it is my turn now. Don't you agree?"

He nodded submissively and backed away from me. It was frightening how easily she could put someone under her spell. A thought came into my head. *Since I no longer have my powers, will she be able to glamour me?* I didn't even want to hint at it in case she hadn't considered the possibility yet.

The thought was pushed to the background when I gazed back at Eli. The deep pain of what he did hurt so much more than throwing myself down a ravine. Eli actually had helped assassinate my mother. The tattoo had not been lying. It had been trying to protect me. She had dreamscaped from beyond the grave, trying to warn me. It didn't matter if I had known her or not. She was my mother, and he had assisted in her murder.

"The Dark Dwellers wanted revenge against me. My poor sister was their way of getting back at me." Aneira patted Eli's arm, almost like she dared him to refute her claim.

Lorcan had stated they were hired to kill; they didn't do it out of revenge. They were appointed to kill a Fay who betrayed her people and her child who was an abomination. If she wanted retribution for her sister, then why wouldn't she have gone after Lorcan, the actual killer, instead of working with him? She wouldn't. Aneira was clearly lying.

"Oh, don't you play the martyr well? They may have helped kill her, but we both know you plotted her murder," I sneered.

Aneira moved so quickly I didn't see her till it was too late. Her hand cracked across my jaw. The strength of the hit crumpled me. My "aunt" followed me down to the floor, grabbing my throat. "How dare you make such a preposterous accusation? I would never have hurt my sister. I loved her." Then she whispered so no one else could hear, "You insufferable brat. You are the reason she is dead. You are to blame. She picked you instead of me. I had to kill her. She betrayed me. She betrayed our kind. Broke the law. I was the one who was wronged." Her words sounded frantic. She was slowly losing her composure. "You will soon be joining her. Finally." She rested, taking a moment as she stood, putting her pleasant Queen-facade in place.

"Now let us return to the festivities, shall we?" She took a step back, placed her hand on Eli, and looked toward me. Vindictiveness simmered in the touch. "Before I kill your lover,

I want you to know I will take my revenge for what his kind did. I will force him to pay. Over and over again."

My stomach knotted at her insinuation. A natural protectiveness for Eli filled me, and a snarl echoed from my throat. If anyone was going to hurt him, it was going to be me. I raised myself onto my feet. When I opened my mouth to respond, agony exploded around my jawbone. It felt like it was broken. But warmth already rolled up my spine as though my powers were at work, trying to heal my cracked jaw. *But, how? My abilities were gone.* That's when it hit me: I was still Dark Dweller. Eli's blood still boiled in my veins. I could feel them stir, sensing the vacant spot my old powers used to fill, and moving in. She hadn't taken the blood from my body, so she didn't receive the blood Eli gave me. The Dark Dweller was in my blood, not an element she could steal from me.

She thought she had the Dark Dweller traits as well as my Dae powers. *She didn't.*

The Queen shook her head in false pity. "Don't worry. I will let you watch me with Elighan for a bit before I kill you. I do not want you to feel left out." Fury hit me and twisted into pain as Eli looked off into space as though nothing were wrong. Her glamour still coated him.

Even if I remained part Dark Dweller, it didn't change anything. I could not defeat her with my partial abilities. Defeat swallowed me. My brain and heart were full of grief. Part of me wanted to lie back on the floor and ask Aneira to finish me off. She had won. She possessed the sword and my strength. Mark and Ryan could never leave the Otherworld, my mom was not my real mother, and the man I loved helped kill my biological mother.

My world and willpower were crumbling into pieces. The only thing keeping me on my feet was the sight of Mark and Ryan across the room, their terrified eyes looking at me with trust and belief. I needed to try and get them to safety. West remained below my feet still locked in the dungeon. I hoped Cal

Blood Beyond Darkness

had succeeded in getting him out since there wasn't much I could do for him right now. The last time I dreamwalked to see West, he could barely keep his head up. I had to believe he would find strength somewhere. If he didn't escape soon, he would die here with the rest of us.

Aneira had no reason to keep any of us alive anymore. She would resort to torture and slow death for the ones she felt had wronged her. For the others, hopefully it would be quick and painless.

A movement behind Ryan caught my attention. Deep in the shadows of the hallway stood Castien. He dressed in the Queen's guard outfit, but he worked for Lars as a spy. A determined expression settled on his pretty features. He had short, shiny black hair and the bright, unique blue eyes of the Fay. His mouth pressed in a thin line and his hand gripped his sword. Would he try and get Ryan out of here? By himself? What was he thinking?

At that moment the windows overlooking the lake shattered in an earsplitting spray of glass. The walls shook as pressure filled the room, wrenching us off our feet. My shoulder struck the ground as my body skittered across the floor. Screams boomed off the walls and mingled with the splintering sound of the breaking glass.

Wind blustered through the opening as five figures floated down, descending from the roof. Through the rainfall of debris, my eyes zeroed in on one humongous person. Rimmon. He jumped to the ground, shaking the room like a goliath. Rimmon being here meant one thing.

Lars.

His telekinetic powers allowed each of his group to hover off the ground. As he let go of his hold on them, they sprang to the floor ready for battle. I quickly recognized Alki, Koke, and Goran standing next to Lars. My heart soared, and I felt the first ray of hope.

The Queen's men scuttled into position in front of her,

some already charging the intruders. Clanging metal rang through the air as swords clashed together. Alki gave a battle cry sending a chill into my heart.

"Ember, come on!" Eli's hand circled my arm and tugged to get me moving. Once up, I searched the room to find my family. Bodies cluttered the space as warriors danced in battle. Blood sprayed and gurgled as Koke and Alki sliced through several soldiers at once, cutting their throats in wide arcs.

"Ember!" I heard Lars call. He moved to me. I wanted to run to him, but I couldn't leave any of my family behind.

Eli tugged on my arm, pulling me toward him.

"I need to get my family out first," I screamed at Eli, wiggling out of his hold. I turned, ignoring both he and Lars yelling at me.

"Ember. No!" Lars's voice came to me again. I ran with no idea where I was headed. A guard jumped in my path; his sword sliced inches from my face. Alki's training remained with me. Even without my powers or a sword, I could still fight.

With nothing holding it back, the Dark Dweller in me sprang to the surface. I pounced, giving him no time to gather his wits. We crashed to the floor, his body taking the brunt.

My family was threatened, and I was no longer shackled. I was pissed. *Kill. Kill. Kill.*

My teeth came down on his throat, ripping at the soft Fay skin. A scream gurgled from his frayed flesh. He had not been expecting me to be a challenge, especially when he thought I didn't have magic. A force collided into me, sending me rolling across the floor. Another guard had come at me, but a body hurtled into him. I looked up and saw Eli had sent the man flying, hitting a post. His neck snapped when his head hit the wall, and he crumpled in a heap. Eli snagged the guard underneath me. His neck snapped under his hold.

My kill! I growled and wiped absently at the blood trickling down my chin.

"Brycin. Stop." A dominant voice broke the kill-hold I had

on the man in his arms. It made me feel uneven and distant. Lost. My gaze went up to my Alpha, searching for direction. Once a Dark Dweller zeroed in on its prey, it was difficult to break the connection. Most people would never get in the middle unless they wanted to become another victim.

"Get her." He nodded behind me. Lily had reverted to a fox and was jumping and dodging the soldiers coming at her. All my senses charged back, crashing around in my brain.

"Mom," I screamed.

The fox's eyes brightened and turned toward me. With a yip, the small animal headed for me.

"Where are Mark and Ryan?" I asked Eli.

Eli shook his head. "They're not here."

"What? They were right there. Where did they go?"

"I don't know."

Another crashing sound took my attention. In the middle of the room, Aneira and Lars fought. Not with swords or with hands, but with their minds. Aneira now had the power of a Demon, and the new attribute was not something Lars had been expecting.

She flung Lars's body in the air, and he collided with the Queen's throne. Both he and the chair rolled off the platform to the ground.

"Lars!" My words were drowned in the noisy room.

He got up, his yellow eyes glowing. With every step he took, they darkened until they were black. Aneira went in the air and sailed back into the wall. He pinned her there, choking her.

"This is foreplay for me, Lars." She forced a smile.

His eyes narrowed on her.

A strangled noise came from Aneira's throat. "You are too late, Demon. I already have her powers." Overhead, flames surged from the broken bulbs, licking the tops of our heads. Lars flew off his feet toward the open windows.

"Lars," Alki called at the same time hands came around my waist, throwing me over a massive dark-skinned shoulder.

Rimmon bounded for the open window with me slung across his back.

"Wait... Eli! My mom!" I ineffectively pounded on Rimmon's back. An object suddenly leaped toward Rimmon and climbed onto his other shoulder. The fox curled its body close into his neck so it wouldn't fall. I let out a small breath of relief. I picked up my head to locate everyone else, but I had no time to latch onto anyone before Rimmon got to the window frame and jumped. His mammoth mitts held me and the fox against his shoulders. A scream locked in my throat as we tumbled into freefall. My stomach and head plunged with dread.

Out of the corner of my eye, a bird the size of a van swooped from the roof, diving below us.

"Hold on." Rimmon's grip held me tighter.

Oh, holy shit. I pressed my lids together tightly in anticipation.

We slammed onto the back of the bird, and it squawked with the impact. Another set of arms wrapped around Rimmon's neck, bumping into mine. I lifted my lashes and peered over Rimmon's shoulder. My mom was back in her human form, naked and shivering, as she clung to him.

A shadow above my head had me eyeing the sky. Another SUV-size bird circled higher and also looked to be carrying people.

Our bird flapped its wings and curved its body, changing direction. Wind jiggled out the last of my ponytail, letting it fly freely in a mass around my head. I moved out of Rimmon's grip and scooted myself to sit on the bird like you would a horse. The feathers were soft and smooth against my skin. It looked to be a huge eagle, but the feathers were black as ebony. It would blend with the night as well as a Dark Dweller and could slip silently up behind you.

FOUR

We coasted for a while before the bird headed for a meadow. It flapped its wings and alighted softly on the ground.

Rimmon, being his usually chatty self, slid silently from the bird's back and landed on the dirt with a thud. Mom followed Rimmon, as I went off the other side. It was a farther drop than I expected, and my knees took the brunt of my disembarking and the pain of impact. I stood, rubbing them. The bird cocked its head and looked at me.

"You are beautiful." I ran my hand over the feathers. Its beak came down, nipping at my fingers.

"Hey! Ow!"

"I would not call *him* beautiful. Ori gets exceedingly grumpy," Rimmon stated. He had slipped off his tank top and handed it to my mom. His top reached her calves.

"Oh." I stepped back. "Sorry."

The bird dissolved in front of me, arms stretched out where the wings had been. The sharp beak melded into a man's face. The large man who stood there was a guard I recognized from Lars's compound but never officially met. He was a shifter. A bird-shifter.

"I am not beautiful," he grumbled. "I am regal." Ori stomped away from me.

I was getting used to seeing people naked. Still, it was hard to make complete eye contact, although shifters seemed to always be extremely fit and not bad to look at.

Luckily or maybe unluckily for me, the other bird touched the ground giving my eyes something else to latch onto. Lars, Koke, Alki, Goran, and Eli were all piled on the second bird.

"Where are Mark and Ryan?" I bolted, frantic, toward Lars.

"They should be here soon." Lars jumped from the bird and landed gracefully on his feet.

"What do you mean? Are they all right?"

"Yes. They were actually first out of harm's way. In the distraction of us crashing into the room, Castien slipped in unnoticed to get Ryan and Mark out." Lars wiped at his cargo pants, straightening them. Everyone dismounted after him. "It was all strategically planned. They are safe."

Air huffed out of my lungs with relief, which filled back quickly with lead.

"Why didn't you tell me?" I glanced between the Unseelie King and the fox-shifter. "Why didn't either of you tell me? I am the Queen's *niece*? My real mother was a princess of the Fay?"

"Technically you are princess now. You are next in line for the throne, which is why you need to kill Aneira."

"I am a princess?" My head snapped around wildly peering at the two of them in utter dismay and shock.

"Ember..." Lily put her fingers lightly on her mouth, appearing to be searching for her words.

"Lily." Lars shook his head at her, then faced me. "I know you have a lot of questions, but now is not the time. We have to get out of here. We are not safe yet, and we barely got everyone out the first time. I do not want to rescue you and your friends again."

He was right. We needed to get to safety before I flipped out.

"We didn't rescue West." Eli said, his voice tight with anger. He walked toward me, while I moved quickly away. Now that we were out of danger, hurt and disgust filled my chest. I didn't want to be near him.

"We don't know yet. Cal could have rescued him." I purposefully kept my eyes off him. I had to keep my emotions intact for a little bit longer, at least till we were all safe and far away from Aneira.

"You trust a pixie and a raven to free a man who probably can't even walk anymore? From a jail cell? Unnoticed?" Eli's eyes flashed red in irritation.

"Don't you dare talk to me about trust." The pain in my heart inched up my throat, wanting to escape.

Eli paused. His mouth opened and then shut before he turned away from me, his hand sliding over his head, rubbing fiercely at his scalp.

Tension filled the space. Mom watched me, but when my burning gaze met hers, she looked away. Finally, I turned back to Lars. "What about Mark and Ryan? They can't return to Earth?"

"Ember." Lars pinched the bridge of his nose. "I have the problem taken care of. At least I did for Ryan. Mark will now have to be a part of Otherworld plan. There is a safe house on the Dark Fae side where they will be going. They will be quite safe there."

I blinked away my tears. "Thank you."

He gave me a stiff nod.

"Also, thank you for coming to get us." Emotion ran over me with the force of a train while looking at my uncle. "I am so happy you are alive."

"I am quite offended if you think Aneira can kill the Unseelie King so easily." Lars frowned.

"She made it sound..."

"I had to let her believe she was more powerful than me in Greece. Her ego is her weakness. If she thought I ran in fear, she would not expect the fight we brought to her front door later. However, this happened before she obtained the sword. I would have played it differently had I known about Josh. I would not have let her take you or the sword."

I grimaced.

"Well, thank you anyway... for coming for us."

"Don't thank me, Ember. The mistake was mine. My own arrogance blinded me. And now she has your powers." Lars looked away from me, his back tall and straight. "I would stop at nothing to get to you. Never doubt it."

I folded my arms across my stomach, trying to contain the emotion which wanted to pour out all over the ground, painting ever surface. I swallowed. "She doesn't have all of them."

"What do you mean?" Lars queried.

Eli's lids narrowed, taking in a breath. "She's still Dark Dweller."

"Are you sure?" Lars looked back and forth between me and Eli.

"Yes," he said as I nodded in response.

Pain must have flashed across my face at the thought of my powers being ripped from my body because Lars said, "I know your loss must be unsettling and unpleasant for you. The only positive you have from this is you no longer have to fear iron."

My eyes widened. I hadn't even thought of the positive side. Not having the Dae magic meant I no longer had the weakness of being half Fay. It did feel freeing knowing an enemy could not so easily restrain me. Well, they could because I was more human now, but not by slapping a piece of metal around my wrist.

A rustle of brush stopped my response to Lars. We all hunkered down, some pulling out weapons, others ready to become weapons. With the diminishing of my powers, any help I could give had been greatly reduced.

Castien broke through the foliage first, followed by Ryan and Mark. A cry erupted from my mouth, my legs moving the instant I saw them. Not knowing who to go to first, I ran for both. Mark reacted immediately, running to me with such determination we crashed into each other. His long, skinny arms wrapped around me and squeezed me so tight I lost my breath. A sob I hadn't expected exploded from my chest. We clung to each other as I tried to get myself under control. When I looked into his face, I saw I wasn't the only one. Tears streamed down his cheeks, disappearing under the growth of his singed beard. Shaking, my fingers touched the burn marks on his face and arm. He didn't flinch. They were no longer red or angry, more like burn scars which had been there for years.

"I am so sorry," I whispered, guilt seizing my vocals.

"I'm fine. They don't hurt anymore." He took my hand away from his face. "You are not to blame."

"But I am."

He pulled me in another hug. "What I care about is you are alive and here. It's all that matters. I didn't think I would ever see you again."

I sniffled. "You will never be able to get rid of me so easy."

I could feel Ryan squirming next to me, eager to get in on the hug. His energy was so different now. It was still Ryan, but after the loss of his cousin and being a prisoner in the Fae world, he seemed less of the happy-go-lucky kid I knew before. There was sadness to him, a loss of innocence.

I pulled out of Mark's arms and went straight into Ryan's, almost knocking him over. There were no words to say, but I still uttered in his ear, "I'm so sorry." Three words could never cover the loss of his cousin, Ian, or the reality that he could never return to Earth again. He responded with a hiccupped cry as he held me tighter.

"You know I am a fairy now, right?" he murmured into my ear.

"You've always been one, but at least now you can say it's official." I teased him.

"Little disappointed there are no wings or a wand. Always wanted a wand. And where is the glitter? I thought fairies came with glitter dust?" Ryan pulled back, wiping his eyes.

"Yeah, I would complain to management." I winked at Castien, who blushed.

"Ember, we do not have time for reunions. Aneira's men are no doubt after us. We need to go," Lars's voice broke in.

Rubbing my nose and eyes, I stepped back but didn't let go of Ryan's hand. Mark rubbed my shoulder. I just got them back. I could not let them go again.

"Hey, girlie, where are you?" A tiny, familiar voice came from a distance. My Dweller hearing picked it up. I could tell by the tilt of Eli's head he heard it, too.

"Cal?" A cross between relief and panic jiggled my vocal cords. "Cal, I'm here." I moved toward his voice.

His little six-inch figure flew through the branches to me, panting and out of breath. I stretched out my hand where he landed. "Did what you said..." He gasped for air. "You were right. The raven... helped me." Cal put his hand on his chest, gasping. "But now... ummm... we have a problem..." He took another deep gulp of air. "Sorry, I flew super speed to get here..."

"What's the trouble, Cal?" I demanded.

He bent over his knees trying to get his breath. A lock of dark brown hair fell into his eyes. "Dark Dweller." He pointed behind him and struggled to get the words out between gasps. "Won't move. Collapsed. Tried to get him up... couldn't."

West.

Eli rushed over to me. "Where? Where is he, Cal?"

Cal pointed again behind him. "That way somewhere. I heard the Queen's men coming. Not safe."

Eli started for the trees.

"What are you doing?" Lars bellowed.

Eli swung around, his eyes burning bright. "Getting my brother."

"Don't be stupid. He has probably already been found. We must get out of here while we can." Anger thumped every word Lars uttered.

"Then *you* go. But I am not leaving here without him."

"Me, neither." I took a step toward Eli. I could feel the weight of my Alpha calling me, needing me. Eli's eyes darted to mine. Not one ounce of emotion flickered through them. I placed Cal's exhausted body on Ryan's shoulder. "Stay here, Cal."

Eli's sense of smell could find West faster than Cal could, and Cal looked too exhausted to fly anyway.

"Absolutely not, Ember," Mom, or Lily as I should call her now, yelled. Her bare feet padded easily over the sticks and rocks on the ground.

I slowly turned to her. My head tilted; my eyes stared at her in warning. "You do not tell me what to do."

Her facial expression looked woeful as she glanced at me and then Mark. His mouth pressed in a firm, stressed line as he watched her. Poor Mark. All he had gone through. He thought the love of his life was dead. To find she wasn't and to learn she lied about so many things had to be incredibly confusing for him.

"I agree. I didn't come here and risk everything to have you get caught again." Lars's chest puffed up, daring me to contradict his order. He was now completely the Unseelie King. As much as I hated the thought, Eli was my Alpha. I followed him first. The moment my other powers were gone, the Dark Dweller instincts took over. My connection to Eli felt even stronger, which pissed me off. But my family was in trouble. West needed me, and I would go get him.

"I'm sorry. We do not leave family behind." With my intentions clear, I picked up my pace. Eli sensed my decision, turned, and ran. I followed.

The ache of betrayal and distrust of Eli had not vanished. I had not forgotten he had taken part in killing my real mother. Yet the power to help my Alpha and my Dark Dweller family flowed over the gnawing pain. I would do what I needed to do. West was the priority. I would deal with everything else later.

Eli led us through the maze of dense woods. The connections I usually had with the earth were now vacant holes in me. It was like visiting an old friend, and finding you no longer had anything in common. The connection you had at one time was gone. It hurt my heart.

Eli sniffed the air and altered direction. Silently, I stayed on his tail. When he stopped, I almost plowed into the back of him. He jerked his head, sniffing again. He turned to his right, climbing over the trunk of a fallen tree. Eli scrambled toward a heap of flesh on the ground. "West? Oh, fuck, brother."

A gasp escaped me. The skinny lump of bones on the ground looked like a shell of what West had been when we first met. Eli grasped his shoulder and tenderly rolled him onto his back. West looked even worse than I remembered from the last dreamwalk. His clothes were soiled with soot, blood, and fecal matter. Excess fabric hung off his emaciated body.

West's head rolled, facing me. Blood dribbled down his chin as he groaned in pain. His neck was shredded with both fresh cuts and old wounds. His eyes were sunken and unfocused.

"Hey. I'm here. You're gonna be all right," Eli said gently to West, his large hand holding West's head. To see such softness in Eli was always jarring. He loved his family fiercely. And privately. Even though I was a part of them, it angered me to see a warm side of him after what happened with Aisling. I wanted to hate him—with every fiber I had left in me. I did not want to struggle with my feelings. I wanted, I *needed*, to despise him.

West's mouth moved, but his voice was too low for me to understand. "What?" Eli leaned down putting his ear to West's mouth. West muttered something causing Eli to lean back and laugh. "Good to see some things don't change."

"What did he say?" I ventured closer to the boys.

Eli's head turned and his eyes pierced deeply into mine, causing my breath to hitch. "He said it took me long enough, and the least I could have done was bring some water fairies to give him a sponge bath."

I guffawed. "Yeah, he can't even lift his head... at least not the one on his shoulders."

A gurgled snort came out from West. "I've missed you, too, darlin'." Every word sounded choked, garbled, and torture for him to get out.

I couldn't help but smile. West definitely possessed the charm of the group. None of them lacked women's attentions, but West, with his southern accent and rugged looks, had panties dropping by the truck load. Interestingly, he had only lived in the south a short time, but he knew the accent drew in the ladies.

Bays and yips of dogs resonated through the forest. I stilled. They were still far off, but I could tell they were moving our way.

"Shit!" I leaped to Eli and West. "We gotta go."

"This is gonna hurt, brother, but we need to get you out of here." Eli slid his arms underneath him. West's face twisted in pain as Eli gathered him up into his arms, carrying him like a baby.

"What do you need me to do?" I looked at Eli.

"I won't be able to shift since my attention is on keeping him alive." Eli adjusted West again. West groaned, his eyes fluttered shut, and his head lolled to the side. "I need you to be the leader and scout. Be fully tuned into your senses. The Fay may not be able to smell us, but their dogs will."

I swallowed nervously. "They're cute little doggies, right?"

"Not quite. They aren't like the dogs on Earth. These dogs are much larger and have stronger senses and teeth. Like an Irish Wolfhound on steroids."

"Great." I plastered a fake smile on my face. "Awesome."

"And they are extremely fast. Let's go."

I closed my eyes briefly and called to the Dark Dweller in me. Not needing to fight all my other powers, it rushed to the surface eagerly. I whipped around and let every sound and smell of the forest wash over me. I bounded forward, sniffing the air. A strong dog-like odor came from my left, cutting the trail we made coming here. The soldiers were dividing us. My family and friends stood on one side, and Eli, West, and I were on the other. It was a risk, but I decided we should circle around slipping behind them. They would continue to move forward and not back from where they came, right? *Please, let me be right.*

Without a word, Eli followed my lead. West had passed out, his body dead weight in Eli's arms. Even as malnourished as West was, he still wasn't a small guy. Eli's strength was beyond reproach, and he didn't seem too bothered by the weight. He was more upset by the actual cargo he carried. His face was stone, but he rushed forward, anxious to keep West alive.

Smells and voices forced me to widen my circle. My stomach knotted with tension. Every step we took was mine to decide, as well as the outcome. I hated the weight it placed on my shoulders. This pressure and anxiety must be how Eli and Cole felt every day.

I stopped dead as a strong scent infiltrated my nose. I turned to look at Eli. His shoulders went taut, curling forward, and a low growl rolled from his throat.

Eyes were on me. I could feel them. I twirled in a circle, my gaze wandering every inch of the forest. Eli sniffed. He was about to place West on the ground when a large mass lurched from the woods, diving for his throat. Both men and the animal crashed to the dirt. West's body rolled, limp as he hit the earth.

I leaped onto the back of the large dog. Its wiry hair rubbed against my skin like sandpaper. I clung to it and wrapped my arms and legs around it. Eli was busy trying to keep its jaws from clamping on his neck. I clutched my hands around the dog's throat and snapped its head back. It wiggled enough so I didn't break its neck, but we both fell. It rolled on top of me and crushed the breath out of my lungs. Its teeth bit and chomped at the air as it tried to reach my face and neck. Teeth grazed my cheek, followed by a warm burning sensation in my face. The weight of the dog pinned my body in place, and I could not move. My lids shut in self-defense. A piercing yelp assaulted my eardrums. My eyes opened to see Eli standing above me, the dog in his hands. With a quick twist of his arm, he broke the animal's neck. It went limp in his arms before he tossed it to the side.

I sighed and let my head fall back onto the dirt.

"Come on. We've got to go." Eli squatted beside me.

I sat up, feeling dazed and dizzy.

"Jesus, Brycin. You're bleeding again." He took his sleeve to my cheek, wiping at the gash.

I jerked away and stood.

He looked at the ground, slowly letting out a huge breath. His shoulders went rigid, and his expression turned to ice as he stood. "Let's move." He picked up West.

We had only traveled ten minutes when I detected another odor. Human. Joy filled me. It smelled like Mark. Old Spice. But now his cologne mingled with a new smell. Fae magic—like the air before a thunderstorm, dense and heavy mixed with fresh rain and earth. There was also sweetness in it—a dash of honey or vanilla. His body was starting to digest the Fae food. Like Ryan, he would get sick as his body took in the foreign substance. We had to get him to safety before his system reacted to the alien element. He would be a lot harder to travel with if we also had to carry him.

Lars was the first to find us. The relief in his eyes quickly changed to anger. The rest of the group shadowed behind.

"Oh, crap on ash bark. Thank goodness." Mom put her hand on her chest, letting out a liberated breath. I could tell she struggled not to run to me, but my guarded expression kept her at arm's length.

Mark didn't have the same problem; he pulled me into a bear hug, kissing my hairline. "Please don't run off again. You scared me and your mother half to death..." Mark trailed off realizing what he said. He stepped back and cleared his throat nervously as he glanced at Lily. Clearly, he didn't know where he stood on the question of my parentage either. What a screwed-up mess my family was.

In the distance, a siren of wailing howls and a frenzy of barking circled us. We froze. By the closeness and the desperate tone of the dogs, I could tell they'd caught our scent. They were coming for us.

"Rimmon, you and Ori head south," Lars said to the two men before pointing at the other bird-shifter. "Deryn, you take Koke and Alki and head east. Castien, you know what you need to do... follow the river northwest from here. Lily, decide now whom you want to go with." He nodded toward her. "Let's hope our strategy divides and confuses them."

Castien herded Mark and Ryan away.

"Wait. What?" My voice was frantic.

"Castien and I planned the escape thoroughly. They will be fine." Lars's body already leaned impatiently in the direction he wanted us to go. The anxiety of separating from Mark and Ryan drilled into my gut.

Another set of high-pitched howls bounded off the rocks and trees around us. They were closer. Everyone strode in their appointed direction except Mom, Mark, Ryan, and me.

"I got them, Ember. Go!" Castien waved me on.

My toes bobbed up and down, still hesitant to leave. Mark's light blue eyes looked pained as he peered back and forth between me and his wife. It stopped me completely and started me moving toward him. *No! I can't leave him or Ryan again.*

"Ember, we have to run! They will be fine. I promise."

Lars pushed my shoulder to get me moving. Eli had stopped and anxiously looked back at me. Mom did not move at all, her gaze going from Mark to me. Her face was pinched in a frown.

"I can't. I will go with them," I insisted.

"No," Lars bellowed. "Even though she has your powers, she still wants you, Ember. She wants you gone and won't stop until your death is accomplished. It is not safe for you to stay in the Otherworld."

"It's not safe for me anywhere." I gritted my teeth. "And if it's not safe for me, it's not safe enough for them."

"The difference is they cannot leave." Lars's yellow-green eyes morphed into a dark olive color.

"Go, Ember." Mark's words halted the argument in my throat. "Your safety is the only thing concerning me. I need to know you are safe, and if leaving here ensures your life, you need to go."

"Mark..."

"No arguments, young lady." He tried to stay stern, but his voice quivered.

Tears stung my eyes and burned in my chest. I ran to him and wrapped my arms tightly around him. "I love you so much. I may not be able to bring you home, but I will make you safe. I promise."

"Come on. We have to go," Lars demanded.

I pulled away from Mark.

"I love you, too, Sunny D. You are my daughter, blood or not." He kissed my cheek.

A guttural cry arose from me as I nodded and turned.

Lily stepped up to us. "Mark, I will be back. I need to get Ember safe, and then I will find you." Her voice sounded unsure.

Mark's expression hardened when his focus landed on her. He nodded and turned away.

I quickly turned to Ryan. "I love you, Ry." Lars grabbed me by the t-shirt and yanked me forward cutting my hug short.

"Please keep them safe, Castien. Do *whatever* you need to do; just make sure they are all right."

Castien nodded. "I will."

Unshed tears gathered behind my eyes. My legs pumped fast as we ran west toward an Otherworld door.

FIVE

We hopped through dozens of Otherworld doors, going in and out of places like Brazil, Australia, and New Mexico. Finally, one brought us close to Lars's property. There were millions of doors all over the world, so it would be hard for them to detect which one we had gone through. I still felt the urge to get safely within the walls of his complex. The Queen could not reach us there.

The adrenaline was wearing off, revealing a void inside me where my powers used to be. I felt empty. My body fought the crippling pain inside, which did not stem from the fight, but from so many things: having to leave Mark and Ryan, the truth of my mom not actually being my mom, the guy I loved being involved or contributing to my real mother's death, and being blood-tied to the Queen. My family. The woman who had killed and hurt so many was my aunt. How could I ever move on from it all?

A small point in my chest burned, growing with every step I took. The woman who was my mother since the day I was born ran next to me, her face solemn.

Eli's expression mirrored hers as his feet hit the ground on the other side of me. West flopped around on his shoulder. His unconscious grunts told me at least he was still alive. This only enhanced my thoughts of Mark and Ryan. In one sitting, Aneira had taken everyone I loved from me in one way or another. I hoped Castien could keep them safe. My head needed to focus on other matters: getting Kennedy back from Lorcan and breaking the curse the Queen put on me.

The electric current from the spell surrounding Lars's compound tickled my skin. Breath huffed out of my chest as I came to a crawl. I felt like I was in a kid's game of tag, and I barely made it to my safety zone. Only heavy breathing filled the air, our group coming to halt. My hands went to my knees as I bent over, taking in air deeply.

"I forgot to ask if you were all right, Ember." Lars turned to me, looking cool and collected, like he had just strolled down a runway and not saved me from the Queen of the Otherworld. He only had one small cut on his cheek. On the other hand, I looked like crap with blood, bruises, cuts, raggedy hair, and torn clothes.

I nodded automatically, still grasping for breath. Then his words hit me. Was I all right? I was far from okay. I stood, ire zinging up my spine. My mom—Lily—seemed to sense my mood shift. The dazed shock and hurt I experienced earlier spiraled into immeasurable wrath.

"Ember..."

"Don't." I cut her off.

"Please let me explain." She took a step to me.

My feet backtracked away from her, and my glare darted between her and Eli. Eli gently placed West on the ground, his attention on me. "What can you possibly tell me to make everything you did better? Anything either one of you did?"

"Ember, I only lied to you to protect you—"

"Stop!" Heat burst up my throat, rage vibrating on the surface. "You only lied to me to protect yourself."

Hurt zipped across her face. Somewhere deep inside it still saddened me to hurt her, but at the moment I wanted nothing more than to wound her.

"You were supposed to be the person I trusted most, and all you have ever done is lie and cause me pain." My voice went up several octaves. It all rushed over me.

"Ember, please understand..." She reached out for me.
Instinct searched for my magic to protect me.
Nothing.
Tears welled in my eyes as I batted her hand away. "Stay away from me!"

Eli had been silently standing to the side, but my thoughts had never ventured far from him. "And *you.*" I pointed, emotion cracking my voice. So many thoughts kept my mouth from opening again.

"Ember, you don't know the full truth." He stepped forward.

A crazed laugh came from my throat. "Truth? What do you know about truth?" I glared at him. "Tell me one thing, Eli. Was Aneira lying? Were you there the night Aisling was murdered?"

Muscles twitched in his neck, his mouth grim. "No, she wasn't lying. I was there."

"Is that why she wanted to protect me from you?" I pointed to Lily. "Is this how you know each other? Why you two hate each other so much? She saw you there, didn't she?" My head pinged back and forth between the two.

Mom looked at the ground and nodded at the same time Eli replied. "Yes."

Any hope I had evaporated into the air. Waves of anger and hate rolled over me, consuming my every thought, leaving no room for anything else. Something in me snapped. All the lies, hurt, and betrayal I had pushed through before dumped down, suffocating me.

"So you helped *kill* my *real* mother, Eli? Were you there to murder me as well?"

"No—" His words were cut off.

Lily's fists clenched at her sides, her face rippling with fury. "I was there, Elighan, remember? I know you were going to try and kill Ember, but Brycin stopped you." The woman and fellow Dae I was named after. Mom had told me how Brycin had helped get us out of the castle to safety. She was later caught, tortured, and then killed for not giving up our whereabouts.

"I won't lie. I wanted to kill that woman with every fiber of my being. She took my family from me." A growl slithered through his teeth. "But I wasn't there for you."

"Is that supposed to make it better?" My arms swung out. My vocals clenched down, trying to keep my voice steady. "Tell me, Eli, every time you slept with me, did my mother's face cross your mind? Did you get off on knowing the truth while you were inside of me?" I struggled for air, the words spilling out in a torrent of emotion. "Did you think I would look past your little transgression? That I could forgive you?" A tear broke free, creating a ripple of them, to streak down my face, blinding me. "You let me fall in love with you."

His mouth went to open again, but I shook my head violently. My body curled with the weight of my despair. "No! Just fucking shut up!" I screeched. Another wave of anger set my muscles on edge. My body moved for him before I even knew it did. My fists smashed into his face and chest. "I *HATE* you!"

He didn't move, but his hands reached for my wrists. "Ember..."

"*No!*" I continued to wail on him. Arms grabbed me from behind, pulling me off Eli.

"Ember, calm down," Lars said and grasped me tightly around the waist. I clawed, kicked, and spit a flurry of incomprehensible words. My brain shut off; my only need was to kill and attack the things hurting me.

"Let. Go. Of. Me." I struggled against his hold. Heat pounded through me.

My Dark Dweller blood wanted to hurt the two people in front of me with my bare hands. To inflict pain externally, like the pain I felt internally. I was no more than a wild animal. Aneira had my powers, but my responses were still there. What I thought of as my "Dark" power—the emotion to shut off and let pure, cold, hatred take over—was by far the scariest part. It enjoyed hurting people. Destroying. It was the part the Queen wanted, and I feared—because I liked it.

"Ember, stop!"

Lars held me tighter against his body. He could easily stop me, even more so now. His power could bind or control me in an instant, but he didn't. He let me flail and thrash against his arms.

Ignoring his words, I reached out again, swinging and grunting.

"Shhhh," Lars murmured in my ear, and his grip turned into more of a tight hug. "Calm down."

The simple difference in his touch broke something in me. My rage deflated, and the fight in me turned back to sheer anguish. A long sob quivered out from the depths of my chest. I slumped back into his arms.

"I think you both should leave." Lars rolled me to face his chest, my tears splashing onto his shirt.

They hesitated.

"Go." I craned my neck to look at the pair in the eyes.

Tears fell from my mother's face, grief raw as she sobbed. Eli was stone.

"Now!" I screeched so gutturally it hurt my throat.

Lily took a few steps back, still not wanting to leave. I could not take much more.

"Do as she asked," Lars spoke, "or I will expel you from the property myself." My uncle's embrace was now the only thing keeping me upright.

With a swift nod Eli pivoted and picked up West, cradling him in his arms. He gave me one last look over his shoulder before he jumped into the brush and disappeared into the thick evening shadows.

Lily choked back a cry and pressed her hand against her mouth. Now not needing to "hide" from me anymore, she shifted to her little red fox form. The top Rimmon gave her fell into a puddle on the ground. The animal turned with its head lowered, trotting off toward the property line. Her orange-brown eyes looked back at me one last time. With a soft whimper she, too, slipped into the forest.

I wanted them to go, but now that they actually had, my heart burst like a dam. My legs sagged underneath me. Lars eased me to the ground, never letting go of me. A river of agony tore into me. I wailed in pain and howled with grief.

Far in the distance, a pained roar of an animal split the air shaking the trees and earth beneath me.

SIX

Rain pummeled the glass door. Gray and black clouds rolled across the late afternoon sky, drowning the earth with water. I stared absently, watching the wisps of condensed air weave and reel around each other angrily. Several weeks prior, the weather would have matched what was going on within me; now I was numb. I lay on my side in a ball, covers to my chin, watching the world move outside my doors.

"I cannot take her unmoving anymore." A tiny foot tapped impatiently on my shoulder. "It has been three weeks. I will remake the bed with her in it if I have to. The sheets need to be changed. They are disgusting."

A snort came from another small figure on my other shoulder. "Good luck." Cal, true to his word, had found me. Lars did not question or react to the little pixie's appearance at my bedside. He even acknowledged Cal, talking to him when I would not answer.

I hadn't spoken more than a couple of words since Eli and my mom left the property. Lars put me to bed after my collapse, and I hadn't moved much since. Depression was so entrenched in my bones it ached to even walk to the bathroom. Food had lost its appeal. Marguerite had gotten me to sip soup, which she enhanced with rich cream and butter to keep weight on me. It still didn't do enough. I looked gaunt and sickly, my hair stringy and unkempt. My problem was I didn't care—about anything.

The simplest things would exhaust me. Not even the thoughts of my friends stirred anything in me—except hopelessness.

Cal curled his arm around Sinnie's shoulder, which he had to flutter up to achieve. He stood only six inches; she was a foot tall. "My sweet dessert, you know how much I adore your determination, but I think you need to let this one go." Sinnie had been trying to change my bed for a week now during the small windows of time when I went to the bathroom.

Sinnie swatted his arm off. Cal had been trying to charm her since the day he arrived, with no luck. "I will do no such thing, little man."

Cal flew to me and landed on my neck. "Sinnie, you are a woman of honor and duty, I get that. But, this one..." His tiny fist knocked on my head. "She is cracked like an egg. Mad as a tree troll. Fractured, crazy, loony, a splintered branch. You will not out-determine her."

"We will see." Sinnie stomped her foot on my arm. "You hear what I'm saying, girl?" She poked at me. "I will remake your bed by the end of today even if I have to push you out of it myself." With that she vanished.

Cal leaned against my head and sighed dreamily. "What a woman."

I blinked in response, most of my attention still on the storm outside my bedroom.

"Soooo... you know *he's* back again?" He didn't have to say who. There was no need. I didn't have the will or energy to tell Cal that Eli had never left. He had been prowling the edge of the compound's border since the day I ordered him away. A few times I had seen the slick black body pacing through the trees.

I'd become accustomed to the sensation of Eli's blood in me. I don't know what it would be like not to feel him. His presence was there, but it was white noise in the background. I didn't even take pleasure knowing he was cold and wet. My hurt went deeper than petty victories could cure.

"Lars let him into the compound last night. Did you know?" Cal sat, using the slope of my shoulder as his back rest.

I did. My hearing and smell had sharpened. More proof, without my powers, the Dark Dweller part of me was taking over.

"They were in Lars's office for over two hours. I tried to listen, but that damn woman, Marguerite, shooed me away."

Over the weeks Lars began to tolerate Eli's constant presence. Even Rimmon and the other guards left him alone, acting as if he were part of scenery as they made their nightly rounds. My hearing and eyesight had caught the guards acknowledging him, greeting him as they passed the terrifying beast at the border of the land. His green eyes glowed from the depths of the forest, watching me.

Every once in a while spikes of hatred hit me at the sight of him, but then the emptiness would claim me. I wasn't quite sure why Lars accepted his presence in the compound. If I didn't know better, I would say Lars possessed some empathy for him. Only a couple of nights ago, I saw Rimmon head to where Eli camped out.

"Hey, Dweller?" Rimmon's deep voice boomed across the property and into my hypersensitive ear canal. "The King would like to talk to you."

"What about?"

I automatically pressed my lids together, hearing the familiar rough timbres of Eli's voice. It rattled my chest and caused it to ache.

"Not my concern. Says he wants Marguerite to give you something to eat and then you're to meet him in his office. He also requested you shower before entering his house. You smell."

What? Lars was letting him into the house? Having Marguerite feed him?

"Better stop sweet talking me, R. Gets lonely out here." Eli's tone was mockingly flirtatious.

"Shut up, Dweller. Personally, I'd sooner kill you, but the King would like to see you first." Rimmon's voice was tight. Humor wasn't something he understood. "Now follow me. There is a shower in the training room."

I jerked up in bed, my head spinning at the sudden movement. Why was Lars encouraging Eli? Why did he want to talk to him?

The heaviness of my depression curled my body back onto my pillow with an angered cry. I picked up my water glass and threw it against the wall. Glass shattered into thousands of pieces, tumbling to the floor. Water dripped in pools down my wall. It did not make me feel better.

Rotting fury molded in my stomach. How could Lars have sympathy for someone who helped butcher my mother and the woman he had loved?

My mother. To think of my mom and not have Lily's image in my mind unsettled me.

Aisling. My biological mother. A royal Fay who died to protect me. I didn't even know what she looked like. I had only a fractured image and a feeling from a dream to hold onto. All those times when Faes told me I looked like my mom, I wondered what they were talking about. Lily and I didn't look anything alike. I had believed they saw something I didn't. My nose and lips, the red streaks in my hair—all those things must have come from Aisling. I had grown up thinking I had a "normal" mother and father. The man I thought was my biological father hadn't been around, but I had believed him alive somewhere out there in the world, when actually I was an orphan. Lily had raised me. Loved me. I did see her sacrifice, but my anger struggled to let me forgive her. Her terror of "losing me" caused her worst fear to come true. Thinking of her triggered a wave of guilt to crash over me. I clenched my jaw and pushed the emotion away.

I was done crying.

"Hey, girlie, are you hearing me at all?" Cal pulled on my

earlobe, bringing me to the present. "Hellooooooo. Hello. Hello," he echoed in my ear, pretending it was a vast cave. He wasn't far off.

"Yeah, I'm getting tired of your constant blabbing all the time, anyway. Why don't you lie there like a lump of rotting goblin dung, and I'll talk?" He leaned into my shoulder, patting it. "Wow, you're really good at ignoring me. Sooooo anyway, this morning, you know when you lay there so distraught with the thought of me leaving? I went to the... the *other* place." He, like others, thought if they limited mentions of the word Dark Dwellers or Eli, it would help me recover faster. "They still haven't tracked Lorcan. He keeps moving around, keeping one step ahead. They found his last hiding spot, but the group had moved on by then. Simmons is out searching for her every day. Don't worry. We'll find her," Cal said. Everyone was out trying to find Kennedy. The fact I wasn't looking myself should have had me feeling ashamed. I was void of emotion.

"Also, I figure you would like to know I took the liberty and went to the Otherworld to check on your father."

My eyes finally darted from the window down to my shoulder. Mark was the only light in my darkness. My heart wrenched in my chest. The torrent of guilt I still felt at hurting him shredded at my soul. People probably kept thinking: *You have so much power, why don't you destroy the Queen and get it over with?"* If it were only that easy. My powers could not kill her, but they could kill and hurt everyone else around. If I ever got the sword back and I found myself alone with her, I would not hesitate. I would forgo my life if I could stop her and all the pain and destruction she caused.

I had barely come to terms with the death of Ian and the fact Ryan could never return to earth. Now I took on the blame of Mark. Mark's job, life, and everything else were gone. His life existed now in the Fae world. All because he came into our family, because he fell in love with Lily. With me.

"Your mother—*Lily*—is there with him." He didn't know

what to call her either. "Lars thought it better if your friend and father had more security. So Torin and Thara moved in as well. They can help Lily and Castien keep them safe."

It gave me some relief. The more protection the better. Actually, it was the only place Torin could go. He wouldn't want to be anywhere near the Dark Dwellers, and he couldn't go wandering around Earth or the Otherworld unprotected. The Queen would still love to get her hands on him. To torture him until he shattered in unrepairable fragments. She had chipped away at Torin pretty good the last time she held him prisoner.

At first I had been amazed Torin hadn't tried to talk to me through our minds or even pull me into a dreamscape, but I finally realized when the Queen took my abilities, she took all those Fay "perks," including the bond between us. I should have been grateful nothing tied Torin to me anymore, and I did not have to worry about pulling Eli into a dreamscape, except I felt lonelier. Isolated. Sorrow carved me into a hollow shell. Desolation was the only thing filling my vacant soul.

My lids squeezed together.

"Some other good news." Cal sat up, forcing a joyful tone. "Looks like the Queen is not out hunting you. Well, not blatantly anyway."

She didn't need to be. She had my powers, and she had the sword. Granted she still wanted me dead and would love to find me, but she could wait for Samhain—the time when the two worlds collided, when the barrier between the two was at its weakest. She planned to break down the wall between them for good. It was less than two months away, or it was when I had last been coherent of time.

Someone knocked and opened the door at the same time. "Hey, little Dae." Nic's voice came through the darkened room. He closed the door behind him. Picking up from where we left off, Nic visited me every day before he left for the night to head out on his Incubus job. He sometimes found his way to my room when he got home from his adventures. Nic was breathtaking, a Spanish god drenched in sexuality. The moment he even got near, you felt like ripping your clothes off. Being a Dae, I was technically immune to his charms, but I still had not been able to deny my attraction to him. I wasn't dead.

Until now.

He crawled into the bed behind me like he always did, his arms wrapping around my waist. But I laid there, indifferent to his hands or lips nibbling at my neck.

Cal smacked at his arm. "Hey! We were talking."

Nic snorted. "I am here *not* to talk."

I knew Nic liked me, but he saw me more as a challenge. Especially now. But I was numb... broken. His hand rubbed my leg methodically, which was actually soothing. I felt tired, and even as he kissed the back of my neck, I drifted off to sleep.

My eyelids rose, and I took in the dimly lit space. I batted my lashes trying to clear my vision. There was no way I should be here. Bars lined in a continuous pattern down the long dark corridor. Wet, moldy straw clumped the floor in each cell and dotted the stone walkway in-between.

"What the hell?" I mumbled to myself. Why was I in the Queen's dungeon?

"Fire has come." A voice came down the aisle.

"Grimmel?" I took tentative steps, following the sound. In the murky corner, the dwarf slept in a rickety wooden chair; the raven stood on his shoulder. "How are you doing this? I thought I could no longer dreamscape or dreamwalk?"

"Grimmel guides all minds." Ravens were powerful dream guides, so he was pulling me into a dreamwalk. He could interact with people in dreamwalks as if they were as real to him as the people actually in the room. No one else would be able to see me, but he could.

"Fire is faint and weak. No flame. No spark."

"Hey, now."

"Build fire. Blaze and burn."

"Can you tell me what you want and why I am here?"

"Dark Knight escape."

"Yes. Thank you for your help, Grimmel. West is going to live because of you."

"Silence."

I wasn't sure if he was telling me to be silent or now West was gone, it was quieter.

"Help baby escape." Grimmel's black beady eyes bore into me. He had adored my mother and helped her get me and Lily out of the castle. "Flame goes out. All for naught. Will lead to destruction."

"What do you want me to do about it, Grimmel? She has the sword. She has taken my powers."

"Baby cry too much." He tilted his head. "Fight fire."

"How?"

"Seek. Want."

"Damn you Fae. Can't you ever say what you mean without the riddles?"

Flapping his wings, Grimmel adjusted his grip on the dwarf's shoulder. "You will know."

With a shove of energy, I tumbled back to my bedroom in Lars's compound.

When I woke, Nic had left. My mind flipped through the conversation with Grimmel, leaving me restless, and even more exhausted. I had no idea what he thought I would know. The raven was bat-shit crazy, so I pushed it from my mind.

The blinking of the clock told me it was nearing dawn. Sleeping twelve or more hours at a time was nothing new to me. Sleep was what I did most of the time. The overcast sky lightened as I continued to drift in and out of slumber.

My room lights flicked on, and my eyes popped open.

"Get. Up." Alki's voice boomed through the silent room. He was dressed in his training outfit of black sweats and black tank top. His body-builder physic rippled through the fabric. With his severe haircut, sharp Asian features, and his muscular form, he was intimidating. Not someone I'd want to meet in an alley.

I jerked with surprise but otherwise did not respond.

"I said get up." He headed for my bed when I didn't react. "We are training today. You are weak, both in mind and in body, especially without your magic. Now rise. I will not ask again."

"Go away," I grumbled, my mouth finding it hard to move after weeks of not speaking. "I don't have my powers anyway. What does it matter?"

Alki grabbed my arm and with a sharp yank pulled me from my bed. I fell to the floor with a thud. "You can still fight. Your body is a tool. And the Dark Dweller is still in you."

"Leave me alone." I curled in a ball on the floor.

He scooped me up. "I told you I would not ask again."

"Let me go." I feebly pushed against his unyielding chest. He carried me downstairs like I weighed nothing.

"I am not training," I protested. "You might as well put me down."

He did not respond and continued carrying me outside. I wore only a tank and pair of sweats, so the chilly morning brought goose bumps to my flesh.

The hot summer was now bleeding into a nippy fall. Leaves of crisp oranges, yellows, and browns sprinkled the ground, most still clung desperately to the trees, holding on to their last bits of life. Time in the Otherworld was such a strange concept. During my first visit, I felt I had only been there for a day or two, and it had been three years. My time spent there recently didn't feel much different, but when we returned it had only been a month. There seemed to be no rhyme or reason to it. As most Fae, it did what it wanted when it wanted.

"Alki, set me down." My voice grew louder and sturdier. It took me a moment to realize he wasn't taking me to the training room. Before I could ask, he rounded the corner and stopped at the pool.

"Noooo." The word came out too late. I felt the release of his arms as I plunged into the freezing water. It felt like a bolt of electricity zapped my heart. Everything in me woke up, coming back to life. I breached the surface with a gasp.

"Do *not* insult the lives of those lost in your name. You think they would not wish to be alive again? If they had the chance, do you think they would squander a moment of it? They did not perish for you to live a half-life!" His words silenced any harsh words I was about to send his way. "Now get out of the pool. We *are* training today and every day until the war," Alki's dark eyes pierced me before he whipped around and headed toward the stone building on the property.

I shivered, moving slowly for the pool steps. His words hurt, but he was right. I had given up. I had always been a fighter, but I had let life beat me. This person was not who I am. I never let anything stand in my way. Yes, I've had a shitty couple of weeks, but I thought of all those people who had died in Seattle, Monterey, along with my biological mother. I'm sure all would have chosen to deal with my problems if it meant they could live again, to see their loved ones and hold their children once more.

I was instantly awake. The icy water dripped from my skin, the cold air lashing through my hair. My heart pumped in my chest, confirming I was *alive*. Determination woke in my body, stirring the survivor in me. I was a warrior—and I would fight.

SEVEN

Every muscle and joint hated me. No, they hated Alki, but I had to feel and hear their complaints. The drills he put me through were agony: running in the mud, uphill; climbing the rope wall; doing pushups and sit-ups till I wanted to puke. I realized I didn't like being "more human." My body did not heal or recover as fast, and everything felt harder and tougher to do. He pushed me till I vomited and then passed out. Alki had no compassion with my lack of powers. I knew I needed to train. I could not depend on my magic supporting me anymore, and I needed to be able to withstand battle without them.

He finally excused me for the day, but training with Alki was far from over.

"You have grown weak in mind and in body." Alki knocked on my scalp and my stomach with the staff he used in kicking my ass in Bataireacht, a form of Irish stick fighting. "But this is the most important." He tapped on my head again and then at my heart. "These are the most powerful weapons you can have."

"Crap. We're in trouble then."

Alki frowned, not the least bit amused.

"Tough crowd," I mumbled.

"Enough. You are in no place to joke. You no longer have your powers to rely on. How do you think you will be able to fight the Queen? There is no way you can beat her in your condition. You are unprepared and doomed to fail if you do not see the seriousness of your situation."

All humor left my face, drawing my shoulders down.

"Your body we can train, and train we will, but your mind and heart are what will win the war." Alki came around me, facing me. "And it will win, Ember. It must."

Alki was right. Since I could no longer out-power her with my magic, I had to outwit her. Find her weakness. And my love and determination were my driving forces. I needed to learn so much more before I faced my aunt. I hated thinking of Aneira as a blood relative. Truth had become a humongous pain in my ass. Part of me thought I had been better off in ignorant bliss when I had no idea what true pain, loss, and betrayal could mean. This was my life. Coming to accept it instead of fighting it was the only way to save my sanity. There were no what-if's; there were only what-now's?

After Marguerite fed me an early dinner, I limped my way to Lars's office. "Was giving me hyperthermia your idea of waking me up?" I said as I pushed open the door, walking in uninvited. A pixie faced the Unseelie King. "Simmons!"

The pixie turned, his face lighting up. "My lady!" He flew to me, but stopped when Lars cleared his throat. Simmons flipped around, standing to attention.

"Everything I told you will get back to Torin and Castien?"

Simmons dipped his head. "Yes, sir."

"You are dismissed, Simmons."

Simmons bowed to Lars and zipped around to me. "My lady, it is so good to see you... talking again."

"I missed you, too." I smiled softly at the little blond-haired, blue-eyed pixie. His 1960s fighter pilot outfit appeared cleaner than I had ever seen it. His swizzle stick sword hung from his belt.

"Simmons," Lars's voice rang with warning.

"Wait for me," I whispered. "I want to see you before you go."

Simmons nodded and headed out. "I will, my lady."

I shut the door behind him and faced Lars again. "You didn't answer my question."

Lars didn't acknowledge my presence. He finished what he was working on before he sat back, his eyes surveying me. "It worked did it not? It got you out of your self-pity coma."

Crossing my arms, I gave him a sour look. "Self-pity? You don't think finding out my mother is not my real mother and my biological mother and father have been murdered by my boyfriend's brother and uncle is not reason to flip out a bit?"

"I did not say whether it was deserved or not." He steepled his fingers. "However, before giving me the credit for getting you out of bed, it was not my idea. Someone else thought you needed a... how did he put it... jumpstart. It was his idea to get you back into training."

"Eli?"

"Yes, or as I am starting to think of him: the lawn furniture."

I couldn't stop the small giggle that erupted. "Did you just make a joke?"

He pinched his lips.

"Be careful you might be susceptible to a thing called humor," I teased.

His eyes narrowed.

"Never mind. It passed."

I sat in the chair across from him. "Now that I am talking again. I think we have some things to discuss. I have a lot of questions."

Lars's head dipped in firm agreement.

"How did Aneira steal my powers? Can I get them back?" I sat forward in my seat.

Lars peered at the ceiling in thought. "Through one of my sources in Seattle, there is a rumor going around in which Fae powers were transferred to a human by your magic."

"What? Me? How is that possible?"

"During the electrical storm a bolt of lightning hit a Fae, going through him and connecting with the human who stood behind. If it had been normal lightning, I am sure it would not have done anything except perhaps kill the human. However, it was not a normal storm. It was strong Fae magic. Your magic." Lars's focus settled heavy on me. "Aneira obviously heard the rumor and was willing to try it." A frown pinched Lars's lips. "Proving this rumor to be fact."

"Something I did caused it?" I placed my head in my hands and rubbed my face roughly.

"We cannot dwell on what has happened. We cannot change it. The focus is on what we will do now."

I looked through my hands then propped my chin in my hand. "Probably better I don't have my powers. I seem to only hurt people."

"Ember, did you think you would be able to contain your abilities?"

"Kinda. Yeah." I sat up straight. "You made it sound that if I continued to train and work hard, I would get a handle on them. Eventually."

"Handle is the key word there. Not control." He tilted back in his chair. "As a Dae, you will *never* stop working to contain them. As you know, Daes were always frowned upon, long before Aneira claimed them abominations and illegalized them. They were too powerful, even for their own good. Too much of something, especially magic, can be a dangerous thing. Daes were not immune to the overdose of magic in their system. Most ended killing themselves."

I was aware of this possibility, but to hear it point blank from Lars, only confirmed my greatest fears. Once I got my powers back, every day would be a fight, a struggle for me to restrain myself. There would be no relief, and there would always be the potential I could hurt, possibly kill, someone again.

"Right now, we need to center you being without them, until we figure out how we can get them back from Aneira. The only way I see you obtaining them again is killing her. Her death will restore them back to you. We need to get the sword in your hands." He tugged at his cuffs, straightening his shirt.

My back curved into the chair. A silence grew between us before I whispered. "I want to know why you let Eli in here. You don't like him, and I don't want him anywhere near me, so why is he here?"

Lars sighed. "You are right. I do not like the Dark Dwellers, although I do not like a lot of people." He swiveled his chair, focus going out the side window where Eli stood watching us. The dimming skyline drew shadows across the rug. "Though I may not be fond of the Dark Dwellers, I respect them. They are loyal and fight to the death for their own. I admire such devotion." He turned back, his eyes narrowed on me. "You are one of them now. No matter what you think he has done or what his deeds have been, he will die for you. As your uncle, I cannot help respect his tenacity. We have all done things we regret. Even you, Ember, have blood on your hands. You unintentionally killed many people's mothers and fathers."

It was the truth. It sliced at my gut like thousands of razor blades. "But it was *my mother* he helped kill, which is not something I can get over."

He pointed to himself and replied, "I killed your father. You find my action all right?"

The logic of his statement slammed into me. "No, it's not okay, but you had to. Devlin was insane. He was killing people."

Lars gave me a side glance. "Remember, tread carefully when you attempt to blur the line between right and wrong. It can be different from where you are standing." He turned back to face me. "Be sure you understand Elighan's side before making any judgment."

"I can't believe you're defending him." There was more shock in my sentiment than anger.

"I am not defending him. I am suggesting there is more to Elighan's story than Lily's side." Lars sighed. "You are so much like your mother. So stubborn."

"Which one?" I snorted. I didn't mean it to come out so derisive.

"Both." One of his eyebrows arched. "You inherited stubbornness from one and came by it in your environment with the other. Aisling and Lily are both extremely tenacious, as you are." His expression softened a little when he said Aisling's name.

"You were in love with Aisling, huh?" I blurted. I put the pieces together, but I wanted to hear the full story from his mouth.

Lars stared at me, his yellow eyes glaring at me. Finally he looked away. "Yes. We were in love."

"Tell me. I want to know *your* side of the story."

There was a full minute of silence before he began. "Aisling was married to Eris, who was abusive and controlling. Aisling was not the kind of woman you constrained. She was independent, determined, and full of life. I fought my feelings for a long time, but even I, a Demon, fell for her charms. There wasn't a Fae who did not. She had a flare about her, and you felt alive in her presence. Our affair was full of passion. I was the one who first took her to Greece. My hometown was a perfect spot to meet. Sometimes Devlin would join us. My brother and I were close back then. With her, we could be ourselves. There was no pretense. The three of us became friends. Light, Dark, Fay, Demon, we let go of prejudices and were ourselves."

He blinked and looked out the window, his voice tightening with control. "I sensed Devlin was in love with her, too. I was cocky and young and did not even consider I could lose her to him. Aisling and I were deeply in love, but my need for power, my desire to have what my brother was achieving as the Unseelie

King, consumed me. The more distant I became, the more she turned to him for comfort. Looking back, I can see how it happened; then, I did not. Let us say I did not react well to finding out Aisling's feelings had shifted to my brother. Devlin and I fought almost to the death. We did not speak afterward. Aisling hated how she tore us apart, but none of us were able to walk away.

"Our feelings for each other did not dwindle, even after she chose my brother. With Devlin she felt safe and loved; with me, it was always a storm of hunger and desire, an addiction hard to break away from."

"You continued your affair?"

Lars nodded. "We tried to stay away from each other, but most times we could not."

My biological mother was married to a Fay while having an affair with two Demons. Go, Mom.

"I think Devlin knew Aisling truly loved me. But I craved power and was too self-absorbed to see what I had. His jealousy changed him. She left him, but by then she was pregnant. Eris believed the baby was his. He was too arrogant and narrow minded to see the truth.

"Aisling wanted to keep the baby. She knew the truth would come out as soon as you were born. She understood from the moment she discovered she was with child she would not be able to hide from Aneira and, thus, her own demise was inevitable. As you know, by Fay law, an association with a Demon in any way is cause for death. Being a princess and pregnant with a Demon's child was the worst deed she could ever have done. Aneira would never let her own sister evade the law. Even if she had wanted to forgive Aisling, she would have made an example of her." Lars turned to me with sadness in his eyes.

"Aisling understood her destiny but did not want the same fate for you. Lily was Aisling's lady's maid and best friend. She turned to her for help. Of course, you know Aneira was aware of the affairs for a long time and planned to secretly kill Aisling, blaming it on the Dark Dwellers." A brief flicker of pain gripped his forehead, then it was gone. "I could have helped her if she had come to me."

"Why didn't she?" I asked.

He shrugged. "Aisling was fiercely independent. She did not want to need anybody or be under anyone else's control. She was too stubborn for her own good. It's why she and Lily became such good friends. They were a lot alike and understood each other like no one else. They were more like sisters than Aneira and Aisling had ever been."

"What happened to Eris?"

Lars scoffed. "He killed himself."

"What?"

"His pride was greatly insulted when he learned his wife had an affair. Not only did she betray him, but she betrayed her Queen and crown with two Demons, one the Unseelie King, and now she carried a bastard child. Eris could not face anyone. His dignity and stature were his driving forces. He did not see a way of redemption after being so greatly humiliated." Lars's tone revealed contempt for Eris. He sounded like an ass, but it was still sad. He ended his life because of what my mother had done, although I did not feel too much pity knowing he had been abusive.

Rez and Lars were together, but I never heard him talk about her like he did Aisling just now. I was pretty sure Aisling had been the love of his life. The one he loved and let get away. Before I found out I was part Demon, I never thought a Demon could love or feel loss. They experience great sorrow, and when they do lose something or someone, the repercussions of their pain are not only personal but global. Fae, in general, seem to behave similarly. They hide their true emotions, though when they do crack, it's a catastrophe.

After learning about my mom and Eli, I shut down; the desire to destroy simmered under the surface. Growing up human allowed me to control my Fae tendencies a bit more. It might have been a good thing I no longer had my powers; otherwise, I may well have leveled another town, without Asim's help.

I squirmed in my seat. My next question had been bothering me for a while, and could not avoid it any longer. I glanced at my hands in my lap. "Is there a chance... perhaps..." I huffed out, holding my head high. Defiant. "You could be my father?"

Lars did not react; he did not even blink. The silence grew, and I wasn't sure if he would answer me. The chair creaked as it turned away from me. He stood and walked to the windows. "I do not know."

"Were you two together when I was conceived?"

Lars cleared his throat, his eyes distant and his face contorted. I had never seen him look uncomfortable before.

"Yes. As I said, Aisling and I could not stay away from each other."

"So, there is a possibility you are my father?"

His only response was a quick nod.

I didn't know what to do with the information now I had it. I wasn't sure how I felt about it. "Is there a way to be tested?"

Lars shook his head back and forth, still looking away from me. "No. My brother and I were identical twins. Human twins may have different DNA, but my brother and I were pure Demon, identical to the last strand of DNA. Only our personalities were different. There is no way of ever knowing who your real father is."

"But she said I was Devlin's."

"Devlin was not certain of our continued affair. If he was, he did not say anything. But my brother was smart. I think he knew the entire time. He loved her and did not want to lose her either. When she stayed with him, he was willing to ignore it. He would have made a better father, before he went insane. Whether it was me or Devlin, she chose the man she thought would protect you better."

"Why did he go insane?"

"Being the Unseelie King is not an easy job. He was not as equipped for it as I am. I think the knowledge of Aisling's inconsistent love also slowly eroded his mind. When she died, he acted completely irrational and did not care about anything anymore. Destroying and killing were his ways of dealing."

Crap on ash bark. Between Aneira and my "father," insanity ran rampant in my family. I didn't fall far from that apple tree. I had thought my life was convoluted. These complications went above and beyond. Writers of soap operas need to take notes on my family.

As screwed up and crazy as they all were, I had a one. Alive or dead, blood or not blood, I could call all these people family, even the Dark Dwellers. No matter what they had done, they were a part of me. I knew I would have to face Eli again, soon. And Lily.

Lars moved away from the window and turned to me. He seemed to pick up my train of thought. "I know you are angry with her, Ember. You have a right to be. However, I think you need to understand what she went through. I may not agree with all the choices Lily made, but I feel she did what she thought was right. Knowing you now, I can see why she chose to keep her life a secret from you. You are far too impulsive and inquisitive. If she had told you anything about who you truly were, you would have looked for more answers. The truth would have gotten you killed. At first I thought it was a foolish decision, but now I think it was wise. She wanted to keep you sheltered."

I played with the ends of my hair, looking down. I didn't want to admit how much he made sense. But it still didn't lessen the betrayal I felt.

"She did her best. She kept you protected for eighteen years, even when she wasn't around. Quite a feat since you were hunted every day since you both escaped from the castle."

Blood Beyond Darkness

I wiggled in my chair with irritation.

"Give her a chance to tell you her story." Lars sat on the corner of his desk.

"Why should I?" Anger spoke the words before rationality got hold of my tongue.

"Because she gave up everything she had for you. Do not forget Lily had family, friends, a future husband, a home... and she left it all. For you. She lost her best friend, all for a baby who was not hers and one who should not have even existed. The prejudice against Daes was at highpoint at the time of your birth, yet she raised you like her own. She was on the run, alone and scared, with a newborn. Lily and I may never get along, but I will always regard her with the highest esteem. I do not think anyone else would have done what she did."

I bit my lip, feeling a wave of gratitude and guilt. Love wormed its way through my hurt and pain.

"She may have made a lot of mistakes, but she loves you more than anything. She gave herself over to Aneira and stayed silent through years of torture to keep you secure. If you cannot find a way to forgive her, then you are less like your mother and more like your real father than I thought."

I kept my head down the whole time he spoke, ashamed of the anguish I caused Lily. A strong desire to see her pounded into my chest, gripping my heart. Now that I was back in the land of the living, there were so many things I needed to deal with. "I need to see her, Ryan, and my dad." Kennedy's face burst into my head. I bolted out of my chair, suddenly restless and angry at myself for not looking for her. What kind of friend was I?

"Oh, my god. I need to find Kennedy."

Lars stood, his shoulders hitching back in frustration as if he was trying to pacify a petulant child. He rounded his desk and faced me from behind it. "In your absence, we have been doing everything we can to find her. She is important to us, too."

"I know, and I am grateful for that, but I need to do something. I've been so selfish. She needs me, and I wasn't there for her."

"She is not aware of your absence."

"But I am." I bobbed on the balls of my feet, my calves constricting in protest.

"There is no way I am letting you leave here. The Queen may appear not to be looking for you, but we both know she is. She will have spies everywhere. Your death has become her obsession."

"Lars, I can't become prisoner here, too. I need to find my friend. I need to see Ryan, my mom and my dad." Panic moved my arms around frantically. "I can't stop my life. I can't."

"Ember!" His voice cut through my rant like a cleaver. "Do you understand the severity of what is happening? Soon, I will have an army here. Aneira is going to tear down the walls with your stolen powers. The destruction will be beyond comprehension. Do you realize you are still the one who has to kill her? We will find a way to get you to the sword. It is our only chance. And if anything happens to you?" He trailed off. "Our chances are exceedingly slim. We need everyone at their best... and alive."

I still had yet to tell anyone the truth about the sword. Part of me wanted to stay silent and let him believe we had hope. The other part needed to get the weight off my chest.

"What if I couldn't kill her?"

His eyebrows drew down. "You have to."

"No. I mean what if something happened, and I could no longer obtain the sword?"

"Not an option." He said it so firmly it almost stopped the words in my throat from coming out.

"Can't anyone kill her? Anyone who has the sword?" My finger curled around the hem of my top. "Why don't you do it? You're the Unseelie King. And don't think I have forgotten about our agreement. I never thought about it till now, but why do you want the sword so badly, Lars? If you are so convinced I am going to become Queen, aren't I handing you a weapon that can kill me?" My stare was full of accusation. "Is it why you want it? Something you will forever hold over me to keep me in line? To manipulate me?"

His jaw clenched as he stared at me. "Your supposition is not the reason I desire the sword."

"Then why? No one would desire a weapon so strong except to use it to control and destroy."

Lars pressed his hands on his desk. "Such a notion will get you killed. Fae and most leaders covet objects and secrets to dominate and keep the game in their favor. What is the human phrase, 'Those with the most toys win'? For Fae it is even more so."

"You will use it to command me if you don't like something I do?"

"Let us hope it does not come to pass."

"You are such a dick," I yelled.

"I am a Demon, Ember. Do not forget the fact."

"I won't." I crossed my arms. "Good thing I can't get you the one thing you want the most."

"You will. You have agreed to the terms." His lashes lowered as his focus drilled into me, forcing my legs back against the chair. "I am sorry, but we do not have time for uncertainty and stubbornness. There is no other option but for us to win. You are going to kill her, Ember. I am not the one who is prophesized. You are. If you do not acknowledge your part then I believe we are doomed."

I swallowed nervously. "No pressure or anything."

"I understand the task is a lot for you. As much as you may not believe what I say, I only want the best for you. You are my blood." *Possibly my daughter* was left unsaid, but I could hear it in the pause. "If I could have it another way, I would take it, but we cannot. The task before us is our fate. Your fate. We must finish the war she forced. End Aneira."

Something in me snapped. "But I can't touch it, Lars! She put a curse on me."

Silence stilled the room, pricking at my skin as he stared at me. "Excuse me?"

Licking my lips, I looked away. "When Aneira killed Eli, she said she would let me bring him back if I promised to never touch the sword again. If I did, he would die. This time for good."

Lars's face flushed red and his eyes swirled brightly. "And. You. Agreed?" He was fighting to control his anger, but his shoulders and chest tensed like steel cables on the verge of snapping. He suddenly seemed taller, looming over me. The room grew tight and small. A chill brushed my bones.

"Yes." My voice sounded small.

His features shifted. No horns sprouted from his head, but his eyes glowed bright yellowish-green, and they outshone the flickering bulbs overhead. The bones under his skin protruded sharply through his now parchment-thin skin. His eyes went entirely black.

I took a step back. I had heard so many people tell me it was freaky when my eyes turned black, and now I saw what they meant. No white remained, just two black pools of fury. "Lars?" My voice squeaked.

He no longer resembled the good-looking, olive-skinned King but a monster from a nightmare. "Lars!"

It looked at me, and it felt like its stare went right through me, tearing at my soul. It took a few steps toward me. My instinct told me to run, but my legs only moved me back against the wall.

The Demon suddenly stood right in front of me, its bony fingers wrapping around my throat and squeezing. My feet lifted off the floor, his hand strangling my throat as he pushed me up the wall. Air tore from my lungs, like it was sucked out with a vacuum.

"Lars, please stop," I choked, my eyes beginning to water.

I could see my reflection in his black eyes, my face red and strained, desperate for air. His fingers dug into my skin, crushing my vocal cords.

"Lars... Uncle." My voice did not make it out of my mouth, but the words formed on my lips.

The Demon stopped, my body sliding back to the floor. It gave a sharp huff of air from its nose, and shook its head. Its features slowly turned back to the face I had come to know so well. Lars dropped his hand and stepped away.

I rubbed at my throat, coughing.

Several minutes passed before either of us spoke. If he needed "time" to control his temper, I would give it to him. Speaking might only piss him off again.

Tension turned the small noises of the house to top volume. My hearing picked up Marguerite setting a pot on the stove. The shrillness of the metal on metal hurt my eardrums.

"All right." Lars turned around and strode to the French doors and looked out into the night. There would be no apologies coming my way. Demons did not work like that. "Nothing has changed."

I blinked, his words sinking heavy in my heart. "What? What do you mean?"

He shifted slightly toward me, but kept his eyes looking ahead. "You can still kill the Queen."

Instant rage pushed me off the wall. "But it will mean Eli dies!"

Lars finally turned and faced me. "Yes, it does."

"W-What?" Even after all he'd done, the mere idea of something bad happening to him, of him no longer existing, launched a terror so deep I gasped for breath.

"You said yourself how you no longer wanted to see him again. You swore you hated him."

"I didn't mean I want him to die!"

Lars sighed. He took slow, methodical breaths. I could tell he was fighting to stay in control. Right now I didn't care.

"How can you even say that? And here I thought you had grown to like him."

"The facts have nothing to do with whether I like him or not. We are at war, Ember."

"How soulless are you? You can't expect me to kill him no matter what he's done. I won't do it."

"Now who is being selfish?" Lars moved to his desk. "Is one life worth millions? Freedom and happiness? Your friends and family? All of it will no longer exist. Is Elighan's life worth all their loss and suffering to you?"

My mouth fell open. Then it closed. My first response was to say yes. Even if I never wanted to see him again, and he had done horrible things, I couldn't kill him. But was I being selfish? Was Eli's life worth the destruction of Earth? I had already killed so many. Could I really doom all to a life of slavery and or death? Was I willing to forgo the lives of millions of innocent humans and Fae for his?

"You are also condemning him to an even worse fate than death."

"What?"

"Let us say you do not touch the sword. Yes, Elighan would live... for a while. So would Aneira. How long do you think his life would last after that? Your way would be quick and painless. Aneira will torture him beyond recognition. I am not talking only physically, either. What she did to Torin would be child's play compared to what she would do to Eli. She feels the connection between you. She will be cruel in dealing with him especially to hurt you. Even if she has already killed you, she will torment him out of spite." Lars's eyes flashed black again, hinting the Demon in him was close to the surface. "Is such a fate what you want for him?"

My lids blinked feverishly, and I stared at my feet, my voice soft. "No." The weight of the world was on my shoulders, crushing my bones into the earth. Both my choices were unbearable. How could one small decision of mine make or break the entire world? Aneira was conniving, and she had been quick to act that day. She saw my love for Eli was enough for her to think she had me, but could she possibly think I would choose him over an entire population? Yes, she did. She had no respect or love for humans and probably could never fathom I would choose their side. As much as I hated him right now, I also cared too much to let him be tortured. I was fated to kill the man I loved, and I knew what my choice would be when the moment came.

"You will not tell him of the curse. I want all heads clear going into war." Lars sat back in his chair, his shoulders tight around his neck.

"You don't want me to tell him he's going to die?" The shrill voice didn't sound like my own.

"No." Lars leaned back. "It will alter his outlook on the battle ahead. He will be impulsive and foolish. His dedication, knowing he will die, would be skewed."

I wasn't particularly crazy about the idea of telling him. How do you tell someone he is doomed to die, anyway? But keeping it from him, from my Alpha, didn't sit right either.

"I bind your tongue, eyes, and hands against telling anyone." I felt the weight of his spell come down on me, wrapping around my throat and tongue.

"Why... why did you do that?" My hand went to my already bruised neck.

"I made the decision easier for you. You no longer have the option. You cannot feel guilty for something you are not able to do. Blame me for Elighan's ignorance. We both know this choice is for the best. There is nothing you can do to change the realities, and Elighan knowing will not help."

Blistering rage rippled between my ribs. Lars was forcing my hand and taking away my choice. I hated it, but at the same time, I felt relieved the decision to tell him was no longer in my hands. Lars was right. It was probably better Eli didn't know. I looked down as a single tear dropped from my eye.

"I am sorry, Ember, but my decision is for the greater good."

My eyelids narrowed as I brought my head up. "I don't give a fuck about what's best right now. Don't worry. I will do what I have to do, but don't give me platitudes about the greater good," I seethed. With a turn I propelled to the door. I grabbed the knob, yanked the door open, and slammed it behind me.

I didn't know what pissed me off more: the fact I felt like I had no choice in the matter, or I still wanted to choose the man who should disgust me.

The world was in my hands? Yeah, good luck, Earth...

EIGHT

I stared out the windows into the darkening sky as I sat on my bed. Syrupy clouds dripped with rain, hiding all remnants of the moon and stars beyond. The pulse of my heart thumped quicker in my chest as the night crushed the walls in on me. I had been here too long doing nothing as my life passed by. My friend was lost somewhere out there. I understood searching for Kennedy at this moment was stupid. Lorcan had taken her far away from here by now. But I knew I could get to Ryan, Mark, and Lily. The need to finally hear my mother's story dominated my thoughts.

"I need you to take me to the Otherworld." My knee bobbed up and down on my bed. "I want to see my family."

"She speaks." Cal flew from the chandelier onto my shoulder.

Simmons followed him, landing roughly on my bed.

"Good girl. Now sit." Cal pointed towards the bed.

I looked down. My rear was already nestled on my bed.

"Goooood girl." Cal patted my cheek. "So obedient."

I flicked him off my shoulder, and he tumbled onto my comforter. "Bad, bad doggie."

"Cal, do not insult my lady." Simmons hopped up on my leg, crossed his arms and tapped his foot on my thigh.

"I'm serious. I need to go now. I need to talk to my mom, to see Mark and Ryan."

Cal padded over and climbed on my other leg. "Are you nuts, girlie? Okay, that is well proven, but are you crazy?"

I frowned.

"Lars will never let you leave here," Cal exclaimed.

Simmons nodded. "My lady, he is right."

"Lars doesn't have to know."

"Right, because his ignorance has always worked out so well in the past." Cal rolled his eyes.

"What I mean is he doesn't have to know till after I leave." The need to go, to move, took all rational thought and stuffed it in a back drawer of my mind. "Better to go now and ask for forgiveness after." I couldn't stay in the room one minute longer. Without warning, I bolted up, taking Cal and Simmons with me.

"Warn a pixie when you are going to erupt all over the place!" Cal yelled as he flew in the air. Simmons settled back on the bed.

My feet moved frantically in front of my patio doors. "Cal, I am going. You can help me or not."

"Without my help, how will you know how to get there, huh?" He flew up to look me in the eyes. His hands on his hips.

A grin grew on my lips as I turned to the other pixie. "Simmons?"

Simmons looked around, unsettled by my smile. "What?"

Cal's mouth hung slightly open. "Are you kidding me? You're not being fair, girlie."

"What?" My eyes widened. "I am only asking. He doesn't have to say yes."

"Oh, come on. We both knew he'll do anything you ask."

Simmons's head snapped between us. "What? What do you want to ask me, my lady?"

"She wants you to take her to the Otherworld." Cal flew down to the bed.

"What? You want me to escort you against the Unseelie King's orders to the Otherworld?" Simmons's eyes grew to the size of dimes.

"Yes," I confirmed.

He gulped and glanced down. I knelt, becoming level with

them. "Simmons, I have been trapped in my own misery for too long. I've been a terrible friend and daughter. I need to fix the mess I made." I paused, knowing the power my next words would have on him. "As future Queen, I ask for your service, soldier. I need your help."

Simmons lifted his head, pride filling his chest and face.

"What a load of fairy farts." Cal let his head dramatically drop back. "Could you tug at his little pixie heart—"

"I will do it," Simmons cut him off.

"Oh, what a shocker." Cal threw up his arms.

I leaned in and gave Simmons a kiss on the cheek. "Thank you."

"What makes you think I am going to go along with you?" Cal stomped toward the edge of the bed; his amber eyes sparked with annoyance.

"I need you to stay here to tell Lars after I'm gone. You can even say you tried to stop me."

"Sprite spit! You really want to shorten my pixie life, don't you?"

"Ahh, it keeps you young."

"Yeah, because if I am dead, I won't age," Cal grumbled. "I'm not stupid enough to go against the Unseelie King."

I wiggled my eyebrows. "Yes, you will."

He eyed me, quick to catch my meaning.

"I cannot be bought, girlie."

With that I started to chuckle.

"All right!" He shrugged and sighed. "You know my weakness. I cannot fight you either, you evil sorceress." He slung his arm across his eyes dramatically.

"Thought so." I grinned.

A few hours later I found myself deep in the Otherworld, through a door connecting the Dark Fae Forest to Lars's property. The forest reminded me of my dreams before I knew what I was. Shadows clung to each crooked tree, wrapping so tightly the lines blurred where one tree ended and the other began. Limbs kinked and twisted, curling into the night sky, only letting the moonlight beam down in rays through the branches. It looked like the dark enchanted forest you always imagined in your head as a child, full of goblins and monsters. I wasn't afraid. As much as I had loved the forest of the light, I found I loved the forest of the Dark even more. The magic filled my lungs with dense air and sparked energy into my body.

"This way, my lady." Simmons's wings vibrated the air, giving off tiny sparks. It made me wonder if this action was where the idea of pixie dust came from. Magic charged their surroundings, and the friction of his beating wings caused the aura to glimmer behind him. I had never noticed it before. If it was because the magic was thicker here or because it was so dark I could finally see it, I didn't know. It was cool nonetheless.

The deeper Simmons took me into the Dark Fae forest, the more I noticed the creatures. A few times I heard mumbling and movement of undergrowth as something dodged away from me. An animal the size of a bunny with red eyes and horns darted into the brush.

"What was that?"

"Probably a horned-hare, tree hobbit, or a ground troll." Simmons waved his hand, dismissing all of them.

"Oh, yeah, of course. Why wouldn't it be?" I said dryly. The Otherworld was still such a mystery to me, and sometimes I would stop and think: *Holy crap! This is my life.*

"Watch your step, my lady. There's a dwarf's burrow here." I tramped around the spot where Simmons hovered. Distorted branches broke through the growth stretching for the ground. They clawed at my back and hair as I bent. There was emptiness now in my soul where I once felt the life of the earth. The trees seemed curious when I passed, as if they felt something different about me, but they quickly lost interest when they felt nothing more inside.

A large leathery winged creature with pointy teeth skimmed my head. "Crap on ash bark! What the hell swooped past us?"

Simmons sighed and turned to see what I was screeching about. The thing buzzed my head again, its soft, bushy tail brushing across my forehead. I hit the ground in defense.

"Oh, yeah, those things are usually nasty." Simmons pulled out his plastic weapon. "But this one is only a baby. Doesn't even have its horns yet."

"What is it? Some kind of bat?"

"No. It's a wolpertinger, a kind of squirrel with wings, antlers, tail, and fangs." He slipped his sword back in his belt loop. "His fangs are too little to do any damage to you, my lady, and he has no horns yet. You are safe."

"A wolpertinger? It doesn't have parents or cousins or anything close by?" I slowly stood.

"Yeah, most likely." Simmons swung back around. Where Cal would have said it sarcastically, Simmons was matter-of-fact. "We should probably get out of its territory."

I quickly followed Simmons. We traveled for a bit as I tried to keep up with him. When we broke through the growth, I paused. My eyes widened at the beauty ahead of me. White light glowed through the mist like Christmas lights. These tiny lit bulbs flickered around me, circling like fireflies. A tickling on my arm caused me to look down. One landed on me.

"What are those?" My eyes examined the dime size creature. It didn't look like a normal firefly; it was more like an oversized ladybug with electric wings glowing every time it started to fly.

"Lamprog." Simmons frowned, shooing it off my arm. "Get away."

"Hey! It wasn't hurting anyone." I scowled at Simmons. "They're beautiful."

"Not as much as you think." Simmons snorted. The one he

shooed away came back around. The closer it got, the larger its fangs appeared, protruding from its mouth.

Sharp pain zapped up my arm as its teeth sunk into my wrist. "Ow!" I screamed swatting at the bug. "What the hell?"

"I told you, my lady. They are not nice. Most things in this forest aren't necessarily pleasant no matter how cute they look."

"Damn." I shook my arm. Tingles infiltrated my arm, as the venom worked itself up. "Are they dangerous?"

"Not individually, but once a year on the full moon before Samhain, thousands of lamprog gather to mate. They get violent and aggressive and can be especially dangerous then. On any other day, they are merely a nuisance. Your arm might be numb for a while, but the venom should not hurt you."

"The 'should' in that sentence doesn't cause me to feel better."

"Come on, my lady." Simmons flew forward. "Don't let them land on you, and you will be fine."

I followed Simmons for what felt like a half hour, but time here felt peculiar. It could have been minutes or days.

"Through here. We are almost there, my lady." He pointed at a cave. It was pitch black, and moss clung to the sides, dripping over the passage like dreadlocks. The divide between the Dark and Light side.

"You want me to go in there?"

"There is no other way." Simmons landed roughly on my shoulder. Without missing a beat, I wrapped my hand around him, steadying him. "You did bring a torch?"

"Yeah." My fingers dove into my pocket, grappling with the small flashlight I stuffed there.

"As you might recall, my lady, pixies do not care for caves very much."

I brought my hair over my shoulder, hiding Simmons underneath it. "Better?"

"Yes, my lady." His wings fluttered against my neck as he tucked in tighter. "But I hate caves. They're full of bats and spiders, all things which tend to consider pixies food."

I shared Simmons's fears of creepy crawly things.

"Big girl pants. Big girl pants." I repeated and stepped into the opaque partition dividing me from my family. Taking me from the Dark side to the Light.

NINE

The mouth of the tunnel swallowed me and dropped me down the throat of the mountain. The walls closed in tighter, my breath clipped in quick reiteration. Simmons stayed nestled in my neck and encouraged me along the way, "Almost there, my lady."

Eventually we came out of the tunnel, which sat at the edges between Light and Dark. The farthest they could go without it hurting them since all were Seelie or at least partially.

The land was a beautiful oasis. A spot at the bottom of a gully. The mountain encased a stone cabin, and a waterfall feeding a small lake sat on the opposite side. It seemed well protected. You had to know where it stood, or you would never realize it was there.

My mom, Torin, and Thara stepped out of the cabin with weapons. All guns pointed at me.

"What is your business here?" Thara clicked off the safety.

"Don't shoot! It's me." I held up my arms.

"Ember?" Mom lowered the gun a little, but she remained on guard.

"Of course it's my lady." Simmons flew out of my mane.

Torin let his arm fall to his side at seeing Simmons. Since Aneira had taken my powers, Torin and I no longer had a bond; he couldn't feel me or sense I was coming.

Mom dropped her weapon back in the holster and ran for

Blood Beyond Darkness

me, but she stopped when she got close. I could see her forehead scrunch and her eyes fill with tears probably not sure how I would react—wanting to wrap her arms around me but not sure if she was allowed to hug anymore. Since talking to Lars, my ire had dissipated quite a bit, though there remained a wall between us, and I knew she was leaving it to me to break it down or not.

"The alarm went off." She took another tentative step to me. Of course. They probably had their place spelled up the wazoo.

"You guys should be on the defensive." I looked at my shoes.

"I am so happy you are here," she said softly, bringing my focus back on her.

I nodded, then returned my attention back on my feet.

"Well, come in." She turned her body and motioned for me to head for the cabin.

"Ember?" I heard a male voice call from the porch. The familiarity of it caused tears to prick under my lids. I ran toward Mark. He came off the porch, meeting me half way. His arms engulfed me in a bear hug and squashed me with the intensity.

"Sunny D," he whispered, kissing the top of my head. I clung to him with everything I had. This man was everything to me. There was no doubt who my "dad" was. "I have missed you so much."

A choked cry burst from my throat, my vocal cords too thick to respond. He was all right. Maybe he could never return to Earth again, but he was alive.

"I love you so much," I finally mumbled. He hugged me tighter before he kissed my head again. When I pulled back, my eyes landed on the burn scar on his face. I flinched, taking his arm in my hand, seeing the mutilation there as well.

"Don't go there, Em. I am fine. Please don't blame yourself." The wrinkled, discolored flesh would forever be a reminder of what I was capable of. No matter what Mark said, the guilt would never resolve itself. I would have to live with it.

Only the sound of Ryan calling drew me away from Mark's embrace. I went from his arms to Ryan's in an instant.

"M&M." He sighed in my ear.

Responsibility hit me like a punch to the gut. "Ry, I am so sorry. For everything." I pulled back to look at him. The glow emanating from him earlier had evened out. It was hard to explain. He looked normal, but I could smell he was not entirely human anymore. His skin had a radiance models would envy. He had lost weight from being sick but was still the warm teddy bear I loved. The big difference was his brilliant smile. He seemed—happy. My gaze went to Castien in the doorway, leaning against the frame. His eyes were on Ryan.

"Em, there is nothing you should apologize for. None of this was your fault." Ryan's gaze penetrated mine.

"We both know that's not true." I shook my head.

"Wow! Hello, self-absorbed." Ryan's hand went in circular movements around me. "This is not all about you." He tried to hold a serious look but failed miserably. "It's about me." A small laugh expelled my chest. Ryan could always make me feel better no matter what mood I was in.

"I appreciate it, Ry, but you and I both know you would not be here if it wasn't for me." I glanced away. "You... we... wouldn't have lost Ian."

Ryan looked at his feet. This time he was all seriousness. "I don't blame you, Em. At first I did. Then I realized you were a victim, too. We can all play the blame game, but the person we should be punishing is the girl who killed him." Samantha. Even the thought of her caused hatred so pure and raw it made me dizzy. "You can throw Lorcan in there for good measure, too."

"I will get revenge, Ryan. I swear to you. Samantha will *pay*. So will Lorcan."

Ryan looked at me for a few moments. A lot had changed since the last time we saw each other. He finally gave a nod, understanding and accepting my meaning. Ryan was definitely more of a lover than a fighter. But Ian was worth the fight. And the kill.

Ryan cleared his throat. "All this seriousness makes me want to get *ar meisce*." He threw up his arms and turned back for the entry to the cabin. "Mead all around!"

"Mead?" I cocked an eyebrow.

"Yeah, Ryan is getting into his new world a little too well." Castien chuckled, nudging Ryan as he went through the doorway.

"I am acclimating," Ryan's fingers curled into quotation marks.

"If that's what you want to call it." Castien snickered. Their banter was familiar and comfortable.

"We were making dinner." Mom came to me. "I hope you will stay."

"Of course she will." Mark's arm reached around me, leading me into the house.

Everyone drifted back into the warm cabin. It was bigger than it looked from the outside with the back part of it built into the mountain. Wooden floors and stone walls gave it a homey feel. Overstuffed sofas were arranged around the fireplace, where a warm blaze danced in the hearth. Fire still called to my soul, twisting around my veins. The flames curled and swayed with hypnotic grace. I stretched my hand out to feel the heat. But it did not acknowledge me or respond to the connection we used to have. I was nothing to it. I blinked and turned away, feeling oddly rejected.

I scanned the rest of the house. A kitchen was off to the left side as you walked in, and a huge wooden table sat between the living space and kitchen. A bathroom and what I figured to be a bedroom were on the right side. A spiral staircase next to the living room led to the second story. It wasn't huge, but it was nice and seemed like enough space for the six of them, especially when most of them probably preferred to be outdoors when they could.

Thara and Mark had made venison stew, while Mom

baked soda bread. I assumed Thara had killed and skinned the deer, and Mark had cooked it. Mark had always been the chef in our house. Mom liked to bake but not cook. Now I knew she had people who had cooked for her most of her life. Her role in the castle had been far away from the kitchens.

Simmons took pride in helping my mom roll and knead the bread. Castien and Ryan set the table. Everyone played a role in this little family, except Torin. He plunked himself on the sofa with a cup of mead in his hand, glaring at the fire.

Even though I could no longer sense Torin, my Dark Dweller senses picked up on a heavy, angry aura which surrounded him. The anger and resentment discharging off him hurt me deeply. He had been so sure of his life's path that when it didn't go the way he planned, he couldn't handle it. It was in his blood to be a soldier and the First Knight. He was no longer either. He also had been so sure of his fate with me. All of this was dumped on top of what Aneira did to him: the brutalizing and torture. How could anybody come back from something so horrible? Especially when the one you did it for falls in love with someone you hate.

"Hey." I sat on the sofa next to him.

His lips pressed together, and his eyes stayed firmly on the fire.

I licked my bottom lip. "Torin, I want to apologize." My sentence trailed off. His jaw clenched, and his teeth ground audibly. "I am sorry for what you went through. What you did for me." I shook my head at the memory of his bruised and bloody face when he had escaped from the castle. His nose had been broken, his eye swollen shut, and dried blood caked his scalp. "I can never repay you for your sacrifice. For always being there for me." I placed my hand on his.

Torin jerked his hand from under mine.

Swallowing back the rebuff, I continued. "Torin, I am so, so—"

"You were the only thing helping me through." He cut me

off. "When she poured boiling tar over me, when she beat me with a spiked club, when she put me on the rack and pleased herself on me over and over as my joints were being ripped apart, I imagined your face, saw your smile, heard your laugh. It took me somewhere else. I could escape my hell for a moment knowing you were out there waiting for me. You were the reason I wanted to survive. Because at the end of it, I would have you."

My fingers gripped each other so hard my knuckles turned white. "Oh, Jesus," I whispered. There was a long, drawn-out pause, which was bursting with tension, sorrow, and unease. His body language expressed he did not want my pity or apology. Finally a hoarse whisper came out of my mouth. "You are free of me now. The bond is gone. You must have felt the truth of it by now. You can move on with your life." *Maybe with Thara.*

Torin bolted off the sofa. His voice sounded low and tight. "Do you think I would stop loving you because there is no more bond? You don't know me at all." He took a step before he turned to me. "Everything I did was because I loved you. Because you were supposed to be my future. *My* wife. *My* love. Bond or not." He turned from me and stormed out of the cabin, slamming the door.

An awkward silence packed the small house. Thara stared at the door and looked like she wanted to follow him. I did, too, but I doubted he would want to see my face anymore. I still couldn't give him what he wanted.

Mom wiped her hands on a towel and came to me. "Give him time," she spoke softly.

I nodded and looked down at my lap. Acid worked up from my stomach as I considered what had actually happened to him. Theories had mulled around in my mind, but the actual truth of what she did to him made vomit curdle at the back of my throat, a breath away from release.

"Uncomfortable moments like these call for more alcohol." Ryan came over and handed me a cup of mead, a delicious wine made from fermenting honey. It was strong and tasted sweet and smooth.

Mark placed the stew on the table, and we all sat around the table. Simmons had been staying here and someone had built him a doll-size chair and table they placed next to me. It looked like Mom's handy work. Like me, she also loved building and creating things. Simmons's mead glass was a thimble. I knew if Cal were here, he would be yelling how his cup was no more than a shot glass and someone had better get him something he could swim in.

The alcohol eased the tension at the table a bit. Torin did not return, which was probably better, and everyone started to relax. By my second glass, even my guard against my mother was softening. I wanted to talk to her. Lars had helped me see I owed her a chance to tell her story.

Ryan, Mark, and I fell into our usual dinner banter. Kennedy and Ryan had spent lots of dinners at my house, and it felt uncannily familiar to have the chatter back. All we needed was Kennedy. As if Ryan could read my thoughts, he cleared his throat. "Nothing on Kennedy yet?"

"No." I shook my head.

"I get reports daily they are out searching for her," Simmons pronounced. "We will not stop until we find her." I bit on my lip. I was too much of a coward to admit I had not been a part of the search.

Later as we carried our dishes to the sink, I leaned over to my mom. "Do you want to go for a walk?"

Her eyes widened, and she nodded.

Mark stepped in and grabbed the plates from our hands. "I got the dishes. You two go." He smiled warmly at us both.

Mom's smile brightened her face as she looked at him. She placed her hand on his arm and squeezed it with affection. He smiled back, and his eyes were full of love as he looked at her. It felt like I was intruding on a private moment. I was happy they were trying to work it out. I knew whatever happened they would get through it together. Love like theirs doesn't go away no matter how angry or hurt you are. It's forever.

An image of Eli's smirk flashed through my mind, wrenching my gut.

Torin sat in a rocking chair on the porch as we stepped outside. The moment we appeared he stood and disappeared into the house. It seemed wherever I was he didn't want to be. The door slammed which left mom and me standing on the porch alone.

"He's been through a lot." Mom looked back toward the door.

"I know."

"He's a good man, but his whole world has been shattered. He doesn't know what to do now. When I told him about your powers being taken, he said he felt the disconnection between you but didn't understand until I let him know. He first thought you were dead, and he went a little crazy. He doesn't know how to adjust to you not being the center of his world." Mom stepped off the porch, her boots crunching on the gravel. "I truly hope he finds his way. He reminds me too much of Eris right now. Black and white. When life turned out to be gray, his pride and stubbornness would not let him move on."

"It is scaring me. Every time I see him, he's getting darker and darker. I don't know what to do." I stopped and turned to face my mom.

"It is not your job to fix him, Ember. He has to find his own way." Lily twirled her long auburn hair into a low bun. "You can only be there as his friend when he decides to accept what has happened. Right now, seeing you only causes things to be worse."

I took a deep breath, the truth of her words settling blade-like between my bones.

"And I think Thara most of all wishes he'd get through this and see there is more to life than you," Mom teased.

I guffawed. "Yeah, I noticed her attention on him from the moment they came to the Dweller's ranch."

Her small hand touched my face. "Because you love someone, doesn't mean they will love you back. Love doesn't work like that. Hearts don't love on command or with logic."

Pinpricks of pain assaulted my own heart; I knew her words held dual meaning: Eli and her.

We walked in silence for a while before she broke it. "I am so sorry, Em, for all the heartache I caused you and the betrayal you must feel from all the lies."

"Tell me. I want to know everything." I stopped walking and looked deep in the shadowy forest. I could hear the surging waterfall in the distance. "From the beginning."

Her shoulders went up as she let out a long breath. She took a few moments to collect her thoughts. "My family had always worked for the royal family. Aisling and I were the same age, and it was a perfect fit for me to become her *searbhanta*, basically a lady in waiting. When I took the role, we were both around twelve in human years. We immediately became best friends and spent every waking moment together. When Aneira took the throne, our friendship became even stronger. We were each other's confidantes and support. She and her sister never got along, though Aneira likes to pretend otherwise. Aneira was jealous of our relationship. She was envious of everything when it came to Aisling. Aisling was definitely their father's favorite. Their mother died giving birth to Aisling, another reason Aneira hated her."

The shadows on Mom's face cleared, and she smiled. "Aisling was beautiful, powerful, strong, sassy, and men fell over themselves to be next to her. Aneira was all these things, but even as a child she acted cold and aloof. She was power-driven and saw nothing else. To be fair, Aisling never had to worry about ruling or being a queen. She had more freedom and less responsibility. Aisling was free to be the wild child and do what she pleased. Aneira had to take on a lot at a young age. The King pampered Aisling but raised Aneira to keep her feelings and emotions locked up. He actually treated her cruelly, acting distant and reserved, preparing her to be the queen.

"The division between the sisters grew every year, filling their relationship with resentment and anger," she said. "Eris had always been betrothed to Aisling, and at first she liked him. She got caught up in the idea of them as a couple and didn't see the true man underneath. After their engagement, things slowly changed. His temper and need for power showed. I tried to get her to see it, but she ignored my advice. Only a month or so after their marriage, she came downstairs with a black eye." Mom stared through the trees at the evening sky. The stars were magnificent and luminous. I wanted to reach out and snatch them up.

Mom's eyes shown with pride for her friend. "Aisling was strong and only let the brutality happen once more before she put him in his place. He never physically touched her again, although he abused her emotionally. Aneira brushed aside Aisling's attempts to talk to her. Aneira liked Eris and tended to ignore anything negative about him. I was the only person Aisling could go to." Mom's lids blinked repetitively.

"So, what happened? When did she meet Lars?"

Mom sighed heavily, sitting on a rock behind her. "Aneira was already obsessed with returning to Earth. Aisling saw what lengths her sister would go to control it, and knew her plans were to kill or enslave all humans. Also, Aneira's fear of Daes and Druids grew into such hatred she tried to annihilate both lines. Aisling knew she needed to do something. No one at the castle had the power or desire to stop Aneira. I mean *really stop* her. Aisling met secretly with Lars since she couldn't go straight to the Unseelie King. Devlin was not easy to find, and it would be perilous if any spy spotted Aisling with Devlin. Fays associating with Demons is so unaccepted it could mean their life. It would be worse for a princess, so she and Lars met when their secrecy could be guaranteed. I knew of their meetings, but it was a while before she told me they were having an affair, that she'd fallen in love with him. As her friend I met him several times. I could not deny their connection, but I knew he wasn't good for her. Nothing positive would come of their relationship. I tried my best to have her see the folly. She was every bit as stubborn and free spirited as you, and she went with her heart."

"Like you're not equally as stubborn and free spirited," I smirked.

"Yeah, I am. But I wasn't as much back then. Aisling was enough for the both of us." Mom smiled. "Their plans to find the sword and kill Aneira were the reasons for meeting, but their love flowered and went on for years. I think Eris knew she was cheating on him, but he would never admit it." She paused for a moment before resuming. "Things might have continued, but Lars was changing. His own obsession for power, for what his brother had, got the better of him. Aisling had become good friends with Devlin at this point and turned to him for advice and support. Everything got quite sticky between them. She fell for Devlin, but I always felt she looked at him more as a friend than a lover. Lars was her weakness; they could not stay away from each other."

Their connection reminded me of Eli's and mine. And my feelings for Torin reminded me of what Aisling might have felt for Devlin—safe and secure but without passion.

"When Aisling discovered she was pregnant, I knew things would never be the same. There was no doubt she would keep the baby. As her friend, I won't deny I begged her to get rid of you." Mom wiped an escaping tear. "But she wouldn't. She understood the repercussions of her choice. There would be no way of claiming you were Eris's child. Nor did she want to. She loved you. She was proud of having a Dae."

"Do you know who my real father is? Did she tell you?" I

kicked at a loose pebble with my toe.

"No." Lily shook her head. "As you know, Aisling was not perfect. She loved two men. Some people might judge her, but I saw her with both of them. Each brought out something different in her. Devlin felt more secure, and he adored her beyond words. Lars and she were connected past time and space. They got each other without talking. They were so intense and in love with each other, and it was what destroyed them. Both men, when you saw her with them, seemed right. There was no right and wrong merely unfortunate timing."

I understood. Love came in many ways and with various people. They fit into your life differently. It wasn't who was right or wrong or good or bad. At the end of the day, it was who made you laugh and feel he was the person you wanted to spend your life with. The image of Eli's cocky grin, his green eyes glinting with mischief, struck me hard. He was there. Always. My throat constricted as I tried to swallow.

"Tell me your side about the night you fled with me to Earth."

"Aisling started planning the moment she found out about you. She didn't tell me anything about when she found the sword or where she hid it. I think she wanted to keep me safe and innocent to her schemes, knowing I would be the first person they would come for. She only asked me one thing: that I be the one to get you out of the castle and take you to Earth, where I could hide you." Mom scooted back onto the boulder, her voice thick.

"We conceived our plan. She contacted the Dae, Brycin. We talked and plotted each day, getting it down to a science. Both of us ignored the truth in front of us... we were planning her death. She knew Aneira would come after her and the baby. Aneira's wrath posed a great threat to Aisling and to you, and Aneira would never let her or you be safe, even on the run. Aisling would stay back and distract her sister while I got you out. She did not fear death. The only thing she wanted was for you to be unharmed and grow up far away from Aneira."

I folded my arms across my chest to hold back the pain and love for someone I would never know.

My mom shook her head. "I resented you at first. You were the reason my friend would die. I understood she wanted me to raise you and love you like my own. But all I saw was a Dae baby destroying our lives. Then you were born..." Mom sniffed, her fingers wiping at her nose. "She laid you in my arms and told me to protect you with everything I had. To keep you away from the Otherworld. The moment I held you in my arms, everything changed. It felt like you were always meant to be mine. Nothing in the world could have kept me from my promise, whether she asked me or not. The bond I felt with you was instant, and I knew it would never change." Mom took a gulp of air, forcing back the tears.

"We had been secretly planning but so had Aneira. She had known about her sister and the Demons for a lot longer than we were aware. She knew the baby didn't belong to Eris. She came for both of you that night. Well, actually she hired the Dark Dwellers to come for you. She could not get her hands dirty in the death of her sister and baby niece. Aneira devised to keep the secret of your being a Dae. If you were dead, she could play the inconsolable queen who lost her sister and her niece. Unfortunately for Aneira, you lived, and the gossip about your two different colored eyes and hair set the castle ablaze. For years she has tried to squash the rumors, but she never could."

"What happened when you were getting us out?" I couldn't say *his* name, but I wanted to hear the truth. I wanted her to finally say it.

"I could smell the Dark Dweller coming. Usually they are hard to detect, but he did not bother to hide his odor or his presence. Aisling kissed you on the head and mumbled something to you. I wasn't paying attention to her words as I was so focused on the beast heading for us. Also knowing I was saying goodbye to her. For good..." A few more tears fell down

Mom's cheek. She took a few moments before starting again. "Brycin waited for us in one of the castle's secret doorways. When Lorcan barged in, we ran. A raven led us to Brycin. The raven adored and was faithful to Aisling."

A raven? It had to be Grimmel she was talking about. He mentioned he had helped get me out.

"He knew every inch of the castle, every secret tunnel and space. He was getting us to a passage, which would lead us out. That is when we ran into the other Dark Dweller." Her eyes squared on mine. "Elighan."

My pulse beat faster, thumping like a drum in my chest.

"Our eyes connected and I saw and smelled the desire to kill, his red eyes, locked on us. He guarded the hall. Brycin pushed me toward our escape route and blocked Eli from you. He lunged for her and he would have killed her, but the sound of Aisling screaming ripped through the palace." Mom took another pause. Her face contorted as if she were recalling another torturous memory. "His attention turned to the room. It gave us a single moment to escape Elighan. Every step I took caused my gut to rip open knowing she was being murdered. But getting you to safety was the rope I held onto to keep my feet moving and leave her behind."

Every time she had tried to tell me Eli was dangerous, or she attempted to get me away from him, I hadn't listened. Now I understood her desperation. She was a mother who only wanted to protect her baby girl. To keep me away from the Dark Dweller who had wanted to end my life. I should have listened to her. I should have run faster and farther away.

Tears dripped off my chin. I hadn't realized I was crying. The sacrifices both my mothers made for me—what they went through to keep me safe.

"This is why I needed you far away from the Dark Dwellers, especially from Elighan. I wanted to protect you from him. From the hurt you would go through when you found out."

Without a word I went to her and gathered her in my arms. A strangled cry broke from her lips, and she hugged me with fierce desperation. She sobbed, letting go years of secrets, painful memories, and lies.

"It's the reason I did everything. I did it for her. I did it for you." Her hand came to the back of my head, and she stroked my hair. "I love you so much. I am so sorry I caused you so much grief."

Aisling gave birth to me, but Lily was my mother. I would always love Aisling and be in awe of what she gave up for me. But the amazing woman in front of me had bandaged my knees when I fell off my bike, held me close and snuggled with me when I had a nightmare, made me peanut butter cookies when someone was mean to me at school. *She* raised me.

I might look like Aisling, but I took after Lily, who had always been my idol. She made mistakes and was far from perfect, but the older I got the more I understood. All the hurt I had felt didn't completely melt away, but it was something we could work through. Lily had sacrificed her home, her family, her life in the Otherworld for the love of her friend and a little girl. She lived her life on the run, always trying to keep me safe and protected. She gave me a home, unconditional love, and Mark. She gave me a father. I no longer cared whether Lars or Devlin was my true father. I had one already; Mark would always be my dad. And Lily would always be my mom.

"Shhh." I patted her back.

"I knew someday I would have to tell you the truth. I thought I was protecting you by hiding it. I hoped ignorance would keep you safe." She pulled back, looking me in the eyes.

"I think it did... until it didn't anymore," I said.

She brushed her nose with the back of her hand. "I was so scared if you knew the truth I would lose you."

"You're my mom. I might get upset with you, but you will never lose me. Ever."

She collected me into a bone-crunching hug. We stayed holding each other for a long time. Mother and daughter, finding a new relationship through sorrow.

Mom gripped my hand tightly as we walked back toward the house. "Aisling would be so proud of you, of the incredible person you've grown to be."

I stopped and turned toward her. "Both of you sacrificed so much for me. *You* gave up everything, and *she* gave her life."

She cupped my cheeks love etched deeply on her face. "And I don't regret a second of it, and I know Aisling would do it again without hesitation."

"Why would you do this for a baby that wasn't yours?"

"Because we're your mothers." She smiled. "And you are worth it. You are worth everything."

TEN

The entrance to Earth slipped over me, tickling my skin. Fog had rolled in, disguising the details of the gloomy forest. The moon peeked through thin spots in the dense moisture. Fall had arrived and a cool breeze wiggled through my lightweight jacket.

I scanned the area as gloomy wisps licked at my feet and curled around the foliage. Dark, creepy forests never scared me. In fact, I usually felt at home in the mysterious darkness. Tonight seemed different. Something felt off. The hair on my arms prickled. Reaching down, I tugged the short blade from my boot. I had learned to trust my gut.

The wish for Simmons to be with me echoed in my accelerating heart. Simmons had stayed behind. Lars wanted him there, he and Cal the carrier pigeons between the worlds.

I had come out a door away from Lars's property line in case someone happened to see me. The house was over eight miles away. I crouched lower, taking hesitant steps. The off-kilter feeling was only enhanced the longer I walked and nothing happened. Bells were going off within every heightened sense I had left. My heart trotted like an anxious show horse in my chest.

Still nothing.

I took a deep whiff of air, my nose assessing each smell around me. There were too many animals and smells to decipher if one was dangerous. I was possibly being hunted. Normally this would not send fear into my gut, but I also was more human than I had been. I remained a Dark Dweller, but it wouldn't stop a bear or mountain lion from tearing into my flesh.

The light of the moon slipped behind a cloud, dipping me in a misty darkness.

Run! My instincts screeched at me.

Along with the thump of my heart, my feet pounded against the earth, pushing me forward. A chilled ripple caressed the nape of my neck and down my back. My nerves heated me quickly, dropping trickles of sweat along my spine.

Run faster.

Intuition lit another fire under my feet. My muscles strained as I pushed my legs to move quicker, jumping and weaving around the wood's hurdles.

Branches of a distorted tree curled down, wrapping around a two-story boulder, blocking my path. I twisted into a new direction but stumbled. Fear leaped into my gut, coiling around it. I smelled what was after me, its scent ingrained in my memory. *Strighoul.*

A branch snapped behind me. I whipped around to see dozens of red, beady eyes staring at me through the gloomy night. I sucked in a breath. Screwed did not even cover it. If I still had my powers, I could have possibly fought them. With so many Strighoul against one partial Dark Dweller, I had no hope. They moved closer as a united front and circled me. My frantic gaze jerked everywhere trying to find an escape.

"You won't get away." Vek's nasally voice spoke through the blackness. "We've only been playing with our dinner until now."

He stepped out of the shadows. His patchy, colorless skin looked even more frightening in the dim light. Thousands of needle teeth flickered as he opened his mouth, showing me his armory. The haze of the moon reflected off the dripping saliva, which drenched each tooth in shiny brilliance.

"You have been a pain to get to in the past. I thank you for making your capture so easy today."

I kept my voice calm. "I'm no good to you now. My powers are gone. You will get no hit off me." I didn't know if informing him of the change was good or bad for my outcome, but I was willing to try.

A laugh came from behind Vek who had clearly taken over as leader. His new Second stepped next to him and smiled at me. He was skinnier than Vek and only had one eye. The other eye would never open again, marred by claw marks entrenched deep into his skin. "I know you are lying. I can smell the Dark Dweller in you. The hit off you will be nice, and so will the revenge for our last leader."

I licked my lips looking at the two creatures. Their former leader had been Drauk. I had cut off his head when they attacked us in the cave while we were in Greece. They had been hired by Lorcan to distract us so he could grab Kennedy.

"Besides our revenge, we were paid to find you. I know she would prefer to kill you herself, but if something went wrong..." He trailed off.

"Wait. Find me? You work for Aneira now?" Confusion laced my words. "But you're Dark Fae. I thought you wanted her dead?"

"We are, and we do." Vek nodded, his red eyes glimmering. "Like your boyfriend, or whatever he used to be, we are mercenaries. We work for the highest bidder. Our revenge on her will come in time, but until then, we have to get by. You are too important a prize to pass up."

Dark Fae were opportunists.

"Isn't anybody faithful to their side anymore?" I tossed out my arms.

Vek snapped his teeth. I recalled, with painful clarity, those teeth ripping into my neck. "We will be faithful when the Dark starts delivering results or pays better. You should tell your *uncle* his workers are going on strike." Vek snorted.

So, the secret of my parentage was out. Worst kept secret in the Otherworld.

"I definitely preferred it when your father was King, especially when he went crazy. Those were good times." Vek took another step toward me.

My body locked in defense. I gripped the handle of my blade so tight it ached. Being threatened brought out the Dark Dweller in me: my eyes shifted, and the night before me sharpened with intensity.

"I see talking time is over." Vek licked his bottom lip.

The rest of his men had moved forward to keep me in a tight space, and the stone wall behind locked me in.

As I turned and gathered my legs to jump on the wall, Vek leaped forward and grabbed my hair. With a yank, my body thumped to the ground. He was on top of me before I could react, ripping the knife from my hand.

"I foresee something going wrong. I guess the Queen won't get you alive. Or whole." Vek's mouth opened, the daggers of his teeth heading for my neck.

Terror kicked in, and my Dark Dweller responded. I tore away from his grip and smashed the heel of my hand into his mouth. Bone crunched, slicing through my skin, and tore at the tendons in my hand. Through the pain, I could feel bits of his fangs falling from my hand to my chest like hail.

He shrieked so loud my ears rang painfully. Vek's body slid off mine to the ground. Blood poured from his mouth as he spit out fragments of teeth.

"You bitch," he screeched. His mouth was a gory, crusted maw full of bloody, broken teeth, dripping with drool.

Shit! If I thought I was screwed before, the retaliation for defending myself would be slow and torturous.

Vek's Second grabbed me under the arms and yanked me to my feet. His grip turned painful as he grasped my neck, bending it painfully to the side.

It took Vek a few moments, but he finally got to his feet, spitting out more blood and bone. "I want to snap your neck like a twig, but it will be more fun eating you alive."

"Then we'll have to get you a straw. You should probably stay away from solids for a while."

Why, mouth, why? Why must you always open and say shit to make things worse?

Vek's fist thrashed my face. My nose crunched, and warm blood poured from it. My cheek throbbed, but I turned my face back toward him, defiant. "Maybe if you ask nicely, they will make a smoothie out of me for you."

I was going to die. They were not going to be nice about it anyway, so I might as well go out being my usual smart-ass self.

A garbled screech came from the depths of Vek's throat, his hands found my neck, and tore me away from his man's hold. We both went to the ground. His hands crushed my air passage, and he banged my head against the earth as he grunted with fury. Dots popped into my vision as I struggled against him. Air no longer entered my lungs, and panic burned in my chest and eyes. Death was inevitable. I thought I had accepted it, but when the moment happened, I forgot to acquiesce.

My hands tore at his fingers, trying to get underneath them and pry them off. His wild rage kept them locked like steel around my neck. Legs flayed as my knees rammed into his back. Out of my peripheral vision, I saw movement. Legs were moving in all different directions around my head. I wondered why. Funny when you were dying, or at least passing out, you paid attention to strange things. It was frantic and irrational.

Blackness devoured my sight. My ears rang with the lack of oxygen. My Dark Dweller fought back with all it had, but the lack of air stole my energy. Something bumped Vek, and a rush of air infiltrated my lungs, blowing them up like balloons. Vek's hands were gone, but I could still feel the pressure of them engraved in my throat. I sputtered and coughed and rolled to my side. My hearing streamed back into my ear canals. A roar filled them along with the sound of screeching and frantic movement. Slick blackness stepped over my body. Four huge paws stood like a fortress around me, guarding.

ELEVEN

Eli. The figures had retreated from the dark killer beast.

"There is only one of you, Elighan. You think you can protect her from all of us?" Vek's words were slurred and choppy.

A growl rumbled the ground. The sound and tremor it caused would have been enough to send me hightailing it out of there, but the Strighoul were tenacious, reminding me of a pack of hyenas.

They slowly advanced, circling him. I could sense Eli's frustration. If he left me, one of them would seize me. If he didn't, they would come at him from all sides.

I had no doubt if alone, Eli would be able to take them all on. With me injured, he was in trouble. It was frustrating for me to be so helpless. Usually by now the earth would be healing me, giving me strength to fight. I still felt connected to the earth, but it couldn't help me.

One of the Strighoul leaped out, biting at one of Eli's back legs. He roared and started to move before deciding against it. Another jumped out and nipped at Eli's front. Eli's beast form bellowed.

They inched closer, getting braver. My throat ached fiercely, but my coughing had stopped. Blood soaked my shirt, drying on my face. I rolled onto my stomach, under Eli, trying to get a better view. I did not do helpless well. I was in a lot of pain, but I could not sit back and be the damsel in distress. If I had an ounce of energy left, I would use it to fight. My knife had fallen too far away from where Eli and I waited to retrieve it. Shakily, I crawled from under him and stood.

His eyes found mine. *What are you doing?*

Fighting back, Dragen. It's what I do.

He snorted with frustration but didn't try to stop me. *Get on my back.*

My eyes widened. *Have you seen your back? Do you want me shish-kabobed?*

You can fit in-between. Be careful.

Be careful. Right. He was talking to *me*.

As I put my foot up on his side, he lunged forward and swiped at a Strighoul moving in on us.

Stop moving! I screamed inside my head. I knew he hadn't heard me as his focus stayed on the threat around us.

His head swung back to look at me. *Now, Brycin. We don't have time for indecision.*

You are not the one going to be sliced in half if this doesn't go right! I yelled back at him.

Would you prefer to get a little cut from me or be torn to bits and eaten by one of them while you are still alive?

Good point.

Eli took another swing at an encroaching Strighoul.

Little cut, my ass, I thought as I looked at the daggers protruding from his back. But he was right; I would rather be slashed by his razor-sharp weapons than theirs.

He lowered himself as I tried to slide in between the sharp blades. Vek wailed and leaped for me, bumping my body as he crashed into Eli's side. Without thinking, my hand grabbed onto Eli's back to keep from falling off. Pain seared into me as my skin sliced apart. Blood gushed from my palm. Vek also screamed and fell to the ground, holding his arm. A chunk of flesh lay on the ground next to him.

Eli felt my weight and bounded forward, knocking down

the Strighoul like bowling pins. Both my hands wound around the serrated edge of his back. I sucked in a pained breath, but I held on. My hands tore as he crashed into each body, slamming them back. Vek grabbed onto my leg, yanking my kneecap out of joint. I yelped in pain. Eli lashed out, and his claw sliced Vek's arm. With a sickening sound, Vek and his hand fell from my leg onto the ground, the hand no longer attached to its owner.

The noise coming from Vek was nothing I had heard before. Vomit shot up my throat as blood sprayed over me. Eli did not hesitate. He plunged into the forest, getting us away from the flesh-eating creatures.

Several miles later, when blood loss made me dizzy, and I slipped off Eli's back and hit the ground with a thud, he finally stopped.

The last thing I remember were green eyes and a naked body leaning over me.

"Brycin!" A voice called me back from the darkness. "Don't you fucking die on me." There was a pause before the same familiar voice spoke again. "Will giving her my blood work again?"

"I think so. She is more Dark Dweller than anything now, but there are still a lot of variables. She doesn't have her Dae powers, so I don't know if it will affect how she takes your blood this time. She absorbed a lot of poison through the cuts on her hands from your spikes; she's only alive now because of her Dark Dweller blood." I knew the other voice as well as the first one. Owen.

My lids refused to open. Nothing responded to my orders to move. I felt trapped inside my body. I could hear, but nothing else. I couldn't even feel my body, making me wonder if I was even in it.

"Take as much as you need. She lost a lot out there."

"You are lucky you found her in time."

"I almost didn't. When the connection between us disappeared this time, I figured she went to the Otherworld. By her scent, I knew what door she went through, so I waited there. I felt our bond come back to life, but she didn't come through the same door." Eli paused. "It was torture when I smelled the Strighoul and knew she was so far away. I nearly lost her to them."

Silence.

"Have you contacted Lars yet?" Owen sounded like he stood directly over me. I heard the soft squeak of wheels being rolled closer.

"Yeah." Eli sucked in a breath. "It was not a pleasant conversation. I'm sure he will be here momentarily. Ouch."

"Sorry," Owen replied. "The needle is thick. We need to fill the IV bag and get it into her system now."

"She's going to be okay, right?"

"I've never seen anyone suffer like she has and still keep getting up." Owen said. "She's a fighter." His tone told me he wasn't only speaking about my physical wounds.

"Yeah. She is."

"You need to tell her the whole truth when she wakes up, and she *will*." I wasn't sure if Owen tried to convince Eli or himself.

"It doesn't matter anymore. She's made her decision. It's over." Eli's voice turned icy.

Owen didn't respond.

Far off, almost like someone else was experiencing it, I sensed a strange stinging in my arm.

"The morphine should keep her out of pain. We will see in a bit how she reacts to your blood. I think she will accept it fine." Owen's shoes clicked on the hardwood. "Sit and relax. I will be back shortly with something for you to eat and to check on her." The noise of the door closing came soon after.

The sound of Eli breathing was the only thing I heard for a long time. A warm feeling started to snuggle in around my mind, pulling me away from consciousness. When a chair skidded across the floor, moving closer to me, I felt my body twitch.

"When I was dying, you probably didn't think I heard you, but I did." Eli's voice sounded gravelly and low. I could sense he was only inches from my face. "I will give you the same inspiring words you gave me. Don't you dare fucking die on me, Brycin. Don't be so damn pigheaded, either. If you really want to piss me off, you'll live. Being alive, so close to me, and I can't have you will punish me enough. More than you dying on me." He sighed. "And I know you love to get under my skin. Torture me."

I grappled to hold onto his words, to understand what he was saying, but they quickly slid out of my head as soon as he spoke them. Sleep wrapped thickly around my mind and created a fuzzy filter.

A distant pressure came down on my forehead before I fell into the comforting escape of sleep.

This time I wasn't surprised to see the rows of cells and dark shadows of the dungeon.

"Grimmel?"

The sound of wings beating came to me before I saw the raven. He swooped down and landed on a wheelbarrow full of soiled hay.

"Fire brighter now. Light inside."

"I'm going to take that as a compliment." *I was pretty sure I knew what he meant, but you never knew with Fae.*

"Know what you seek, Fire?"

Lily's voice suddenly came to me: *"A raven, Grimmel, who adored and was faithful to Aisling, knew every inch of the castle, every secret tunnel and room."*

The splinter festering in my mind since my last dreamwalk with him finally dug in. "You can help me locate the sword. Find out where it is hidden," I exclaimed.

Grimmel's claws padded to the edge of the barrel. *"Flame finally kindled."*

"Why didn't you say it straight out a long time ago?"

"Because."

"That's it? Because?"

"Greatness only found in brightest spark."

I rubbed the bridge of my nose. "I am going to clip your wings."

Grimmel tilted his head, looking like he didn't understand my comment.

"All right, will you help me find where Aneira has hidden the sword?"

"No."

"No?" I sputtered. "But you said..."

"Queen feels Fire's flames."

"You mean she will sense me here?" His black eyes continued to stare at me. "Then can you search for me?"

"Grimmel do. Grimmel help." He squawked and flew up to the barred window. *"Grimmel knows all secrets."* He glided out of the room at the same time I felt the thrust of being propelled out of the dreamwalk and back to my body on Earth.

Light slowly bled under my lids as they lifted. The glittering of a chandelier above my head attracted my eyes, sharpening my focus.

"It is all right, Ember. You are home and safe." A voice spoke next to me. My head jerked to see Rez sitting in a chair next to my bed with a damp cloth in her hand.

I opened my mouth to speak but nothing came out. I

winced at the slightest movement of my head, my neck badly bruised.

"You should not try to talk. Your vocal cords have been damaged." Rez sat forward and placed her hand on mine. "Because of the Dark Dweller's blood, you will heal. But the injury was bad, so it will still take some time."

A fuzzy memory of Eli and Owen dipped into my consciousness. My veins buzzed with new Dark Dweller blood. My senses were so sharp it was almost uncomfortable for me to keep my eyes open. The smells of antiseptic, blood, and sweat were so potent I felt nauseous.

I pushed myself up and rested against my headboard. When I felt less dizzy, I reached for my nightstand drawer. Inside was a journal. I snatched it and grabbed a pen. Finding a blank page, I scribbled a note.

How long have I been out?

Rez's eyes ran over the page. "You have been sleeping for three days. But you've been gone from the compound for two weeks."

My eyebrows arched up. Two weeks? Damn Otherworld time difference. *Lars pissed?* I wrote.

Rez tilted her head. "What do you think?"

Yeah, that's what I figured.

"Lars had you brought back here a few days ago."

"Brought back?" my voice strangled.

"Don't talk." Rez scolded me. "Elighan saved you and took you to their family's physician. You do not have the power to heal like you used to. We almost lost you."

The memories dim at first became more concrete in my mind: Eli saving me from the Strighoul, getting on his back, the sharp daggers on his back slicing my hands to shreds. Then it got cloudy. I peered down at my hands. Thick white lines crisscrossed them like a checkerboard.

"I'll have Marguerite fix you a special soup. It's Sinnie's family recipe, and it will help heal your throat." Rez stood and her hands brushed out the creases in her tight leather pants. The woman was beautiful, with her long dark hair, dark chocolate eyes, and olive-colored skin. It was hard not to stare at her with your jaw on the ground.

She gave my head a quick kiss. "You scared us to death. Don't ever do that again."

I nodded. It was foolish. I was aware of the stupidity going in. *Never seems to stop me from acting.*

She left me to stew in my foolishness and pain. Soft rain pelted the French doors of my room. Swinging my legs over, my feet touched the lush rug and my toes curled into the velvety wool.

The need to move to the doors tugged me forward. I could feel him. The strength of his blood propelled me to the window. Pressing my hand against the glass, my gaze scanned the gray, soggy landscape. The tingling of my skin told me his eyes were on me. Watching me. My heart pumped under my ribs, thumping loudly in my chest.

The last time he gave me his blood, I recalled the overwhelming connection I had to him. It lessened over time, but at first it felt extreme. Again I knew exactly where he was, to the tree he was leaning against, even though I could not see him.

He called to me. Not just because he was my Alpha, but because my body longed for his. Every sense in me felt overstimulated. My skin could feel his eyes crawling over every inch of my body. It was as if his fingers were actually touching me. I leaned against the cool window, my legs shaking underneath me, and my breath quickened. Desire consumed me. I felt embarrassed when a low moan came from me.

No. I can't. At first it was my hurt which made me not want to hear his side. After my mom's story, I felt right about despising him. But seeing him again, having his blood swim through me, warming my body, I realized the truth. It was the pain I would feel if I let him back in which stopped me. He would die. I could see no way around his death. I understood what I had to do. Saving millions of lives compared to one seemed like an obvious choice. But when it came to Eli, nothing had ever been clear or obvious. It would be easier to continue to hate him, to keep him at arm's length.

With a sharp intake I shoved myself back away from the doors. My trembling legs were not ready for the movement; I plummeted to my ass. My shoulder blades knocked into the bedframe. A startled laugh came out of my throat. Instantly, I grimaced in pain. No matter how much I trained, no matter how graceful my sword wielding had become, I was a klutz, through and through.

"Ember?" Rez's anxious voice bolted through the room.

"*¿Donde estás, mi dulce nina?*" Marguerite moved quickly into the room.

"*Aqui*," my voice croaked out. A dry, sharp pain sliced my throat. I leaned my head back against the down-filled comforter and regretted trying to speak.

Rez came around the side of the massive bed. Marguerite's head popped around Rez.

"What are you doing on the floor? Did you fall out of bed?" Rez asked.

I sighed deeply.

Rez frowned but leaned down to help me stand. "You need to take it easy. Your body is weak. A lot more like a human's now."

I frowned, feeling the Dark Dwellers blood coursing palpably through my veins. A deep sorrow crammed into my heart. I missed my Dae powers so much. A piece of me was gone, and I felt hollow and cold without them.

After Rez reinstated me on the bed, Marguerite bumped her out of the way. Her hands cupped around a bowl. "*Mi dulce*, you need to drink." She handed me the soup.

My nose crinkled. It smelled like rotting compost. My lips pressed together, and I shook my head. Marguerite's worried expression shifted, and her eyebrows narrowed in on me. "It will help heal. Drink."

"I know it smells bad, but it will help your throat mend." Rez gave my ankle a squeeze through the comforter.

Marguerite kept motioning for me to drink. I closed my eyes and tipped the cup into my mouth. Instantly my gag reflex kicked in, wanting the foul flavor off my taste buds. Marguerite placed her fingers on the bowl pouring it further down my throat. "Drink all."

My eyes watered as I forced the last of the liquid down my throat. I groaned, needing to wipe my tongue clean of the nasty taste. The smell already stuck in my nose.

"Just wait." Rez winked and a smile twitched her lips. Marguerite swatted at her, her glare telling her to shut up.

It was then the burning started. It felt as if someone doused my gullet with kerosene and threw a match on it. "Ahhhh!"

"I'm sorry. I forgot to warn you about the after burn." Rez smiled and patted my leg again.

"Ahhhhh!" It was all I could get out and not very well, as my hands clawed at my chest and throat. My nose and eyes leaked liquid in retaliation.

"Water," I squeaked out.

Marguerite was the first to shake her head. "*Mi dulce*, sorry. No food or *agua* until it finishes healing." She rubbed my arm.

The scorching sting moved down to my stomach and then made its way back up my esophagus. A whimper worked its way out of the incineration that was my throat, and I curled on my side. It felt like the pain would never end. Finally, coolness replaced the heat, like aloe on sunburn. I cried in relief as it caressed my throat and soothed the irritation.

"There, there." Marguerite hand stroked the side of my head. "*Mejor ahora.*"

It took me another moment before I sat up, feeling nothing of the burn, which had tortured me barely moments before.

"What the hell was that?" My vocal cords wavered, but it no longer hurt as much to talk.

"It is a Brownie remedy." Rez sat at the foot of my bed. "I figured it was better not to tell you what you would go through. I hated the first time Marguerite fed it to me, but now knowing what it does... it is just as hard to take, even when you know it will cause you to feel better in the end. Being ignorant is sometimes a blessing." A flicker of sadness hinted in her eyes. "In my line of work, I've had to drink a lot of her remedy."

"What do you mean?" Rez was a Siren. I never asked the details of her "job" but figured most men went willingly.

Her gaze went to the chandelier. "A lot of them fight me in the end. Trying to strangle me is how they think they will be able to get away. They never do."

Oh.

The faraway look disappeared from her expression as she bounded back on her feet. "We'll let you rest, but you probably will start feeling a lot better."

Marguerite grabbed the empty bowl with one hand; her other reached for my face, stroking it. "We worry. *Feliz que esté en casa segura.*" She leaned over and kissed my forehead before turning. Her short and stocky statue shuffled to the door.

"Get some sleep." Rez pulled the blanket higher on me, then headed for the door.

"Rez?"

"Yeah?" She turned back, holding the door.

"Do you like being a Siren?"

Her eyes widened before she glanced at the floor. A soft breath puffed out of her. Her eyes looked back into mine. "There is no like or dislike; it is what I am." She stepped back and closed the door.

I lay down, chewing on what she said. Unlike humans, Fae didn't question what they were. They accepted it: good, bad, or ugly. I didn't know what was better: trying to be someone you were not, or accepting what you were.

I laid there for a while, my thoughts drifting back to my dreamwalk with Grimmel, still vivid in my mind. I needed to tell Lars that Grimmel was searching for the Sword of Light. Hopefully, the raven would find something soon and get back to me. Knowing the location of the sword would be so helpful. At least we'd know where we were going once inside the castle. If we made it that far.

Eventually my brain tired at the endless thoughts going around inside, and I fell into a deep sleep.

TWELVE

It was barely dawn when my lids blinked open. My stomach growled in hunger. I shifted and sat up. Rez had been right; I felt much better. My toes pressed down on the cushy rug as I got out of bed. My stomach screamed for food. My brain sent images into my head, my mouth instantly watering.

Deer. Raw.

My Dark Dweller part perked up, giddy and licking its lips.

Hunt.

I scurried to my closet and pulled on a pair of sweats, tank top, and a hoodie. Shoving my feet into tennis shoes, I raced out of my room. I quickly drew my hair into a ponytail as I bounded down the stairs. Hunger dominated every thought. I didn't encounter anyone as I moved through the silent house and exited the kitchen door. Fog clung solidly to the ground and trees in the early dusk. The smell of fresh rain and wet dirt infiltrated my nose.

He was there, too. The constant scent of him blended in with the familiar smells of the land. The Dark Dweller in me needed to hunt and eat more than I desired to stay away from Eli. He probably sensed I was outside. I didn't care.

Letting my nose track any whiff of game, I moved into the forest. The broadcasted odor of a deer far in the distance caught my nose. My legs tore after it. Normally I would let my Dae powers lead me across the terrain when it was so foggy and dark. This time I couldn't. Even with sharp Dark Dweller skills, I stumbled and bumped into things I would never have if I had my Dae magic. I had taken for granted the maps of my surroundings which had been laid out in perfect detail in my mind. The loss of my abilities only caused me to move faster, anger pumping solidly into determination.

The deer was close by, pulsing with life. I jumped off a boulder as my focus zeroed in on my kill. The musky stench of wet fur and the tang of blood coursing through its veins whirled up my nose. Everything else went to the background. My breath sounded loud in my ears as my heart thumped with adrenaline. My calf muscles clenched with stiffness as I pushed off at a sprint. The old war wound would always be a reminder of Lorcan's attack.

Then a semi-truck, or what felt like one, slammed into me. My body twisted in the air toward the attacker, taking it with me to the ground with a brutal crunch. Bright green eyes locked on mine, snapping my focus from the deer. For a moment I felt confused and dazed.

When Dark Dwellers lock on something, they get tunnel vision. It's hard to break them off their course. It takes a moment for them to clear their minds and readjust, like pressing a restart button and waiting for the data to reload.

It didn't help that Eli was between my legs, every part of him pressed firmly against me. I was overtaken by the basic Dark Dweller urge to hunt, kill, or screw. With him between my thighs I felt an instant and desperate need. My desire for him pissed me off. I struggled underneath him.

"Where were you going?" His tone sounded sharp.

"Why the hell should I tell you?" His weight atop me grew heavier. He would only let me up when he was ready.

His mouth tightened in a clenched line. "I swear, Brycin, if you are doing something stupid again, I might take you out myself."

Fury generated a hiss from me. "Go ahead. Do us both a

favor. You know you've wanted to for a long time now."
Please, then I don't have to make an impossible choice.

Eli closed his eyes briefly, his jaw clamping harder. He tugged air deeply through his nose. "You on a suicide mission lately? Is that it?"

"What the hell do you care?" I wiggled underneath him. His eyes glowed brighter, skimming with red.

"Stop," he warned.

I did. He was rock hard against my hip. His urge between the three instincts was even more dominant than mine. He would probably want to do all three at the moment.

"Then get off of me."

He stayed in place, staring at me. His hair had grown even more since I had last seen him and touched his shoulders. It reminded me of when I first met him. How I longed to run my hands through the silky, brown locks.

I had to force back every impulse and keep my hands to myself. His gaze drilled into me. My heated breath moved shallowly in and out of my lungs. My mind and heart were telling me one thing, as my body and nature desired him to rip off my pants, slip inside, and take me right there.

"Tell me where you were going," he said through clamped teeth.

"Crap on ash bark! I was hunting," I belted at him. "Okay? Is it all right with you, Dad?"

He blinked and moved off me, replacing his warm body with the coolness of the morning air. "You were hunting?"

"Yes." I scrambled up and put distance between us. "I seem to be craving raw meat even more now."

He looked at me. No emotion showed on his face. He knew I was telling the truth. With his blood so entrenched in me, he could probably sense everything I felt. The knowledge disturbed me. I didn't like him knowing he had such a strong effect on me, especially because it was not killing I wanted to be doing right now. "What were you expecting to do once you caught it?"

Huh. I hadn't thought past my craving.

"You gonna tear into Bambi's neck while it was still alive?"

I grimaced with the visual. He was right. I couldn't have killed it except if I slowly tore at its throat till it bled to death. Wow, I hadn't planned that through.

"Marguerite keeps steaks in the freezer. Think that would be easier for you to stomach right now. I will kill a fresh one later for you."

I folded my arms, rubbing one of my shoes over a pebble. "Thanks."

He smirked, shook his head and leaned back against a tree. He wasn't leaving. I looked around. We were still inside Lars's property line.

Eli sensed my emotions and responded, "Lars thought it smart to have another pair of eyes on you. Especially belonging to one who could feel you and know when you are trying to leave."

Gripping my elbows tightly, I moved away. Indignation rose up my throat.

"I am your personal bodyguard now." His smile looked anything but friendly or nice.

As I watched him casually resting against the tree, I could not deny the part of me which wanted to beg him to tell me the whole truth and deny his part in killing Aisling. But if he did that... *No, Ember, stay strong. Keep him away.*

"I don't want you as my bodyguard. I don't want you here at all. You need to leave." My voice came out softer and more cracked than I wanted. To counter my weak voice, I shoved my chin higher in the air.

He blew out some air and looked off to the side. "Tough."

"What?" Outrage pushed up my shoulders. "But I don't want you anywhere near me. For once respect my feelings and go!"

He turned, his eyes blazing, pleading. "Ember..."

"No!" I rubbed at my skin like bugs were crawling on it.

His eyes burned into mine. We stared at each other for a long time. Neither of us relinquishing our stance. Nothing was said, but it didn't have to be. We both understood the meaning in our posture, in the cool gazes we delivered.

Finally his gaze shifted to the side; his jaw clicked as he moved it around. "I guess you've made your decision." He shook his head and turned.

"*You* crushed *me*. You ripped out my heart!" I screamed, as he walked away from me. My healing vocal cords strained, breaking up my words.

Anger tore across his face as he whipped back around and strode to me. He got inches from my face. "And you just ripped out mine."

"You don't have one." I could feel the burn of tears behind my lids. His familiar smell wafted deep into my nose.

"Then we are done here." His jaw moved stiffly as he spoke, his voice low and gruff.

"We were done the day we met."

He gave no response as he headed for the property line. My heart felt like it was drowning in agony. *The break will be easier, Ember. You are making the right decision. It will hurt much more if you let him in again.*

Then why didn't it feel that way?

THIRTEEN

My determination to cut Eli from my life was short lived. Later in the afternoon, Nic came and retrieved me from my room.

"Lars demands your attendance in his office." He motioned for me to follow him downstairs.

Usually Nic would leave me at the door with a slap on my ass or a sexual comment. Instead, he knocked and let Lars know of our arrival before opening it for me. The large office was stuffed full of people. The feel of Eli's blood pounding through my veins was so prominent after my second dose, it oversaturated me, leaving me numb to when he was really close. Like now.

All the Dark Dwellers were here. So were all the members of my Demon family, along with Torin, Thara, and my mom. All eyes turned to me. I felt like I had walked into a warped version of an intervention. Cal zoomed across the room to me and landed on my shoulder.

Eli's eyes were the first thing I locked on, but I quickly shifted away and focused on Lars. "What's going on?"

Don't say intervention. Please, don't say intervention.

"Many things have happened since your little venture to the Otherworld." Lars's words were sharp and meant to stab at me. He still hadn't confronted me about it. "We only have a month until Samhain. We must prepare for the war ahead. Starting tonight, we will build our army and train." Lars looked at Alki and Koke, acknowledging them. "Our land will become a camp. Thousands of Dark Fae have been summoned here. Rimmon has already noted a few arrivals."

I was surprised at Lars's plan for the impending war. His home was his sanctuary, and I knew he hated the idea of bringing thousands of Fae into his backyard and into his world. But times were desperate. We needed a secure place to train, and this was the most fortified location on Earth.

"Security will be extremely tight. It will be harder to get in here than it would be walking into the White House's Oval Office uninvited. Rimmon and Goran will be sure everyone who enters is faithful to our cause." Lars did not go into detail, but knowing the Unseelie King, I didn't want to know specifics as I knew of his penchant for violence when necessary.

Lars stood tall behind his desk, commanding the room although his was not the power thrumming against my spine. The pull to stand with the Dark Dwellers and especially next to Eli was almost crushing. I took in a few shaky breaths, holding my limbs still so I wouldn't give in to the desire.

"I invited the three of you." Lars nodded toward Mom, Torin, and Thara. Torin snapped his gaze back from a certain Dark Dweller to fix back on the Unseelie King. "I need you to be aware of what is happening. Tension is going to rise in the Otherworld, and the Queen will be aware something is happening. The three of you will stay at the cabin and protect the humans." Lars's yellow eyes drifted to mine before returning to them. "If I need you, I will summons you through Simmons or Cal. These are the only messengers I will send. If someone else comes, kill them." He looked at my mom's shoulder where Simmons stood straight, saluting Lars. "Simmons has agreed to continue his residence with you in case you need to reach me. Cal will remain here."

They nodded, but Lars didn't wait for their agreement before he turned to the Dark Dwellers. "Cole and I spoke earlier and have come to the conclusion that all of you will stay here until the war and will participate in Alki's and Koke's training sessions."

"What?" The words fell from my mouth.

Eli's head jerked in my direction, his lids narrowing. "Guess you're gonna have to get used to the idea of me being around."

My mouth opened to counter, but I couldn't come up with one single completely unselfish thing about me not wanting them here. My problems were going to have to go to the wayside till the war was over. If we even made it out alive.

Eli saw my struggle. His lips quirked into a cruel smile. "Life's a bitch, Brycin."

"And you're the reason she became one," I retorted.

He shrugged. "It's the Dragen charm."

"Charm is not the exact word I would use for it."

"Oh, I love when they do this." Cal sat on my shoulder his head ping-ponging between Eli and me. All in the room fell silent as they watched our repartee. Eli had a way of making the entire world disappear, leaving the two of us, whether it was fighting, screwing, or talking. Embarrassment flooded my cheeks. I frowned and looked away from the gawking stares.

"Back to the reason I brought you here." Lars pushed one hand into his pocket, irritation simmering in his tone. "As we all know, there is more than fighting on the battlefield. Aneira now has the sword in her possession. We must retrieve it and kill her. Otherwise, we are doomed. Everything will be destroyed." His eyes glared at me, and meaning was heavy in his gaze. Not able to hold it, I stuffed my hands in the back of my jeans, looking at the floor.

I knew what Lars's look meant—a reminder Eli would be sacrificed. My lashes flicked to where Eli stood. Invisible fingers curled around my throat, squeezing the air from my lungs. I would lose him, and he would never have told me what actually happened that night in the castle. How selfish was I? Didn't he deserve to be heard? To have his story out there?

Even if in the end it hurt me more.

"While the Dark Fae fight, we must have another group heading for the palace. Ember has to get into the room where the sword is held. I have spies searching the castle. They have yet to discover its whereabouts."

I shuffled my feet. "I also have someone searching for me. He will find it."

"What do you mean? Who?" Lars eyed me suspiciously.

"The raven that helped Mom and me escape. If anybody can find it, it will be him."

"Grimmel?" Mom piped up. "That old bird is still alive?"

Lars shook his head, brushing off mom's comment, his laser gaze on me. "How do you know the raven isn't a spy for Aneira?"

Mom took a few steps toward his desk. "He was faithful to Aisling, Lars. I know Grimmel. He hated Aneira and adored Aisling. He will not turn Ember over to her."

"You are sure?" Lars placed his hands on the desk and leaned toward Lily.

She nodded. "Yes. He would not betray Aisling's memory or her child's."

"All right. Good news, then." Lars straightened. "The moment he contacts you, Ember, you come straight to me. Understand?"

"Yes," I acknowledged.

Lars moved toward the French doors. "Before we can get the sword, we need a Druid to break the protection spell. Aneira has certainly charmed it. Besides the Queen, a Druid is the only one to break her magic. We need to find Kennedy. She is imperative to our plan. Cole, I need you to intensify the search for her."

Cole held his head up defiantly, a strand of his long reddish-brown hair falling into his face. "We have been searching every day. Lorcan has been good at moving right before we find his location."

"Well, then, it is time to try a new plan. I say we agree to work with him."

"Oh, hell, no," Cooper barked.

The bristling energy from the Dark Dwellers condensed, and my skin itched to run to the group. *My family.* I rubbed at my temple trying to dislodge this thought.

Cole stepped forward, acting first. "We do not trust the possibility he is not working with Aneira. I will not put any of my family or yours in danger."

Lars challenged Cole. "Well, do what you need to do, but if I don't see results soon, I will take matters into my own hands."

Cole stiffened at Lars's words but did not refute him.

Lars flicked his hand. "All right, the meeting is now adjourned. I have things to sort with our new arrivals. I will want some of you back here tomorrow night. We have a great deal to plot." He slipped around his desk, heading out the door with Rez, Alki, and Koke right behind him.

I gave my mom a hug before she hurried to leave. I could tell she was anxious to get back to Mark. Leaving Ryan and Mark unprotected probably made her nervous. Castien was there, but he would not be enough protection if there were a true threat. As he left, Torin didn't even acknowledge my existence when he walked by, Thara trailing him.

Cooper rubbed my head, and Gabby punched my arm softly as they passed. "Roomies again," she teased.

Cole squeezed my shoulder. "I'm glad you are all right."

"Yeah, me, too."

Owen approached behind his brother.

"I guess you are the one to thank for saving my life, again." I smiled at Owen.

"I only stuck you with needles and sewed your wounds. You would have died if not for Eli's blood."

I peered at the floor again, a rollercoaster of emotions rippled through me. Eli had saved my life twice, without hesitation.

"Thank you anyway." I wanted to hug Owen, but he seemed awkward with physical contact that went beyond doctor-patient. He leaned away, his body stiff. I clasped my hands together and smiled appreciatively.

Eli walked by me last. Electricity crackled in the air between us. He huffed and headed for the door. I closed my eyes and let out a sigh of relief. Even if I knew I couldn't stay away from him much longer or deny him the chance to explain, I wasn't ready right at the moment.

The sound of the door slamming shut popped my lids back open. Eli stood there staring at me. The door firmly closed behind him. His green eyes perforated my skin, inflicting a storm of emotions. Being near him was more difficult than I thought. I wanted to be able to shut off my longing for him.

Pain wrapped around my heart. My walls were raised, defending it. *No, I am not ready. Not yet.*

I headed for the door. I was not running... only moving extremely fast. I stepped to the side and tried to get around him. He countered my step. His body was close. Heat flowed off his physique, hitting mine. I tried to dart around him again, but he blocked me. His hand reached out and brushed my arm. A zing of electricity clutched my chest. I jerked back. "Don't."

He stayed silent, his expression neutral, but didn't step away. Everything inside and outside of me tingled. He was too near. My conscience and body each battled for what it wanted.

"Brycin." My name came out low and husky. His voice felt a dagger to my heart. Tears threatened under my lids, but I would not cry again. I was done with tears.

I took several steps back, hitting the desk. "I-I can't do this."

"Hear me out." He reached for me again.

I slapped his hand away. "No." If I let him touch me, I would lose the fight within myself.

"Listen to my side," he demanded. His forehead lined with

a scowl.

"Screw you." My shoulder knocked into him as I bee-lined for the door. Panic jumped my muscles into movement. He was getting too near. The wall within wanted to protect me, but it teetered, faltering under his gaze. "I don't have to do anything you ask."

"Yes. You. Do." Eli seized my arm tightly. He pushed me back into the wall, pinning my wrists. "You have hit me, daggered me with wooden spears, screamed at me, ignored me, used your powers against me... and I have taken it." My breath caught in my throat as he pressed into me. His eyes flashed bright green, and his jaw clenched in determination. "You *will* listen."

My heart thumped in my chest. He still could scare the crap out of me. I felt angry, terrified, and hurt, but my body was unfaithful to my mind. Being so close to him again only made it yearn for his. I looked away biting my lip, trying to rid myself of the images of him yanking off my jeans and slowly dragging my underwear down my legs, his fingers trailing across my skin.

"I didn't kill your mother. Lorcan did," he shot at me, his eyebrows furrowed.

I seethed at him. "I know that, but you were still there. Helping, right?"

"Will you let me finish?" he growled.

My breath was heavy, catching in my lungs. I glared at him but didn't respond.

"I was there to stop him."

My world came to a halt. "What?" I whispered.

He released his hold he on me and stepped back. He had my attention.

"After what happened with the Daes, the Dark Dwellers lost respect. People no longer feared us like before. Other groups wanted to take advantage of our perceived weakness and because we lost so many of our group. Lorcan had always coveted the leader role. He was too young after my father died, so it fell to Cole. It's fair to say Lorcan and Cole never got along. Lorcan was offended because the new leader was not true blood. He became even more agitated when Cole groomed me to be his Second."

He rubbed at the thick stubble on his chin. Eli still seemed too close. I crossed my arms, putting some sort of barrier between us.

"Lorcan took it upon himself to find a way to 'redeem' our clan. The Queen told him she had a secret mission no one could ever know about, and if he completed the job, she would not only restore our legacy but inundate us with riches."

I swallowed my sadness and anger. I knew what the mission was. Kill Aisling and me.

"Cole was against it. He and Lorcan got into a huge fight about who should be the true leader. Cole, in his anger, let it slip he would never choose Lorcan as his Second, and he wanted to nominate me. Let's say Lorcan was not pleased. He 'challenged' me. I won." Eli turned away from me and shoved his hand through his hair. It curled slightly at the ends.

"I should have known Lorcan wouldn't let it lie. I don't know if he thought fulfilling the quest would prove he was the proper leader or what, but he went on his own to accomplish the task. My gut told me to follow him." Eli paused, letting out a breath of air, and his shoulders lowered. "By the time I got there, he was already in Dark Dweller form, and Aisling lay on the floor." He fell silent again and seemed to struggle with effort to continue. "When I got to the private quarters, Lily was trying to escape the castle with you. Lily figured I came there to kill you and Aisling. The Fox clan is Light Fae, and we are Dark. Our clans have never liked each other. Seeing me there only deepened her hatred. Her prejudice is probably rightfully earned, but not for that night. I wanted nothing to do with killing any royal Fay or baby. Unfortunately, the Dae who had killed my family, the woman named Brycin, stood with you guys. I

Blood Beyond Darkness

reacted. I wanted to kill her for what she did to my family. I got distracted when I heard Aisling scream. The Dae slipped away with both you and Lily."

His gaze fell on me. My focus broke away and targeted my shoes. My hair curtained my face, walling me from his penetrating eyes.

"Lily always had it wrong about me. By the time I got to Lorcan and Aisling, I was too late. Aisling put up a fight, and she wounded Lorcan enough to draw blood. As she lay there, she chanted something and wiped the blood from Lorcan across a small blanket she clutched. At the time I did not understand it, but now I know she was placing a curse on the Dark Dweller line and attaching it to you. This is why your family symbol reacts to us, especially Lorcan. It would respond to all Dark Dwellers, but mostly to Lorcan and me. We are of the same bloodline, blood spilled near your mother's body the night of her death."

My glance drifted up to Eli, and I let go of the breath I didn't realize I was holding. "Then why did you tell me you killed her? Why did you lead me to believe you helped?"

His face contorted and his eyes became distant. "Just because I didn't kill her doesn't make me the good guy here. I want you to know this. I didn't try to save your mother because I had heart, or I suddenly became moral. I didn't. I only tried to stop Lorcan because I knew the Queen was up to something, and it was a bad deal. I did it for *my* family. Lorcan likes to blame me for being the one who got us exiled to the Otherworld because I messed up the mission, but I knew we would be exiled no matter what, especially if we completed the assignment. The Queen could not kill us, but she did not want us around for liability reasons. What would happen if anyone ever found out she had her own sister killed? Instead, her popularity and power skyrocketed as she played the grieving Queen who lost her sister to the ruthless Dark Dwellers, exactly how she planned it." His Adam's apple bobbed as he swallowed. "I cannot say given different circumstances I would have acted differently than Lorcan. Your mother could have easily been another mother I killed on another night. We were assassins. That was who we were in the Otherworld. I won't apologize for it."

I tried to absorb the new revelation. Lars told me earlier that truth is a funny thing. A story is not one dimensional. Each has many layers and versions and realities. I couldn't deny Eli's truth changed my feelings, weakening my resistance to keep him distant.

No, Ember. Hating him will be easier.

"But I was a different person then. We have changed since being on Earth. *You* changed me." He licked his bottom lip. "I've made a lot of mistakes. I've never had someone who has completely undone me." Eli sucked in a ragged breath. "I probably won't ever do the right thing, but I won't be without you. Not anymore."

I blinked, clearing my eyes. "You could have told me."

Eli snorted and shook his head. "Would it have made a difference? I was still there. I didn't stop him."

"But you could have told me you tried to save her."

"I wasn't saving her, Ember. I was saving *us*." His hands flew to the middle of his chest, emphasizing his point.

"Whatever your reasons, you were still trying to stop Lorcan. You could have said something, denied it," I yelled back, aggravation assembling in me.

"I did," Eli barked back. "You didn't want to hear my side, remember?"

The night in the woods after the first time we were together, when Lorcan showed up, came hurtling into my mind.

"Is this true?" I asked, my voice catching in my throat. *"D-Did you kill my mom?"*

"Em, it's not wha..." Eli finally spoke.

I cut him off. "It's not what, Eli? Did you or did you not kill my mother?"

"It's not that simple."

A crazed laugh burst from my lips. "Oh, I think it is that simple."

I had a hard time trusting people and automatically thought the worst of them. I hadn't let Eli explain. I jumped to a conclusion. Even if he had tried to explain, would I have listened? Probably not. I hadn't been ready to hear the full truth, especially about Lily and my real mother. "What about after?"

He glanced away. "The first time you returned from the Otherworld, Lily wanted to talk to me, remember?"

I nodded, already knowing what was coming.

"She begged me not to say anything. She wanted to tell you in her own way. I agreed. It was not my place but hers to say something to you. We take oaths extremely seriously in the Otherworld. Until the truth came out, I could not reveal anything."

"Why didn't you tell her then? You could have at least told her the circumstances," I yelled. "It could have relieved her of the hatred and pain she felt for you. All those months she had to watch you and me together, thinking you were Aisling's killer and nearly mine."

He rubbed his hand at the bridge of his nose. "I don't know. I was angry at her, too. I felt no matter what I said she would not believe it anyway. She would think I said it so I could get into your pants."

Suddenly all those strange expressions and odd comments that had passed between the Dark Dwellers and my mom made sense. I was no longer mad at her for keeping reality from me, and I was not upset she kept Eli from revealing the truth. It had been her place. Not his. But because Eli did not tell her, due to his pride and stubbornness, my mom went through months of silent torture. He was probably right—at that point she was too obstinate to hear his side. She probably would have thought it a lie. *Like mother, like daughter.*

Learning what Lily went through to get me out and protect me from Aneira helped me understand her choices. I also couldn't be upset with her belief that Eli had helped kill Aisling. If I had seen a Dark Dweller blocking the hallway and attacking the Dae named Brycin, I would have come to the same conclusion. And Eli let her continue to believe it.

All the new information felt as if my thoughts were wandering through paste. Space. I needed space.

Being close to Eli didn't help me think clearly. I had missed him. Too much. Rubbing my head, I went around him, the door within my grasp.

"Don't walk away from me," Eli boomed, his Alpha authority stopping me in my tracks.

"Don't do that! Don't you dare command me!" I whirled on him, glaring. "Because you suddenly aren't Aisling's murderer doesn't mean my feelings have abruptly changed. I need time."

"No."

"What?"

"I said no," he growled.

"You don't tell me no!"

"Yes, I will."

"Why?"

"Because."

"The best you can do is *because*?" My feet moved toward the door again. "*Because* is not good enough."

"Because... you are mine, Brycin."

"I am no one's property," I hissed, keeping my gaze on the door.

There was a slight growl in his throat. "You. Are. Mine."

Pain burst to my chest, my head slightly shaking. I reached for the doorknob.

A frustrated cry came from him. "*Ta gra agam ort.*" His words stormed out. The Gaelic phrase suspended my hand on the knob. I understood what he had said.

I love you.

My eyes grew wide, rounding back to face him. "What?"

Blood Beyond Darkness

"You heard me." He rubbed the back of his neck. "I've *never* said those words to anyone, and certainly never thought myself capable of it."

There was a strained pause before I spoke softly, "How do I know it's not because I have your blood?"

Eli frowned. "My blood creates a bond, but it does not create feelings. Let's say, hypothetically, I gave my blood to Thara, I would know where she was, but it would not cause me to like her anymore. *Believe me.* That's not how it works."

His words were a mixture of fire and ice. Happiness and agony. I had waited so long to hear him say something even close to this. I understood a bit more why he reacted so harshly to me when I first told him I loved him: he didn't think I would feel the same after I found out the truth. My heart didn't work in such a way. If we stayed together or not, I would never stop loving him. I punched the wall as frustration suffocated me like a corset. "Dammit!"

Everything seemed so twisted and turned upside down. The man I loved finally told me he loved me back, and I was going to get him killed. Fucked up didn't even begin to cover it.

I kicked and hit whatever stood in my way.

"FUCK!" I screamed again. The release felt like a drug, and I needed more of it. Something in me snapped. My hands went for anything not nailed down, throwing, hitting, and kicking everything in Lars's office. Books were torn from the shelves, chairs thrown across the room. My hands ripped the printer cords from the wall. The printer sailed into the air, hitting the door. Chips of paint and bits of plaster crumbled out of the dent it caused. Anger. Rage. The darkness, which still resided in me, was finding its way to the surface.

"Stop!" Eli grappled for my hands, trying to block me. Blood covered his palms. It took me a moment to realize the blood was mine, from cuts on my knuckles and palms.

"No, let go!" I tried breaking from his hold. He had no idea the sick twisted truth. Would I even be able to do it in the end?

Choose between Eli and the world? Without my powers, it was like punching a cement wall. I didn't like it. I let my beast rush to the surface. I shoved at Eli. Not expecting my Dweller strength, he stumbled back and crashed into the door He barely hit before he popped forward, coming for me again. His eyes glowed bright.

"*Damnú ort!*" He barreled into me, slamming me into the opposite surface. Air was crushed out of my lungs. My Dark Dweller flared further to life.

I didn't want to be stopped. My fury sought to break, destroy, and tear apart everything in my sight. So much I needed to let out. So many emotions I could not handle. He stood in my way. Literally. My knee came up, and he twisted to the side.

"I won't fall for that one again," he rumbled, forcing me harder against the wall. It only riled me more. Turned me on. His green eyes flashed red as he took in a whiff of my hormones filling the room. My want for him only flamed the fire of my anger.

I kicked at him again, clawing against his hold. "Get off me!"

"Stop!" He roared. I could feel the authority in his words weighing heavily on my impulse to bite and hit him. Anger ballooned in my chest.

"Stop trying to control me." I stomped my foot on his. His grip loosened, and I took advantage, kicking at the joint in his knee. His leg buckled, causing him to fall. I stepped hard on his calf and leaped over him. He grabbed my ankle in mid-air and tugged down. I dropped hard, and my shoulder slammed into the wooden floor as I spun.

The beast in both of us was becoming more apparent, though only one of us could fully change. Breathing heavy and growling, I kicked off his hold and jumped back up. He moved faster. He wrapped an arm around my waist and jerked me back, throwing me onto Lars's desk. Papers scattered like butterflies off the desk.

"I said stop," he ordered.

I stilled as Eli's hand went behind my head, sharply yanking my hair back. His eyes were now completely red and full of feral need. A sound came from his chest, as his knee pried my legs apart. His grip on my scalp tightened, almost to a painful, thrilling level. My lungs pumped air quickly in and out. He brought my bloody knuckles to his mouth, licking them. Even the slightest graze of his skin on mine was hitting painful levels. He tilted my head, turning my face to his. His lips moved down, only a breath from mine.

My hands smashed into his chest, and he stumbled back. Before he could respond, I pushed him again. This time he hit the glass and splintered the French doors. His eyes glinted as I stepped up to him. He licked his lips. A smear of my blood still clung to his bottom lip. My fingers hooked around the collar of his t-shirt and tore at it. The fabric ripped in half, falling from his body and showing his chiseled torso. His chest moved in and out rapidly.

His gaze linked on mine, steady and piercing. We both held our breath for a moment before we crashed into each other. His lips moved over mine ferociously. The need to feel him deep inside me was unbearable.

Ripping the shirt over my head, he gave us only a short break before our mouths found their way back. My bra hit the floor as he backed me to the table. The noise of his jeans' buttons being torn open sounded like a machine gun. He scooped me up and dropped me on the desk. Everything crashed to the floor as he forced me back. With one tug, he pulled my jeans off. Our desire for each other was not soft or delicate. There was no "let's take our time" here. It was now and desperate. Violent. I clawed at his shoulders, drawing blood, bringing him down on top of me. He slipped off my underwear, which joined his jeans on the floor. I wanted him so badly it felt painful. My body shook.

"Brycin. Look at me." He rasped.

My gaze turned to his. I could feel cock drag through my folds, hitting at my entrance, teasing me.

"Eli." Desperation throbbed my pussy, digging my nails into his skin. "*Now.*"

He clutched my ass, holding me in place as he angled himself and slammed into me.

A cry cut up my throat, my eyes shutting at the intensity and pleasure burning through me, my body trying to adjust to his massive size.

"No. Open your eyes and keep them open. I want you to watch me fuck you."

I inhaled, opening my lids, turning my focus down, watching his cock, covered in me, thrust in and out. Over and over. It turned me on so much. Everything about it was erotic. The sound of my wetness, our groans, the feral hunger in his eyes, the way our bodies moved together.

"Fuck, Brycin." He picked me up, and my legs wrapped tightly around him. He stayed inside as he walked over slamming me against the office door. With one hand he pinned my arms above my head, arching me into him, slipping him in deeper. Pounding. Unrelenting. His mouth covered my breast biting at my nipple.

"Oh god, Eli." I squeezed around him. I wasn't close enough. I needed more. I needed all of him. "Fuck me harder… *destroy* me."

A deep growl came from his throat. He lost all control, plunging into me deep and rough, rattling the door, sliding me up and down, parting me over the doorknob. The metal rubbing into my ass as his cock hit an angle so deep in me, a sob racked up my throat. His free hand wrapped around my neck, holding me in place as he unleashed himself. My climax raced for me, and then he clenched down on my throat, cutting air from my lungs. Everything escalated, ever nerve flamed, every thrust was like an electric shock.

I exploded.

And so did every electrical object in the room.

FOURTEEN

I curled into Eli's side; our legs and arms intertwined. The dark bedroom was illuminated only by the hazy glow of the moon filtering through the thin curtain and softly crossing the floor up onto my enormous bed.

I sighed contentedly. The first time might have been intense and aggressive; the last time had been as passionate but slower. We took our time rediscovering each other. Both ways had been amazing. I could never imagine getting enough of him.

His lips touched the space between my eyebrows, making a sound like he was going to speak, but nothing came out.

"What?" I placed my chin on his chest and gazed up at him.

"What, what?"

"You were going to say something."

"Was I?"

"Yes. So talk."

"The bed is amazing. And sturdy."

I frowned.

He sighed. "I am done—"

"What?" My head shot up.

"Brycin." He tipped an eyebrow at me.

"Sorry, continue."

He took another breath. "I was gonna say… I am done with being without you. Ever again."

"But what if I am done with you?" I placed my hand under

my chin, teasing.

"You won't be."

"Oh, really?"

He cupped the back of my head, rolling me underneath him. "If you do, you will find yourself with one unrelenting stalker. A shadow on your ass."

"Oh, goodie. My own personal butt brigade."

He smirked as he leaned in and kissed me. "I am serious. Never again."

"You think you can handle me full time?"

"I know so. And I hear there's a great benefits package in it for you." His lips slid across the skin between my breasts, while his heavy erection brushed my leg. The torture of knowing what lay ahead of us twisted my gut. I couldn't think about it, not tonight. Most likely neither of us would live through the battle. I had to enjoy the time I did have with him.

I touched his face, turning it to mine. "Don't say it unless you actually mean it. Will you feel this way when you get sick of sleeping with me or I annoy you one too many times?"

"You might tire of having sex with me first." He kissed my neck softly, moving up slowly. *Doubtful*, I thought. "Let's enjoy right now." He nipped at my top lip. I could feel his smile tickling my mouth.

I forced my smile to match his. "All right, but if you ever even think about cheating on me, especially with Ms. Tits and Ass," I paused dramatically, "fried bacon bits, *deep*-fried."

"Shhhh." He peered under the blanket. "I told you they can hear you."

I grabbed the blanket, yelling down there. "Then hear me! You wander elsewhere and you will become a charred beef kebab with a side of meatballs."

Eli cringed, making me snicker. He then turned back to me, his hands touched my face, and his expression grew intense. "Believe me. My dick isn't going anywhere else. It's got squatters' rights now." His lips met mine fervently. He found his way back inside of me, showing me exactly what he meant.

"Dammit, Ember!" Lars thundered, banging on the bedroom door the next morning.

My lids cracked open; blurrily, I looked around in confusion. People pounding on the door cursing us should be normal to me by now. "What the hell did you two do to my office?"

Crap.

Eli rolled over grumbling.

"I will not subject Marguerite to cleaning your mess, especially when your underwear is on the floor. I want you both up now. I won't use my desk until I know it has been sanitized thoroughly."

Marguerite picked up my underwear all the time, but I got his meaning. This was slightly different.

"Did you touch the door handle?" Eli yelled back at him.

"Yes... why?" Lars asked skeptically.

"Uh, no reason."

Lars groaned and muttered something incomprehensible and stomped off.

I looked over my shoulder at Eli. "Think we're in trouble."

Eli's eyes were closed; his head snuggled back into the pillow. He didn't look like he would move anytime soon. Only his hands reached out, pulling me back into him.

"I smashed his printer, didn't I?" I laced my fingers through his, which were wrapped around my middle.

Eli snorted. "Yeah, you sure did. We kind of pulverized his office."

"We are starting to be quite expensive."

"You are." He winked when I turned over to look at him. "Because of you I had to buy Cooper a new bike."

"What did it have to do with me? I wasn't even here when he lost it."

"Exactly."

I scowled.

"You don't want to know." He stuffed his arm beneath his pillow, rolling to his stomach.

"I'll take your word for it." I sat up, pushing the covers off.

"Uh-oh." The sheets had fallen off him as I rose, showing off his entire sculpted body. Normally, I would have found the sight enormously pleasing to the eye, except for what I saw now—all over Eli's backside.

Pixies held grudges and did not forgive so easily. The juniper juice lover had certainly not forgiven the Dark Dweller yet. I did not want to think about when he snuck in here to retaliate. Hopefully, it was well after Eli and I passed out from exhaustion.

"Oh, crap." My hand went to my mouth, blocking the half groan, half laugh.

"What?" Eli's lids splintered open.

Ink and glittery Tinker Bell stickers were stuck all across Eli's ass and back. "Sprinkle Pixie dust" and "I believe in Pixie power." were written across Eli's back in glitter.

"What?" Eli followed my gaze and looked over his shoulder. "What the hell?"

I couldn't stop myself. I curled forward with hysterical laughter. Eli scrambled out of bed, chasing his own tail as he tried to get a better view of his backside. His hand went to one of the stickers and tried to tug it off.

"Ow." He flinched. "Damn, the li'l fucker super-glued them on!"

Tears spilled down my cheeks. "Oh, Cal, you are my hero."

Eli shook his head and yelled into my room. "This is war, you winged girlie toy!"

"How did you sleep through that?" I wiped at my eyes. How did we both?

"Guess someone really wore me out." Eli winked at me then returned to glued objects on his back.

As I watched him wincing while he struggled to tug off a sticker, a grip of sadness and guilt washed over me. This moment of happiness would end, and I would never have it back again. He would die, and if I decided I couldn't do it, then the world would collapse. Millions would die. My shoulders curled in. I felt like I would crack under the pressure of the responsibility. Even against my will, I was keeping secrets from him. In a way I was thankful Lars had taken the choice from me. My tongue had been bound by him before. I couldn't even tell Eli through our eye communication. Even if I could have told him, what would I say? How did one go about telling someone the only way to vanquish the Queen would kill him? There had to be a way around it. Could Kennedy be able to break it? Could a Druid end the Queen's spell? I was desperate. I would try anything.

The thought of Kennedy brought more shame. I needed to find her. A shiver tiptoed across my heart at the thought of Lorcan having Kennedy. I hoped he hadn't hurt her, though I wouldn't put anything past him.

"I need to jump in the shower. Only way to get these things off." He grinned, clearly a little impressed with Cal's creativity.

My laughter dried up as my thoughts drifted to the dark realities ahead of me. I got out of bed and headed to my walk-in closet. Here I was enjoying the best sex of my life with the love of my life who would soon be dead, and Kennedy was possibly being tortured. I yanked open a drawer and grabbed one of my t-shirts. Eli sensed my change in mood and followed me. "We'll find her." He wrapped himself around me.

My eyes darted over my shoulder.

He smiled. "You are not hard to read, and I can still feel your emotions." His arm looped my waist, twirling me to face him. His hands ran down my bare skin. "We'll track Lorcan. We'll get her back."

I nodded.

He pulled me closer. I threw my arms around his neck and

fell into his engulfing hug. I hoped he could only sense my anxiety for Kennedy and didn't think he had something to do with the decline of my mood.

He squeezed tighter. These moments were rare with him. I had to enjoy them while I could. Our naked bodies melded together as we embraced.

He sighed deeply and gave my shoulder a kiss, then smacked my bare ass. "Now get dressed and go clean your mess, woman."

"And we're back," I said dryly, shaking my head.

FIFTEEN

Later in the day I was startled by the movement at the top of the hill. The inundation of Dark Fae on the Unseelie King's land was beginning. I seemed to be the only one in awe of all the strange looking Dark Fae flooding in. They came in all shapes and sizes, from tiny forest gnomes to large mountain trolls. I had no clue what many of them were, but most Dark Fae were human in appearance. No surprise since the Unseelie needed to blend in with humans more since the Dark needed them to live off of.

Lars had set up a field of tent-cabins, but many brought their own version of portable homes, and some even dug holes in the ground.

"Oh, no. Anyone want to poke my eyes out?" I was on my knees, peering through the curtains of the window behind the breakfast nook.

"Why?" Eli chomped on a huge bite of the sandwich Marguerite made for lunch.

"There is a goblin peeing on the lawn," I said. "Guess six inches of man applies to all Fae creatures."

Eli smacked my ass.

"Eating here, darlin'." West slapped the other side of my rear.

I flipped around and slipped down the curved booth, plopping into a sitting position. Eli, Cooper, West, and I all sat together.

Marguerite was making more sandwiches at the counter. Rez grabbed one and walked to the table, sliding the plate to me. "You are probably going to see worse than Fae peeing." She pulled out a chair and sat across from me. "And a lot of it. There are going to be thousands of Fae heading here in the next couple of weeks."

"How will the Queen not notice?" I squashed the ciabatta bread, trying to get it flatter to fit into my mouth.

"Lars made it clear they glamour themselves, use different doors, and space out their arrival." Rez snatched a pickle from my plate. "Most Dark Fae are eager for the fight. They want Aneira destroyed. They do not want anything to screw it up either."

Cooper mumbled through a mouthful of food. "Damn, this sandwich is amazing. I am already in love with you, *mamacita*."

"No kidding. You want to move in with me?" West winked at Marguerite. She blushed and batted her hand at him but hummed happily.

The sound of someone tapping on glass flowed over to us. "Ummm... girlie? Help here?" A muffled voice spoke. "Come on, Marguerite, you won't let them leave me in here, will you?" Cal's voice came from the middle of the island. Marguerite looked at the pixie then at Eli. She smiled at the two of them, and then turned back to her sandwiches.

"Sorry, Cal. This is between you and Eli." I held up my hands.

Eli chuckled and took another bite of his sandwich, looking smug.

I tried to keep the smile off my face as I peeked at Cal. He sat at the bottom of a glass jar, tugging on his feet, apparently glued to the base. Eli had taken a jar and slathered the inside bottom and sides with honey. He poured an inch of juniper juice into the bottom. Cal, of course, could not resist the temptation. As soon as he entered, his wings and feet became trapped in the sweet confection. He had been stuck in there most of the morning. The juniper juice had long since been drunk. Left at the bottom stood a bitter, pissed off pixie.

"Your ass is mine, Dark Dweller." Cal smacked the glass.

"Bring it, Princess," Eli muttered through bites.

The situation was going to get bad. Pixies were not sweet, forgiving creatures. They were little, but mighty. Eli really was asking for it.

"Should you be calling him a princess when you still have glitter covering your ass?" Cooper smirked, causing West to laugh.

I tried to hold mine back, but a smile lit up my face. Eli had taken several showers since the morning and shimmer still clung to his skin.

Eli shot a warning at his brothers. "Better watch it. I have pixie power now."

We all burst out laughing; even Rez and Marguerite couldn't hide their amusement. When we quieted, Rez pointed at my plate. "Ember, eat. You are still weak."

My gaze stayed glued to my plate, but I could feel Eli stare at me before he turned away, shifting in his seat. He knew he was one of the reasons I stopped eating.

"Eat, darlin'." West's shoulder knocked into me "So your boobs will get bigger."

Cooper snorted into his plate. "I second that."

Eli sat back, his hand stroking my thigh. "Wish all you want. You're still not going to be touching them."

"Eating won't help. They're a lost cause now." I shrugged.

"Ember needs to eat. And you need to behave." Rez pointed at West.

"Good luck with that." I shoved part of the sandwich into my mouth. I munched for a few bites. "How is our property going to hold thousands of Fae? Two hundred acres is not enough to hold so many."

"Glamour and lots of it." Rez munched on the chips.

"We're extending our property line and glamouring it from humans, as well, to dissuade them from hiking or coming through our area. *If* by chance someone still does, they will not be able to see anything out of the ordinary."

The reality of the impending war was becoming real. We had talked about it, but seeing the invasion of Dark Fae coming onto the land made it tangible. And I knew a lot of these Fae standing in our field would not be alive in a matter of weeks.

My stomach knotted. I pushed my plate away.

"You better finish your food." Rez stood, grabbed another plate off the counter loaded with a large sandwich and chips, and headed for Lars's office.

"If you don't, I'll eat it." Cooper licked his fingers, getting every last crumb.

Eli huffed. "I get priority, right?" He squeezed my knee.

Silently, I slid my plate across to West. He chuckled as we both fist bumped each other.

"I see how it is." Eli stood. "Watch out there, Brycin. I know where Marguerite stores the peanut butter. You might find yourself out of it soon." A conspiratorial grin edged his lips as he looked at the small force of nature. Marguerite tried to hide the smile, but her face flushed with it. She loved me, but I had no doubt Eli would win every time when it came to her.

"Those are fightin' words, Dragen." I slithered out from the booth, standing in front of him.

Eli hands clutched my waist, and I went into the air. My body slumped as he placed me over his shoulder.

"Oh, no, not again." I fought against his hold.

"*No. Sin payasadas en la cocina.*" Marguerite flailed her knife in the air at me and Eli.

"If you would only learn your place, woman, I wouldn't have to do this. You know, you should be docile, sweet, and subservient."

Cooper and West exploded in laughter.

"Speaking of submissive. Take me to the training field,

boy." I let my arms and head dangle freely down his back. "Straightaway."

Lars had mentioned several times after I cleaned his office that he better find my behind on the training field after lunch. He meant partly to punish me, but I sensed he was as nervous as me about my fighting Aneira without powers.

Eli turned us toward the door. "Are you lifting my wallet again?"

"Shush, boy. You do not address the future Queen in such a manner." My fingers tugged at the leather case. I picked my head up and winked at West and Cooper, as I sifted through Eli's wallet and pulled out the cash, stuffing it into the back of my jeans. Cooper and West shook their heads, chuckling.

"Wait!" Cal's arms flailed around his holding pen. "Girlie, you better get me out of here, or I'll pee on your head tonight, as well,"

Pixies were not known to make empty threats.

"Guys?" I looked at the boys and motioned to Cal.

"Yeah, we'll get him. I endorse anyone who wants to urinate on Eli." West winked at me.

Thank you, I mouthed to him. I waved and blew Marguerite a kiss as Eli stuffed us through the kitchen door. Stepping outside, the cool air brushed at my exposed skin, invigorating me out of my food coma. Eli carried me for a few steps before he stopped and glided my body down his, standing me back on my feet. "You know what I do to willful future Queens?"

My fingers wrapped around his belt loops, pulling him against me. "Do tell."

"I tie them up and use my mouth to torture them." His stubble brushed against my cheek, his lips skimming my neck.

I rose on my tiptoes, taking his head in my hands. "I think I will need a preview to see how I will respond in situations like those you mention." My mouth just met Eli's when a voice spoke behind me.

"Hey, little Dae." Nic trotted to us, his brown eyes glinting as he stared at me and Eli. "Alki sent me to retrieve you. He says you need to be on the field now."

"Yeah. Thank. You." Eli's teeth ground together as he glared at the Incubus.

Nic's eyes drifted slowly along the length of Eli, with an expression of challenge and interest. Nic did not discriminate between gender, race, or status. Sex was sex to him.

Eli caught Nic's look. "See something you like?"

"More like what I want." His lip hooked up. "Now I see why my little Dae is so content. The sex vibes coming off you..." Nic breathed in.

A lot of human men would have felt threatened or uncomfortable by his statement, but Fae did not grow up with the same sexual biases. Even as "manly" as Eli was, another male's attraction didn't faze him.

"Sorry. Spoken for." Eli shrugged.

"Oh, I want her, too. I say we make it a party." Nic winked at me.

Eli's shoulders bristled. "Yeah, you're not going to be touching her or crawling into bed with her ever again. You got it?"

That's what Eli found offensive? Nic hitting on *me*?

"Got it." Nic held up his hands. "I won't deny I will miss it. I've enjoyed the time with you, little Dae." Nic turned to leave. "If you ever get bored, you know where to find me." He winked and headed back for the field.

Eli's lids lowered, glaring after Nic. "She won't."

My fingers twined with Eli's. "I think he was talking to you." I teased and hauled him toward the field. We both needed to work off some extra energy, but with Alki it would not be fun. Hours of pain and agony lay stretched ahead.

Alki's torture session extended for four hours. My legs barely worked to climb the stairs to my room. Eli turned on the shower and shoved me in. The hot water loosened my muscles and stopped them from shaking. Eli joined me, washing my hair and holding me upright. Times like now I missed my Dae powers with such a fierce passion it hollowed out my heart. My Dark Dweller part kept me standing and would get me moving faster than any human but nothing like my Dae magic used to. The lack of healing instantly and having abundant energy and strength buzzing from my magic left a chasm in my soul.

"I hate this." I pressed my head against the tile wall. Water plummeted on me from above. "Without my powers, I am weak. I feel like I am missing a part of me."

Eli grabbed my hips and turned me around. His hands curled at my jaw, tilting my head back. "You may not have your magic, but you are anything but weak." Water coursed down his shoulders and face. "Believe me. With or without your powers, you are still the same stubborn, pain-in-the-ass girl I met at Silverwood." He smiled and licked the excess water off his lip. "They don't define you. You define you."

My gaze lowered, watching the pelts of water slip off his arm. He grabbed my chin, turning my face to his. "You got what I'm saying?"

"Yeah. I got it." A soft grin tugged at my mouth. "And you're right. Even if you weren't a Dark Dweller, you'd still be a dick."

A smirk pulled up his mouth. "Absolutely." His fingers seized my hips. "How about I show you how much of one I can be."

Fresh from a shower and in the middle of getting dressed, a piercing wail filled my ears and vibrated the ground. Eli clapped both hands on his ears, wincing. I knew exactly what caused the sound, having experienced something similar at the Dweller's ranch. The property's spell had been crossed without permission. Before I could even react, Eli ran out of my room. I pulled on a pair of sweats and ran after him, my aching body not carrying me as fast.

"Hey, girlie. Where do you think you are going? I have a bone to pick with you." Cal spoke as I ran through the kitchen. He was probably there following Sinnie around as she tried to do her chores. He was lonely without Simmons. Simmons's absence affected both of us more than I imagined. I missed the bugger.

"Stay here," I ordered as I caught the closing door Eli had gone through.

"And miss all the fun?" He zipped to me. "Not a chance."

"Then promise me you will stay quiet and out of the way."

He settled on my shoulder. "Don't I always?"

I peered at him; my brow arched.

"Yeah, yeah, okay. I will this time."

It was Lars's property, and he would deal with whoever tried to get in, but I couldn't stop myself from going. I had always been protective of my family and friends, but since becoming part Dark Dweller, those traits had heightened even more. This was my home, and I would defend it.

Halfway there I picked up a scent.

Lorcan.

This time I did not dread seeing him. He was the only connection to my best friend. A nagging feeling pressed on my heart. *Oh, please, say she is okay.*

The tendons in my legs stretched, aching with the strain as I sprinted after Eli. Cal flew next to me. My heart thumped with fear and anxiety. *What if something happened to her? What had he done to her while she stayed with him? Had he hurt her?* So many awful scenarios ran through my head as I made my way through the forest to the property line. Lorcan's scent muddled with Kennedy's pulled me in a definite direction.

I slowed to a jog when I saw Lars, Rimmon, Goran, Cole, Eli, Cooper, and Gabby standing on the inner ring of the property line. Lorcan, Dax, and Dominic were easy to spot across from our group.

"Not that bastard again." Cal hovered in the air, his arms folding over his Woody Woodpecker t-shirt.

Loathing slammed into my chest the moment I took in Lorcan's smug face. *He* killed my mother. He took her away from me. Then I spotted long, red hair contrasting like a flare against the green leaves of the trees. Samantha.

A growl vibrated in my throat.

Cal snuck under my hair at my neck. "Easy, girlie."

Another rumble climbed my throat. Then Kennedy came into my sight line. "Kennedy!"

Her head cocked toward me, and she smiled but did not move from Lorcan's side. My feet came to a stop next to Eli. Something seemed wrong, like brushing the feathers of a bird the wrong way.

"Lorcan, I swear to God if you harmed her..." I spit out, my furor almost pushed my feet over the invisible line dividing our groups.

"Does she look hurt to you?" Those familiar green eyes narrowed on me, looking me up and down in contempt. His physical likeness and mannerisms to Eli always unsettled me.

"Just because I can't see—"

"I'm fine, Ember." Kennedy's usual sweet, soft voice rang boldly through the air, cutting off my rant.

Lorcan opened his arms. "We heard you were recruiting people for your war. Thought we'd come and offer our services."

I snorted. "You're kidding me, right?"

Lars stared at Lorcan before he gave a nod.

"W-Wh-hat? Are you serious? But he killed Aisling!" I sputtered like a cat in water.

Lars turned to me slowly. "This is war, Ember, and we have to sacrifice." His eyes glowered with meaning. "I may not like it, and when the war ends, some alliances may end. Until then, we must work against our common enemy."

Lars and his men turned to leave but stopped and faced Lorcan. "Our personal feelings have to come second if we want to achieve our goal. We cannot win unless we are all willing to compromise in some way or another." He glanced at Lorcan. "You are welcome to join; however, if you make one move out of line, I will kill you myself."

As cocky as Lorcan could be, his Adam's apple bobbed nervously as he nodded in concurrence. The Unseelie King did not make threats he did not intend to keep. Lars and his men disappeared into the forest.

"He can't be serious." Cal stomped his foot on my shoulder.

I turned back to Lorcan. His superior grin returned to his lips as he strutted across the property line. With a word from the King, the enemy was inside the walls.

When Kennedy crossed the line, she did not run to me like I thought. She stayed next to Lorcan.

Again my stomach twinged with uncertainty. No one held her or had a weapon menacing her. She had no restraints and didn't even look scared. She stood strong but relaxed in her stance. She held her chin high, and her demeanor revealed her as part of the group, not against it.

My gaze met hers questioningly, looking for a secret SOS or sign she was being terrorized in some way. Maybe they had dangled her family or possibly Jared as a threat for her to behave. She would send me some small signal. We knew each other well. She only had to blink funny for me to catch on.

Nothing happened. Kennedy did not turn away from my gaze but held it. A wall blocked any emotion from her expression. I had seen Kennedy change and grow after finding out she was a Druid, but this felt different. The confidence caused her tiny frame to stand taller. She didn't appear frightened or unsure.

A lump formed in my stomach, which I tried to deny. But the thought kept coming. She was not a prisoner. She stood with them on her own.

"I don't buy the fact you are here to help." Cole stood at his full height, every inch a powerful creature.

Lorcan's eyes darted to Kennedy then quickly looked back at Cole. "I have never been opposed to us working together. You were. I feel we can be stronger cooperating than apart against Aneira."

Eli's booming laugh filled the air. "This comment coming from the guy who betrayed his family, crawled into bed with the one enemy who banned us to Earth, abducted Ember, turned her over to the Queen, and then kidnapped Kennedy." Eli motioned to my friend. "And you want us to trust you? I don't think so."

Lorcan rubbed frantically at his shaved head. "Believe what you want about me. What I did was for you guys. You think I wanted to go to Aneira? Eli, you couldn't see straight when it came to her." Lorcan pointed at me. "I knew going to the Unseelie King would only cause a war. And it did. I wanted to avoid combat so I went to the source. *I* tried to keep my family from this. I did it for you."

Cooper coughed a short laugh. "I think we can all do without your version of being there for your family."

Dominic moved toward the line. "Get off your fuckin' high horse, Cooper. Lorcan was the only one who truly sacrificed anything. Elighan only sacrificed his judgment and ethics to be with *that* abomination. He was only for himself. Not us."

"I absolutely love being talked about like I'm not here. So good for the ego." I mumbled. No one listened to me. "Was killing my mother only out of love for your family?" I spewed at Lorcan. Eli quickly wrapped his fingers around my wrist. The feel of his hand on me calmed me a little, but my need to make Lorcan pay for his crimes pressed in on me with greater force.

"Yes," Lorcan replied. "I was doing a job. We were *mercenaries*. It's what we did. We killed for a living, Ember. We have killed a lot of creatures and people who had mothers and families. Your mother was not personal to me."

"She was to me!"

"If you want to hate someone, hate Aneira. She wanted your death and planned Aisling's murder down to the last detail. I happened to be a pawn she used to do it."

But Aneira wasn't here, and Lorcan was. Was there a difference between the one who actually committed the crime but had no ties to it, and the person who didn't get her hands dirty but had planned it all out?

Dominic puffed his chest out at Eli and said accusingly, "Too bad Eli screwed it up, and you lived. Otherwise, we wouldn't be standing here in this mess."

Eli roared and barreled for Dominic. In that millisecond everyone moved for the opposing group of Dark Dwellers. I saw it as a perfect opportunity to go for Lorcan, but Samantha stepped in my path. She'd do just as well.

A cruel smile twisted my lips. My hatred for her was stronger than for Lorcan. Yes, he killed my mother, but it hadn't been personal to him. Everything about Samantha was offensive. She killed Ian because of her vengeance toward me. She had sliced his throat with sheer giddiness only coming from the truly sadistic.

Cal sensed me coiling. He flew into the air as I zoned in on Samantha's throat. I wanted it.

Your death is mine. Her words entered my mind.

What the hell? I hadn't expected her voice inside my head. She dove for me, catching me in a vulnerable moment.

"Ember!" Cal yelled, snapping me back into focus. He grabbed the ends of her hair and yanked her head back. She yelped, and I pounced. The feeling of my pupils shifting into thin diamonds, eyes of a killer, spiked my adrenaline higher. My teeth craved her throat; my mouth watered for the kill. The need to tear her apart was there, but Samantha was the real monster. I was just a wannabe. There was little chance I could hurt her, but I was willing to try.

Mid-leap there was a pop. Defusing pressure in the air

broke my focus on Sam and launched both of us back to the ground. We landed only a few feet away from each other. Air huffed in and out of my lungs as I got my bearings.

What just happened?

"NOW STOP!" Kennedy voice thundered through my haze. My head popped up to look. Everyone except Kennedy had landed on the ground in unruly clusters. All were now gaping at the girl standing in the middle.

Crap on ash bark. Kennedy did that? Her powers had grown a great deal since the last time I saw her.

"It was my idea to come here today." She spoke confidently, and her gaze swept around at all of us. "We will be better together than separate. So get over the past and your issues. All of you!" She directed her last words at me, sensing my rebuttal. "And you will behave." She pointed at Lorcan when his mouth opened to speak. "I agree with Lars. Let us deal with the real problem. Right now we need to work as a team. We need to defeat Aneira. You will have the chance to kill each other after."

Lorcan shut his mouth with a click. His eyes bowed away from her weighty gaze on him.

If I were standing, my jaw would have hit the ground. I had never seen anyone shut Lorcan up nor have any sort of control over him. What had happened to turn the captive into the leader?

Cole stood first. "She's right. Our grudges need to go on the backburner for now."

"Easy for you to say!" I sprang up. "One of them didn't kill one of your good friends and your mother and turn you over to the Queen!"

Ember, enough. Cole's voice popped into my head. I could hear him. He seemed to understand the widening of my eyes. *Without your other powers you will become more Dark Dweller. You are linking to us. It will start out sporadic but will become more solid as time passes.* His voice came clearly into my mind.

Of course. Just as I had once linked with Torin, I was now joined to the Dark Dwellers since losing my Fay magic.

Cole had spoken in his head to me but now addressed the rest of the group out loud in a soothing voice. The Alpha had the power to calm others with his voice. The deep tenor of his voice settled us all back. "But Aneira is a far greater foe. She will destroy Earth and everything you have grown to love. We will all be slaves, not only the humans. I'm not saying you have to get along or even be cordial, but I need us to have a truce."

"But—" My words were cut off as the Alpha raised his hand. My voice died in my throat.

Back down, Ember, he commanded in my head.

"Don't put up with that." Cal perched on my arm. He didn't understand I didn't want to but had no choice.

Cole continued, "Only until the conflict is over, like Kennedy recommends. Then we can deal with each other. Until then, we need a truce between us."

Everything in me wanted to protest, but I had to respect my Alpha's authority. If I didn't feel deep down somewhere that Cole, Lars, and Kennedy were right, I probably would have disputed him more.

Eli crossed his arms. "Fine. But it doesn't mean I'm going to trust him... or any of them. Not by a long shot."

"Same here, brother." Lorcan sneered.

Lips moved against my ear. "And the moment this little truce is over, I am going to relish ripping you into shreds," Samantha whispered.

"Ditto." I jeered back at her. "With pleasure."

SIXTEEN

"Kennedy!" Jared bellowed as she and I walked onto the training field. I noticed as he ran toward us how his body was beginning to develop from a boy's to a young man's, filling out his hand-me-down t-shirt more. He was slowly catching up to his actual human age. Jared would be turning nineteen in a few months, but his body and mind were still young. He didn't appear much older than fifteen or sixteen. Almost four "Earth" years had passed while he was locked in the Otherworld before I got him and Kennedy out.

Age didn't usually matter to Fae since we lived for thousands of years, but Jared was half human. He was also raised on Earth, growing up differently than the rest of the clan. Because of his human half, they tended to coddle him too much. Now a war was upon us, and Cole seemed overly aware of the pampering Jared had received.

A few nights after the Dark Dwellers' arrival on Lars's compound I heard Owen, Jared, and Cole arguing. I could blame my inquisitiveness on my heightened Dark Dweller hearing. But, hell, let's be honest. I'm purely nosy.

"You want me to train but not fight?" Jared's voice rang through the thin wooden wall of the temporary cabin they inhabited into the chilly night air.

"It's my fault." Cole spoke. "I should have been more adamant about your training from the start, but blame is all hindsight now."

"Jared, I understand you are upset with us, but you have to know we are only doing this for your benefit." To me, Owen's tone always felt like ointment on a sore. Soothing and calming.

Except Jared didn't seem to take it in the same way. "You think keeping me out of the battle is a benefit for me? No, it's only for your sake because you don't think I can hold my own out there. To you I am weak and useless!"

"Jared." Cole huffed in irritation. "It's not that we think you're weak. But as much as you'd like to deny it, you are half human. Your heritage does cause you to be more vulnerable than us. You weren't raised like your father and I were, which is a good thing I promise you." A small sigh came from Cole's throat. "You are going through a rough time right now. I speak from experience in raising three teenage Dark Dwellers. You even more so. Both your human and Dark Dweller hormones are out of control. Everything is heightened, and you cannot think clearly. You are aggressive and impulsive." Cole paused. I could see his outline drift back and forth by the window. "I stand by my decision. You are too young and inexperienced to be on the battlefield, but I still want you to train every day."

"Bullshit," Jared spoke. Something hit the wall making the cabin shake. Most likely his foot or fist. "So, I do all the training but don't get to put it into action?"

"As of right now. Yes," Cole replied.

"Right now?" Jared's voice rose with optimism. "Is there a chance if I work really hard and get really good, you will let me go?"

There was a long pause before Cole spoke. "Maybe." *Maybe* was all Jared needed. Every waking moment, Jared threw himself into training. Trying to stuff years of education and practice into a few weeks. There was always one of his fellow Dark Dwellers out training with him.

Today's opponent was Owen. Alki's booming voice came from down the field as he and Koke displayed their moves on stage. Thousands of Dark Fae moved simultaneously together, creating a moving piece of art on the lawn.

"Baby!" Jared dropped his sword. Pure happiness shown in his eyes when he saw Kennedy walking to him. He ran to her, almost knocking her over. He wrapped his arms around her. Words caught in his throat as he cupped her face and stared at her. He leaned in and kissed her hard. His arms latched on, touching every bit of her.

"I can't breathe." Kennedy's lips turned into a smile, but the same happiness didn't show in her eyes.

"I am so sorry. Damn, I've missed you. Are you okay? Did they harm you?" He looked her from head to toe frantically.

"No, I'm fine." She stepped out of his arms.

I waited anxiously for the moment Jared noticed Lorcan. When it came, Jared did not disappoint.

"You asshole! How dare you show your face here?" He flew at Lorcan. Eli could have easily stepped in to block Jared's punch, but he stood back, a half-smile on his face.

Lorcan also could have shifted aside; his reactions were a lot faster than Jared's. But Lorcan let the hit make contact, only causing him to stumble a step or two back. Jared turned his shoulder and rammed into Lorcan's stomach. I was amazed, but Lorcan took it. He didn't fight Jared or try and stop it. It was the first decent thing I'd seen Lorcan do. He knew he deserved it.

I looked at Kennedy. I expected her to be in the middle trying to prevent Jared from getting hurt, but she only stared at them, her forehead furrowed. Kennedy was usually so sensitive to people fighting. When watching movies with extreme violence, she would always hide under the covers while Ryan and I enjoyed them. So her lack of action surprised me.

"Now things are getting good. I should tell Sinnie to cook popcorn." Cal leaned against my neck. I brushed him off. He fluttered next to me and huffed.

"Jared, enough." Cole finally stepped in and pulled him back.

"Let me go," Jared seethed, his eyes still latched onto his target.

"Cooper?" Cole nodded his head.

Cooper moved forward and wrapped his fingers around the back of Jared's neck, steering him toward the forest. "Let's take a walk. Cool down."

"I don't want to cool down. How are you guys letting him come here after what he's done? He kidnapped my girlfriend. Betrayed us." Jared's aggression rose again. Cole gave Cooper another pointed look, and Cooper pushed Jared forward. Jared stumbled as he tried to turn around and come back, struggling to get out of Cooper's hold. They finally disappeared into the trees, but we heard Jared's rants for a long time after.

"I think we need to discuss some matters," Cole said coolly and turned toward the temporary cabins Lars had built on the other side of the field. Most Fae camped outside, but a few demanded some sort of housing whether it was a tree house or a burrow in the ground. The Dark Dwellers took over some cabins and made a huge fire pit where they sat most nights.

Gabby, Samantha, Dax, and Dominic followed Cole. I continued to watch Kennedy. Her eyes and lips were tight as she stared between Jared's disappearing form and Lorcan. Lorcan wiped the blood from his lip. He looked briefly at her then turned away.

She snapped around and, without a word, trudged to the cabin, her shoulders rigid. My legs moved to catch up with her.

"You sure you are all right?" I grabbed her hand in mine as we walked.

"I wish people would stop asking if I'm okay." She replied without even looking at me. "As you know, I'm not easy to keep down now." I had said the same thing to her months ago. I didn't know what caused the gulf between us, but something was wrong.

Lorcan's scent wafted close behind us, flaring my predatory nature. The urge to turn and tear out his throat was so appealing I had to force my free hand into a fist, which I stuffed into my pocket. Eli's presence behind me helped act as a buffer between me and Lorcan.

I didn't know how I was going to have a truce with Lorcan or Samantha.

We gathered outside Cole and Owen's cabin. Tension crackled at the edges of the group, straining the precarious treaty. Lorcan swaggered next to Cole in defiance to show he still had authority over his own group. Things would never go back to the way they used to be. Lorcan made it clear he was Alpha in his pack, and he would never return to being a Beta. Eli clenched his fists at Lorcan's audacity but kept his mouth shut.

Cole's body tightened, but he did not say a word to Lorcan. "I know working with each other will be difficult. But we need an alliance between us to defeat our common enemy. I know none of us want Aneira to have control of Earth and the Otherworld. Her powers are already too great. Her ideas of freedom and supremacy have destroyed ours and many other dark clans, and her dominance over both Humans and Fae will only get worse. We may not see eye-to-eye on a lot of issues, but I think we can come together on this one." Cole's voice soared through the assembly, rendering us still.

Lorcan nodded. "Yes, I agree with Cole. We need to let go of the past and focus on the future."

"*You* forget the past?" Eli scoffed. "I find what you say amusing when all you do is bring it back up and put the blame on everyone else as to why you do the things you do. You stand there pretending to be Alpha, saying we need to fight against Aneira, when it was you who worked with her. Not us."

Lorcan shifted his weight and moved around under the scrutiny. "I understand your feelings, Elighan. As a leader, you do what you feel is best for your clan. At the time I felt I was doing just that. I quickly realized the choice may have not been the most effective option. I have made amends and moved on. It is you who won't let go. Neither you nor Cole can stand here and say you have always made the best decisions for the family. Our divide proves this."

Eli's hands clasped even tighter. Cole looked at the ground, taking in a deep breath.

"How ethical you guys have become here on Earth. Do you think Father would even be questioning me? He understood the true acts of a leader and how far you sometimes needed to go."

"Father wouldn't have done what you did," Eli said.

Lorcan shook his head. "You have no idea who Dragen really was, Eli. You were young and idolized him. I saw what he was capable of. Ask Cole. He knows what I am talking about. You have a notion of Father that is a fantasy. Mother as well. She was equally cruel and conniving. You only saw what you wanted and only remember what you want. They were Dark Dwellers through and through, which is why Cole has tried so hard to raise you differently. He never liked how they led. He hated them. Right, Cole?" Lorcan turned to Cole.

Cole stood stock-still, though I could feel the vibrations of his every muscle struggling not to pound Lorcan into the ground.

"I was older, already too far in following good ol' Dad's footsteps, huh, Cole? Is that the reason you chose Eli? I was too much like the man you despised?" Lorcan twisted to Eli. "On the other hand, Cole could still save you."

Deep, raggedy breaths came in and out of the man next to me. Eli stood still, but the violence underneath was thundering.

"And do you want to know why Cole hated Father so much? The man you looked up to as a hero?" Lorcan shot Cole a pointed look, full of meaning. And Cole seemed to understand the unsaid words.

"Lorcan, don't." Cole shook his head and glanced quickly

at Eli.

"Don't what? Tell the truth? Don't you think it's time he knew?" Lorcan hand gestured in Eli's direction. Eli's body twitched, his glare going between the two men.

An eerie awareness suddenly slammed down on me. *Oh, no.*

"*When* did you find out you were Father's bastard child, Cole?" Lorcan folded his arms as a united gasp fell over the group.

Owen jerked forward. "What?"

Cole ignored Owen's outburst, and his jaw muscles tightened. "When did *you*?"

"A long time ago." A fleeting emotion flittered across Lorcan's expression. "One night I caught Father sneaking to your mother when your supposed father went off on a job—a job which my father assigned him. It didn't take long before I realized the affair had been going on for a while. After you were born, I could see it in how Father looked at you and how he addressed you. The toughness he showed you was a red flag. And every once in a while, I could see him in you. Your mouth, in your mannerisms."

"What? Is this a joke?" Eli's chest rattled next to me as he tried to speak. When neither brother would look at him, he turned to Lorcan. "You knew and didn't tell me? Did Mother know?"

"Yes." Lorcan's usual smug expression evaporated, and the corners of his mouth turned down, like a hurt little boy. "One night I overheard Father and Mother arguing about Cole. She forced him to keep quiet about the affair and his bastard baby. It was easy when he looked so much like his mother. He could easily blend in as Donovan's son." Lorcan's voice came out low, anger tinting his tone. "She wanted the title of Alpha more than she wanted a faithful mate."

I could see the storm brewing in Eli's mind, his emotions a squall of hurt, betrayal, and shock. He held his body rigid, his eyebrows pinched.

"You're my brother?" Eli's eyes were on Cole, his voice came out a whisper.

"Half," Lorcan stated.

"Holy shit," Gabby mumbled under her breath. Her eyes did not shine with excitement as they normally did around drama. Even she could not make light of Lorcan's revelation.

Owen took off his glasses, rubbing his eyes. "How come you didn't tell me?"

Cole whirled around, his temper flaring. "Because I didn't want it to be true. I knew you would look at me different if you knew." Owen took a step back. Cole closed his eyes before reopening them. "You are my brother, Owen. Nothing will change the fact, and I didn't want it to change for you."

Owen bobbed his head. A few moments passed before he found his voice. "It won't. Half or full, you are still my brother."

Cole took one large stride and engulfed Owen in a hug, pounding on his back. "I don't want Jared to know." I heard him whisper into Owen's ear. Owen nodded, his hand moving to Cole's shoulder as they separated.

Lorcan's hatred of Cole now made more sense to me. Lorcan had taken out his anger at his father on the innocent boy, a result of an affair. This had made Cole's ascent to Alpha even more of a sting to Lorcan, especially when Cole chose Eli.

And here I thought my family should be on a reality show.

Eli's feet held resolutely to the ground as he looked at his two older brothers. I knew Eli thought of his whole clan as his brothers and sisters, but this was a little different. Cole was blood—a half-brother he hadn't known about. A deep family secret finally found its way to the surface.

Cole's gaze landed on Eli, softening. "I'm sorry I didn't tell you. I didn't want to be the one who destroyed your views of your father. I thought it better to keep everything the way it was."

"You still should have told me." Eli's hands went up, as he

roughly scoured his head. "Why now, Lorcan? Why bring it up now?"

"Because I felt it was time you knew the truth. You are so determined to have me be the villain even though you have no idea how many times I protected you, how I stood in front of Father when he became abusive and cruel. I took the beatings when he got drunk and his temper needed an outlet." Lorcan rapped his fingers on his chest. "You still want to make me the bad one? Fine."

Reaction to Lorcan's words contorted Eli's face. His fists clenched and his shoulders twisted down. A palpable hush enveloped the group. We entered the eye of the storm, waiting in trepidation for Mother Nature's wrath to resume.

Cole's low voice finally cut through the invisible barricade. "I do want to talk about it, Eli. We have a lot of things to discuss, but I think we should do it later, privately." Cole scratched at his scruff. It was his gesture when frustrated or nervous.

Eli clasped the back of his neck with one hand. I wanted to comfort him, but I knew he needed to process the facts first. Right now he would reject any comforting. His instincts were on guard and defensive.

"Yeah. We need to get back to what is *really* important—killing the Queen." Eli's tone sounded cold and clipped.

Oh, yeah, he is going to need some time with this one.

"Eli?" If I could sense Eli shutting down, then Cole could sense his Second's mood shift, as well.

"No, you are right." Eli rolled his own shoulders, his neck rigid. "We can't change the past. Let's focus on what we can alter."

Nervousness crawled over my heart, as I felt his mood veering down a vicious alleyway.

Eli cleared his throat and adjusted his stance, a clear sign he was changing subjects. "You all know I was recently taken to the Otherworld where Aneira lifted the curse so I could get through the doors." He paused. My feet felt like they were standing over a trap door, not sure where he was going with this. "I figured it was temporary, but to my surprise, when we escaped, I could once again get through the doors. I began to wonder, if Aneira granted all of you," Eli's hand waved around in the direction of Lorcan's group, "the same liberty when you were working for her. What did you need Kennedy for? Why kidnap her and talk of your need for her if you could already get through the doors to the Otherworld?"

My head wrenched up as his point completed its circle in my brain. Everyone, except Lorcan's clan, snapped to look at Lorcan.

"Holy shit," Gabby belted out. "Why did you kidnap her?"

Multiple questioning stares landed on Lorcan. He tugged at the bottom of his jacket, a pained smile on his face. "Because the curse is not lifted."

My hand went to my hip as I shifted my weight to the side. "What are you talking about? Did she put it back on you? I've seen Eli go in and out of those doors."

"No, you stupid bitch." Samantha edged herself in front of Dax and Dominic.

Heat burned up my neck as ire filled my bones, and Eli quickly stepped in front of me and glared at Samantha. "I'm looking at the stupid bitch, if you open your mouth again." His voice iced so quickly it chilled my fury.

Samantha's eyes grew wide, and then narrowed to slivers. "You are no longer my Alpha, Eli, and no longer the man I am supposed to obey. Cole ruined you. He took your true destiny away."

Eli's eyes never left hers, his voice even. "And I am thankful."

Samantha's eyes flourished into a deep red, and a snarl hissed from her teeth.

"Stop!" Lorcan raised his arm at Samantha. "We don't have time for your petty temper tantrums."

She scowled in his direction, before skittering back in between the two thugs next her. Her glare danced back and forth between Eli and me.

"Now to answer your question." Lorcan curved his body to face me. "We can still get in and out of the Otherworld doors, but it doesn't mean the curse is lifted."

"Get to the point, Lorcan." Cole restlessly rocked his body back and forth.

"I also thought when Aneira gave us entrance, we no longer had to worry. I thought my plan had worked, and we had got what we wanted. I went back to the Otherworld, thinking we were home, where we belonged. We were there only one Otherworld day before we felt it." Lorcan paused with dramatic flair. "It was like the land rejected us. After a while, it became too painful. We had to retreat to Earth." His clan all nodded in agreement to his story. "We may be allowed to go in and out of the Otherworld, but we are still banned from the land. The curse of Aneira's will never be lifted off us. Either we have a Druid break it, or Aneira has to die. We knew if Ember were the prophesized one, then it would be pointless to take the sword away from her. If she succeeded, then the curse would be broken. If she didn't, I still had backup. Kennedy. It was the best of both situations."

Eli shook his head. "But I was there in the Otherworld, and I didn't feel anything."

"You were only there for a few hours, and you were already hurt. How do you know you didn't start to feel it?" Lorcan's brow lifted, challenging Eli's statement.

"It's true." West said quietly beside Eli. "I didn't understand at the time, but it makes sense. The lack of blood had weakened me, but it was more than that. Being there destroyed me, tore me apart on the inside. I thought it was because I had been on the Light side too long." West had been bones by the time we got him out of there. His quick decline was caused by more than blood loss.

Eli rubbed absently at his elbow, frowning.

"He's telling the truth." Kennedy's tiny legs carried her to Lorcan, standing defiantly beside him. "I did a revealing spell, and the curse was locked tight around his aura."

"Then nothing has really changed," Cole said. "Breaking our curse is important to us, I know, but it will be all for naught if we have no Otherworld to go back to, or we have either become Aneira's slaves or are on the run from her. We are a self-centered species, but we cannot forget the war is beyond our little problems. We fight for a bigger cause. We battle for all of the Dark Fae. Breaking our curse is icing on the cake if we kill her."

"Thank you." I threw up my arms. "Finally you admit it." Since the day I met the Dark Dwellers, they had been obsessed with getting back to the Otherworld. It didn't seem to matter who they hurt or what else was going on around them. It was nice to hear Cole recognize their fanatical tendency.

"What?" Cole's mouth quirked up.

My lids lowered. "The whole 'egotistical can't-see-beyond-your-own-assholes' part."

Snickers broke out through the gathering.

"The 'it's-not-all-about-you' section."

"I did not get the memo." West leaned out past Eli to see me.

"Okay." Cole clapped his hands. "For now I think we can take a break. Lars will be meeting with Lorcan and me later, and we will let you know what the plan is. Until then, let's stay out of each other's way and try to get along when you do."

Murmurs hummed through the clans as people dispersed.

"Eli?" Cole called. Eli gave a swift nod and move toward the other Dark Dwellers.

"Hey." I grabbed his hand. He looked back at me, emotionless. I didn't say anything out loud or through my eyes. I didn't need to. His head lifted ever so slightly and he squeezed my hand. Then he turned away and walked to his new family.

Owen, Cole, Lorcan, and Eli headed into the cabin and shut the door behind them.

SEVENTEEN

Kennedy roomed with Gabby, so I headed directly there after the meeting. We had much to catch up on. My last encounter with Kennedy left me uncomfortable, shut out, something I hadn't experienced with her. I never thought Kennedy capable of resentment or anger, but she was no longer the girl from school, no longer vulnerable. *What if she found out I had never looked for her?* My guilt alone was enough to put a partition between us.

My knuckles drummed the wooden door.

"Come in," Kennedy's voice soaked through the cracks.

I stepped into the small, cozy cabin. Gabby's clothes were draped everywhere, over a chair and oozing out of her dresser like it was retching up fabric, but she was not in the room. Kennedy stood with her back to me. She placed her folded clothes from her bag into a neat pile on her bed.

"Hey." I shut the door but didn't venture past the entry.

"Hey." Kennedy kept her back to me. She pulled out more clothes from the canvas pack than she had before. Lorcan probably gave her the bag full of clothes he had acquired for her. The thought of him buying her things like shampoo or tampons did not settle properly in my mind.

"Hope Lorcan had better fashion sense than Gabby or Owen did." My attempt at humor fell flat as she wordlessly continued to unpack her suitcase. I shifted, feeling the uncomfortable silence building between us.

"Ken," I faltered. "I-I am so sorry."

She stopped, not turning, her arms bunched to her chest. "For what?"

"For what? For not protecting you. For not stopping Lorcan from taking you. And not finding you fast enough." *For not even looking.*

She slowly turned to face me. "None of that was your fault. You couldn't have stopped him, and you can't protect me every minute of every day. I am not a helpless baby. I can look after myself."

"I know."

"Do you?" Friction bounced between us, spreading into every corner. I didn't know what to do. The sensation twisted my hands against each other. Unspoken words crowded around us like bullies, tormenting and smashing at our friendship. The only way to deal with a problem was head on.

I took a breath and leaped. "Are you all right?" My shoe scrubbed at the thin planks of wood. "Did he hurt you?"

Sitting on the edge of her mattress, Kennedy shook her head. Her shoulders lowered along with her defenses. "No."

"What happened then?" I grabbed a wooden chair next to the bed.

"I don't want to talk about it."

"Ken?" I sat and leaned forward to take her hands in mine.

Kennedy moved from my reach, stood, and walked to the window. It hurt my heart. I felt responsible for what happened to her. I'd been too caught up in my own turmoil.

"Kennedy, talk to me." I turned to stare at her back.

Kennedy whirled around, and her eyes narrowed on me. "You want me to talk? Fine. Why didn't you tell me about Ryan?"

It felt wrong to see her look at me like this. Anger and betrayal mirrored deep in her brown eyes.

"I—"

"You kept the truth from me." Kennedy cut off my sentence. "Don't you think I had the right to know *my* best friend, the boy I have been friends with since kindergarten, would never be able to return to Earth?"

"Ken—"

She waved her hand, cutting me off again. "Lorcan told me the truth. Do you know how stupid and betrayed I felt being the last person to know? You of all people should know how it feels, but you were the one who kept it from me. You complain about Fae keeping secrets from you, and yet you're exactly like them."

A sharp breath snapped in my lungs at the truth of her accusations. I knew exactly how she felt.

Her face now showed pain and sadness. "I believed all our work was to get him out, and for one of us at least to be free of this mess and the Otherworld. But Ryan can *never* come home. He can never see his family again or move to San Francisco like he dreamed." Kennedy paced the room.

"I know. I'm sorry." My head lowered. "You probably won't care, but I actually thought it was for the best and knowing about Ryan would distract you."

She stopped, her nose flaring. "You had no right to decide for me. How little you must think of me that I wouldn't want to help. I also have a stake in the war. Ryan or not, I am going to fight. Aneira killed my entire family and would like to see me dead, as well. You are not the only one who has reason to hate her."

Kennedy was not a sweet, timid girl anymore. She was fierce and strong. She had always let Ryan and me dominate. Not any longer.

"You're right." I nodded. "All I can say is I am sorry, and I will never keep anything from you again. You can handle much more than I ever gave you credit."

Her shoulders relaxed. "Thank you."

I didn't know what to do. I wanted to hug her and have

everything go back to normal. But we weren't normal. There still seemed to be a fence between us. "Are we okay?"

She looked up, meeting my gaze. "We will be."

My lips formed into a sad, thin smile. I understood. I would have to earn her trust over time. A long, drawn-out silence filled the room, neither of us knowing what to say or do next.

"Lorcan kept me safe. He didn't hurt me. He actually helped me." She spoke softly, wrapping her arms around herself, retaking a seat on her bed. "He's taught me a lot. My magic has grown so much."

"Lorcan?" My eyes narrowed.

Her head jerked up, her face becoming defiant. "He's the only one who has been truthful with me. Cole and Owen never told me the full truth, even though they knew. Lorcan told me about my family and the true power of our magic. He's made me stronger."

"Because he wants to use you."

Kennedy bolted off the bed. "I already know what he wants from me. He never kept it a secret. Can you say the same about Eli? Or Cole? They want me for the same thing. What makes him different?"

"Because it's Lorcan."

She pressed her lips together so hard they turned white. "He's not what you think he is."

A sputter came from my throat. "Wha-what? Lorcan is the guy who kidnapped you, had Ian killed, and murdered my mother."

Her chest grew as she sucked in a bucket of air. "Samantha killed Ian. Lorcan did not actually want to hurt any of us. He was bluffing to get you to act."

My mouth opened and closed. "Lorcan doesn't bluff. He didn't give a shit if Ian died or not. He doesn't give a damn about anybody but himself."

Kennedy's expression went hard, the barricade falling

thicker between us.

"What the hell is going on?" I looked around like something in the room could answer my question. "Is it the Stockholm syndrome or something?"

Kennedy tilted her head and glared at me.

"What is this, Ken? Why are you defending Lorcan?" Then with one thought, ice trickled into my chest, freezing me. "You have feelings for him."

"Of course, I don't," she refuted.

Her denial felt too fast. Too defensive. "Oh, no." My eyes widened more as I watched her. She fidgeted under my gaze. "But Jared?"

Fury flashed through her eyes. "I may have come to understand Lorcan better, but I love Jared." Her fists tightened against her legs. "Do not confuse your situation with mine. I am not you. Though, I don't see how you have room to judge. You fell for a killer. But that's okay because you let yourself believe Eli is different." She brushed past me, stopping at the door. "You have kept secrets and lied to me. You say you're different from the Fae, but you aren't. You claim they only want to use me. I'm not stupid, Ember. I can *feel* you came in here for your own motives. What do *you* want to use me for?"

My mouth couldn't get out more than, "I—I..."

"That's what I thought." Though she looked at me, her eyes had a faraway glint. She grabbed the door, threw it open, and then turned back and spoke softly, *"What has been done cannot be undone, not by my hand. His death will come by yours."* She blinked, coming back to herself, then stomped out the door. It slammed with a deafening bang.

What the hell just happened?

Her words twisted around my stomach, clamping down as I stood in shock. Consciously I had not come in here to ask for her help, but her seer saw my true desire. I felt sick and agitated. My emotions rotated through mad, hurt, devastated, and guilty.

Kennedy was a huge priority of mine, but I could not deny

Eli held an even bigger urgency. To find a way to break the curse on me so he wouldn't die.

Shame sat heavy on my conscience. What kind of friend was I? Not a good one lately. Her reaction toward Lorcan also bothered me, the way she defended and talked about him. It felt wrong, but nothing about our fight seemed right.

EIGHTEEN

Ugliness leaked into my soul. My last hope of saving Eli's life while still killing Aneira had perished, turning my heart cold. Also I had never fought with Kennedy before, and not once had she been mad at me. Not like this.

Even without my powers, the darkness still part of my DNA blinded me. It barraged my body because I could not release it. I craved to let the power take over and push me past feeling or caring. That kind of power only happened to me a few times, but the rush of complete control and strength—not caring about anything around me—was addictive.

With the desire to destroy crackling in my veins, I headed to the stone building on the property where Alki trained me. I blew up the first training room, and a stronger stone structure now replaced it. Lars had forbidden anyone but his family to go there. It held some extraordinarily powerful weapons, one being the sword now belonging to me. It was ancient and had seen many battles in its time. The rapier had shown me images of a few of its crusades from the past. They were bloody and gruesome, but the weapon never bowed to any other blade. It was proud of its conquests, and pleasure crawled up my spine to have a sword that would not hesitate to kill.

The more time away from the argument with Kennedy, the darker my mood became. The blackness went nowhere and clogged my rational thoughts leaving only anger and frustration.

The hopelessness of my situation with Eli moved my soul to hate. We were doomed. *Life's a cruel, twisted bitch.*

When I muttered the magic word to release the lock, the door swung open in welcome. My fingers caught it as I stepped in, and I slammed it behind me. I headed straight for the wall. With a touch of my finger, the cupboard doors opened, revealing the gleaming metal display of the recently honed swords hanging in their leather scabbards. A saber etched with intertwining Celtic symbols called to me. It wasn't the most beautiful sword there, but it was one of the strongest. My hand grasped the hilt. Feeling my touch, magic buzzed through the blade, down the handle, and into my hand. Sensing my dark energy, it vibrated as though anxious for a battle, or perhaps the weapon was tired of sitting on the shelf.

Me, too. My nerves were frayed with the thought of what was to come: the moment when, even if I were victorious, after hundreds or thousands died, I plunged the blade into Aneira's cold heart, and Eli would die. Part of me wanted it to begin so it could end.

"Sorry, my friend. No battle today." I swung it around, cutting through air, then whirled in a circle and plunged it into the training dummy.

Over and over I twirled, swung, and drove my blade into the training objects. I could hear Alki in my head, *"Not quick enough. You do not have the luxury of your powers anymore. You will not live if you cannot beat them in a duel. Again!"*

Drips of sweat wandered down my face and trickled into the space between my breasts. My fury grew with each stab, the sword enticing the anger from me; it took pleasure from my fury and wanted more.

The door hinges creaked. I spun around; my blade prepared to meet a live threat. The end point whisked to a throat, blood trickling as the piercing tip broke the intruder's skin.

Eli only stared at me, his body tight, but his arms stayed at his sides.

Stepping back, I lowered the sword. "You're lucky I didn't kill you."

The moment the words came out of my mouth, I flinched. He tilted his head, his expression unchanged. He had no idea how fateful those words were.

My shoulder hit his arm as I darted around him, headed for the weapons wall. "What are you doing here?" I slipped the blade back into its sheath.

"You're kidding, right?" He turned to face me. "With the level of emotions you are throwing off, I would be able to feel you half way across the world right now. I'm in the middle of talking to my *half-brother*, and my dick goes hard as a rock."

I smiled at his comment but then immediately winced, aware he was going through a lot, as well. Today had been a tough day all around.

The new dose of blood I received from Eli had evened out in me. I could not feel his emotions as intensely as he could feel mine. I had the urge to hide from him, already too open and exposed.

I grabbed a towel from the clean laundry stack on the counter and wiped the sweat from my face. He sauntered to me, plucked the towel out of my hands, and tossed it to the side. He gripped my hips, pulling me in close. "You gonna tell me what has you so wound up?"

I shook my head and looked away. "Are you going to tell me how your talk went with Cole and Lorcan?"

He closed his eyes briefly, his voice growing forced. "I've had a hell of a day, and you're throwing off a lot of endorphins right now. If you don't want me to act on them, you better talk quick. If not..."

Frustration still rippled through me and made me want to beat the pulp out of someone. He could sense it, but he took my sidling up to him as an answer.

He widened his stance as he slowly unzipped my jeans. His hand slipped beneath my underwear as his fingers slowly moved lower, soft and teasing. I still kept my eyes on the wall, feeling my breath pick up. My anger held tight. I tried not to react as his fingers moved in deeper, harder. My lids fluttered as he hit the spot. "Stay there." He mumbled as he dropped to his knees and yanked my pants and underwear to my ankles. The slight breeze from the window hit my nakedness. He opened my legs more, his tongue finding its way inside.

    I groaned, and when my legs threatened to give out, he grabbed me by the waist with one arm. He pressed me harder to his face, licking, sucking, and nipping. I grabbed the back of his head. My fingers curled around his locks of hair. His mouth was so hot the cool wind only stimulated me more. My legs could no longer hold me. He brought me down as he laid us back, his tongue never leaving me. I felt on fire. Every nerve ending throbbed.

    Bucking hard against him, I let out a loud moan, his tongue darting in and out faster. "Now. I want you to fuck me." My anger turned into violent passion. He pulled down his pants with one hand as I moved over his body, straddling him, already shaking with need. He normally liked to take control, but he stayed underneath me, letting me be the leader. He seemed to understand my level of aggravation translated into a need to dominate him. I pinned his arms back onto the mat with one hand as my other guided him into me. His eyes flared red as my pussy slammed down on his thick cock, and surrendered to the aggression. Nothing in me was sweet, kind, or quiet. I tore into his shirt, my nails leaving marks on his chest. Screaming out, I rode him relentlessly. I took out all my anger, regret, and frustration on him. His hips lifted higher, hands gripping my hips as I leaned back, until my head almost touched his thighs. Lifting my legs, I spun around on his cock, my pussy strangling him, until I faced the opposite way.

    "FUCK!" Eli howled underneath me, both of us feeling our climax coming as I continued to ride him backwards. My rage wasn't ready to let go yet. I clamped harder around him. He let out a roar, standing us up, he flipped me around, lifting me up, my legs clamping around him. His hands clamped around my ass, sinking back in, fucking me harder. He pushed my back into the wall of swords, rattling all the weapons with the force. My hands flung back and wrapped around the blades, cutting into my palms and spine. The rapiers felt our passion, tasted my blood, and came to life in my grip, sending their power through me. He slammed so deep into me my eyes watered. I wanted more. He pressed even farther. Pieces of the stone wall crumpled to the floor as the door banged on its hinges. The sheer ecstasy escaping my throat sounded more animal than human. He plunged again and again, sending me over the edge where I could no longer see or breathe. Then, everything shattered. All my anger. All my sadness. All my worry. Eli let out an earth-rattling roar. The window cracked into a spider web of lines and several pieces shattered. Clumps of the roof rained down on our heads. We both fell back to the floor, panting and sweaty.

With my body too limp to move, I only heard our heavy breaths before I caught voices outside.

"What was that?"

"Have no idea."

"I don't know about you guys, but I am horny as hell. There is a lot of intense magic around right now."

"It sounded like it came from there."

"Something being tortured and killed?"

Eli's lip went up in a cocked grin. "Hear what they're saying, Brycin? Something in here is being brutalized. Think the something was me." Eli rolled onto his side. His shirt was torn in shreds. Angry red lines tracked across his chest from my nails. He still had on his boots, his jeans circling his ankles. Eli had been gentler with my shirt.

Before I had the chance to respond, the door banged open. Several human-looking Dark Fae and what appeared to be a troll stumbled into the room, weapons ready for battle.

They stopped short, and their eyes widened. Then slowly smirks crossed their faces.

"You caused this?" The troll looked around in disbelief.

"Ember?" Cal's nervous tone hit my ears before he flew through the broken window. "Lars is look... Ahhhhh," he screamed and covered his eyes.

I yanked at my pants and sat up. Eli followed suit but did so slowly, not concerned if anyone saw him.

"Oh, sweet juniper nectar. I am blinded for life," Cal wailed, covering his eyes. "So much bare Dweller ass seared into my brain now!"

"Like you haven't seen it before." Eli zipped his pants, a frown on his face, probably recalling when Cal put stickers all over his butt with super-glue.

"We thought someone was being tortured in here." One of the human-like Fae stepped farther into the room. His eyes scanned us and stopped on me.

"You aren't far off." Eli smirked, leaning back on his hands.

"That is some serious fuckin' magic. Pun intended," a bald, dark-bearded Fae declared. "Shit. I am impressed and envious. Never felt anything like it before."

Cal continued to whimper, his face covered.

"Cal, we're dressed," I said to him then turned to our audience, my face flushing with embarrassment. "Thank you, guys, but we're fine."

Most of them snorted, making snide comments under their breaths.

Lars barreled into the room. "What is going on? No one is allowed in here." He stopped, and his eyes latched on me, then Eli. Understanding filled his expression, and his mouth tightened. The Unseelie King addressed the men at the door. "Return to your training or whatever you were doing." They scurried out of the room like cockroaches when a light is turned on.

"Ember, Elighan, I need you in my office. *Now.*" Lars took a breath, opened his mouth again, looking like he wanted to say something more and then scowled and stalked out of the room. He shut the door with a firm bang.

A breath and then laughter suddenly burst from my chest.

"You're laughing?" Cal whizzed to my ear. "There is not enough juniper juice in the world to block the image from my mind. I am scarred for life."

His comment only made me laugh harder. Eli lay back on the mat, one arm tucked behind his head. "I might be scarred for life, too." His free hand fingered the holes in his shirt. In-between the tatters, I noticed the nail marks on his chest were dotted with blood.

"You." Cal pointed at me. I tried covering my mouth to keep back the giggles. "You owe me a pool-size amount of juniper nectar. Enough to drown the bad images."

"How about my bathtub. Is that fair?" I countered.

Cal tilted his head and then nodded. "Yes. The tub will do. But I am still very much traumatized here." He flew, stopping at Eli. "I'd sleep with one eye open, Dweller. Revenge will come. I'd watch your extraordinary firm ass."

I could not hide my grin. Cal gave an enraged huff and darted out the window, singing, "I like big butts, and I cannot lie..."

Hysterics overtook me. "How does he even know that song?" I gasped between breaths.

"It's Cooper's and West's influences there. Introducing him to American culture."

I curled on my side facing Eli, still chuckling.

He reached for me. I placed my hand in his and slithered to him.

"Feel better." His eyes glistened. It wasn't a question.

I snorted, "Your ego is enormous."

"So are most parts of me."

I swatted at his arm with a groan.

He shrugged. "I have you."

My mouth fell open. He was not wrong.

"And you have me, woman. Completely." His lip hitched up.

I know I do. I tried to say in his mind without looking at him.

His eyebrows arched. "I heard that. You're linking with the Dark Dwellers now?"

"Looks like it."

"Crap, now I have to be careful what I say to my brothers behind your back." He smirked.

"Me, too." I leaned and kissed him.

"Funny."

"I think right now it's still pretty sporadic."

"We are able to direct conversations to certain people and block others. So you might only hear what others want you to, or when thoughts are directed at you personally. No different from your Fay connection to Torin."

"I don't have a bond with him anymore. It went away when my Fay powers were taken."

A smile grew on Eli's face. "You can't link to him anymore?"

"Nope."

His grin grew wider.

"Don't look so happy there. My powers are gone, which is the sucky part."

"Yeah, but I just found the silver-lining. If you can't communicate with fairy boy, then you also can't dreamscape or dreamwalk with him."

"I can't at all." *Unless Grimmel pulls me in one.* It hurt to talk about my lost magic. My happy mood dampened. I turned the conversation back to him. "Are you okay? With the Cole thing?"

He looked at the ceiling. "I won't say it's the greatest news I've ever found out. The father I idolized was a cheating asshole, but it's certainly not the worst. It shocked me more at first, but now..." Eli's shoulders lifted toward his ears. "It kind of makes sense. Cole always felt like an older brother to me. Now, he actually is."

"And Lorcan?"

"I understand his actions more. I still don't trust him, but he has gone through a lot. I didn't realize how much he shielded from me."

I propped my head on my hand. My heart thumped painfully in my chest as I stared down on him. After a while, he turned to look back at me, catching my exposed emotion. Hastily, I averted my eyes to the far wall.

He stayed quiet before he blew out some air. "Damn, woman, you can fuck. I will give you that."

"Well, if you need any pointers or anything..."

His eyebrows went up. "Pointers?"

"Yeah, you know if you need any tips or technique advice, I can help you out. Might be good if you knew a little more about what you were doing." I strained to keep my lips from breaking the line I was forcing them in.

He grabbed me and pulled me into him. I squealed as he tried to tickle me.

"No, stop!" I attempted to wiggle away from him, my cheeks hurting.

He yanked me roughly to him and kissed me. "Still think I need to muzzle you. You can get really loud," he whispered huskily.

"You broke the building!" I pointed to the shattered glass and chunks of debris.

"It wasn't only me. You contributed."

"Second time Lars will have to fix our training room because of me." My hand went to my forehead. "Lars probably wants to lock me in a padded room."

"From the look he gave us, I imagine Lars would prefer to castrate me or have me banned from the property." Eli stood, pulling me with him.

"Think we remind him too much of his past." I looked out the splintered window, remembering what he told me about his passion with Aisling. Their level of desire was rare and probably hard to live without once you experienced it. The way he talked about my biological mother, and the way his eyes glinted in memory revealed he had loved her but was too stupid to see it when he had her. I would not do the same with Eli. My heart was being shredded apart knowing we only had a brief time together. I would enjoy every minute of it.

Eli's hands cupped my chin, turning me to face him. "Now that I'm able to think properly, you want to tell me why you were so mad?"

Oh, man, where do I start? I pulled away and stepped back. "Kennedy and I had a fight. A bad one."

He frowned. "What about?"

"Ryan." I fidgeted with the hem of my shirt. "She knows he can't come back, and she is mad I didn't tell her. Rightfully so. I should have."

"Maybe." Eli's eyes studied me. "Is that all?"

No. But my lips pressed together, holding in my thoughts. *Only the fact I will kill you, and no one can help me.*

My mouth opened to try to tell him, just a hint, anything I could, but the spell closed my throat. No words came. An uncomfortable squeezing twisted my vocal cords.

I took a shaky breath to shrug off the spell's clenching grip. "That's all."

He watched me. Skepticism heavy in his green eyes. When I didn't elaborate, he released a sigh, and his shoulders sagged. He rounded and headed for the door. "Come on. Let's go see what Lars wants."

I followed, my bliss giving way to the buzz of frustration coming off him. He could sense I was lying.

NINETEEN

Lars's office was packed with people lined against the wall. Shoulder to shoulder bodies jammed in the free space in front of the desk. All eyes stared at the corner of the room where Lars's flat screen TV hung. Pictures of destruction and turmoil flashed on the monitor. Fire shot out of building windows, crumbled concrete and wood piled in huge heaps sprawled in every direction down streets. Cars were crushed by trees and poles. Blood covered the faces of people who were crying and screaming as they ran in the foreground of the screen. A sick *déjà vu* feeling set in, spiking fear in my chest, which squelched any euphoric emotions I had left, leaving me empty and cold.

No... not again.

Cole, West, Cooper, Gabby, Owen, Torin, Kennedy, Lorcan, Dax, Alki, and Koke stood staring at the images. Simmons stood on Torin's shoulder. Torin's eyes caught mine briefly before looking away. I ignored the hurt flashing in his eyes and directed my attention to the activity on the TV.

My stomach dropped. A headline ran across the monitor: 9.0 EARTHQUAKES HIT NEW YORK AND LONDON. FIRE DAMAGE DESTROYS CITIES, KILLING HUNDREDS OF THOUSANDS.

"Oh, my god." I clapped a hand to my mouth. Nausea rushed into my stomach and curled up my throat. An aerial view showed New York as a pile of rubble, burning. Central Park was a bonfire. The image changed again and displayed the Statue of Liberty as a massive, crumpled piece of metal, lying more in the Atlantic Ocean than on land. A split screen showed London burning. Big Ben was a heap of debris next to the remnants of the Parliament building. People were screaming and wailing as loud as the sirens trying to get to the wounded. I gripped my stomach, holding back the bile rising in my throat. Tears streamed down Kennedy's face. All the faces in the room were twisted in horror.

It was happening again—Aneira proving who was in control.

Lars stood at his desk. His tone sounded grave as he addressed the room. "My sources say she used Ember's powers, magnified by Asim, to cause this devastation. With the power of earth and fire along with her own power of air, she caused a huge earthquake and the destruction after. Earthquake plus fire with massive winds are all she needs. The heart of both cities will burn in a matter of hours. She has all the elements she needs to destroy."

My brain could not keep up with the idea of both London and New York being taken to their knees. The torment of people in pain reverberated through me in a wave. I felt like I was standing right beside them.

"We have to do something." I advanced into the room. Simmons heard my voice, raced for the door, and landed on my shoulder.

"What do you want us to do, Ember?" Lars's yellow eyes lifted to mine, challenging.

"Something! Anything!" I cried. "We can't let her get away with this. She can't be able to kill and destroy again... with *my* powers. We have to stop her."

Lars came from around his desk. "What do you suggest? Go to the Otherworld and fight her right now?"

"Yes!" I screamed, turning to look at the others in the room.

"Then, she will win." He clasped his hands together. "The Queen on her own land is too powerful. Neither myself nor any Dark Fae will be able to fight there for long."

"What do you mean? You fought her when you rescued me."

Lars rubbed the bridge of his nose. "Only for a brief time. I could not have stayed for much longer without feeling the effects."

I blinked at him in disbelief. "What effects?"

"Dark cannot fight too long on Light's land and visa-versa," he said. "The Dark takes Light's energy and the Light depletes ours. It is why all our battles take place during Samhain. It reduces all land, Earth and the Otherworld, neutral and equal in a fight."

The other Fae nodded their heads in confirmation. Suddenly I understood what West said earlier about being on the Light side too long. It wasn't only the blood loss and the Dark Dweller curse weakening him. He had three consecutive energies working against him. *How had he lasted as long as he did?*

I grunted and rubbed at my forehead, a drill-like headache boring down on me. Simmons patted my neck gently. I looked away from the TV. More death. More destruction. And there was nothing I could do about it right now. Aneira was crippling Earth, making it weak, so when the wall came down during Samhain, there would be no fight. She would take over. Even if we fought her and won, Earth would never be the same. The damage she already caused around the world would leave deep scars.

"What do we do?" I breathed in. "What's our next step?"

Lars nodded as though he had been waiting for me to get through all the emotion and finally ask the right question. "We will fight her, Ember. And we are going to defeat her. The prophecy *will* be fulfilled." He tapped his knuckles on the desk, emphasizing his words. "As the Light's future Queen, I want to know what *you* would do next."

Air caught in my throat. If the prophecy were fulfilled, in only a matter of days I could be ruling the Otherworld. I shook my head. Nothing in me felt qualified to be Queen. Nor did I want to be. Everyone turned to me, as though waiting for me to say something brilliant or lead them. My brain stayed blank.

"We need to strategize every move, every role people will be playing. We do a few practice runs so we all feel comfortable with what we are doing," Kennedy spoke up. The tears had dried. Her voice turned every head to her. "Familiarity with our roles will keep us on target instead of letting fear take over."

I couldn't stop my mouth from dipping open. I shouldn't be surprised. Kennedy liked to plan. She wanted to be prepared before going into any situation. I was more a by-the-seat-of-my-pants type of girl.

Lars smiled slightly. "Exactly what I was thinking." He nodded at her in approval. Embarrassment flooded my cheeks. Here I was the so-called future queen, and my mind went blank. "Aneira is attempting to weaken us. I have received an influx of calls from Dark Fae who survived and are fleeing London and New York. They will be heading here. Magic caused the destruction, so it not only killed humans, but hundreds of Dark Fae have perished, as well.

"The stakes have been raised, and we must be prepared for what is ahead. Training is no longer enough. With Cole's help, I have started planning the best approach for war." Lars made eye contact with each person in the room. "The most vital are Ember and Kennedy. They will need to be where the sword is located."

"Has the sword been located yet?" Cole stood in the middle of the room, his arms crossed.

"No," Lars said. "Not yet. I have informants searching. I do not doubt we will have the information before the battle begins." Lars had a precise way of speaking that completely captured you. You believed whatever he told you.

Come on, Grimmel. Come through for us.

"As you all know, Ember does not have her Fay powers. At least she is no longer affected by iron while Aneira is. My spies have told me she is daily trying to test herself around iron, which leads me to believe she thinks she has the Dark Dweller powers in her along with Ember's. She is frustrated as to why Ember could push through the iron, and she cannot.

"The sword will be protected with spells and guarded around the clock. The essential plan is to get Ember, the sword, and Aneira all in the same room. I will be sure to always have eyes on the Queen. When she heads back for the castle, I will follow. Until then, I have to be with my men. Aneira has to be sure of my presence on the field. Yet I understand in lieu of Ember not having her powers, I am the only one strong enough to help contain Aneira long enough for Ember to kill her with the sword." Lars clasped his hand together. "Just in case, Cole and I have developed a plan. I want us to be prepared for all circumstances which may arise."

Lars lifted his arm, gesturing to Cole. Cole dug into his pocket and pulled out an intricately woven metal band. "Ember, you will carry an iron bracelet. There is only one of these armlets in existence, and it is extremely powerful. It's goblin-made, and it will help debilitate Aneira."

I pointed at it. "Is that..."

"Oh, I've missed your doggie collar." Eli reached for it and sighed with nostalgia. "Can't take you for walks like I used to."

My elbow met his gut.

Holding my breath, I tentatively took it from Cole's hand and let the cool metal slip over my fingers. I gritted my teeth in reflex, waiting for the pain to come. But the iron sat innocuously in my palm, and I let out my breath. The experience was bitter-sweet. It was nice not to feel the agony of my insides being ripped out every time iron touched me, but this only solidified a part of my soul had already been taken from me, leaving a vast empty hole.

"Don't you love the idea of locking it around Aneira's wrist and using it to restrain and deplete the bitch of her powers?" Cooper said from behind me.

"If you don't, can I, darlin'?" West spoke from against the wall, his tone sharp and full of hate and bitterness. "I have a few complaints about the dungeon I would like to file with her."

West's hatred for her probably spiked as high as mine. He may never forgive Lorcan, but his true hatred was for Aneira. He wanted her dead and by his own hand. I knew it frustrated Eli not to be the one who could kill her. I couldn't even imagine the aggravation West felt about it.

"We are hoping you will not have to use the bracelet, but I want you to be prepared. And now you can carry it without repercussions."

Lars strolled back around his desk and settled in his chair. He clicked off the TV. The horrific visuals of pain, fear, and devastation disappeared. "We have a lot to discuss so everyone get comfortable."

We spent another two hours in Lars's office before he dismissed us. I was reaching for the door, needing air and a moment to myself, when I heard Lars's voice dart over to me. "Ember, you and Elighan stay." His tone held a tinge of displeasure. Could he seriously be upset at us for what happened in the training room earlier?

I stepped back into his office, moving to the side to let people get by. Torin and Kennedy passed me without a glance. My shoulders slumped with their rebuff.

"Goodbye, my lady." Simmons gave me another pat on the neck and flew off after Torin, heading back to the Otherworld.

Everyone else walked out, leaving Eli and me alone with Lars.

"Kennedy will be a fantastic leader of the Druids

someday." Lars adjusted in his seat.

I moved toward his desk. "I thought she was the last of the Druids?"

"I have a feeling Kennedy was not the only one hidden. After the war, I will not be surprised if others emerge." He waved to the seats in front of his desk. "Both of you sit."

"Lars, you can't be upset with us for what we did in the training room?" I plopped into the chair. Eli's lowered himself on the one next to mine.

Lars sighed and stared at me. "Really, Ember. I think we have more pressing matters than your sexual endeavors with Elighan. You are part Demon and Fay and very much your mother's daughter." He glanced out the window into the hazy autumn light. "I am not like your human father, upset you are having sex. Sex is a natural part of who we are. We are not embarrassed, shy, or shocked by it like many humans are."

"Okay, so what do you want?"

Lars leaned back. "I want to know we are on the same page and that you will follow your destiny, kill Aneira, and become Queen. I want *nothing* to get in your way of accomplishing it." His gaze darted to Eli.

My mouth clenched in a line while my eyes tapered to slits.

"Nothing will get in her way. Ember will kill Aneira and take the throne." Eli sat further into the curved back of the chair.

I clamped my teeth tighter to keep from crying out. Every moment I fought with the idea of what I would choose in the end. Most scenarios ended with me picking Eli. But that image was only a fantasy. After the devastation shown on TV and the volume of people's lives Aneira shattered within minutes—babies, mothers, fathers, sisters and brothers—how could I forgo all those human lives and the freedom of Dark and Light Fae for one person? For my own selfish desire? Even when I tried to picture myself as a Queen, I didn't see Eli by my side. Whether he survived or not, he would never be able to live with me in the Light. He was Dark Fae.

No matter what fate had in store for me, if I were crowned, the seat next to me would be vacant. Always. For the welfare of the Fay, I would have to go on. But every time I looked at Eli, I didn't trust I could.

"What if I don't want to be Queen?" I whispered.

Lars slammed his fist on the desk. "It doesn't matter what you want. It is your destiny. You must accept it and run toward it with both arms, or we will fail," Lars countered. "And you play a part, Elighan."

"How can I help?" One eyebrow curved up on Eli's face.

My hackles rose. Did Lars enjoy taunting me?

"You are the only one I trust to get her all the way inside. I know for a fact you will fight and kill anything standing in Ember's way."

Eli tipped his head in agreement.

The burden of what was coming weighed heavily on me. A minute ago I wanted to proclaim war and attack Aneira. Now I realized what the declaration meant: a fight to death. For all of us.

"Now we have the goal clear. Go. I have some business to do and need to deal with what has happened in New York and London." He reached for the phone, his yellow-green eyes flashed brightly, a sign of anger. There was a faint tremble in his hand. I had been around Lars enough to know he hid his feelings, retaining a composed exterior to keep everyone else around him calm. He was anything but relaxed on the inside. Aneira's taunt bothered him more than he let on.

Eli and I left his office, the screams of agony still echoing through my head and heart.

TWENTY

After leaving Lars, we found most everyone downstairs in the family room, continuing to watch the updates on the news.

The same footage of the devastation replayed over and over. There wasn't much new except for a mounting death toll. Once again, I felt the weight of what happened descend on me, the blood coating my hands, because my powers had caused it. The pain I felt for those suffering consumed my soul, placing me into an immobilized state. I felt powerless. Useless. Aneira could destroy the world with a flick of her wrist. Who was I to stop her, especially now? She had my powers. And she would flatten us.

My attention strayed to the TV showing a child crying, dried blood crusted her blonde braids. After a moment, my heart could no longer listen to her wailing for her mother. It was too much. My throat closed, cutting back my air. My hand went to my chest as I rushed to my feet and left the room.

"Em?" I heard both Kennedy and Eli call after me.

I had no idea where I was going until I sought the safety of my bedroom, my own bubble of protection. I went around my bed to the windows, facing the world outside and leaned against it, breath-ing shallowly. The view spun, and I let my body slip to the floor.

Kennedy's face swam into my vision. "This isn't your fault." She leaned down, putting her hands on my knees. "Breathe.

Concentrate on me. On my eyes." Her fingers dug into my jeans, which helped me focus. She mumbled something, and right away a slight numbness soothed the agony and cleared away the garbled mess in my mind.

"Did you just work your Druid mojo on me?"

"Yes. You were having a panic attack. I could see it coming, and it was not going to be pretty." She rubbed my leg. "I understand why you feel what Aneira did is more on you than anybody else, but it is not your fault. You did not wreak the destruction we saw. Don't let Aneira get into your head. We need you to be at your best. Aneira took your powers, but she did not take away who you are."

"I feel like those powers are who I am."

Kennedy shook her head. "No. They add to you, but they are not you. You are much more than your abilities."

Tears gathered under my lids. Eli had said something similar.

"You are the girl I befriended in junior high who is strong and feisty, loves deeply, and will fight to the death for those she cares about. That is who you are. You are the person I love and have missed so much." She pushed her glasses up the bridge of her nose, and her brown eyes filled with tears.

I lurched forward, hugging Kennedy. "I've missed you so much, too. I hate you being mad at me. It's something I hadn't experienced before and never want to again. I love you so much."

Kennedy sniffled, and her arms enfolded me. "Today gave me a huge dose of perspective. I was being silly. Right now all I care about is both you and Ryan are alive and in my life. All the rest can kiss my ass."

I jerked back, my eyes wide with mocking shock. "Kennedy, you swore."

She giggled through a weepy snuffle and sat back on her heels. "Yep, I mean it that much."

"Shit suddenly got serious."

We both broke into hiccups and giggles. The release felt

better than any drug could provide. Sometimes in the most tragic or sad situations, laughter was a necessity.

When we calmed somewhat, Kennedy moved next to me, leaning back against the bed. "Today made me realize I want to do something. Even if it's really foolish."

"What?"

"See Ryan." Kennedy curled her hands in her lap. "I know Lars will deny us, but I need to see him. To hug him. He can't come back here, so the only thing I can do is go to him."

I related to the urge to go to our friend, but I shook my head. "Ken, I did and was almost killed by the Strighoul. It's too danger-ous."

Did those words actually come out of my mouth?

Kennedy pivoted her head to look at me. "I know, but when did it ever stop you before?"

"Uhhhh... good point."

"Em, please." The need in her voice sounded palpable.

"Fine. Fine." I stared at the ceiling in defeat. "I don't have the right to tell you not to do anything."

The idea of seeing Mark, Ryan, and my mom developed in my head. A slow smile came to my lips. "Let's do it."

Her whole face lit up.

I winced at the reality of doing it. "Problem. There is no way I can go without Eli knowing. He will have me chained down in the basement faster than I can blink. And not in the fun way."

Kennedy twisted back away from me, her gaze going to the outside. "Yeah, those Dark Dwellers make it hard to get away with anything." She frowned, and her eyes narrowed.

I couldn't decipher her expression. My gut told me she wasn't talking about Jared.

"They are a pain in the butt."

Kennedy nodded, her gaze faraway.

We sat in silence as a smile grew over my lips. "My birthday is tomorrow..."

Kennedy's head popped up, a conspirator glint sparkling in her eyes. "The birthday girl should get to do what she wants."

"And I want to have a party with my friends and parents in the Otherworld."

"Good luck." Gabby's voice spoke from the door. She stomped into the room and flopped across my bed, resting her chin between me and Kennedy.

Since our time in Greece, she seemed a lot more comfortable hanging around us. Deep down I knew she enjoyed the girl time, even if she would never claim the fact.

"Come on, Gab, it's not like you are a rule follower." I craned my neck to look at her.

"No, but I like my life, and Eli would kill me if he found out I knew and let you girls go."

I shrugged. "And Eli knows I do what I want. No one *lets* me do anything."

Gabby snorted.

"Besides, I'm planning to tell Eli. I can't get far without him knowing anyway."

"You think he'll be okay with it? After last time?" Gabby turned on her side and propped her head on her hand. "I thought we were going to have to commit him. You are about as dumb as an imp if you think he will agree to your leaving."

I grinned. "I have my ways of persuasion."

Gabby's eyebrows arched.

"Okay, they're called blackmail and guilt."

"Now, that is a true Fae answer." Gabby picked at imaginary lint on my pillow, her demeanor becoming shy and hesitant. It looked all wrong on her. Especially in her punk-rock outfit, dyed purple and black hair, and knee-high, shit-kicker boots. "I'll back you with Eli if..." a trace of blush spread across her cheeks. I hadn't seen her blush or get embarrassed. Ever.

"If what?" I encouraged, curious as to what I could offer her and what would cause her to react this way.

"If... if you could find out if Alki is seeing anyone and

maybe put in a good word for me. I know it's a bad time, but all that's happening made me think... you know?"

My jaw slackened. "Was not expecting that."

She continued to pluck at the pillow, her face flaming.

"I'm sorry. The voices in my head were jabbering loudly because I could have sworn you asked me for a favor to talk you up to my sexy Demon trainer, Alki?" I patted my ears.

"Yeah, yeah. Go ahead, enjoy yourself, *páiste gréine*."

"Oh, I will." I rubbed my hands together. Kennedy giggled beside me. It felt good to break away from the gut-wrenching tragedy and be girls for one moment.

Gabby rolled her eyes but smiled softly. She must really like him to take any kind of teasing from me.

"Okay, I will help you with Alki, but instead of helping me with Eli, you have to keep Lars distracted while we go to the Otherworld."

She frowned, contemplating my deal. She sat up, tucking her legs underneath her. "Agreed."

TWENTY-ONE

Before I considered the Gabby-Alki arrangement, I needed to talk to Eli. I found him hanging out in Cooper and West's room. They probably needed a break from watching the bleakness of what was happening across the country and world. Something I keenly understood. The need for the comfort of friends and family in a time like this was powerful. The desire to feel his arms around me tingled in my veins, drawing me to Eli.

West called to me as I stepped into the doorway. "Hey, darlin'! Always nice to see your gorgeous figure walk through my door."

I smiled, leaning against the frame. West lounged on his bed. Eli lay against the wall on the other end, and Cooper stretched out fully on his bed across from them.

"Let me guess. You didn't know Eli was here, and you were coming here secretly for me?" West winked.

A suggestive smile curved my lips. "Eli who?"

Cooper and West both laughed. It got quiet again, my focus still directed on West. Eli cleared his throat.

"Oh, Eli. Hi. Didn't see you there." I feigned embarrassment. He snickered, shaking his head.

I leaped from the door, crashed onto the bed between the two men and tackled them. "Doggie pile," Cooper shouted and jumped on top of me. The springs and I both groaned in retaliation.

"In this case it's not far from the truth," I squeaked under the weight of men on me. Their answer was to tickle me. I wiggled against them, trying to get away. "Stop. Stop." I laughed. Like two older brothers and a man who lived to torment me, they didn't. They ignored my pleas.

Finally, I slithered off the bed onto the floor, getting away from them. I pulled down the hem of my top, which had crept up while trying to escape. Panting, I tried to catch my breath. "You guys are so not fair."

"What would be the fun in that?" West scooted back, propping himself against the wall.

Cooper stood and got out from between his two large brothers. "Fair would be you getting naked."

Eli chuckled as he moved to the edge of the bed, his feet on the uneven wood planks. He leaned his elbows on his legs. As I stood up, Eli grabbed my belt loops and tugged me between his legs. "Need something?"

I nodded.

"All right, boys, I'll see you at training later." Eli stood, his fingers still curling around my pants.

"Again?" Cooper's head fell back in anguish.

"What can I say? Duty calls." Eli smacked Cooper on the shoulder while herding me out the door.

"West, I say we go get drunk and find some deviously horny Dark Fae women," Cooper's voice followed us out of the cabin.

"Sounds like a brilliant plan." I heard West chuckle.

I led Eli from the cabins toward the forest. We stopped at the edge of the woods. "You know it's my birthday tomorrow."

"Wow, it must be a big favor." He crossed his arms.

"Since I can't lie to you like a normal person, I have to try the honest, but in a full-of-shit, flattery way."

Eli's mouth quirked into a side grin. "Get to the point, Brycin."

"Kennedy and I both want to go to the Otherworld to visit

Ryan." Seeing the frown cross his face, I held up my hand, stopping him before the rebuttals started. "Like I said, it's my birthday, and I would really, really like to have a dinner with my family and friends. Like regular people do."

Eli stepped closer to me. "First, we are anything but normal; second, there is no way Lars will let you."

"Already taken care of."

His forehead crunched in surprise. "He's allowing you to leave?"

"Honestly? No, but I have someone who's going to distract him for me."

"Who did you cajole into agreeing to do the impossible?"

"Gabby."

"What?" The shock on his face looked comical. "How the hell did you get her to go along with your scheme?"

"The secrets are between us. Just know I did." I felt a smirk spread across my face. "And I'm not asking for your permission. I thought I would tell you beforehand instead of you finding out when I disappeared from your radar. This way you won't send out a search party and get Lars involved."

Frustration lined his forehead. "Only you and Kennedy?"

I nodded.

His brow furrowed deeper. He pressed his lips together and glowered at the ground. Neither of us spoke. A deep, heavy exhale came out before he spoke. His voice low and commanding. "Being an Alpha, I always have to think for the group. Whatever I do concerns them. Good or bad."

"O— kay."

He rubbed his hand through his hair. "The point I am getting at is you need to realize you are no longer alone. You are with me. You are in a clan. You have a family, several actually. Everything you do, say, or don't say affects them. It affects me."

I glanced at my feet. He was right. I wasn't used to checking in with people or thinking for anyone other than myself. I had always been independent. But after my mom's so-called murder, I had become an island, letting no one in, except Mark. But even with him, I kept some distance. Now my solitary island had bridges to all these other places, and I could no longer only think of myself.

My shoulders fell with a heavy slump.

"Hey." Eli placed his hands on my face, bringing my head back up. "I suppose since it is your birthday, you can do something foolish and precarious."

My grin stretched greedily over my face. I pushed up on my toes and kissed him. "Thank you."

"I am always ready for wicked behavior. You just have to include me."

"I did."

"No, you told me, but you weren't including me."

I leaned back, really taking him in. "You want to go with me and hang out with my mother and Torin?"

"I think it's time Lily and I come to an understanding."

I blinked in shock. "We're going to be sitting around a dinner table, and you will have to talk to people."

"Will there be alcohol?"

"Of course. And knowing my mom, there will be cake."

"Then I want to be there for your birthday."

The words felt strange coming from his mouth. I suspected he actually didn't want to be there, but he was doing it for me. Talking to my mom was also for me. I doubted he cared if he was on my mom's good side, but he knew I did.

"Be careful, Dragen, the dark horse you're riding on is developing white spots."

His eyes narrowed, and a deep growl gargled from him. He grabbed me and pressed my back into a giant boulder. My pulse zipped through my veins at the thrill of his actions. In the far distance I saw figures moving, practicing drills.

"People can see us."

Eli shoved me harder against the rock, pinning my arms back. "I am a beast. I don't care." His eyes turned red, his breath hot on my neck as he leaned in. "Don't forget what I really am and become complacent with me or think I'm someone I'm not. Ever."

Later I found Alki heading for the training field. His face seemed tired, a look I had never seen on him. Dark smudges circled his eyes, and his shoulders were starting to droop. I suspected one of his powers was he could fight endlessly without tiring. The amount of people he trained, day in and day out, would have any other Fae keeled over after the first day or so. It had been weeks, and he only now started to show signs of exhaustion.

My legs caught up with his pace.

"Grab your sword. You need to train more." He scowled at me.

I turned toward the field. Thousands of Seelie and Unseelie mingled in clusters, swinging axes and swords. Fae were mostly old-fashioned in battle, still preferring swords to guns or their own teeth and claws to either. There would be a few on the field who didn't follow those rules, but for the most part, it seemed like a strange honor code. To them, it was a truer fight if you could beat someone with your own hand than by a bullet.

"Actually, I came to offer help." I huffed and had to run to match his brisk pace.

Alki slowed. "You want to help me train the soldiers?"

"Not me. I have someone else in mind."

"Koke is helping me."

"You are training over a thousand Fae at all hours of the day and night. Koke and you could use some help, especially for those bodies who can change into weapons."

Alki's eyebrows curved up slightly at me. "And who do you recommend?"

"Gabby." I practically shouted her name. "She would be

perfect to assist with the shifters, helping them train to be more lethal in combat." My plan might not work, but I wasn't about to pass him a note asking him to check the box if he thought Gabby was cute.

Alki stopped and rounded on me. "You want a Dark Dweller to assist me?"

The request was as awkward for him as it felt to me. "Um... yeah. She's an incredible fighter." His narrowed eyes told me he wasn't falling for it. "Never mind, you're right. You and Koke have everything covered. I am sure we will be ready for war with two people training hundreds of different types of Fae, totaling over thousands." I nodded and stepped back. "Sorry to bother you."

Either he would ignore me or take the bait. It was up to Gabby now. Matchmaking and being indirect were not my specialties.

Eli and I walked to meet Kennedy. In the distance a tall figure stood next to her. The evening shadows kept the person's features hidden. My first instinct assumed it was Jared, but quickly I realized the person was far too tall and powerfully built to be Jared.

My stomach plummeted to the ground. I grabbed Eli's arm, knowing he could smell who it was. He stiffened under my touch; a low growl discharged from his chest.

"Easy, little brother," Lorcan's voice seeped calmly into the evening air. "I am not here to cause a problem."

"Then why are you?" Eli's shoulders muscles compressed together.

"I'm here to keep Kennedy safe if anything happens."

Eli and I came to a stop only a few feet away from Kennedy and Lorcan.

"I can take care of it," Eli gritted out.

"I am not saying you can't, but if a group of Strighoul comes after Emmy again, who will you protect?"

"Hey!" My hands went to my hips. "I am not a damsel here and neither is Kennedy. We can take care of ourselves."

Lorcan's smug smile hitched his lips higher. "I never said you were a damsel. I've heard you are quite the tiger." His unsaid implication of "in bed" sat heavily at the end of his sentence. "But you know without your powers, you can't help as much as you'd like. And Kennedy's powers aren't for hurting people. Hers are to heal and protect."

"I said he could come." Kennedy shuffled her feet. "Lorcan's right. I can't fight like you guys can, and if something did happen, I trust he will have my back."

Trust? Lorcan? Those two words didn't belong in the same sentence.

"What about Jared?" I asked.

Kennedy frowned. "He was training and seemed quite happy there. I thought it would be better if he stayed. If we do come across trouble, I know he can't change like you two can." She motioned at Lorcan and Eli. "I don't want Jared to get hurt. I could not live with myself if anything happened to him." Her words sounded sincere, as though she meant every syllable. There was little doubt she loved Jared. Her feelings toward him didn't take away from the nagging feeling in the pit of my stomach there was some connection between Kennedy and Lorcan. Whether it was only a shared respect or more, I couldn't tell.

I shifted my weight. My mouth opened to refute the need for Lorcan, when he cut me off.

"I understand your wariness of me, Ember. I killed Aisling. It is a plain and simple fact, but I will not apologize for what I did. To me it was a job. It might seem cold and heartless to you, but it's how we were then. Even your boy here cannot be excluded. Eli killed a lot of people, too. Someone's mother or father."

It was true, and I was being a hypocrite, but it felt different because Lorcan killed *my* mother.

"I'm not going to ruin your night and go inside. I know Lily would have my head served as the entree. I'm planning on staying outside, keeping guard like the good little obedient beast I am."

I glowered at him. He did not back down or look away from me. Time was ticking, and we didn't have much as it was. We had to be careful since time was different in the Otherworld. Lars would not be distracted beyond tomorrow afternoon before he came looking for us.

"Fine. But you stay far away from the house. I don't want my mother to get even a whiff of your foul scent; I will not stop her if she tries to kill you."

Lorcan raised his arms in surrender. "Agreed."

Eli stepped forward, getting in Lorcan's face. "You try anything or do anything I don't like, and I will kill you this time, Lorcan. I will not hesitate. Got it?"

"I get it." He waggled his eyebrows and sneered. "Lorcan farts too loud, and he is a dead man. Memo received."

Grumbling, I pushed my way past the two guys and headed for the property line. "All right, Cal, come on out. You can show us the way."

"H-ho-how did you know I was here?" Cal's voice came from a tree.

"Because I know you." There was a silence. "Cal?"

"You are wrong. Cal is not here right now. You can leave a message at the beep. Beeeeep."

"Cal, get your little pixie butt down here now."

Leaves rustled over my head before a winged nuisance fluttered down to me. "Damn, girlie. You are good." Cal hovered in my eye line.

"No. You are predictable." I smiled. "And an eavesdropper."

"My *listening* skills have come in useful many times."

I guffawed. "Spying you mean?"

"Labels, labels." He waved his hand.

"Can you show us the way to the house?"

"For the sweet nectar of the gods, girlie, I will do no such thing. I almost became a Pixie pudding last time."

"How about I get some flypaper, pixie?" Eli moved behind me.

Cal's eyes narrowed on him. "And how about I get my sharpie pen and a glittery glue stick, Dweller?" Cal brought his fingers to his eyes, then pointed at Eli as though to say, "I'm watching you."

"Boys! Truce for now, all right?" I sighed, rubbing my neck. "Cal, I will get Marguerite to let you use her huge kitchen sink for the juniper juice, and how about one of those kisses I still owe you?"

Cal turned red, a dreamy look glazing his eyes. Then he looked back at Eli, his eyes became hard again. "Follow me." He grabbed his plastic sword and pointed forward.

If we all didn't kill each other tonight, I would call the evening a success.

TWENTY-TWO

Cal led us through the doors into the Otherworld. Eli and Lorcan moved cautiously as they still mistrusted the aspect of being allowed into the Otherworld. Lorcan had mentioned they couldn't be there more than a full Otherworld day without it starting to become painful. We were only going to be there for a few hours. They should be fine.

When Cal guided us into the crooked forest, I realized how easy it would be to get lost in these woods. Everything looked exactly the same. A break in the trees or a stream appeared no different from the ones we crossed earlier. "Should I be leaving breadcrumbs?"

Lorcan and Eli peered at me with confusion, only Kennedy seemed to get my joke. "Was thinking the same thing."

"Breadcrumbs?" Lorcan said. "How about you put out a sign saying: 'Here's an appetizer that will lead you to your entrée.'" He pointed to himself.

"She was kidding." Kennedy laughed. "It's from a children's fairytale we grew up with, *Hansel and Gretel*. They get lost in the forest before getting caught by a witch, then eaten. You've never heard of it?"

Lorcan and Eli both shook their heads. "No, but if they were leaving breadcrumbs in a forest full of Dark Fae, they should have been eaten." Lorcan raised a sharp eyebrow as though affronted by the notion.

"Yeah, too stupid to live anyway," Eli added.

Kennedy and I grinned at each other. "Wow, someone's taking *Grimm's Fairy Tales* a little seriously." I regarded the two brothers.

"Because this shit is serious," Eli said as he continued to trek through the foliage. "A fairytale means something different to you than it does to us. It's real and a bitch."

Thinking of Aneira and what she did to London and New York, I had to agree. The Fairy Queen is a ruthless bitch.

When we got to the cave, Cal crawled into my hood, preparing for the entry. Creatures like wolpertingers, bats, and spiders looked at Cal as lunch.

"So, I figure I will be staying right here." Lorcan motioned to a rock next to the cave.

"It will be best." I nodded.

"Thank you, Lorcan. We'll try not to be long." Kennedy touched his arm gently. He looked at her hand, then away.

"I am watching the moon. If it moves past those trees, I am coming after you."

"I'll watch it, too. We have to be extremely careful about the time we spend here," Eli said as we stepped into the mouth of the cave, tapping at his temple. "Let me know if anything happens," he added, referring to their link. Lorcan did not know I would also be able to hear him. "Or our warning call."

Lorcan watched Eli for a moment before he gave a nod. "I will."

"Warning call?" Kennedy asked Eli, as we entered the cave.

"It's a specific howl our dad taught us if he couldn't reach us through our link." Eli's pupils enlarged as they adapted to the darkness around him. We started into the cavern leading us to our family and friends.

We crawled out of the tunnel and moved into the protected

parcel of land where the cabin sat. The sound of a waterfall thundered in the distance. It was afternoon here, but it still wasn't light. The Dark Unseelie side of the Otherworld stayed in perpetual evening/night intervals. The mornings and afternoon looked more like dusk before the night enveloped you in blackness again. My missing powers had nothing to do with my preferences, but my Demon side still favored the darkness, while my Fay longed for the light.

Simmons glided out of the door with Torin and Castien close behind. We had set off the wards, letting them know there were intruders. "It's only me," I yelled, waving my arms at the two men.

"My lady?" Simmons darted to me.

"You said you wouldn't call me that in public," Cal said dryly from under my hair.

"Cal!" Simmons bee-lined for his friend, crashing into him. They both tumbled off my shoulder, almost hitting the ground before they caught air and flew into the sky, laughing and jabbering. I bet they had never been apart this long.

"Ember?" I heard my mom's voice come from behind them. "Ember's here?"

"Yeah, Mom. I came to celebrate my birthday with you."

She rammed Torin and Castien into the wall as she pushed past them, running to me. "It's your birthday today?"

"Yep." I knew they were not on the same time as Earth and probably didn't have much idea what day it was.

She had me in her arms in a matter of seconds. "Oh, my baby girl. Happy birthday!" Then her body tensed in my arms. I knew exactly what made her react like she did. Or who caused it. Good thing Lorcan had stayed at the entrance of the cave, or she would be having a conniption fit in my arms. "Elighan." She stepped back.

"Lily." Eli nodded.

Before I could say anything, Ryan came out on the porch. "Kennedy?" His voice rang across the cool air. "Oh, my god.

Kennedy!" Ryan rushed headlong down the steps.

"Ryan!" Kennedy tore off for him. The two almost knocked each other over as they came together.

"I-I can't believe you are here." Ryan's hand petted the back of Kennedy's head. "You're safe."

Kennedy pulled away to look at him. "We made a pact in third grade we would be friends forever, and we'd always be there for each other no matter what. I took the promise seriously. There isn't anything that would keep me from you." Tears streamed down her face.

"Except when kidnapped by Fae." Ryan squeezed her arm.

"Except that." She laughed.

"Teaches us not to read the fine print in our pact." Ryan rolled his eyes back dramatically.

My heart soared watching them together. Reunited. They had been best friends since kindergarten and had been through so much. I was glad we came for Kennedy.

Ryan looked over Kennedy's shoulder. "Hey." He pointed at me. "Get your salty ass right here and join in our reunion. You're a part of us."

"But I didn't sign any best friend contract."

"Your contract was signed in blood." Ryan put his hands on his hips, tipping his head. "Now get your butt over here."

I ran to them. The three of us intertwined with arms and tears. It was already the best birthday I could ask for.

"Now, get the smoking hot, happy meal over here so I can slyly squeeze his ass." Ryan whispered in my ear. I burst out laughing and looked over my shoulder.

Eli smirked, opening his arms. "All you have to do is ask, Ryan."

Ryan's cheeks turned several shades past embarrassed.

"He has exceptional hearing." I winked at Ryan. "And a firm ass. I highly recommend feeling it at least once tonight."

Ryan let his chagrin roll off him. It never lasted long with him. He searched the porch where Castien stood. "Do you mind, honey?"

Castien shook his head and waved his hand, giving him the go-ahead. Mark stood next to Castien smiling at all of us.

I hoped it took him back to the many nights Ryan and Kennedy came to the house, and we bantered very much like this.

Mark was my next hug victim. "It's my birthday. Eli-ass for everyone," I exclaimed as I headed for my dad.

"Feeling like a piñata," Eli mumbled.

"Now you being a piñata is something I want to get in on." Mom's tone was less than humorous.

"Me, too!" Cal raised his hand.

I sighed, but kept my eyes on Mark. "Hi, Dad." I threw my arms around him.

"It's good to see you." He squeezed me tightly. "Happy birthday, Sunny D."

Torin had been standing there the whole time, his body filled with tension, and his eyes locked on Eli. "You brought him here?"

I wanted to have a good night, but things needed to be dealt with before the fun could happen. "All right. Before we go on, we need to get something straight." I turned and faced my mother. "I know you believe Eli was there to harm us in the castle, but he wasn't."

Mom's contradiction already formed in her mouth.

I held up my hand. "He came there to *stop* Lorcan. When you saw him in the hallway, he was on his way to try to prevent his brother from following through with Aneira's plan." I kept my voice strong as I looked at everyone. Then my eyes landed on Mom and Eli. "I think you two need to go hash out all the details because you are both in my life. You will have to learn to get along since I will not choose between you or be sandwiched in your feud. The rest of us will start getting drunk." I turned and went in the cabin.

Torin's face contorted with a frown, and he hurried down

the stairs. His arms swung stiffly at his sides as he disappeared into the forest.

"Well, no birthday cake for him." Cal swooped into the room.

"Sir Torin has been through a lot," Simmons contested. "You cannot deprive him of cake as well." I snorted. To them, depriving anyone of either sugar or alcohol was a sin beyond measure. Cruel and unusual punishment.

"I hope we have the ingredients to prepare a cake." Mark headed into the kitchen. "It's not like you can run to the store or get a box of cake mix around the corner."

"Do you have stores here?" I hadn't even thought about how they were getting their food.

Thara leaned against the counter. "Of course we do, but the closest town is about twenty miles away. And they don't have boxed anything. Nothing is processed here like it is on Earth."

In some aspects, Fae were quite advanced, but in others, they were still in medieval times with their consumer markets. At least now they had refrigerators, lights, and other appliances which ran off solar power and magic. In a lot of ways, they were far better off without all the human devices. If the Queen didn't murder humans, fast food would kill them for her.

Kennedy, Ryan, and Castien came into the house, but Eli and my mother didn't. I peered out the door and saw the two of them walking off. Good. They would never like each other, but I wanted them to at least know the other's story and come to some kind of truce.

Mark and Thara gathered everything they needed for a simple cake and dinner. I didn't care if there was cake or any food. I only wanted to be with them.

For the next hour Kennedy, Ryan, and I caught up, laughing and crying through our adventures and stories since we last saw each other. As he cooked, Mark would pipe up with his version every once in a while. I was diligent about keeping the chef's cup full. Mark's cheeks were pink, and he was in an especially joyful mood by the time dinner was ready.

Ryan and I set the table while Castien and Kennedy sat on the sofa trading stories about Ryan.

"No, no, he does that when he gets mad." Kennedy giggled.

"Does what?" Ryan dropped the silverware on the table, looking at them.

"Nothing." Both Kennedy and Castien said in tandem, their eyes wide and innocent.

"At least have the decency to talk *behind* my back," he teased.

"Then, how would you know what we thought of you," I kidded as I set the plates around the table.

"I already know you think I am funny, devastatingly handsome, and have impeccable taste in clothes."

I grinned. "I never said we told you the truth to your face."

"Ha, ha." He laughingly mocked and then tried to look serious.

"Dinner's ready. Where are Eli and Lily?" Mark grabbed the pot from the stove and placed it on the table.

Eli and my mom still hadn't returned. "I'll go see if I can find them."

Cal and Simmons, who usually wanted to go with me, were already at their places, their empty drinking cups pounding on the table in revolt. "Fill de cup or we piss in de pot!" Okay, Cal led the chant, but Simmons hit his cup on the table along with him.

"Better do as they ask, or we'll have pixie pee in our stew." I grabbed the door handle and headed into the dark. The late afternoon had turned black. Stars glinted overhead, but the moon cast enough light to allow me to see where I was going. My gut pulled me to Eli, and I knew he could feel me coming. Stepping into a clearing, I saw them standing there. Both had their arms folded over their chests and no smiles on their faces, but they were alive. A good sign.

Eli's head curved in my direction. "No, we haven't killed each other."

"Yet." My mom snorted. Humor. The situation seemed better than I hoped.

"Dinner's ready." I stepped closer.

"Okay." Mom came to me, taking my hand in hers. "I'll see you both inside." She gave my hand a squeeze before heading away from us, back to the house.

When she left, I rounded on Eli. "So?"

He walked to me, widening his stance, and his hands came to my hips. "Your mother will never like me. She will always want better for you. But I think we have come to a ceasefire."

I nestled myself into him. "That's all I can ask." His lips came down on mine, sparking my body. When we broke apart, I asked: "How are you feeling? Has the curse started to affect you yet?"

"I don't know. I feel restless, but I don't know if it's the spell or because I am anxious about the time here."

"How do you feel being back in the Otherworld? You wanted it for so long. Is it strange to return?"

"Yeah, it is odd to be here again." He pressed his lips together in thought. "Part of me feels like I can finally relax, that I am home. But it's not exactly what I remember. My memories built it up to something no longer fitting with who I am." He rubbed his brow. "I'm also realizing there are things on Earth's realm I would miss."

I nuzzled closer to him, kissing his lips gently. "Like peanut butter."

"Yep, I would definitely miss that." He nipped at my bottom lip.

"What else?"

"My bike," he mumbled between kisses. "And you on it. Both my girls between my legs."

"I'd miss your Harley, too. When we get back, we should give it a tribute." With that sentence, ice filled my lungs. He would not be the one leaving Earth's realm in the end. I would be sitting on a throne without him.

Oh, hell, no.

"Your idea makes me want to start now. We can add the bike in later." He shut down my thoughts as his kiss deepened, his mouth desperate against mine.

"We. Have. To. Get. Back." I said during air breaks.

"In a minute." He nipped at my bottom lip. "I got you something."

Leaning away, I sputtered. "You got me something? Like a birthday present?"

"Uhhh... sure." He kissed me again. Sarcasm thick in his tone.

"Okay, what is my non-birthday present?"

He pulled away from me and lifted his shirt.

"I do appreciate the sentiment, but I can have that package any day." I winked at him.

"Damn, woman, have you already grown weary of my body?" He shook his head, grabbing at something stuffed in the waist of his pants. "As much as I think I'm a better gift, I got you this." Unceremoniously, Eli plopped a sheathed blade in my hand.

I stared at the supple leather before sliding the six-inch knife from its cover. The blade curved slightly and was designed with delicate and beautifully woven patterns and motifs. My fingers couldn't help reach out and touch the etchings. It hummed under my hand, coming to life. Pictures flashed too quickly through my mind, but power and pride filled my chest. Instantly, I felt the connection. It was made for me. It claimed me as I claimed it.

Air sucked through my lips. "It's beautiful."

"It's goblin-made with the finest Fae metal." Eli kept his eyes on the weapon. "It will fit perfectly in your boot."

My head wrenched up to look into his face. Some girls might hate getting a dagger for a present, but I loved it. He had made it especially for me. I dove into him, my arms wrapping around his neck. "Thank you."

"I knew you were the kind of girl who would prefer something able to gut a Fae rather than getting flowers."

My grin widened. "You know it." I pulled his mouth to mine, showing him my appreciation.

"I say, since I gave it to you, there should be some unwritten promise you can't use it on me, no matter how much you want to."

"Oh, I never make those types of promises." My mouth returned to his; our kisses deepened.

"Lasssss? Purtty waddy," Cal's voice slurred from the forest. "Mr. Marky saed no mourn mead till ewe comb my back."

I leaned my forehead against Eli's with a chuckle.

"I am gonna kill that little flying Barbie," Eli growled.

"Come on. There's alcohol and cake." I tugged on his hand as I slipped my new present into my boot. It fit exactly like he said.

"Only way to deal with your family."

"If you're not going to be nice, I will demand we play pin the tail on the ass."

Halfway through dinner, the door opened and Torin came through. He grabbed the empty chair and sat down. "Happy birthday, Ember." He nodded at me.

"Thank you," I replied, a little stunned at Torin's greeting. Thara beamed at him as she filled his plate. I wanted to tell him I was glad he returned, and it wasn't the same without him here, but I kept silent. His being here was a big step for him. Eli sat far on the other side, but they were at the same table together, sharing a meal. It meant so much. Happiness ballooned in my heart as I looked around the table at all the faces so dear to me.

Laughter and stories overflowed the room. Every one of these people belonged to my family. With every new person who became part of my world, my fortified heart opened wider to receive them.

Later when the cake was brought out, Cal plunked down on my head, pretending to be a birthday hat. The more I tried to get him off, the more he threatened to poop on my head, so I gave in. But I drew the line at people singing. Those not born on Earth were familiar with the annoying tune, but the Fae world did not have the same birthday song as humans. For which I was grateful.

Restless energy bobbed Eli's knee relentlessly against mine, and he stirred in his seat. He wasn't usually fidgety.

I glanced over at him questioningly. *The curse?*

He answered me with a swift nod. Between being on the light side and the curse, he had to be suffering far more than he let on. It was time to go. We had already been away longer than we should have, but I found it hard to leave. Today was the first time I had a birthday with all the people I loved, and sadly I knew it would probably be the last. The night was amazing, but a war sat on the other side of it—coiled and waiting, like a snake.

"We have to return," Eli whispered in my ear. I nodded, the smile falling from my face. "You have another gift waiting for you in your room later, if it makes you feel better." He nuzzled my neck, placing my hand high on his thigh.

"Eh." I shrugged, playing indifference.

"You know that is only going to cause me to be more deter-mined."

My eyes widened. "Really? I would never have thought you could so easily be manipulated."

"So full of crap."

I winked.

Cal poked his finger into my head. "Sorry, everyone. They do this a lot. Please continue on as if they are not here because they certainly aren't aware of us and how awkward they can make a room." My response was to flick him off. He tumbled into the air. "You are so going to get pooped on later."

"Try it pixie, and I will tell Sinnie you were the one who unmade every bed and hid all the sheets in the house so you could see her."

His eyes turned the size of saucers. "You wouldn't."

"Oh, I would. And she was pissed. I remember her threatening to disembowel the culprit if she ever found out who it was."

Cal glowered at me. "You win this one, girlie, but only because I am more scared of her than you."

"Smart man." I chuckled. "I hate to bring it up, but we have to go. I'm sure it's way past the time we should have started back." I pushed my chair from the table.

"Mom, walk me out." I took her hand in mine. I hugged everyone, with a double for Mark. Kennedy's eyes filled with tears having to leave Ryan. She was much more aware than he this might be our last moments together.

"My lady?" Simmons came level with my gaze.

"You need to stay here," I said. "Protect my family. Lars will call for you soon."

"Yes, my lady." Simmons bowed.

"Why do you call me that? Why have you always treated me like your queen? Did you know about the prophecy?"

"No, my lady, but I always knew you were meant for great things." Simmons tilted his head. "I knew the moment we met you in the woods you were someone special. There was no question I would follow you."

A lump knotted my throat. "Thank you, Simmons. It has been an honor having you as my friend. And soldier." He stood taller, brushing his fighter pilot's jacket. "You are a fierce and faithful warrior."

From the tips of his ears to his bare toes, Simmons blushed.

"Oh, crap on a beetle butter biscuit, is the syrup poured thick enough, girlie?" Cal flew next to Simmons, his wings carving a spark in the dense Fae air, which twinkled every time his wings flapped.

I swiped Cal out of the air and gave him a sloppy smooch. He turned lobster red and sputtered, tongue-tied at my action.

"That will shut him up." Simmons grinned from ear to ear and flew to me giving me a high-five. His little hand hit the middle of my palm. "Always a good thing."

Smiling, I headed out of the house. Cal flew quietly toward the cave. Kennedy and Eli started to follow him, while I drifted back with my mom. "Lars and I both agree we want you to stay here during the battle."

Mom shook her head. "No. No, way."

"Mom, listen to me. We both know this fight is going to be bad. People are going to die. And we're wise enough to know one of them will probably be me."

Lily grabbed for my other hand. "Don't say that."

"Admit it or not, it's the truth. Mark lost you once, and he barely made it without falling apart. I don't have a choice in fighting, but you do. He will not be able handle losing us both. He has already been through too much."

Liquid filled Mom's eyes, her voice choking. "I will not lose you again, either. I can't sit back and do nothing."

"I have some of the best warriors beside me. I love you, but you are not a fighter. And I can't handle if anything happens to you. And what about Mark? Please, Mom, stay for me. For him." I gulped past the tightening in my throat. She looked at the ground, hesitation in her determined armor. "Plus, the layer between the worlds will be thin at best, and what if Aneira starts breaking holes into it? You might have to defend your place. Torin and Thara are going to be with us, leaving only Castien to protect Mark and Ryan."

Mom's head drew up, her orange-brown eyes reflecting the moonlight. Deep in them I saw the struggle raging inside her heart to either remain with Mark or go with me.

"Do stay for me, please?" I begged.

"Ember, do you know what you are asking of me?" A tear slid down her face. "You are my daughter. You will always be my first instinct to protect."

"I know, but there is nothing you can do to help me once we are on the battlefield. You being there will only distract me. Do you think I could continue on if anything happened to you?" I dropped her hands, reaching for her shoulders. "Stay here and defend the man we both love. Being here is how you can help me. I want to believe you two will have your happily-ever-after. Let me have this hope."

A small cry twisted out of my mother's chest.

"Promise me." I tightened my grip.

She stared at me, and her eyes appeared tormented. Then, slowly a resolve flowed from them. "Yes, I promise."

I yanked her to me, my arms crushing her. "Thank you," I whispered.

We held tightly to each other; words were no longer needed. She pulled back, went up on her toes, and kissed my forehead. "I love you."

"I love you, too."

"You kick the bitch's ass for me, all right?"

I laughed. "I will."

Mom's eyes watered again. "Aisling would be so proud of the woman you've become. You are the best thing to have happened to me. I am so thankful for you and every second you blessed my life. Live. Live for all those who love you." She stepped away, taking my cheek in her hand. Her eyes quickly darted to where Eli stood. "All I could ask is for someone to love you wholeheartedly. And he does."

We hugged again. With a heart-wrenching sob, she turned from me and headed to Mark on the porch. He took her into his arms as she wept into his chest. He kissed the top of her head, his eyes full of love and sadness.

Turning back, I headed for the tunnel. I had to leave now or I never would. When I reached Eli's side, his thumb came and brushed away the salty water pooling under my eyes. "You will see them again."

"We will all be with each other again." Kennedy reached for my hand, pulling me into the passageway.

TWENTY-THREE

"What the hell took you so long?" Lorcan demanded the moment we walked out of the cavern. "I actually thought about coming in and getting you guys."

"Your presence would have gone over well." I brushed at my back, feeling the whisper-thin tickle of cobwebs covering me.

Cal zoomed from the hood of my jacket, wiping frantically at his head and wings.

"Like I give a shit," Lorcan grumbled. His body twitched and jerked, reminding me of Eli's knee at dinner. "You guys were there much longer than you were supposed to be."

"Getting lonely and scared here by yourself, Lorcan?" Eli quipped.

"Yeah, that's it." Lorcan looked at the sky.

"Sorry, we had a lot to catch up on." Kennedy touched his arm lightly. "Thank you for waiting."

He scoffed. "Not like I had a choice."

"You didn't have to come at all," I stated as I walked past. I had only taken a few steps when I heard a humming sound. "What's the noise?"

"Not sure, but in this forest probably nothing good." Lorcan started to trek through the foliage. "Let's get out of here."

For once I agreed with him.

The longer we walked, the louder the buzzing became. As I broke through some bushes, I heard Cal stammer, "Um... Ember?" He hovered midair with his attention ahead. My step faltered, and I came to a complete stop.

"Holy shit," Lorcan said from behind me.

A few feet beyond where we stood were thousands of lamprog. Light flickered off them in pulsing beats and ignited the night around us, making everything glow and twinkle in the dark forest. The drone of their wings rattled at my chest and limbs, consuming the air.

Simmons's warning of their breeding habits and timeframe steamrolled back into my mind. It was several nights before Samhain. A full moon.

Crap.

"I remember these things from when I was a kid." Eli spoke next to me. "We avoided the forest on nights they were procreating. Mean little shits."

Kennedy, too busy staring at them, lost her balance as she took a step. She tumbled down the mound we were standing on and crashed into the wall of lamprog, disrupting the courting bugs.

"Kennedy!" Lorcan yelled and leaped below to reach her. The firebugs sensed the threat; their already passionate mood turned furious. A wave of bugs crashed onto Lorcan and Kennedy, while more headed for me and Eli.

Kennedy let out a cry as the bugs bit into her.

"Cal!" I yelled for him to retreat, but instead, he pulled out his sword, slicing at the angry insects. There were too many to fight. Eli jumped down next to Lorcan, trying to get Kennedy out of the swarm. The bugs quickly surrounded us. I plunged next to my friends. I pressed my lips together, shielding my face with my arm. They flew at us from every direction, climbing into our clothes. Welts from their bites bubbled over my skin. Strands of my hair got tangled as bugs caught in its tendrils struggled to free themselves. Numbness zipped through my limbs.

"Run!" Eli pushed me forward. Lorcan picked Kennedy up, her arms swollen with bites, her body limp in his arms. Lorcan tucked his face into her and barreled through, insects bouncing off his head and shoulders as he ran ahead.

My gaze darted around. "Where is Cal?" I could barely speak; my lips were going numb as more fangs delved into my skin. A small body lying on the ground a distance away caught my attention. "Cal!" I propelled my way through the storm to get to him. My anesthetized legs struggled to move, like I was pushing through mud.

"I'll get him." Eli grabbed me. "You get out of here. Now!" He didn't wait for my response before he turned deeper into the throng. It was hard to do, but I forced myself to do what he said. My shoes skidded across the dirt; my legs wanted to buckle under my weight. Stumbling and tripping the whole way, I finally cleared the horde of bugs. I fell on the other side of a small stream next to Lorcan and Kennedy. The water seemed to be a barricade, keeping the bugs on one side of the brook.

"Where's Eli?" Lorcan demanded the moment I collided onto the damp embankment.

"He went to get Cal," I muttered through lifeless lips. Forcing myself to sit, I looked back across the water. "He should be right behind me."

It was only a few beats, but it felt like forever as we waited for Eli to break through the barrage of bugs. Nothing. *It shouldn't take him so long.* My legs were shaking as I tried to pull myself up, ready to go back after him.

Before I could move, Lorcan stood up and was already crossing the stream. "Eli?" he bellowed, his arm covering his face as he dove back in, the mass engulfing him.

"Are you all right?" I faced Kennedy, trying to distract myself from running after Lorcan. *He will get him. He will.*

Kennedy's head flopped on the ground as she tried to look at me. It lolled around in a form of a nod. The poison affected her more than it did us. We were from this world. She was still human, and her body reacted differently.

"That was a yes, right?" I brushed back the hair off her forehead. My attention again fell to where Lorcan disappeared. Panic crept into my heart. Normally, lamprog poison was nothing more than a bee-sting, if you weren't allergic; but if a swarm as big as this attacked you at once? How many small doses of poison could a body take before it couldn't process anymore?

With wobbly legs I stood and trudged into the middle of the stream. The panic turned into full blown terror.

"Eli?" I screamed. "Lorcan?"

No one answered. My feet plunged onward, taking me to the barrier of the buzzing swarm. I took another unsteady step, ready to plunge in when a massive force slammed into me, knocking me on my butt. Lorcan twisted to the side, the limp body he carried slipped off his shoulder and crashed into the stream. Lorcan fell face first next to Eli. Water and pebbles soared into the air as the two big frames hit. Lorcan groaned and rolled over. Both he and Eli sprawled on their backs, the trickle of water finding its way around the new dams their bodies created.

Kennedy grunted. I could tell she was trying to sit up, but doing a poor job of it. I rolled over and crawled to them, my hands and knees plodding through the water as I placed myself between the two men.

"Eli?" My hands went to his face. A low sound came from his chest. I let out a relieved sigh. "Oh, thank God you're okay."

"Yeah, I am fine, too. No, really, it's sweet of you for asking. Thanks." Lorcan blinked deliberately, his gaze on the sky above.

"I hoped you were in there long enough they would at least numb your mouth for a while," I snorted.

"No such luck," Eli mumbled. When I looked back at him, his eyes were open but unfocused.

"Nice, brother, see if I save your ass again."

"Where is Cal? Did you get him?" If Eli and Lorcan were this affected, then how would a six-inch pixie handle it?

Eli's lips smacked together, as he tried to move his arm. Neither worked. He grabbed his shirt and tried to lift the fabric. My fingers went to his to help, and he showed me my answer. Tucked in the sheath where Eli had hidden my knife, between his pants and hip, was Cal. He was unconscious, but I could see the tiny flutter of his chest. He was breathing. I dipped my head on Eli's chest in respite. Cal was all right.

"If you..." Eli stopped. I sat back. "Ever tell him. He was this close. To my dick. I will chain you up."

"Hmmmm... foreplay." I leaned to him and kissed his forehead.

Movement on the bank caught my attention. Kennedy had gotten herself into a sitting position and sluggishly crawled into the creek, stopping on the other side of Lorcan before falling next to him. Her body facing his, her head even with his shoulder. It didn't look like any of us were ready to move for a bit. I placed my head on Eli's chest, curling in next to him. The water actually felt soothing against the bites. Gazing at the stars, I found the silence peaceful. Even the humming of the lamprog was a hypnotic sound lulling me deeper. Sandwiched between two warm bodies, the soft trickling of water, and Eli's heartbeat steady in my ear, it didn't take long before my lids became heavy. The poison pulled all of us into deep lassitude.

"Grimmel?" I called the moment my lashes raised.

"Baby fire," Grimmel said from the shoulder of the dwarf. The little man's back was to me as he pitched old straw out of a cell, grunting with the effort.

"Did you find it?" I asked.

Grimmel's sleek black wings ruffled. "Flame doubt?"

"No. If anyone could find it, you could."

Grimmel fluttered, his feathers puffing out. The dwarf continued to work not aware or uncaring his raven talked to nothing.

"Can you show me?"

Dizziness came over me as I plunged from this room to another. The space was dark except for the glowing sword hanging midair in the middle of the space. The area had only one window with thick, wooden shutters barring any light from getting in. Doors leading in and out were in the far corner.

"What is this place?"

Grimmel's clawed feet, curled around my shoulder as he landed. "I know not."

"Then how will I find it?"

"Follow hidden paths. Down below world. False night will light way."

"What? What the hell does that mean?"

"No time. Go, Fire. Before squall unearths you."

"Oh, no!" Kennedy's voice pierced the gentle morning air. "Guys, we fell asleep. Get up. We have to go!"

My eyes flew open at the disturbance in my sleep. *Morning?* I sprang up, my soaking hair hitting my back in a clump. Kennedy and I dueled in our wide eyed, "Oh, shit" expressions.

"Eli, wake up." I shoved at his chest. He didn't stir. "Crap on ash bark. We are in so much trouble." If it were morning here, who knows how many hours had passed on Earth? I hoped Samhain had not come yet. Surely, Grimmel would never let me sleep so long.

Eli groggily turned over on his side, a side that held a pixie. "No, you don't." I grabbed the sheath from his waist. Cal was curled in it snoring. I strapped the cover to my belt loop. "Wake up." I splashed water on Eli's face. His eyes sprung open. He looked around in confusion before sitting up.

"I thought it was all a dream." He rubbed at his face, water dripping off and slipping down his wrist.

"Unfortunately, not." I stood, pulling him with me. He winced and grabbed his stomach.

"Hey, Lorcan, wake up." Eli kicked at Lorcan's foot.

While we were sleeping, the gang of lamprog had dissipated, their night of frolicking over. The big welts had disappeared along with them, and only red splotches showed where we had been attacked.

Lorcan opened his eyes and blinked at Eli, similar confusion in their identical green eyes. He looked even more startled when he saw Kennedy sitting next to him.

"Not a dream." Eli grabbed for Lorcan's arm and pulled him up.

"Hell." Lorcan shook his head, looking like he was trying to de-fuzz his mind. He reached out to Kennedy and helped her to her feet. Lorcan then hissed, bending over.

"What's wrong?" She grabbed for him.

"We got to get out of here." He took in a deep breath and straightened. Eli rubbed at his arms and neck, breathing heavy through his teeth.

Kennedy and I looked at each other with knowing looks. Nobody needed to say it. We had been here too long, and the curse drilled hard into them.

We headed toward the opening, the dim morning sky barely light enough to be called dawn, although my body felt it was later than it looked. As we plodded through the forest, Eli wiped the sweat from his forehead and ground his teeth. Cal stirred as we walked. Eventually his head poked out, but he kept quiet. We all looked like hell, with one side of us dry and the other matted with muddy water. Red blemishes covered our skin, and our pants sagged with muck, chafing us. Lorcan stumbled, his knee hitting the dirt. Eli staggered to him and hauled him back up. Agony was turning both of them ashen.

"Thanks." Lorcan gripped Eli's arm tighter.

"And thanks. For last night. Saving me." Eli breathed heavily, as his eyes set on what stood in front of him.

Lorcan didn't respond, but there was something unsaid going on between them, something not needing words. Lorcan had not hesitated to go after Eli. When Eli needed him, he had been there. His actions were not something even I could overlook.

When we finally reached the door, I was no longer happy to see it. Our escapade should have been fun and something Lars would not know about. The possibility of him staying ignorant was now nil. The only thing saving me was the new information about the sword's location.

"Maybe we should stay." I looked back wistfully at Eli.

"If I didn't feel the Otherworld splitting my insides and shoving me out, I would agree." He grunted, nudging my back, and herded me through the door.

The moment Eli and Lorcan walked through, relief exhaled from their lungs. I had no idea how much discomfort they had been in, but knowing Eli, it was more than I could even fathom.

We were only feet away from Lars's property line when I heard a voice. "Sir, they've returned." Goran, the head of Lars's security, stepped out. Rimmon stood stalwartly behind him.

"Crap." My last sliver of hope we hadn't been gone long enough for Lars to find out dissolved.

"Oh, I think you will be saying a lot more when Lars gets ahold of you. Don't think I've ever seen him so pissed. Right, Rimmon?"

Rimmon snorted. I gulped.

"Come on. Boss is heading our way now." Goran jerked his head behind him. As we crossed the property line, the spell skated over my limbs. Goran escorted us through the forest, and with every step, dread sank in deeper.

"How long were we gone?" I asked.

"Five days."

This meant it was only three days until Samhain.

Double crap.

The first sounds came from Cal as he slipped out of the sheath, flying to my shoulder. "You are so screwed, girlie. And not by him." He thumbed back at Eli.

I agreed. Lars's anger was valid, but the punishment might exceed the crime. Most feared him and not without reason. He was a Demon with the power to control your body to cause you to do things against your will. If you tried to disregard his bidding, it felt like your insides were being scraped over a cheese grater. It was pointless to ignore him anyway; his power was too much to fight. All my brain pictured for my punishment was me being forced to lash my own back with a spiked ball. Or drowning my head in a boiling pot of oil.

"Stop." Goran halted us. "He wants to meet you here."

"Why? So there will be no witnesses?" I exclaimed.

Goran only smiled.

Kennedy looked like she wanted to vomit. Eli and Lorcan stayed expressionless.

The person who walked out to meet us was not whom I expected.

"Gabby?"

"Came to see you guys get spanked."

"Think you have done enough, Gabrielle." Lars, dressed in a crisp suit, strode over the foliage like it was a Manhattan sidewalk.

"Yeah, Gabrielle." I placed my hands on my hips.

"What?" Gabby shrugged. "I distracted him. You didn't specify how long I had to divert his attention. I am good, but I think five days is past even my ability."

"Thank you, Goran. You and Rimmon may return to your duties." Lars gave a dismissive nod to the men.

Goran bowed slightly and headed back to his post. As he passed me, he grinned. I didn't know him well, but he seemed to be taking great delight in my reprimand. Clearly not one of my fans.

Lars plucked at his shirt cuffs under his jacket sleeves; his voice strained. "And I think Alki is expecting you on the field, Gabrielle." The hint was clear.

"Alki?" My brow went up.

Gabby hands went to her hips, and a tint of color dyed her cheeks. "I am now assisting him in training."

"Really?" My little talk with Alki worked.

"Yes." Gabby's face turned red, then she rolled her eyes at me.

"And you should go, Gabrielle." Lars ordered. When Gabby didn't move, Lars glanced at her, his pupils converting into black orbs. "Now."

Gabby shuffled backwards, her eyes wide. "Think Alki needs me on the training field. I'll leave you to catch up." She turned and disappeared into the forest. Wanting to join her myself, I stood my ground, my body rigid, waiting for his wrath.

"I'm sure Sinnie has missed me. Better go ease her worry." Cal pushed off my shoulder and waved at me from behind Lars.

I glared at him. "Weenie," I muttered.

"No. Smart." He headed in the direction of the house.

Lars's skin paled, and his Demon fought for control. He clenched his fists, taking deep, slow, methodical breaths as he glowered down at me.

"You must have been designed to test my patience."

"Funny, it's what I think, too," Eli laughed as he nudged my arm. He was suddenly in the air, his fingers clawing at his throat.

"You find it a joke, Elighan?" Lars's teeth snapped; his face contorted more into a hideous creature.

"Stop it," I screamed at Lars. My instincts wanted to combat his powers. Once again I felt helpless.

Eli wrestled for air, his legs twitching as he dangled. Lorcan was sent flying into the dirt, his hands going for his own throat, choking himself. Kennedy shrieked, her legs crumpling beneath her as though by force.

"I know your weaknesses." Lars must have tightened his hold around Eli's and Lorcan's throats because a gargled croaking sound came from both of them. "Do not forget what I can do if you disobey me again."

"Please, stop!" I pleaded. "I know where the sword is being held. Grimmel showed me." Sort of. I couldn't get much from Grimmel's enigmatic words *"Follow hidden paths. Down below world."* It was still more than we had known before.

Lorcan froze. "Where?" His black eyes were intense and unsettled.

"Beneath the castle." I think. "I will tell you every detail of the dreamwalk if you let them go."

"Your information does not make your disappearing for five days acceptable." His white lips moved tightly, but Eli dropped to the ground, and his mass quaked the earth under my feet. Eli pushed himself up, his own eyes flaming red. A growl shook his body.

I heard Lorcan gasp for breath and move quickly to Kennedy. "I'm fine," she mumbled to him.

I placed myself between Lars and my friends. "Enough. Our disappearance was my fault. I wanted to spend my birthday with family."

Lars's head jerked slightly at my words. "You put yourself in danger and disappeared for five days so you could have a birthday party?"

"Yes. I wanted one night when I didn't feel helpless or scared. One night I could forget all I am destined for, all the people I might lose, and have fun spending time with some of the people I love."

Lars did not move, but his normal yellow-green eyes filled his pupils. His skin took on more of an olive tone. Finally, he broke the heavy air suffocating the space. "I want the four of you in my office in ten minutes." He spun and walked away.

I turned to Eli. His hand lay on his neck, but his focus locked on the back of Lars. "Eli, are you okay?"

He gaze snapped onto me. "Yeah. Fine."

He was pissed, and I knew better than to be overly concerned. It would only heighten his anger. Eli didn't like being the less superior one in a fight.

"Fuck," Lorcan muttered under his breath, rubbing his own neck.

"And he was just irritable. You should see when he really gets upset." I sighed, relief sliding off my shoulders.

"He was just *irritable*?" Lorcan remarked.

"Believe me. If he were truly angry, none of us would be breathing right now," I replied.

Eli rumbled behind me. "The raven visited you last night?"

"Yeah." I faced him. "I was going to tell you, but our first priority was getting you two out of the Otherworld. Now we need to go deal with a pissed-off Demon."

His lips curved down, but gave me a curt nod. I turned in the direction of the house with a sigh. There was a good chance a pot of boiling oil waited for me. My feet shuffled toward the house. The rest of them followed begrudgingly behind.

TWENTY-FOUR

The warm sun shone down on a beautiful fall day designed for relaxing. Mother Nature painted each leaf with a brilliant pigment of color. Bright reds and oranges dyed the trees into a rainbow of auburn shades. Fall was my favorite time of year, and I took in a deep breath, seizing all the spicy smells of the season. My enjoyment of the perfect day was marred by the uncertainty of what Lars's punishment would be. He had not let us off the hook.

We only made it to the beginning of the field on the way to the Unseelie King's office when a voice shouted, "Kennedy!" Jared jogged to us from his workout spot on the grass. His sweaty face lit up at seeing his girlfriend. "Where have you been? I was really worried about you." He faltered as his focus went from her to the man behind her. "What the hell are you doing here?"

Kennedy put her hand up. "Calm down. It's not what you think."

Jared didn't respond, keeping his attention locked on Lorcan.

"Hey." Kennedy grabbed his chin and turned it to face her.

Jared seemed to finally see his girlfriend. He reached for her and gave her a quick kiss. "Where were you? You've been gone a *week*."

Kennedy cupped Jared's cheek with her hands. "I'm sorry.

We went to see Ryan. We were only supposed to be gone a day, but some bugs attacked us, and we were extraordinarily lucky to get out."

"You went to the Otherworld without me?" His body stiffened, and his eyes widened at her words.

"You were training, which is more important than you com-ing with me. I wanted to see Ryan and spend time with him. You needed to stay here and train." She gave him another quick kiss.

He nodded in excitement, his anger dissolving. "You should see what I learned." He moved away from her, bounced and made a skewed flip to the side. He landed and did some punches in the space in front of him.

"Impressive." Kennedy smiled and moved back to him, kissing his cheek.

Eli grabbed the back of Jared's neck, playfully squeezing it. "Think you can fight me now?"

"Oh, I can take you, old man." Jared took the bait and bounced about like the Energizer bunny.

Eli's arm wrapped around Jared's torso, which hit the ground in a matter of seconds. "You sure?"

Jared's ego was all Dark Dweller and boy. He didn't like being shown up, especially in front of Kennedy. His eyes narrowed as he bounded up, jabbing Eli in the gut.

"We need to go. Lars is furious enough with us." I flicked my matted hair off my shoulder, twisting it into a low bun. My skin itched with drying mud and grime. I longed for a shower.

Eli brought Jared into a head lock, rubbing the top of his head.

"Keep working on those moves. I'll come out later and practice with you."

"Where are you guys going?" Jared scanned the four of us.

Kennedy motioned towards the house. "Lars wants us in his office."

"I want to come." Jared wiggled free of Eli's hold and

sprung to Kennedy, taking her hand in his. A possessive gaze was directed at Lorcan. Kennedy looked at me.

"No, sorry, J. But I am saving you from getting strung up by your intestines with the rest of us." I patted his back as I walked past.

"Sorry." Kennedy squeezed his hand.

"I'll come find you after practice." He gave her a quick peck and ran back to his spot on the field.

We made it to the house where Cal sat in the spoon holder on the stove next to Marguerite as she cooked. "You turncoat." I pointed at him as I walked through and gave Marguerite a quick hug.

"Self-preservation," he hollered back at me.

"Deserter."

"On scrumptious brownies." Cal giggled.

I groaned, shaking my head. The four of us continued to Lars's office.

When we entered, Rez stood at his desk, tablet in hand, while Lars was on the phone.

Rez turned and gave me an exasperated look. "You need to stop making him crazy. I swear you have given him his first gray hairs."

"But then why would I get up in the morning?" I retaliated.

"You look awful. What happened?" She frowned.

As I was about to answer, Lars put down the phone, and she snapped her gaze back to him.

"The Selkies are arriving soon. Be sure they are housed near the river," Lars said to Rez.

Her fingers tapped on the screen. "Is that all?"

"Yes, you can go." He relaxed in his chair. She nodded and swept out, never once smiling.

Lars's regard fell on each member of the foursome then bored into me. "As the future Queen, I expect you to act a certain way, especially after recent events in London and New York. You need to stop thinking of yourself and start thinking for the kingdom."

Ouch.

"You will have obligations, people to lead, and an entire court looking to you to guide them through the aftermath of the war. Start acting like you are the ruler of these people and not like a spoiled, selfish, little girl. You are an adult now. Behave like one."

Angrily, I strode to his desk, placed my hands on the top, and leaned into his space. "That is why I needed to do it. If, and it is a strong *if*, I live long enough to become Queen, my entire life is all wrapped up in a bow. I will have my existence planned out for me, down to when I go to the bathroom. I am willing to do it because I don't want the Light to suffer. They need a ruler, and they need someone to get them out of Aneira's mess. I know I am her blood, so if it is meant to be me, then I will do it. But it is not because I *want* to." I tilted even farther into his face, my voice a harsh whisper. "You know better than anyone what I am *giving up*, to do the right thing. Aneira's massacres and destruction made it exceptionally clear I needed one last night with my family and friends. Don't make me feel bad for wanting to be with them."

Our eyes were deadlocked before he shifted and nodded slightly. "Tell me everything about what the raven said and where the sword is."

I filled him in on every aspect of my dreamwalk with Grimmel.

When I finished, he swiveled his chair and stared out the window. "You all look and smell horrendous. Get cleaned up, and then I would like the four of you to go through different scenarios and strategies of getting into the castle. All of you must be ready for every situation thrown your way. I have set up a mock battlefield downstairs in the family room. No one will interrupt you there. I do not want you to leave until you have fleshed out a dozen plans to infiltrate the castle. And even more of how you will escape." Lars scooted back to his desk and picked up the phone. "You are dismissed." He had pardoned us, but his gruffness told me it could as easily swung the other way.

I hadn't gone to the Otherworld to anger him or be rebellious out of spite. Seeing my mom and my dad meant everything to me. If I were going to die, I wanted them to know how much I loved them and to have those last moments with them. Still, I hated upsetting Lars.

Everyone filed out of the room. When I reached the door, Lars called to me, "Ember, I do understand how it feels, and I know about loss and sacrifice. But it must be done, and the faster you come to accept it the better it will be for you."

I turned to look at him. "That's the difference between you and me. Sacrificing people I love will never be something I will accept." I stepped out of his office and shut the door.

After our showers, the four of us met in the large family room downstairs. Upon entering, I spotted Lars's mock battlefield. It was the size of a ping-pong table and placed in the center of the room. A miniature castle and field sat in the middle, replicating the Seelie fortress. It was detailed to perfection even to the bridge and landscape. Dozens and dozens of tiny plastic figures painted with the Queen's insignia lay in a pile, one of them larger than the rest, representing the Queen. On the other side were black figures, most of them blank, except for a handful with initials on them. I found the EB figurine headfirst in the moat.

"Looks about right." Eli snickered. I snagged the ED model and threw it in the painted lake.

"Nice." He grabbed for his piece.

I set my miniature self down at the beginning of the pass. "All right. We need to start. Let's say we get to the bridge, but it's blocked. What are our other options?"

Lorcan and Kennedy moved on the side of the table across

from me and Eli. Lorcan handed Kennedy her model. She plucked it from his fingers, her eyes focused on the table before speaking. "The bridge is our only way in and out, unless..."

"... we come from the water." Lorcan finished her sentence.

"Right." She smiled at him and placed their characters in the lake.

I put my piece on a spot by the lake. "This is how I got in before. There are sewage tunnels here. Let's hope no one told Aneira how I entered last time, or she hasn't thought of it."

"Someone will think of it," Eli said.

"I don't know. Torin would have, but Josh is her First Knight now. He would have no idea they are there."

"Her other soldiers would."

"Probably, but it's an option. It might be our only way."

"I agree. *On* the water, we are too exposed." Eli assessed the board.

"Not if we're *in* the water," both Kennedy and Lorcan said at the same time. They looked at each other and laughed. He bumped her shoulder. "We need to stop doing this."

"I know." She chuckled again, nudging him back. "Dax wanted to kill us one night, remember."

"Oh, yeah, I remember." Lorcan rubbed the back of his ear; a smirk played on his lips, and he became lost in a memory.

Eli's brows furrowed, his gaze going from one to another.

"There you are. I've looked everywhere for you guys." Jared pounded down the last few steps into the room. Kennedy's head sprang up, the smile falling from her face. She quickly moved away from Lorcan.

"Oh, cool." Jared sauntered to the table and picked up a figurine off the board. "Where's mine?"

"You don't have one." Lorcan placed his LD figure on the board.

"Why not?"

"Because you won't be going with us. You know that."

Kennedy placed her hand on his arm, rubbing it.

"Right. I am to stay here with the women and children." He glared.

We girls immediately put our hands on our hips. "Excuse me?" My eyebrows cocked up.

"You know what I mean," he grumbled.

"You're staying here and protecting people like Marguerite and Rez, which is a huge job."

There would be protection spells on the property, but if the wall came down, the enchantments would be rendered useless, leaving the house and people who needed to stay back vulnerable. Marguerite and Rez could handle themselves, but we needed Jared to believe his was a legitimate duty.

"Dude, my girlfriend gets to go into battle, and I have to stay home with the babysitter. It's not fair." Jared banged his fist on the table. Sometimes I could see and feel the age difference between them. Kennedy had grown so much. She'd always been advanced well beyond her years, but Jared and Kennedy had still seemed to see eye to eye. Now Kennedy's furrowed brow revealed she might also be feeling the years growing between them.

"When has life ever been fair?" Lorcan rolled his figure between his fingers.

Jared's chest expanded, the muscles in his face twitching. "Fuck off."

"Jared, stop it." Kennedy massaged her temple. "You know if I could stay back, I would, believe me."

"Yeah, but they *need* you." Jared spat at Kennedy, his eyes narrowing on her. "You are 'special' in a good way. I'm only a nuisance and a liability, but they can't do without *you*."

"Hey!" Lorcan's voice boomed through the room. "That's enough, Jared. You're mad at the situation, at me. Don't take it out on Kennedy." Lorcan's hand touched Kennedy's lower back protectively. It was only an instant before he noticed what he did and dropped his arm. But it was enough.

Time froze for a breath, and tension grew in the room until it exploded all over the walls, peeling away in chunks.

With a roar, Jared flew at Lorcan, at the same instant Eli sprung and blocked Jared from reaching Lorcan. "Whoa." Eli grabbed Jared's shoulders.

"Get out of my way, Eli," Jared snapped, his hazel eyes burning a dark red color.

"You need to calm down, J." Eli gripped Jared's arms tighter, restraining his push forward.

"How about you fuck off, too! You are really no different. You also treat me like a kid. I am almost nineteen!" His face twisted in fury at Eli, and then it turned back to Lorcan. "And you keep your hands off my girlfriend. Why are you touching her? She is *mine*. Not yours!"

The possessive tone did not go unnoticed by Kennedy. Her brows slid down at an angle. "Jared. Stop." She moved in front of Lorcan, trying to be in Jared's sight line, but his head kept twisting and craning to the side to keep his target in view.

"Why in the hell are you even here anyway? Shouldn't you run back to the Queen like the trained lap dog you are?" I could hear the influence of Eli in every insult Jared flung at Lorcan.

Lorcan clenched his jaw but didn't move from his spot.

"Why don't you leave, Lorcan? No one wants you here. No one likes you." Jared fought against Eli's hold.

"Please, Jared." Kennedy took another tentative step closer.

"You want him to go, too, don't you?" Jared's chin flicked over towards Lorcan. "I know you can't stand him anymore than the rest of us. Tell him."

"Jared..." Kennedy clasped her hands together, her eyes wide with pleading.

"Dammit, Ken, tell him!"

Her mouth opened and shut.

Jared rocked back on his heels. Eli's hands dropped away from him as Jared's confusion turned quickly to realization. His shoulders sagged, pain pinching the muscles in his face.

"Jared, I..." Kennedy reached for him.

He jerked away. "Don't!"

She drew her hand back, holding it against her chest. Kennedy's eyes reflected the unshed tears building under her lids.

"I get it now." Anger filled Jared's voice.

"No." Kennedy's head shook. "You don't."

"I must have been blind not to see it." Jared's body was rigid, his tone vicious. "Did you enjoy making a fool of me? Leading me on? Pretending you cared?"

"What are you talking about? I love you." Kennedy still clung to her wrist, keeping it tight to her body.

Jared ignored Kennedy and resumed. "Him?" He pointed at Lorcan. "Really? You'd rather be with him?"

"No." Kennedy shook her head.

"It's not what you are thinking," Lorcan said behind Kennedy.

"Shut up!" Jared seethed. "You don't get to talk."

We all stayed silent as Jared stared at Kennedy and Lorcan before he swore under his breath and headed for the stairs.

"Jared?" Kennedy turned to follow him.

He continued to storm up the stairs, without a glance back. Kennedy's feet shuffled tentatively after him. "Jared..."

"Let him go. He needs to cool off," Eli said to Kennedy. "He's got the hot Irish temper like the rest of us. He'll be fine once he calms down."

Kennedy half turned toward Eli and nodded. Her lips trembled, her eyes heavy with liquid. She took a breath but could no longer hold back the stream of tears. Her hand went to her mouth, a sob erupting from her lips. She whirled towards the hallway leading to the bathrooms and ran.

"Shit." Lorcan mumbled rubbing his forehead, and his head turned to where Kennedy disappeared. "Maybe I should go talk to him."

"No!" Both Eli and I said in unison.

"Tell him it's not like that." Lorcan waved his hand in the direction of Kennedy.

"It's not?" Eli crossed his arms, his gaze locked on Lorcan. "Jared would see through the lie."

Lorcan's chest filled with air, his mouth opened, holding Eli's gaze. He appeared to be about to protest Eli's claim. Then he locked his jaw, and his eyes darted to the side. Lorcan's movement was so minimal, I almost didn't notice it, but his head dipped slightly in acknowledgment. I was sure Kennedy cared about Lorcan more than she let on, but I didn't know how serious her feelings were. It was clear, Lorcan's were deep.

"You will only make it worse right now." Eli ran his hand over his hair, his attention on the door. "I'll go."

"And I'll check on Kennedy." I was already halfway across the room, heading for the hallway.

It didn't take me long to find her. When I turned the corner, she was sitting on the floor, her back against the wall. There was no way she didn't hear what we had said. I slid down the wall and sat next to her. My shoulder bumped hers. "You okay?"

She let her knees fall, tucked her legs underneath, and balled her hands in her lap. Tears slid down her face. "Not really."

"I am so sorry, Ken." I placed my head on her shoulder. "You didn't deserve that."

Her shoulders shook with a silent sob. "Don't I?"

I lifted my head and waited for her to continue. When she didn't, I finally asked, "Did something happen with you and Lorcan?"

Her head stayed bowed, her hands coming to her face. "I am a horrible person, aren't I?"

Oh, holy crap on ash bark. It's true.

My chest constricted, but I forced my own emotions to the side. "No, of course you're not." I wrapped my arm around her shoulder and pulled her to me. "You're human Ken. Well, mostly," I teased. "We all make mistakes, but we get up, brush ourselves off, and try to learn from our mishaps. Or so I've heard."

She wiped frantically at her eyes. "That's the thing..."

"You don't feel it was a mistake?"

"No. Yes. I don't know." Her head went back, tapping the wall. "I love Jared, but I feel a huge gap between us now. I've changed, and maybe he has also. But in whatever way we have changed, it is pulling us apart. Not together. I've been feeling it for a long time now, but I've been trying to ignore it. I thought we could get through; we could make it work."

"So, what happened with Lorcan?"

Her ponytail brushed against the wall as she moved her head back and forth. "I don't want to talk about Lorcan. What's going on has nothing to do with him."

"Nothing to do with him?" I echoed as I turned my body to face her. "It has everything to do with him."

"No. This situation has to do with me and Jared and me being honest with myself." Her face was streaked with tears, but her eyes were now dry. "The last thing I want to do is hurt Jared, but I can't lie to myself, either."

"No, you can't," I agreed. "That wouldn't be fair to either of you."

She placed her hand over mine and squeezed my hand. She didn't say a word, but she didn't need to. We had been friends too long for me not to feel her love and thanks.

"You're not going to tell me what happened?" I peered through my lashes at Kennedy.

"I need to figure some things out on my own first. Okay?" She replied, taking back her hand. Her fingers twined around each other, knotting on her lap.

"Yeah. Okay."

She shook out her fingers and pushed herself onto her feet. I stood with her.

"There is no doubt I love Jared. I don't know if it is enough to keep us together."

"Lorcan?" I tried again.

She sighed. "I care for him. A lot. I don't know what it means yet, though. I won't deny I am drawn to him. But I will do whatever it takes to have it work with Jared."

My stomach dropped hearing her confessions. I could not deny Lorcan had changed since I first met him. To me there was little doubt Kennedy was the reason. I still felt sick at the thought she wanted to be with Lorcan. But I didn't want her to stay with Jared because she felt she should.

Whatever her choice, I would be there for her. She was my friend, and her happiness came first.

TWENTY-FIVE

The following couple of days were a blur of strategic fights, preparations, and running drills over and over. Kennedy hadn't spoken to me about what was going on with her and Jared, but the tension between them was obvious. Before, they were constantly touching and kissing, being all gooey and sweet. Now, they stood feet apart. On breaks, they would be near each other, but they were either silent or quietly arguing. It broke my heart to see them quarreling. It hurt even more to think they were trying to force a relationship no longer working, for either of them. Sadly, with the war so close, their relationship woes were not high on the priority list.

On the last day before Samhain, our group—which included Dark Dwellers, Demons, and Kennedy, Cal, Simmons, and me—stationed ourselves on a back lot of Lars's property, away from the other training Fae. Lars put me in charge, wanting me to get used to the leadership role. I did not feel comfortable being the one in command, although I had always taken care of myself and dealt with what I needed to. Leading a mass of people who were better trained and had more knowledge and experience was daunting and awkward. Watching Lars and Cole, I realized a good leader recognizes limitations and delegates. Kennedy was a huge help in dividing people; her seer insight could pick out their strengths and weaknesses.

Alki, Koke, Nic, and Maya were to lead the main battle on the field with Lars and the rest of the thousands of Dark Fae who had been training here. Only a handful of us would be making our way to the castle. Thara, Dominic, Dax, and Samantha were in the first group who were to hold off the opposing side. They would be our most important defense, so the rest of us could get around the main battle and closer to the castle. The next unit contained Cooper, West, Owen, and Gabby who were to hold the line of Seelie back. The final team helping us break inside consisted of Lorcan and Cole. Eli and Torin would be the ones to take Kennedy and me, along with the two pixies, all the way to the room where the Sword of Light remained hidden. Thanks to the raven, I had some idea where it was. And with Torin's intimate knowledge of the castle, he knew ways of getting into the room none of the rest of us had.

Rez and Marguerite planned a "last" meal on the night before Samhain. My stomach did flip flops with the mere thought of food. Without uttering a word, we knew it could be our final moments together. If we lost the war, it would be the last dinner for all of us.

It was an amazing thing to see—my Demon family alongside my Dark Dweller family. No one would have believed these groups could be working so closely together, let alone eating a meal, laughing, and telling stories with each other. There was tension in the air. Old prejudices don't go away overnight, but the fact they were all here together was enough. They were gathered because of me—the unexpected adhesive bringing these two groups together.

Lars sat at the head of the table, Rez to his right, Marguerite's open chair to his left. Alki and Koke sat next to Rez with Nic and Maya on Marguerite's other side. Kennedy and I were across from each other in the middle, the buffers and the connections between the factions. Eli, Cooper, West, and Cole sat on the same side as me. Jared, Owen, and Gabby sat on Kennedy's side. Lars made sure there was no other "head" of the table. He was King and wanted to keep his role clear.

Marguerite brought a steaming bowl from the kitchen. Cal and Simmons trailed closely behind, following the scent of the dish like they were on a leash. Cal's time in the kitchen following Sinnie around had bonded him and Marguerite.

"You sure you don't want to add some *berries* to the top of it?" Cal fluttered around the dish. "I think it would really advance the flavor."

"And your alcohol tolerance." Kennedy laughed. Sets of eyes turned to look at her. The quiet mouse was roaring like a lion lately. I loved it, but it still took me aback, forgetting the strong change in her, especially since returning with Lorcan's team.

Cal only nodded. "Exactly."

Simmons flittered down next to my plate. "Cal, if you advance anymore tonight, I'll have to retrieve you out of the toilet. Again."

"I *fell* in. And it happened one time." Cal swung around, flying to me. "Okay, okay, twice."

Cal landed beside Simmons and drew his arms around his friend's shoulder. "What would you do without me?"

"Probably be respectable."

"*Phhhhtttt.*" Cal disregarded this notion. "Respectable maybe, but bored out of your mind."

Simmons tilted his head and sighed deeply. We both knew Cal was right.

Marguerite placed the dish she was carrying near Lars. His back relaxed into the chair, and he regarded us as if we were his subjects.

"I smell molé." Nic rubbed his hands together. Catching my eye, he gave a wink. I smiled back. Nic would always be Nic.

Marguerite swatted at his hand as he tried to grab for the

dish, uttering something in Spanish to him. I smiled at the familiarity of Nic and Marguerite bantering. Her adoration for him was so clear it put tears in my eyes.

It struck me as I glanced around the table watching everyone together, in a warped way, this was what a holiday would be like with my newly blended families: laughter, vast amounts of drinking, and massive discussions between the sides. What holidays were all about, right? It seemed like the perfect idea to me. Except it would probably never come to pass.

I gripped Eli's hand harder under the table. He looked over, giving me a faint smile, his thumb running over the back of mine. We didn't need words. He was aware of our odds. He just wasn't aware of his.

I could sense Lars glaring into me. My head popped up to look down the extended table. His expression was clear. *You will do this. He will die either way. Quickly by someone he loves or by someone who will force him to suffer for a dreadfully long time.*

My lips pressed together, and my gaze jerked back to my plate.

"Um... my hand." Eli's voice shot into my ear. My gaze jerked over to his lap, realizing I clutched his hand in a death grip.

"Sorry." I released it.

His brow curved up. "You okay?"

A gruff snort barked from my throat. "Oh, yeah. Awesome." I grabbed the beer in front of him and downed it. I could not hide a frown of displeasure at the acrid taste. "Uck."

Eli stared at me.

"What?"

"Beside the point you drank beer?" He leaned back farther in his chair, which creaked as though it might not hold. "You drank *my* beer and didn't even appreciate it like it deserved. That was a limited brew from Bruges."

I picked up the bottle and shrugged. "It still tasted like troll piss."

Eli made a squeak of offense.

"It's *special* troll piss." I patted his arm. "Better?"

His hair brushed his shoulders as he shook his head. "You are gonna pay for insulting and disregarding my beer."

"Put it on my tab." I leaned in closer to him.

"Your account is going to be paid in full tonight," he mumbled against my ear.

"Seriously?" Gabby declared from across the table. "I'm eating here. Or at least trying to."

In true Eli fashion, wanting to torment his sister more, he pulled my face to his and kissed me sloppily, making annoying smacking sounds.

"Ewww." I laughed and pulled back as Eli licked the side of my face.

"Elighan!" Gabby threw a tortilla at him.

He grabbed it midair and stuffed it into his mouth. Munching happily, he smirked across the table at his sister. Gabby glared and stuck her tongue out at him. It was like a step into their past. I could see them so clearly as kids, taunting each other till someone became truly mad. Probably poor Cole.

Family and siblings. I had missed out, even though I'd had Mom and Mark. Now I was finally part of a huge extended family, and I was so afraid it would be taken from me. I loved every one of them. There was nothing I wouldn't do for them.

Lars cleared his throat, standing. "Before we start to eat, or dinner turns into a food fight, I want to thank Marguerite for once again making our delicious dinner." He gave her a nod as she slipped into her seat, setting down the last dish.

"I do not know how I survived before Marguerite came to this house." Lars's voice or face did not show emotion, but he spoke the words warmly and fondly. A Demon showing any kind of sentiment was a rarity in itself.

Marguerite blushed and swished her hand at him.

Lars actually smiled at her. "This is not something I ever thought I would say or feel, but whatever happens tomorrow... I am proud of all of you here. I never imagined working with some of you." He motioned down the table to the Dark Dwellers. "Though times like these produce interesting bedfellows. It has been an honor to work with you." He nodded at Cole who tilted his beer in acknowledgement. "Ember." My name jolted me stiffer in my seat. "You have been the biggest surprise of all. Good and bad. I never thought I could care about anything, especially after losing your mother. As a Demon I never desired a family. The moment you stepped onto my property, my feelings changed. I finally understood Aisling's decision to protect you, choosing to save you over herself."

My lids were flimsy dams, barely holding back the torrent wanting to break through and pour down my face.

"Daughter or niece, it does not matter to me." He kept his face like stone, but I saw past the façade. It didn't matter to me, either, whether he was my father or my uncle. I loved him enough for both. "Aisling would be so proud of you, and so am I. I believe you will fulfill the prophecy tomorrow and become an excellent queen." He raised his cup while everyone at the table joined in. We clinked glasses and dove into the meal Marguerite had prepared.

As I sat there and looked around, bile crept up my throat. The becoming-queen part always seemed to slip my mind, focusing purely on getting through the war. Not thinking about what would happen afterwards if we did win. Neither outcome, win or lose, was a good one for me. Eli was not a part of either scenario. Happiness would be elusive to me. But *my* happiness wasn't the point, was it? In some ways, fate had never let my life be completely mine. I had to make the best of whatever happened. For Earth and for the people who survived.

My reflections drifted away as dinner went on. The number of times glasses were raised and filled along with other speeches lightened my mood. We probably shouldn't have been drinking before the battle, but it could be our last night together. We were going to enjoy it. When the tequila shots came out, so did the stories. My stomach ached as West told us about the night he, Cooper, and Eli hid in a church to get away from the cops.

"Eli jumped into the confessional booth to hide." West's eyes glistened with amusement as he recalled the memory. "It would have been perfect if there wasn't already someone in it. Do you remember Eli?" West burst out laughing.

A chuckle came out of Eli. "Yeah. The little old woman grabbed me by the ear, made me sit down, and confess." Eli shook his head as everyone roared with laughter. "Damn, she was a mean old bat."

"The best was when we came to find him." Cooper took a gulp of air. "She was hitting him in the shin with her cane when he stopped talking. She kept saying, '"Don't roll your eyes at me, boy. Keep talking. I can tell you're slicker than a snake in soap.'"

"Don't forget she sat *both* your asses down after mine." Eli pointed at both Cooper and West.

West wiped at his eyes, chuckles rolling from his chest. "Even if the cops had found us, they probably would have let us go. Her punishment was much more severe than what they could have given us."

My stomach muscles were cramped and sore, my face a mess with tears after listening to their stories.

Lars stayed longer than I thought, even after dessert was finished. He sat back, taking in his assembly of people around his table. Once I could have sworn I saw amusement flicker in his eyes, but it could have been the alcohol making me see things. Goran eventually came in, whispering something in Lars's ear, which took the Unseelie King away. Rez followed. Maya and Koke disappeared soon after, never being ones to relax and have fun.

I'd been sure Alki would be the first to leave; his entire philosophy stood opposed to having fun. Well, at least this kind of fun. He usually got his enjoyment in torturing me with drills and endless hours of training. But here he sat. Gabby went to the bathroom, and when she came back, she sat down in the vacated seat next to Alki. He only acknowledged her with a slight shift of his head but a smile filled my face. I looked down, so my hair would curtain my reaction.

Cal wind-milled his arms around. "My new floaties!" Sliced olives circled his biceps like mini inner tubes.

Eli reached over and broke off a piece of olive and plopped it in his mouth. "Tasty floaty."

"Heyyyy!" Cal threateningly pointed at Eli as the other half of the olive slid off his arm and onto the table.

I grinned and looked at Eli. "I wouldn't mess with the man's new floatation devices."

Eli scoffed. "I'd like to see him stay afloat with those."

"Don't worry, Cal. I will get you real ones." Barbie had a pool collection, right?

He nodded in response, deflated, and glared at Eli before he broke a chunk of olive from his other arm and chomped down on it.

"Multi-functional." I grinned.

Cal turned his glower on me, then shrugged. "Aye."

Kennedy's peal of laughter brought my attention across the table, but she didn't hold it. In the large, arched window behind her I caught a pair of glowing, green eyes. The intensity of the gaze was so familiar I had to look at Eli to reassure myself he sat beside me. When I looked back, the eyes were gone.

Lorcan.

Lorcan watching us didn't bother me like it normally would have. I didn't know if it was the tequila talking or whether I had gotten to know him better. It pissed me off and made me feel guilty, but I no longer despised him. There were times, if I didn't think about his past or mine, I would say I might even acknowledge he was okay.

Oh, yeah... it's the booze talking.

Kennedy laughed so hard at something she slipped off her

chair, knocking Jared over with her. Everyone at the table roared in amusement, while the pair giggled so hard every time they tried to get back up, they failed.

Jared pulled her to him and kissed her on the forehead. "See, this is how we are supposed to be. We belong together." His lips met her head again, forcefully. "I've missed you. You. Are. *Mine*. No one else's."

Kennedy yanked out of his hold. Friction swelled between them, overflowing to the rest of the room.

"I am not yours, Jared. We've been through this," she said quietly, sitting up, her back straight. "I am not something you own. Especially now."

Like a switch, Jared's entire demeanor changed. He sat and leaned back on his hands; his aura filled with cocky aggression. "And how many times have I explained to you? I am Dark Dweller. You are mine. I claimed you. It's how we work."

Kennedy shot to her feet. "You seem to easily forget you are also part human. What is with you lately? You are trying so hard to be something you aren't." Arms folded, her gaze shifted to the floor. "I-I thought we could still be friends..." She pushed at the middle of her glasses, and with a big sigh, she returned her attention to Jared. "Yes, you are Dark Dweller, but you are also human. You used to be Jared, the boy I loved, which doesn't seem to be enough for you anymore."

"Funny, I seem to be the one who is not enough for *you* anymore." He got up, his shoulders tight and hunched. He moved over her, his words accusatory. "Plus, why the hell do I want to be 'just Jared'? It's weak and pathetic. Everyone treats me either like I am going to break or I'm stupid."

"I am human also. Would you say I'm weak or stupid?" Kennedy exclaimed. Her tiny figure did not cower under his looming body.

"No."

"Then why would you say those things? You are anything but them." Her brows wedged down, pinching the bridge of her nose.

Jared snorted. "Really? You of all people are asking me why? When you are the one who treats me the most like an idiot. You don't think I can see the truth, but I do. I am not blind." He stepped away, their gazes locking. Jared didn't elaborate, but at least three of us in the room knew what he meant. The whole room probably did.

Jared's face was tight, straining the skin across his forehead. He cocked his head to look around the room. "You are all about me accepting my human side. Then, fine. I am eighteen. An adult. I make my own choices."

"Jared, you lost a few years in the Otherworld. You are not emotionally eighteen yet." Owen pushed back his chair and rose.

Cole shoved his seat back. "I know you're upset with my decision, but I'd rather you hate me than get killed. We talked about it. I can't afford for you to be rash or reckless. Not with something this serious. You are young, and you think you're invincible." He got to his feet. "As much as you hate it, being half human does cause you to be more vulnerable. I will not risk losing you because you are careless and untrained for what lies ahead."

Dark Dwellers were never ones to coddle someone emotionally. They might try to keep Jared protected physically, but they were nothing but direct when it came to emotions.

Jared's chest filled with air. "You think I *want* to be half human? An embarrassment to the clan. I want to be full Dark Dweller, so I can be treated like one of you."

Owen's chair crashed to the floor as he charged around the table, propelling all of us to our feet. "Don't say that!" Owen growled, his voice deep, rumbling the room. In the time I had known Owen, I had never seen him lose his temper. You could almost forget he was a Dark Dweller. But now the beast was vivid in him. His pupils became diamond shaped, and his shoulders curled forward as he stomped to Jared. Muscles twitched under his skin, responding to his emotions. The beast wanted to come out. He stood a few inches taller than his son, and he used it to his full advantage. Jared retreated a few steps. "You are half your *mother*, one of the strongest people I have ever known. Do not be ashamed of what she was. Do not insult her memory."

Jared's nose flared, his jaw tightening. "But I've done all the training. I thought you'd change your mind when you saw how good I am. And I *am* good."

Owen lowered his head, and a shudder went through his body as he took a deep breath. The beast was being reigned back in. "You are. But it's not enough."

Jared's face turned a deep shade of red as his hands clenched tighter to his side.

"I lost your mother. I will not lose you, too." Owen whispered, veering back to the table.

A silence hushed over the room before Cole broke it.

"You are anything but an embarrassment to us. You are the glue keeping our family together. You are our life blood, and if anything happened to you..."

Jared's eyes filled with tears. He looked away. "You can't keep me in a bubble forever."

Cole let his head drop. "I know. But this is not the time. I would prefer if Kennedy stayed, too, but she has to go. She's vital piece in the war."

"Yeah, yeah. Not wanted." Jared shook his head and walked to the doorway. "Message received." His fist hit the wall as he stormed out, putting an exclamation mark on his departure. Jared's fury was not only about not fighting in the war. I didn't know for certain, but it seemed pretty obvious he and Kennedy had broken up, and Jared was not too happy about it.

Kennedy didn't move to follow him. She turned towards the glass doors leading to the outdoor patio, yanked them open, and disappeared into the darkness.

"What a total bumblebee kill." Cal sauntered across the table.

"Huh?" I replied.

West rolled his eyes. "*Buzz* kill, tinker-toy, as in inebriated. Not as in the sound a bee makes."

Both Simmons and Cal tilted their heads.

"Oh, yeah, I kinda wondered about that one." Cal put his hands on his hips.

West and Cooper were teaching slang to the pixies. The results were pretty humorous.

Cole placed his hands on the table and leaned into them. "Jared will eventually grow out of this stage." Cole nodded at Eli, Cooper, and Gabby. "I've been through this before with you three."

Eli nodded. "Yeah, we were probably even worse than him. It's a hard time for adolescent Dark Dwellers, but one that is also going through human puberty as well..."

"He's still mentally and physically fifteen, even if he wants to already be eighteen. He will eventually catch up with himself, when all the hormones even out. He will be fine." Owen clasped his hands together. I could feel him hinting at the end of the evening. Eli noticed it, too.

"All right." Eli moved away from his chair. "Think the party is over." He leaned into my ear, tension from the earlier scene taut in his vocals. "Except ours. Time to pay in full, Brycin."

Sleep was impossible as my brain ran through each scenario and everything that could go wrong in battle. I rolled over for the tenth time in fifteen minutes and punched my pillow before flopping my head back down. Eli's impending death ate at me. The thought of never waking up next to him or hearing his voice again made vomit burn my throat. To never feel the warmth of his body pressing against mine, how he slept with one hand always on me. A spasm clenched my lungs. The thought of being without him was too much, and every minute brought me closer to the moment I would have to act it out.

"Will you settle, woman?" His hand pressed on my leg, pushing me into the bed. I peered over my shoulder. Eli lay on his back next to me, staring at the ceiling.

"Sorry, am I keeping you up?"

"Wasn't sleeping." He shifted his head to look at me. "But you're driving me crazy tossing and turning."

I rolled over to watch him. "Sorry." My hand reached up to trace the scar that cut from his chin to his hairline, his scruff tickling my fingers. He closed his eyes, letting me touch the contours of his face. Tears blinded me as my fingers and eyes outlined every nuance of his features. My heart ached with my feelings for him. We had come so far, been through so much, and I could lose him in the next twenty-four hours. I choked back the wail wanting to surface.

"I love you." I was trying so hard not to cry I could barely get the words out.

His eyes opened—bright green lights in the dark room. His hand brushed back the loose strands of hair falling around my face, curving around my jaw. He pulled me to him, his lips finding mine.

"Ditto, Brycin," he muttered between kisses. He curved his arm around me, pulling my body to his. His arms felt so warm and protective. It made me both dizzy and sick to realize they would not be holding me after tomorrow. His lips moved lightly kissing my forehead.

"Whatever materializes tomorrow, you know I will always follow you, woman, wherever you go. Even in death."

My head jerked up looking at him. My throat felt clogged. Eli was not one for sentiment. He did not understand how ominous those words were. My lids blinked rapidly trying to keep the water works back. It didn't work.

"Nothing is going to happen to you." I felt the need to say the lie aloud, as though it might be possible. I had to believe, or I wouldn't get up in the morning and go into battle.

"You are strong and will turn out to be a great Queen."

"Why does everyone keep saying that? I don't want to be one." I shook my head.

"Hey." He grabbed my chin. "Sometimes we choose destiny and sometimes destiny chooses us. The day you came strolling into my life at the police station it picked me." A mischievous grin curled the side of his lip. "And I am glad since I was far too stubborn and stupid to see what was in front of me."

My feelings pushed me forward, my mouth finding his. I was out of words. He told me once the only way he wanted to die was to go out screwing me. For the rest of the night, I made sure his wish was satisfied in every possible way. We took our time, worshipping each other's bodies.

As though it were the last night of our lives.

TWENTY-SIX

Past midnight, Samhain

The night sky glowed with blues, yellows, purples, and reds. Magic's tango spun and swirled in the atmosphere, igniting sparks as our worlds collided. Thanks to me and Asim, the Queen's "extra" power was breaking down the lines further. Even humans would notice the changes. It looked like the northern lights had waltzed across our skies using Earth as their dance floor. Lightning cracked and ripped around the heavens in enraged bolts of energy and light.

The magic ebbed higher and larger, sizzling at my skin. The field of Dark Fae stood motionless, weapons in hand, waiting. Lars made sure we were in the right spot so the castle would not be far from us when the wall went down.

The day was tense and filled with restless energy. Waiting. Every minute was agony. I struggled between trying to enjoy the last minutes I had with loved ones to actually wanting the damn thing to start. Anything had to be better than waiting. With time differences across the world, the layer between the worlds began to come together early in the day. To humans it probably looked like dense humidity rippling the air, but I could feel the enchantment swelling in the atmosphere, pushing and wrinkling as it collided with the Earth. As the day went on, the more the sensation heightened.

Midnight was when the barrier would reach its weakest point. Magic pumped heavily through the air right before. At twelve, the sky exploded into an art show of lightning and colors.

I stood now in the cool darkness looking above my head as the Earth lit up as if fireworks were being tossed into the air. Deep in my soul an ache rolled around the vacancy where the core of my power had been. *Fire. Earth.*

Cal stood on my shoulder, tugging at the small bag attached to his belt. "You sure I can't have one lick of juniper juice powder? I think it might calm my nerves. I mean it might be my last one, ever. Do you want to deny me of what could be my final bit of happiness?"

"Cal, you cannot drink during battle." Simmons was perched on my other shoulder. His foot stomped onto my collar bone.

"Who says?" Cal snapped back. "Anyway, it's not technically drinking." His fingers poked at the contents inside the pouch.

"Because we are soldiers. We must have our full wits about us."

"Jumpin' juniper juice, *this* soldier has the wits to know he should be drunk."

My eyes were still locked on the colors tumbling around in the sky.

"Cal, I promise if we get through this, I will fill the gigantic pool at Lars's with juniper juice."

"Oh-oh, you have to get me real arm floaties and a lounge chair... and... and a curly straw. I always wanted one of those."

"Done and done." I smiled.

"My lady, you are only encouraging him." Simmons huffed next to me.

"I'll get you a floaties and curly straw, too."

There was a pause before he uttered, "I'd appreciate your gifts, my lady. Thank you."

My grin widened.

I detected Eli walking up behind me. He still could make my body tingle, although the reaction to my tattoo was almost gone. If I really allowed myself, I could ever so slightly feel it prickle in warning when he touched me. It would probably never truly go away. A reminder of the past, which was no longer a bad thing.

His fingers brushed mine. In my peripheral vision, I saw him next to me, looking at the sky. My fingers found his and curled around his large, warm hand. He grasped mine back. Eli turned his head to me. Lightning and the vibrant glow of the atmosphere reflected in his eyes. He didn't utter a word, but his strong presence was enough to calm me. It would be too hard to talk. To say all the things we left unsaid between us. I couldn't let my mind land on the idea I would lose him.

Cole stepped close and clasped Eli's shoulder. Eli glanced at him, and their eyes met. The love ran deeper than mere pack mentality. They were family and loyal brothers.

Another sharp crack ignited over us. In the light, an outline of a castle loomed in the distance, more than a half a dozen football fields away from us, perched on a hill surrounded mostly by water. The already fragile wall between the two worlds diffused and thinned even more. Aneira planned to shred the barrier so it could never return to normal. If we didn't stop her before the day was out, Earth's atmosphere would never be able to heal itself. The worlds would be fused for good. She had already broken holes in it when she destroyed Monterey, London, New York, and with my unwilling help, Seattle. Magic spilled over. No matter what happened, I doubted we Fae could hide our secrets any longer. All over the world, humans would experience and see things they could not explain with science. The panic of the masses would create a doomsday effect. And they wouldn't be wrong for reacting this way. I had to stop Aneira; her death was my destiny.

On the other side of the frail wall separating the two

worlds, thousands of Seelie soldiers and Light Fae stood dressed for battle. A rumble shook the ground as both sides pounded their weapons on the damp earth. Deep, guttural battle cries sent the hair on my arms and neck straight up.

"Crap on ash bark," I mumbled. Out of the corner of my eye, I saw Cal stick his fingers in the bag and lick them quickly. I couldn't blame him. My free hand stuffed into my pocket touching the cool metal of the goblin bracelet. It was an anchor, keeping me grounded in what I needed to do.

The level of energy emanating in the air between the two sides flowered in my chest. Terror like I had never experienced clapped down on my muscles. I had been nervous and scared before. But being here, seeing the other side with their weapons, feeling their desire to kill us made me want to run like hell. But the fear riding through my body weakened my muscles. I fought against the urge to fall to the ground, curl up, cover my head and hope no one would see me. I had seen these kinds of battle scenes in movies and always imagined what it would be like in real life. They didn't even come close. Death would find many of us today. Stealing us away from our loved ones and soaking the field with our blood.

An object flew over my head, and I spotted Lars on the back of Ori. The sleek, regal bird cut through the sky like a ballet dancer. Lars was dressed in full battle gear, and his commanding presence sent gasps through the crowd. The wall would be thin enough to walk through soon. The Unseelie King was here to rally his troops.

Lars held out his arms, and immediately everyone on our side hushed. "My fellow Dark, for too long we have been under Queen Aneira's control, suffering under the Light's prejudices and rules against us!" A wave of cheers and weapons being struck in agreement reverberated through my shoes, tingling my feet. "She wants to *enslave* or *kill* our energy source." Boos and hisses broke through the cheers. "She wants to see us destroyed!"

Lars's powerful voice thundered. I wanted to cheer and pound the ground along with everyone. "The Dark will no longer be controlled by the Light. This is our world, and she will not take away what belongs to us. Today we fight. For our lives, for our freedom, and for our world!"

The Dark exploded in united harmony of songs and battle cries that shook the lungs in my chest. The energy was addicting, pumping my adrenaline higher.

All we needed was Mel Gibson in Scottish attire on horseback.

Another fractured bolt ripped through the night and collided with part of the wall still up. The layer between worlds shriveled, curling in on itself and creating a gigantic hole like plastic wrap in fire. I could feel in my bones Aneira was breaking down the barrier with my powers. Anger and outrage filled me. It was my magic. She used *my* magic to control the worlds.

The ear-splitting sound of shrieks pummeled me, almost knocking me over. Both pixies went into the air, hollering. There was a rush towards the opening from both sides as Aneira sent one more blast of lightning and tearing another crack into the atmosphere.

Alki sounded the horn from the back of the bird-shifter, Deryn.

The war had begun.

Eli grabbed me by the collar of my jacket and tugged me into his body, aligning every part of us. His hand came up, cupping the back of my head, bringing me in. His lips crushed mine, and he kissed me so passionately and deeply everything around me disappeared. He pulled back abruptly, turning his body forward again. I wobbled at the intensity of both the kiss and the departure. Now, I was battle ready. Aneira would not take him away from me. No one would.

"Let's go kill the bitch," Eli declared. Lorcan, Eli, Cole, Owen were staying in man-shape while the rest of the Dark

Dwellers were going to be in beast form. It was easier for the non-Dwellers to communicate if some Dwellers could speak. But in case Eli had to shift, I had an extra set of clothes inside my tiny backpack attached to my sword sheath for when he needed to return to man-form. The Dwellers didn't seem to like the idea of parts of them so accessible to being stabbed or sliced off. I backed the sentiment heartily.

The Dark killers emerged, slick and black as night, and surrounded me. I knew without looking it was Cooper, West, and Gabby. My connection to the Dark Dwellers was burrowing so deeply in the fibers of my soul I could no longer imagine what it felt like to not be one of them. Without seeing, you could feel each one. Their individual presence crawled over you, declaring their voice. My connection to them had gone from a spindly rope bridge to a concrete, steel enforced roadway. I heard full conversations between them.

West bumped my leg, and our eyes met as I looked down at him. *I wish I could be the one to do it. When you kill her, make her feel the agony she inflicted on me and so many others.*

I nodded. *I will.*

West's eyes glowed red as he roared his own form of a battle cry and charged ahead. My skin prickled at the sound. It was the call for death.

The blade on my back whooshed as I drew it from its sheath. Cal and Simmons both drew their tiny swords, which was for show as their job had to do with juniper powder and getting us into the castle.

Kennedy stood behind me and also carried a pack and sword. Torin stayed to the side, Thara next to him. They were dressed like warriors: thick leather pants, impenetrable long-sleeved black shirts, with a silver-plated metal shield. These did not have the Queen's insignia, nor the King's. They were fighting for themselves and for all our freedoms. Their swords hung from their right hands.

"Kennedy, stay close to me." I gripped the handle of the

blade tighter. She also held a Fae gun. It was her best defense till it ran out of bullets. She could only carry one extra round as they were pure iron and extremely heavy. The girl was not built for battle. Her first weapon was her magic, but she could do nothing more than knock someone out for few moments. It would have to do. Behind her was Lorcan's group. As much as I disliked the thought, we were a united front today. Samantha sidled up to Lorcan. She and I would have our time, and one of us would be dead by the end of it. Her red eyes met mine, glinting brighter as she snarled. Her feelings for me were mutual. But right now was not the moment.

The echo of metal clashing, armor clanging, and people shouting dominated my senses. Lars led his troop from the sky. The Queen was nowhere to be found on the field, but she had to be there somewhere. She would want to be close but also in a space where she could safely use *my* magic to destroy the layer between the worlds.

"Let's move," Cole called out. "You know the plan. Let us see it through."

Holy crap! This was actually happening. My insides twisted into knots, and my shoes struck the dirt as I trotted with my group. The occasion we had schemed and trained for had arrived. There was no do-over. No trying again tomorrow. We had one chance to succeed... or fail.

Our group skirted the main battle trying to blend in while appearing to be part of the fight. Sounds of loud, bone chilling screams of pain, metal clanging, bones crunching into dust, screeching beasts on the field and in the air dominated the sky around the battlefield. There were hundreds of creatures before me, from the beautiful to the most hideous, slicing their blades across the others' throats. Trolls and goblins tore into willowy elf-looking Fae, who seemed like they came from a Disney movie. The odor of blood wafted up my nose.

I looked around at my strategic partners. Each pair had a different part of the plan to get Torin, Kennedy, Eli, and me inside the castle.

Glancing one more time at the daunting fortress looming over the land, where a prophecy stated I would be ruling from, I took a breath, sucked in my heartache and ran furiously for the fate that lay before us.

TWENTY-SEVEN

The swarm of soldiers crushing into our first line of attack came with the wet sound of blades slicing through bodies and the grinding of metal and bone. Flying shifters with riders on their backs dotted the sky. Birds and bats the size of vans circled overhead as arrows rained down from them. Breathtaking moths of creamy white and fuchsia alongside butterflies swirled with colors of cobalt blue, neon green, and vivid orange packed the sky. Even these goliath-size insects were killers. Their teeth, which could puncture holes in a car, surged from their mouth as they grabbed victims and bit into them, ripping off their heads.

Crap on ash bark. We were not in a sweet fairytale anymore. Okay, we never were.

Our group slipped around to the side, continuing to the far end of the field. Light Fae swinging swords and axes drove at us. Thara, Samantha, Dax, and Dominic sprung after them, keeping the path clear for us. Thara didn't hesitate as she plunged into the torrent of Light. I could see Torin wanted to join, but he kept running. Our destination remained in the distance.

Alki and Deryn swooped overhead, tailed by a huge moth-shifter. The bird-shifter was much bigger, but it only made him a larger target. The moth took flight above Alki and dive-bombed the back of the bird. Alki twisted and shoved his sword at the fanged moth. The blade came out the back of the insect's head. The thing chirped in anguish and tumbled on Alki, knocking him off Deryn. From way up in the sky, Alki's body plummeted to the earth below, the moth shadowing him to the ground.

Alki! The scream of Gabby's voice in my head rocketed my nerves and caused me to put my hands over my ears in defense. Her claws spit up the dirt as she spun, tearing across the field to where his body hit.

"Gabby!" Cole yelled after her, but it was useless. She didn't falter at her Alpha's voice. There was no stopping her from getting to Alki. Cole's eyes narrowed and concentrated on her; he was trying to communicate with her through their link before she blended with the shadows and disappeared.

Lightning shot across the pre-dawn sky, and the bolt collided with the Otherworld shield near us, knocking us to the ground. Electricity lit up and trailed over a portion of the invisible wall like veins, ripping a chasm into it. Magic poured out of the wound, invading Earth's air. A group of Light Fae headed for the opening.

"Come on." Eli clambered onto his feet, helping me scuttle away from our proximity to the sizzling wall and encroaching soldiers.

Hundreds of gnomes and wolf-shifters poured out. A single gnome was not a threat, but hundreds of them with weapons, moving with their stealthy speed, sent jolts of terror into my legs. Lars had taught me there were Light and Dark of every species. It was a choice.

"Run," Torin yelled at us.

Blood pumped frantically in my body. There were more attackers than we expected, and we couldn't outrun them, especially the wolves.

As the challengers came for us, West and Cooper turned to them, arching their spines as they growled. The blades on their backs reflected the colors running through the night sky. Without hesitation they dove for the foe, zeroing in on the biggest threat to us with the grace of an exquisite but raw ballet.

West and Cooper moved together with lithe beauty and slipped to the head wolf, tearing into him with a ruthless magnificence. It was brutal, chilling, and incredible to watch.

"Brycin, move," Eli yelled at me. I did as he said and bolted. We only made it down the hill before we spotted additional troops coming for us. More gnomes, wolves, and Light Fae swarmed at us from over the crest and one side. Dense forest lay on the opposite side.

"Shit." The only way we could proceed was through the forest. We couldn't let anyone see that we were trying to get in the castle through the sewer tunnels, or hundreds of creatures would follow us in.

Cole stopped and turned, waving us to keeping running. "Go. I will stall them."

My mouth opened to protest that he could not hold them all back, when a form darted through the brush, settling next to Cole. "I can help you, Uncle." Jared, dressed in cargo pants and a t-shirt, held a sword in his hands. Another knife hung from his waist, but he wore no protective vest or anything.

"Jared. No!" Both Kennedy and Owen screamed.

Cole turned to his nephew. "What are you doing here? Go back, Jared. It's too dangerous."

"This is my fight, too. I'm a Dark Dweller; let me act like one." Jared firmly stood his ground.

"No. This is not pretend. People are going to die, and I will not let you be one of them." Owen grabbed Jared's arm. With every second we stood there, our opponents gained ground on us.

Eli seized Jared. "Go! We can't worry about you, also."

Jared glanced back at Kennedy, his face flushing red. "Then *don't*! I can fight." His pupils elongated, his eyes burning fiery red, taking on some of the Dark Dweller appearance. His jaw clenched in a strong defiant line, trying to hide the true fear I saw in his eyes.

"Guys?" Kennedy nervously pointed ahead of us, the wolves and gnomes only yards away now.

It was too late for Jared to leave. He was in the battle now, whether we wanted him or not.

Owen pushed Jared toward Eli. "I will stay. You go with them."

Cole and Owen shifted into Dark Dweller form, ready for the attack. Jared rolled the handle of his blade between his fingers. Both excitement and fear shown in his eyes.

My head jerked around when I heard Torin bellow from the lead. He hopped back with his blade swinging. More soldiers of the Light crashed through the trees near us and blocked our path.

Cal and Simmons flew back toward me. "My lady, we are surrounded," Simmons announced.

"Crapping cupcakes, there is a mess of them coming our way." Cal yanked two swizzle swords from his belt.

I drew my blade; it zinged with anticipation of the fight. "Let's lessen their numbers, boys."

Kennedy turned, her eyes darting nervously from the group surrounding us to Jared.

"Kennedy, don't." Lorcan also clearly sensed the panic growing in her.

She held out her hands and muttered something. A compression of magic bowled out of her. Everyone in fifty-foot radius went tumbling to the ground.

Rocks hit my tailbone as I landed on my back. The yells and rustling of the other members of our group told me they also were trying to struggle to their feet. Kennedy's spell blew out of her like a sonic wave. It didn't discriminate. In trying to help us, she took all of us to the ground, which made us more vulnerable to attack. We scrambled quickly from the dirt.

"I'm so sorry. I was only trying to help." Kennedy put her hands to her mouth.

Lorcan widened his step, holding his sword. "Please, don't *help* again."

She looked at him, remorse in her expression, and nodded.

Roars from the opposing side blasted through my eardrums

and into my lungs. I sucked in a breath as the mass of fighters broke through our border, coming at us from all sides.

I swirled, slamming my blade into the metal of my challenger. My rapier sang with life, rushing with energy as it clashed once again. A beautiful, blond haired, blue-eyed Fay soldier stood across from me. His exquisite chiseled jaw held firm as he reared back and came swinging at me again. I ducked, feeling the rush of air zing a breath away from my scalp. He knew exactly who I was, and I could see the rage and disgust deep in his eyes every time his sword missed me. How proud he would feel if he could take my head back to the Queen. He must already taste the reward—the riches and fame he would have if he could only find a way to my neck.

My weapon would have none of this. It did not like the idea of losing. It sent a current of energy through my arm as I sliced up. The tip kicked at his armor. Light soldiers wore the uniforms I had seen on Torin when he was First Knight: leather pants and the thick long-sleeved black shirt with the Queen's insignia on the chest shield. Both the pants and shirt were thicker and harder to penetrate than they looked, making for great protection.

I danced around my enemy while grasping a quick overview of the scene around me. Lorcan and Eli stayed close to Jared, taking on the bigger fighters. Kennedy fired at anything coming near her. The sound of gunshots had long grown to white noise in my head. She'd reloaded already, so she would be out of ammunition soon. Torin and I, along with Cal and Simmons, covered the other side. We stayed in a circle formation, our backs to each other.

"Ha! Another baker's dozen." Jared bounced on the balls of feet, cutting down a stream of gnomes. The more he took down, the more animated and eager his movements became.

"Good, J, but don't get too cocky," Lorcan commented.

Jared declared over his shoulder, "Yeah, you're the one to teach me not to be an arrogant prick."

There was an almost inaudible scoff from Eli as his half-formed, clawed hands sliced through a Fay guard and threw the body aside.

The Fay I was fighting slipped on the blood drenching the soil underneath our feet. He stumbled into me, both of us falling to the ground. I knew if he fell on top of me, I was done. My Dark Dweller kicked in, and I went into a low crouch with my shoulders hunched close to my ears ready to attack. I snarled and flung myself to the side and rolled before his body landed on mine. His face hit the damp earth, and I leaped on his back, my teeth snapping as primal instinct took over. The world disappeared around me.

Kill. Mine.

My teeth went for his throat, tearing into the soft flesh. He wiggled violently under my hold. Fight seeped from his body before he stilled.

"Ember!" A voice rattled into my head, but I paid it no heed, still locked on my kill.

Gunfire rang out close to my ear before a body collapsed on me, breaking me out of my zone. The sharp smell of blood and the cacophony of screeching bird-shifters, battle cries, and the clanging of swords as people fought flooded my senses. I twisted to see Kennedy standing near me, her gun still smoking. The soldier who rolled off me onto the ground still held the sword he had been ready to swing down.

My eyes widened. *Holy shit.* My head had almost been cut off because I had let my Dark Dweller part take over. Very little gets in the way of breaking the contact. Their focus is why Dark Dwellers are good at being assassins but perhaps not perfect for war. Well, at least not me. I didn't have the years of training and learning to see and feel beyond my prey.

"Thank you." I jumped up, wiping the blood from my mouth.

She nodded, but her attention was centered behind me. I whipped around to see Cole and Owen heading down the hill, taking out creatures as they moved to us.

Cole, our Alpha, spoke through our link. *More Fay are coming, Eli. They carry spears and arrows. You need to go now.*

Cole and Owen got close enough so I could see their sleek black coats were soaked in blood. Wounds were entrenched deep into their bodies, legs, and faces.

"Dad!" Jared's attention dropped away from the fight as he spotted Owen's injured body.

"Jared!" Kennedy cried, pointing ahead of him. I followed Kennedy's finger. A man-creature two times the size of Rimmon hurtled from the trees, a giant axe descending on Jared.

A growl came from Owen's beast-form as he leaped, knocking Jared out of the way. The axe found its new target as it sunk deep into Owen's body. The blade of the axe burrowed into the dirt.

I screamed. Horror ripped its way through my heart as Owen's body fell on Jared's. The weight took Jared to the ground.

Everything happened in a split second. Cole's eyes flashed such deep burgundy they appeared almost black. His beast-form dove into the giant and slashed into his neck, tearing the head from the goliath with his teeth. He jumped off him, the blades on his back bristling. The giant's bloodied head fell to the dirt. Eli pulled Jared from under Owen. Jared struggled and fought against Eli, straining to go back for his father.

"Retreat," one of Light Fae soldiers yelled. The group of men, gnomes, and the three wolves that were left, fell back, running. Cole howled and rushed after them. His rage was thick in my thoughts. No words, just a red craze.

"We have to go. More men are coming." Torin spoke first, nodding to small figures in the distance heading for us. Soon the ones withdrawing would see they had reinforcements and come back for us. Cal and Simmons zipped to Torin, ready to head out.

Jared sobbed and clawed at Eli's shoulder, but Eli's face

stayed stone-like. "Jared, we have to go. We can't stay. Owen would not want you to."

"No," he wailed.

"Do it for your father. He did not save your life for you to forfeit yours." Eli gripped him harder. "I need you to stay alive, kid." Those words stilled him. Eli lowered Jared to the ground and hugged his nephew tightly. Kennedy stepped behind Jared and touched his elbow. He stiffened and wiped his face, erasing the signs he had been crying before he turned to her. He wasn't fooling anyone, but it was a Dweller trait—never show weakness.

Kennedy wrapped her arms around him and kissed his forehead. We gave them a moment. Eli and Lorcan both kneeled next to Owen's body, their heads bowed. I heard them mumble something before they stood. "Let's go," Eli said, his voice detached and bitter. Lorcan's expression mirrored Eli's. His jaw clenched tight and his eyes dead but determination set on his forehead.

I hadn't moved, still not believing what had happened. My brain and body were detached from each other. Owen, the doctor who saved my life, the man who was always so kind and caring, was dead. Until now, I didn't believe Dark Dwellers could actually die; they seemed invincible. The loss of him, of one of my family, was gut-wrenching. It felt like a bullet tore through my heart, taking a good chunk of it out. In that gaping hole was Owen. There would always be a piece of me missing.

TWENTY-EIGHT

Our dwindling group stepped into the forest, getting closer to the sewer tunnels. We slipped noiselessly through the undergrowth, every step taking us away from the battle. Our eyes were sharp and trained on any movement jostling the leaves. Jared was not as stealthy as the others. He sniffed loudly while his feet dragged through the brush.

Torin and the pixies scouted the way with the rest of us on their heels.

"Do you think anybody followed us?" I mouthed to Eli.

He held his finger to his lips, his head tilting to hear better.

"Let them come," Jared swung his sword in a slashing motion. "I will kill all of them."

"Jared." Kennedy touched his arm, as though to quiet him.

"Don't tell me to be quiet. I just lost my father. They. Killed. Him." He whirled on Kennedy, his anger shaking his body. "I'll tear them limb from limb!"

"Shhhh." Torin glared back over his shoulder at Jared as he cut a path through the foliage.

"Jared. Be quiet," Lorcan warned.

"Don't. Tell. Me. What. To. Do!" Jared screamed, his muscles twitching around his neck. "Why are you even here, Lorcan? You don't care about anything but yourself. Oh, except stealing my girlfriend. Or should I say ex-girlfriend."

"Jared, stop." Kennedy reached for him again. He ripped away from her, and she stumbled back.

"No, I will not stop it. I don't give a fuck about any of you right now! My dad was sliced in half in front of me." He held out his arms, waving his hands. Anger crawled up his neck, twisting his features. He was hurt and lashing out. "Come out, you fuckers. You want to kill us? Come get me!" Sadness filled his eyes while a deep frown etched his features. "He died trying to save me." He breathed in, his face burned red, and his veins struggled against the skin in rage. "And it's his own damn fault! It's all of your faults! If I had trained more, been treated as an equal, this never would have happened."

"Jared," Eli's voice sounded stern.

Jared leaped to Eli so fast and suddenly Eli flinched. "I was never good enough. You guys always thought of me as less than you, as your weakness."

"*Stop!*" Eli roared. "You are our weakness, but not in the way you think. You are the one we all love more than anything. We may have protected you too much because we could not fathom how we would carry on if something happened to you. You made our exile to Earth the best thing to happen to us. You were our glue when most of us wanted to kill each other. You are the reason we still try to be a family." Eli glanced at Lorcan.

Lorcan bowed his head in agreement. "He's right. I never stopped loving you, kid. Never."

Jared stood in shock, his head darting from one brother to the other.

Lorcan's and Eli's heads snapped around and cemented on a direct spot in the forest. Their demeanors altered, growls simmering from their throats.

"Get down!" Eli yelled. A high-pitched whistle struck the air. We barely had enough time to react when a spear shot through the trees. A triangular Fae-blade burst across the space and propelled straight into Jared's chest, nestling deeply. His body flew back. The long shaft broke through the other side of him mooring into a tree, pinning Jared's body with it. The throw was so firm and precise little blood splattered. Jared's eyes were open in horror. Life slipped from them fast, turning his hazel eyes vacant and hollow.

My throat burned with a guttural scream which tore from my lungs. Vomit filled my stomach, burning.

"Jared!" Eli bellowed as he sprinted to where Jared's body hung limply.

Oh, my god. This can't be happening. The shock of Owen's death still deadened my thoughts. Shouts and shrieks from both Lorcan and Kennedy filled my head, registering anguish beyond words. They ran to Jared. Devastation paralyzed me, keeping my legs from moving toward the group.

A handful of Seelie soldiers broke through the brush. Torin dashed back, leaping over the bushes, his sword clashed with the enemy, the two pixies flanking him. It took Eli and Lorcan longer than normal to respond to the threat.

Everything was happening so fast. My brain couldn't even comprehend my surroundings when a hand came around me and covered my mouth. Fingernails dug into my cheek and my hip. "If you make a sound, I will snap your neck right here," a familiar voice hissed in my ear. Samantha, back in her human form. "Now move."

Samantha? Why was she here? She should be fighting on the field. I didn't realize what was happening, my mind still firmly on Jared's limp body. Kennedy was on her knees next to him, sobbing. She did not notice Samantha's entry. The guys were too busy fighting their opponents to observe my abduction. My muffled scream went unnoticed. *Eli!* I tried to call through the link, but he did not respond, his attention still on the several Fae coming at him.

Pulling me away from the group, Samantha hauled me into a small stone maintenance shed and slammed the thick metal door. She slid a heavy bar across it and dropped the barrier into its holders with a sharp clank before turning to me. Rage and loathing distorted her features. "Jared is dead..." Her voice trembled. "I felt Owen die. Our connection abruptly ended. And

Dominic was slaughtered in front of me," she screamed, rubbing at her head like she was trying to scrub away the thought. "I lost three members of my family because of you. It's your fault!" Her eyes burned bright in the darkness. "Everything that has happened to my clan is your fault, and I am done with it." Her calm but seething tone snapped me out of my cocoon, which had sheltered me from feeling or realizing what was transpiring.

"What are you doing, Samantha?" I took a step back.

She snarled. "You think I want you to be Queen?"

Ice slipped down my throat into my lungs. "You're on Aneira's side?"

"I'm on *my* side." She stepped closer. "I don't want either of you. But for the time being, would I prefer to have her or some disgusting abomination sitting as a leader? That's a no-brainer." Her long red hair hung over her bare breasts. She looked like a battle-worn Venus de Milo, not a killer. "I would rather know you are dead and in little chunks sprinkled across the ground than allow you to become Queen. I should have killed you a long time ago... the moment you walked into Elighan's life and destroyed him."

Understanding settled over me like a gentle rain. Or maybe an acid rain. Her hatred for me stemmed back to Eli. She had always despised me, but I figured her abhorrence for Aneira overshadowed her hatred of me at least a bit. It didn't. She was acting against her own pack. She would be an outcast.

"You took everything from me," she spit. Her eyes burned with hatred, her face twisted with anger, and her teeth bared. "Since we were little, I was meant for Elighan. We were going to continue the pack line and become the Alphas. This was the life I was supposed to have. Eli was to be my husband. *Mine!* You took everything away from me. You stole my life, my future."

My jaw fell open. *What?* No one had told me about Samantha and Eli, though I had little doubt it was true. It made sense. She would have disliked any girl moving in on Eli but would have looked at the "Natashas" of the world with a wave of her hand, thinking he would outgrow them and eventually come back to her. I had ruined her plan. And to top it off, I was a Dae.

"Do you know how long I've wanted to kill you? All the ways I dreamed of hurting you? My favorite fantasy is the one in which Eli watches, finally seeing you for what you truly are."

Samantha's stability had always been off, but now the teeter-totter had tipped and fallen hard on the crazy side. "Why wait then?"

She tilted her head. "If I killed you before the war, I would have the Unseelie King and his band of idiots after me. Doing it here and now will appear like you are another casualty of war. A lot of people are going to die today. And one of those will be you."

The most frightening thing of all was how sane she sounded. Inch by inch, I moved back. It would not be a fair fight. Without my powers, I would be dead in minutes. And it would only last that long because she'd want to play with me first. My Dark Dweller could not fight hers.

But it would try. I gripped hilt of the saber tighter.

She smiled, baring her teeth. "You ready to die, Dae? Because I'm ready to kill you. You can join your useless human friend I killed."

My teeth clenched, and I snarled. Her back curved, her body shifting into a deadly beast. Red eyes met mine as her claws swung for my body. I ducked and twirled, wielding my blade. Samantha's nails clipped my sword, and her teeth snapped at my arm.

Her body rolled gracefully onto the floor before she sprang and came for my throat. My sword slashed at her, but she zipped past, my blade missing her completely. Eli had warned me long ago Samantha was skillful fighter. Even if I had my magic, I was out of my league.

Sam barked a laugh as she swung around, her claws

lashing out for my thighs. I jumped back, hitting the wall. In the small space, I found it hard to protect myself properly. She lunged for my legs. I dove over her, spinning to land on my back, my sword pointing in her direction.

Coming up short, my shoulder hit the rickety wood floor. Pain shot up my arm. The sword fell from my hand, clanking loudly on the boards. Her back leg kicked at my face. Ducking my head under my arm, my side took the brunt of her kick. Nails sliced through my jacket, digging into my arm. I screamed. Samantha wheeled her sleek body to face me. Pushing through the pain, I grabbed my sword and scrambled to my feet.

She stepped closer and batted at me with her claws playing with me like a mouse. Blood dripped onto my hand as I tried to lift the sword. The blade slipped out of my wet fingers, hit the floor, and skidded across the space. In that instant her beast-weight knocked me down. Her body shifted on top of mine, and her human body now pinned mine.

"I wanted to take my time killing you, but sadly I do not have the luxury." Her hand hadn't fully changed back—it bore one deadly, shiny beast claw, which dug into my throat. "I need you to look at me when you die. To know I won. Someday Elighan will get over you, and he will find his way back to me and to what we were supposed to have. I want you to know in the end it will be my name he'll be screaming out."

"If he's screaming out your name, it will be to get your attention before he kills you." I needed to keep her talking while my hand bent toward my foot. "Eli has always had better taste than choosing you. How awful do you have to be if he'd prefer to screw a Dae than be with you?"

Sam's eyes flared a deeper red, and a rumble rolled up from her stomach. She pulled my head up and banged it on the worn wood. Spurts of light exploded across my vision. Her clawed fist smashed into my cheek, and pain exploded into my eye and head. "You really think angering me is wise?"

Almost there. I stretched my arm farther.

"I am going to die anyway." I scoffed. I could feel blood coating my teeth. "Might as well piss you off while I do it."

"Ember?" The door rattled as Eli pounded on it. "Samantha, stop. You do not want to do this." Eli couldn't see us, but he could smell and sense us both, especially my blood.

Samantha snarled toward the entry, then roared. Eli had upped her need to kill me. She shifted to Dark Dweller again, nose and mouth protruded, fangs dripping with need for retaliation. "I am going to enjoy this. Your time to die, Dae."

Eli's body slammed against the door over and over, as he tried to break in.

My hand grappled for the edge of my boot. *Come on. Get it!* I screamed in my head as her teeth reached the artery in my neck, crunching down. Pain slashed in my body, immobilizing me. Blood sprayed from my throat across her face causing her to yip with excitement. Sam drew her head back, her mouth covered with my blood, her eyes burning deep red. This would be how I die? By Samantha? No. Freaking. Way.

My arm shook, weak with trauma and blood loss, but stretched farther toward my foot. Her daggered mouth opened snapping eagerly for the other side of my throat. Drips of saliva dripped onto my skin. Her mouth hot and inches from the artery she zeroed on. Spots blurred my vision, and with agony I pushed hand toward my leg with everything I had. My fingers curled around the hilt of the small dagger tucked in the side of my boot, the Fae-welded one Eli gave me for my birthday. I clenched desperately to the knife and swung my arm up, aiming for her heart. The blade plunged deep into her back, through her heart.

Her head lurched back, and a nerve chilling wail arose from the depths of her body. I twisted the blade deeper. Samantha's eyes went wide, turning back to blue. Her face and hands became human. Loathing emanated from the depths of her eyes. Blood trickled down on me from her mouth as she still tried to fight.

"It's not my time yet. But it's definitely yours," I sneered, and I could feel my face contort in revulsion.

Her body slipped off mine, and I pushed myself up and whispered into her ear. "That is for Ian. And as you die, know not only will I become Queen but a Dae got the better of you—in every way, you psychotic bitch." I hissed. "Also, Eli gave me the blade that killed you. Call it poetic justice."

Samantha lay there, blood pouring out of her and into the cracks of the floor. Her lips moved and faintly, and I caught the word, "whore," before she stilled for good.

"Been called worse." I pushed the rest of her off me. I crawled to my feet and wobbled from my own blood loss. If I had my powers, I would have been healing already. At least the Dark Dweller in me slowed the leakage.

I leaned over her and tugged my blade from her back with a slick, sucking sound. Using a piece of my torn shirt, I wiped off the steel and stuck it back into my boot.

"Ember," Eli's voice hit the wood along with his body. The metal from the broken door clattered throughout the room.

I scrambled to the opening, unhitching the bar. As the door swung open. Eli barreled into the room and stopped short. His eyes went from me, to the body on the floor, back to me again, landing on my neck. "Are you all right?"

"I'm not dead."

He frowned and came to me; his arms pulled me into him. His hand going to the seeping wound on my neck. "I am so sorry. If I'd known what she was doing..."

"It's no one's fault." I pressed my cheek against his chest. "Our time was a long time coming. I'm glad it's finally over."

The shock of killing her kept me numb. Someday it might hit me, or maybe it never would. I did not feel joy or sadness, only relief I had survived.

"I am so sorry about Jared." I bit on my lip, keeping the tears at bay. There would be a time to mourn.

Heart wrenching sadness carved into Eli's expression. His larynx bobbed as he swallowed back emotion. He kissed my head and squeezed me tighter. Besides Jared's death, I knew Samantha's hurt him more than he let on. For all her bad qualities, Samantha was still his clan. Like Torin for me, she had been destined for Eli, but fate stepped in and changed the path. Similar to Torin, she did not handle the change in plans well.

Eli's and my life together would never have been the easy one, but it certainly would have been the right one. Now because of Aneira's oath, we would never have a chance to see it through.

"We have to go. Kennedy, the pixies, and Torin are waiting for us down in the tunnel. Lorcan is going to stand guard and make sure no one follows us."

"What about the men who killed Jared?"

Muscles in Eli's jaw twitched. "Taken care of."

I nodded against his shirt and stepped away. Turning, I looked back and saw him squat next to Samantha. He leaned over, closed her eyes with his fingers, and gently touched her face. His eyes closed briefly before he stood and followed me out of the room.

Lorcan stood at the opening of the tunnels waiting for us, his posture tall and erect. The mold of his mouth strained. He looked to be struggling to hold back emotion. Sam mentioned earlier she had felt Owen's death. No doubt Lorcan had experienced Samantha's. She was one of his pack mates. The Alpha of the group connected stronger to everyone is his group. His link to her died the moment she did.

"I am sorry, brother." Eli's voice sounded solemn, but his body stayed rigid, his muscles primed to react to whatever Lorcan would hurl our way. Lorcan did not move to attack. His agitation did not seem to be directed at us.

Lorcan massaged the back of his neck, looking at the ground. He slugged in a deep gulf of air. "I should have seen it coming." His voice wobbled with anger and grief. "It was Samantha's decision, not yours. A true Alpha would know what was going on with his clan. Samantha was always emotional and unpredictable, but in the end, my ego held no doubt she would follow my orders. That is my failing."

My mouth gapped at Lorcan. He actually sounded remorseful. What the hell happened to the ruthless, arrogant prick I had come to know?

"Lorcan—"

He held up his hand, cutting me off. "You did what you had to do, Ember." He rubbed his palm roughly over his face, when his eyes found mine, they were back to the emotionless, cold state. "Now we each have killed someone we loved. One of our family members."

I sucked in a sharp gasp. The bullet of realization to my chest felt acute.

"You guys need to get going. We don't have time for talking." Lorcan waved to the tunnel.

Eli nodded, grabbed my hand, and took a step to the entrance.

"Good luck, brother." Lorcan's voice sounded unemotional, but his eyes carried deep concern. For the first time, I could see the affection Lorcan felt for his little brother.

Eli paused before pulling Lorcan into a hug, pounding his back. It was a manly hug, but I could feel the love between them. Losing Jared and Owen changed my perspective, too. My abhorrence for Lorcan softened. Hate drained me and kept me from seeing what was truly important—family. Although I would never forget, I needed to move pass it.

The men broke apart. Eli pressed his hand to my lower back, herding me into the tunnel.

Lorcan gave me a deep nod. "Stay safe, Ember."

My foot stumbled, and my head jerked toward him. We held each other's gaze, and something I couldn't explain passed between us. Maybe it was understanding. Maybe it was forgiveness. I didn't know, but something had changed.

"You, too, Lorcan."

We would never be friends, but he was the brother of the man I loved and a fellow Dark Dweller. In some way, he would forever be connected to me.

TWENTY-NINE

Eli and I left Lorcan and made our way into the channel. We jogged the long corridor with the sound of our feet reverberating in unison off the walls.

"My lady, are you all right?" Simmons and Cal both winged to me as soon as they saw us.

"Yes. I'm fine." I grabbed Simmons as he tried to land and placed him on my shoulder.

Cal settled himself on my other side, touching the blood crusting around the tear in my neck. "I can't leave you for a moment, can I?"

The moment we rounded the corner, Torin snapped, "Where have you guys been?" He stood with a stiff-back, arms akimbo, and eyes narrowed to crinkled slits.

"Sorry," I snapped back. "I was trying not to become a meal of vengeance served with a side of abhorrence."

Torin silently narrowed his gaze on me, then turned his back to us.

Kennedy sat on the ground next to Torin's feet. Her arms wrapped around her legs, while she rocked. Dried tears lined her face as she stared off into space. I knelt and folded my arms around her. She stayed nonresponsive, her body in shock. I touched her face. I could say nothing to take her pain away. Ken's gaze drifted to me, empty. It made my heart clench. She gave me a small nod and took my hand. I helped her to her feet.

I know we both wanted to curl in a ball and say screw the war. But we would have to grieve later. Kennedy's will and strength continued to amaze me. It took extraordinary strength to keep going. It was something I understood well.

I pulled out a light from of my backpack to illuminate our way as we traveled through the tunnels.

Torin felt the walls as we walked. After a short time of moving through, he stopped. "Here." A castle with secret passageways didn't surprise me. I had a feeling this place was full of them. His hand pressed at different spots in the wall, but nothing happened. "Dammit. She's blocked me from entering the passages."

"What do we do?" Kennedy's voice rose in frustration.

"Find another way in." Eli peered down the dark hall.

Torin twisted to stare at Eli. "Another path? We don't have time to find another way."

"What do you expect us to do? Stand here and wait for it to open? Sorry, but I forgot my garage door opener." Eli shifted closer to Torin, getting in his face.

"What is *your* great plan?" Torin stepped to Eli.

"Stop it, both of you." I tugged at their arms, trying to get them to back down. "We don't have time for the testosterone crap."

"No. You don't." A voice came from the other side of the door as it swung in, opening.

Fear hardened the air in my lungs. I recognized the voice instantly. "Josh?" I spun and faced the figure.

"You seem surprised." Josh tilted his head. He stood there, dressed in the outfit of the First Knight: black leather pants and a long-shelved shirt covered with the crest of the Queen. He was even taller and more filled out than the last time I saw him. He kept his eyes locked on me. "You actually thought I'd turn my back on the only person who ever cared about me? I'd actually fallen for the Queen's tricks and wasn't the one playing her like a fiddle?"

My mouth went slack, eyes wide, as I continued to stare at him.

Josh shifted his feet. "I know you don't trust me, but I swear I never planned to betray you."

"You're right. I don't believe a word coming out of your mouth." Eli stepped closer to Josh, his chest extended, using his height difference to loom over Josh. "How do we know it's not a trap?"

Josh's lips clenched tighter together, and he threw back his head to look at Eli. He kept his eyes steady on Eli's. "You don't. Except for my word." He swung again to me. "Ember, you know me. I mean really know me. *Believe* me. I am on your side."

"You turned me and the sword over to the Queen." I shook my head. "How can I possibly trust you?"

"I had to. She watched my every move. I needed to make her believe I was faithful." Josh went to step around Eli, but Eli blocked his path to me again. "Believe me!"

I hesitated, wanting to believe his words, but I had been burned too many times before.

"I'll admit, I fell for the idea of her and what she could offer me at first, but what she did to you is when I saw her for what she truly is." Josh nodded to Torin. "I could easily be the next guy she tortured. But by then it was too late. She was in my head." He brushed absently at his temple. "I had to do what she wanted, or we would all be dead. But I swear to you, Em. I always planned to backstab her in the end."

"He's telling the truth," Kennedy spoke from behind me. I twisted to look at Kennedy, her lids closed. *"The false Knight will guide the way."*

Why does this phrase sound so familiar? I faced Josh again and looked deep into his eyes, now seeing the certainty written deep in them. My brain spun in a whirlpool of confusion and questions before it bottomed out, pouring the answers down on me. I was probably doing the stupidest thing, but my gut told me I was right.

My lips quirked up. "It's about freakin' time you got on the right side, Josh. We have so much to talk about, but right now we are kind of in a hurry here."

Josh tilted his head at me, his jaw dropping. "Me? I've been standing here waiting for you. Do you know what it took to slip away from 'my men' unquestioned? At least Aneira is too distracted by Lars and the battle to be in my head."

"Wait. What?" Eli's protest fell on my ears, but I ignored him as I ploughed into Josh.

My arms wrapped around him as I choked out a sob. "I knew it."

"I am so sorry, Em. It was necessary. She was in my mind every single second, compelling and threatening me. I had to play like I actually was betraying you. She needed to believe she had me completely under her spell." He stroked my hair. "I didn't know she would be in Greece. I freaked out, and in overplaying it, I almost got us killed."

"Are you fuckin' kidding me, Brycin?" Eli interrupted. He threw out his arms, his gaze going to me then Josh. "Whatever Kennedy says, are you are actually going to trust him? Are you insane?"

"Yeah. I guess I am." I stepped out of Josh's embrace and swiveled my neck to look at Eli. "I believe him. And I need you to have faith in me."

Eli's head slanted to the side, his jaw moving back and forth, grinding his teeth.

"What other choice do we have?" I pleaded with Eli. He kept his attention fixed on my face before his shoulders sagged.

"Fine." He said to me, then turned to Josh. "But if you betray us, I will tear you to pieces before you can even blink. Do you get me?"

Josh's Adam's apple bobbed before he nodded. "Yes. I understand."

Eli gave a slight nod back.

I faced Josh. "You're all right, though? She didn't hurt you or anything?"

"I'm all right." He looked down. There was heaviness behind his words. I couldn't think about what he meant by "all right" or what Aneira might have done to him. It would have to wait. "She has no clue I've been tricking her the whole time. She never doubted for a second I was some dumb, gullible human who fell for her hook, line, and sinker. She let me overhear things... like where the sword was kept."

"How'd you know we would be here?" I pulled out of his arms.

"Let's say a little birdie told me."

"Grimmel?"

"Is that the crazy raven's name?"

I nodded.

"He would come to my window every night and jabber nonsense. I even dreamed about him, and every time he would lead me down here, saying 'I see you, false knight. You help fire flame.'"

"False is the night that will light your way." Grimmel's ambiguous words came back to me. *Oh, holy crap. He meant knight, not night.* He had been intimating Josh's true intentions and hinting he would be the one to help us get through the passages and into the sword room.

I pulled Josh to me again. "You don't know how happy I am to see you. I have missed you so much."

"I have missed you, too." Josh's arms wrapped tighter around me. "You are the only one, besides Mrs. Sanchez, who ever really cared about me."

"All right, all right." Eli nudged us. "We have to go before all of Josh's acting skills are for naught."

"Don't forget, Dragen, who saved your ass," Josh declared over his shoulder as he stepped away from me. "I even fooled you. Double crossed the double crosser. You can't say you aren't impressed?"

Eli glowered at him.

Not being totally blinded, a part of me also understood

Josh didn't do it entirely for me. He still had a "human" complex, and there was some part of him getting off because he had tricked all of us. A human out-fooled the most notorious tricksters, the Fae.

Right then, I didn't care. He was here, and that's what mattered. Josh grabbed my hand as we headed down the tunnel. "Sorry about having to pull a knife on you in the cave and handing the sword over to her. She was watching. I had no choice."

I nodded. "Not happy about it, but I see it now. I could handle the blade to the jugular, but the drop in the cave? Never going to forgive you for the free fall."

"Yeah, because I planned almost dying." Josh rolled his eyes and waved us forward. "It should be pretty clear, her majesty only left two men guarding the room." He instantly grimaced. "Sorry, I've had to say 'majesty' so much, it's hard to stop."

"Cal, you and Simmons are on." I nodded toward the pouches around their waists. "It's bedtime for some guards."

"Aye, my lady." Simmons flew ahead.

Cal frowned, staring at the contents. "I am so sorry, my love. You being misused like this is wrong. Please forgive the violation I am about to commit."

"Cal," I warned.

"Yeah, yeah, girlie. Clamp those britches between your cheeks. I am going," Cal snipped, before heading after Simmons. They disappeared into the darkness, which swallowed the path in front of us.

Kennedy, Torin, Eli, Josh, and I trotted down the path with only the light from Kennedy's and my tiny flashlights leading us.

"Here," Torin suddenly called. All of us halted at the space. A vague outline of a door interrupted the seamless stone wall.

"Crack it, so they can get in and out." I pointed to the

pixies hovering at the gap.

"Yes, let the little pixies out so they won't pee on the carpet." Cal huffed.

"Someone is bitter," I chided. "Fine. One lick before you go."

Cal's face beamed as he licked his entire hand and stuffed it into the bag. It came out caked in powder.

"Cal," I placed my hand on my forehead. "Not quite what I meant."

"To be fair, you said one lick. You didn't specify how many fingers he could use. His tongue has yet to leave his hand." Eli shrugged.

"Yeah, I walked into that one." I rubbed my temple and nodded to the opening. "Do it now before he gets tipsy... tipsier."

Torin stepped back, letting Josh take over. Only the First Knight had access to the doors. Josh shoved at a protruding chunk in the stone. The wall shifted, revealing another swinging door. He carefully nudged it and opened it a sliver.

"I am counting on you guys. Okay, mostly Simmons." I glowered as Cal finally rolled his tongue back into his mouth and hiccupped.

"I will not fail you, my lady." Simmons saluted me before darting into the gap.

Cal went to the aperture, dropped his pants, and mooned us before he flew out.

"I am sure in some cultures showing your naked butt is a sign of respect," Eli said with a grin.

"Yeah, yours." I bumped his shoulder. Torin exhaled deeply, his head falling back with annoyance. I pinned my lips together, looking away from Eli. I didn't need a connection to Torin to see his distress and irritation with Eli and me.

We waited a few minutes, giving Cal and Simmons time. Torin bounced on the balls of his feet, eager to move. "I think it's been enough time. Let's go." He barely finished his sentence before he was sliding through the door.

"I'm getting the distinct impression he doesn't enjoy my company much." Eli smirked before he slipped through the opening. The rest of us followed, silently sneaking into the room. It was a large space with several hallways leading off. Seeing the small windows at the top and smelling the dank odor, I knew we were at dungeon level. But rugs and tapestries covered the walls of the space. Nothing like the actual dungeon.

Josh pointed to the nearest hallway. "This way."

"No. This way." Torin headed for one of the antechambers. We paused. Eli turned and followed Torin.

"Sorry, Josh. Torin was raised here." I trusted Torin's knowledge of the castle more than Josh's. Josh grudgingly trailed the rest of us down the corridor.

The moment I saw the large wooden doors at the end, my instincts launched warnings: my skin tingled and my heart picked up pace. There were no guards and no Simmons or Cal.

"Guys, what...?" I trailed off as Eli spun around, his harsh growl shuddering off the rock walls, his focus on the shadows. The sound of Torin's blade being unsheathed raised my flesh.

"You shouldn't send pixies to do a man's job." A deep, velvety male voice spoke, his outline appearing out of the gloom. The closer he stepped, the more I could see he had something clutched in his fist.

"Cal!" I rushed forward. Eli grabbed my arm, pulling me back. Cal lay limp in the guard's hand. "What did you do to him?"

"He got a taste of his own medicine." The man chuckled. "A lot of it. Poured it down his little bitty throat until he gagged."

I could feel rage igniting my chest. Cal's chest moved slowly. He was still breathing. The juniper plant dust put Fay to sleep and got pixies drunk, but how much of the compressed substance could a pixie handle? When the lamprog attacked us, Cal's metabolism could only burn off so much. He could die of an overdose. Eli gripped me tighter, feeling my need to take the guard down and grab Cal. Where was Simmons?

"Let him go, Quilliam." Torin pointed his blade at the man.

Quilliam? The name sounded familiar. Then a memory of slamming this man's nose under my palm darted into my mind. He'd been a casualty of me trying to sneak into the castle the first time. His hateful glare told me he remembered me clearly.

"I don't think so, Torin. This guy seems strangely important to you. How many times did I beat you at cards? You know I don't give up a good hand." Quilliam stuffed Cal into his pocket and patted it. "I'll keep him safe, right here."

"You play cards the same way, by slipping some in your sleeves and pockets to cheat with later." The muscles of Torin's jaw strained against his skin.

"You are such the hero, aren't you? You pick right and wrong, while I pick winning." Quilliam sneered. "I think the Queen will prefer my way."

"Speaking of Aneira." Eli's shoulders hunched as he scanned the room. "Where is your owner?"

"She is kicking the ass of the Unseelie King right now. Soon he will be dead and so will you."

Eli chuckled beside me. "You think you can take all of us?"

A handful of the Queen's men hustled in behind Quilliam. "I do." He nodded again. A yelp had me spinning around. A few guards had snuck behind us, seizing Josh.

Impulse moved me toward him. The guard holding Josh poked his blade into Josh's throat. My feet halted, glued to the ground.

"Quilliam. Let him go. The argument is between us." Torin challenged him and the guy holding Josh.

"You're right. My real hatred is at you," Quilliam snarled back.

A tight smile pulled up Torin's mouth, "Does having to play second fiddle still eat at you? Must have hurt when the

Queen passed over you again, especially for a human."

Quilliam's shoulders pulled tightly back. "At least I didn't disgrace myself for a Dae."

"Looks like your nose has healed." I tilted my head. "Though I have to say it looks crooked. Suits you."

Torin snorted and looked back at me. It was the first time I had seen humor in his eyes for a long time. Our eyes connected. Torin and I smiled at each other, the only two in the room, not counting Quilliam, who got the joke. Something flashed in Torin's eyes, but before I could decipher it, his gaze broke away from mine. He faced Quilliam, and his expression grew dark.

"You used to be something, Torin. You had everything. I looked up to you. Now you are nothing. And it seems you didn't even get the girl. So was *that thing* worth it?" Quilliam nodded toward me.

Eli immediately held me back, keeping me from charging the guy like a bull.

Torin gripped his sword tighter. "Yes."

Quilliam laughed. "Seems both First Knights have a weakness for Daes." Quilliam sauntered to Josh and grabbed his face with one hand. "This one should never have been the First Knight. A human. What a disgrace to us."

Josh gulped. He kept his chest up, a stoic front, but I could feel his terror like little darts shooting off him. Quilliam was a soldier through and through. He was raised to put himself in harm's way to protect his Queen. Josh had been a prop, and they all knew it.

Quilliam turned his head to Torin, pushing away from Josh. "Has this finally come down to you and me, Torin? Student versus teacher."

"You were never any good at listening or learning," Torin declared.

"Let's say the student knew he could outfight the teacher at an early age." Quilliam curled his fingers at Torin, beckoning him to move closer. "Come on, Captain, let's see who has the better skills."

"I am still the First Knight. Back down." Josh addressed the soldiers. "You have to obey me."

What is he doing?

Quilliam unhurriedly turned his back on Torin and stepped to Josh. "Do I?"

"Yes. It is Fay law. You obey your First Knight without question." Josh pushed strength into his words.

Quilliam stroked his nose, nodding. "You're right, I do." Without warning he pulled his sword and stabbed Josh through the throat. Blood sprayed back onto Quilliam's face. "Now you are no longer the First Knight."

"Josh!" A scream tore from my mouth as I watched my friend's eyes bulge, before his body realized what happened, and he fell to his knees. Eli caught me as my body wanted to collapse and move to Josh at the same time.

"You never really were. You were nothing to her and even less to us." Quilliam twisted his blade before yanking it out of Josh's neck. Bubbles of blood gurgled from the open wound. Josh twitched as he fell on his side. "The Queen was looking forward to killing you herself. She could not stand the sight of you, human. But she will have to forgive me. I couldn't bear listening to your irritating voice for one more moment." Quilliam kicked Josh's body. Josh struggled to breathe, gasping for air, as his life force flowed from his body. His gaze flitted across the room and landed on me. It was only a brief moment his eyes latched onto mine, full of fear and sadness. Then they glazed over.

Josh was dead.

THIRTY

My body shook. Eli held me close to him. He was the only thing keeping me from crawling to Josh. The boy who lay dead on the floor had been my first friend at Silverwood, gawky and funny, with a big heart. All his life, he had been betrayed and abused. All he wanted was for someone to love him and to be more than the nothing his father made him feel. He could have easily fallen for Aneira's words and falsehoods, but he came back to me. He had always been my friend, even when I no longer believed it. I hoped he knew he had been loved.

The scene in front of me blurred as tears filled my eyes. Quilliam and his men moved toward us. "Now it's your turn."

"Go, I've got it." Torin waved us toward the door. "I'll hold them off."

"What?" I shook my head. "We're not leaving you, Torin." There were eight of them and only one of him.

"He won't be alone." Simmons nosedived from the ceiling, where he had been lying in wait. "Go, my lady. Sir Torin and I will take care of them." Simmons drew his plastic sword and dove for a guard's eye. "No one messes with my friend!" I adored Simmons, but the help Torin needed went way beyond him.

"Elighan, get her out of here." Torin gave Eli a fierce look communicating more than I could decipher. Torin stepped up, going into battle mode. Eli hauled me and Kennedy toward the opening. It took me a moment to identify Torin's expression. He was sacrificing himself for us. For me.

"No! Eli, stop. We need to help him," I wailed. "He will die if we leave him." I thrashed against Eli. He prodded Kennedy through the door with him and me right behind. He slammed it after us, barricading it. "Eli! We can't leave them. There are too many guards. Torin and Simmons will die."

Eli gripped the sides of my face, forcing me to look at him. "It's his decision. Simmons', too. They are doing it so you can finish your quest and others may live. Torin understands your mission is bigger than his life."

My legs bowed as a silent sob cracked through my chest. I had lost three people I loved in a matter of an hour. Torin and Simmons would soon follow. And possibly Cal, if he wasn't already. And if I continued, I would lose one more. I couldn't do it. I wouldn't lose him, too.

Eli kept his arms wrapped around me, helping me stand. He enfolded me in his arms, giving me a moment to mourn.

I gathered all the strength I could, drawing from the sacrifices of my friend's deaths, and pushed back away from his chest. "Let's finish this." The girl who had come into the battle was never going to leave. Even if I lived, most of my heart would never go beyond the walls of this prison. It would stay, along with the ones who died here.

Eli clawed through several more locked doors, moving up a severe set of stairs. Eli's hand jutted out, halting us. He put his finger to his lips telling us to stay silent. This is when I caught the sound of soft snores coming from the landing above us. The three of us tiptoed to the corner.

Eli peeked around the wall then quickly pulled back. "Two guards. Asleep."

I sighed with relief. This must have been Simmons's doing.

We crept by them like wisps of fog in the night before we came to the room from my dream. Enchantment swirled around the three of us, crackling the air. In the middle of the room, the Sword of Light levitated, glowing and pulsating with a protection spell.

Kennedy stepped closer to it, and her hands felt the air. "I don't usually say this, but *fuck*."

I faltered at her language. I said the word all the time, but it felt wrong and frightening coming out of Kennedy's mouth.

"I'll second that." Eli stood on the other side of her.

"Yeah, but when she says it, I know we're screwed." I tried to laugh, but it came out more a whimper.

"The spell is quite powerful and complex." Kennedy's brows furrowed, and her hands shook. "The magic protecting it is beyond my capabilities. I don't know if I can break it."

"You have to," I pleaded. We could not get this far and lose so many people for nothing.

Fear consumed Kennedy's face and body. "What if I can't, Ember? What if we got all the way here, and I'm unable to break it?"

Eli's hands clamped on her arms and turned her to face him. "Jared believed in you, and I have faith in you, too." Kennedy's eyes were wide and dilated with panic. "Close your eyes and take a deep breath," he demanded. For a few agonizing seconds she stood staring, panting slightly, and I worried she had finally cracked and all was lost. But then, she took one solid inhale and nodded. He let her go and turned her toward the sword. "Ignore everything outside of you. Forget the room exists or anybody else is here. Only concentrate on what's in front of you. Feel the magic and let go. You can do it, Kennedy."

As if Eli worked a magic of his own, her shoulders relaxed as she inhaled. My skin itched as the magic heightened in the room. Kennedy's voice started low, but her chants filled the room, strong and determined.

It was like being back in the cave in Greece. The spell thickened around my windpipe, suffocating me. Heaviness pushed down on the room as her voice rose in volume. Spit shot out of Kennedy's mouth the deeper she fell into her magic. It grew around her, thrusting into the room and building up pressure. It felt like a noose strangling me. Sweat slid from

Kennedy's forehead, and her eyes clenched tightly.

Weight rammed on top of me, and my legs collapsed. A strangled cry broke free as another block of energy crushed me. Spots impeded my vision, and bile climbed up the back of my throat. Eli grunted as his own legs were brought to the ground. Kennedy was in a bubble. Wind I did not feel swirled her hair as her words became more feverish. She fought against the burden of the magic. Her mouth tightened the words pushing from her lips. Tears flowed freely from Kennedy's face, blood trickling out her nose. The incantation was killing her. I wanted to scream for her to stop, but the words could not travel to my mouth.

Then, I heard a pop. Like a joint being put back into its socket. A blood curdling scream coiled out of Kennedy before she dropped to the ground. The room's pressure dissipated. The glow around the sword dissipated. The protection spell was broken.

"Kennedy?" I scrambled on my hands and knees to where her white body lay crumpled on the floor. "Oh, God, no!" I pulled her head into my lap, leaning over her, listening. Nothing.

Eli was on her other side. "Kennedy, come on." He shook her. "Come on," he roared.

"No-no-no-no." My hands frantically pumped at her chest. If I had my powers, I could save her, pour my energy into her. I was helpless. "Eli, do something." I knew he couldn't do any more than I could, but my wild desperation did not care about logic.

He bent her head back and breathed into her mouth as I pumped at her chest. "Please, Ken, don't die. You can't leave, too."

The thought of losing both the people in the room stirred terror so deeply in me I could no longer even see or think. I was already lost to the agony. *No.* My heart could not take the pain.

"Stop!" Eli shoved my hands off Kennedy's chest. He bent over, his ear to her chest. His eyes closed, relief spreading over his features. "It's beating."

The sound that came from me was nowhere near human, but it was filled with relief. Her chest moved in weak, shallow breaths. She was alive, which was all I cared about. Eli stood. He gave me a moment before he spoke. "The Queen will be heading our way soon. She will know the spell has been broken. Kennedy almost died for this. It's now your turn to ensure today's sacrifices are worth it. Jared, Owen, and Josh's deaths can't be for nothing."

My feet pressed into the ground as I stood. Looking at the man in front of me almost had me collapsing again. I could not go through with it... to be without him.

"You better go grab the sword." Eli's eyes were bright and focused on me as he moved around Kennedy and stood before me.

I looked at him, then back at the sword. My head shook before I even thought of my answer. "I-I can't."

"Yes. You. Can."

"No! You don't understand."

"You don't think I know?" His voice rose, cutting me off. "I know what will happen to me if you do."

"Wha-what?" I sputtered. "How?"

"The 'lawn furniture' has exceptional hearing. I overheard you and Lars talking about it one night."

"That was a month ago. You've known the whole time?"

He grabbed my shoulders, peering at me. Through the sharp, hard gaze, I saw a slight softness. "My life isn't worth the millions of human and Fae lives lost if you don't. There is no option. You grab the fucking thing now." His expression turned fierce.

Anguish so deep tore through my heart and up my throat, blocking me from speaking. Only a guttural cry came out.

"Eli, I can't lose you. Not now."

He cupped the back of my head firmly forcing me to look at him. "It is not a multiple choice. You are picking up the sword. It's an order from your Alpha."

A tear slid down my cheek, my chest heaved and another noise erupted from me like a wounded animal. The fate of the entire world was riding on my shoulders. It was beyond fathomable. He was trying to make it easier for me by sacrificing himself and telling me I had no choice in the matter. But I did. I could choose him.

If the prophecy was right, I would kill the Queen and take her place. It was in my bloodline. Everything about it felt wrong, especially without him. I didn't want to become Queen. I didn't want to sit on a throne and give orders, not without him. I wanted to be out in the world, hunting the bad guy instead of sentencing them. Eli was supposed to be my future. My always. He was a part of me.

But fairness was something the Fae knew nothing about. It was not the cards dealt me. I knew what I had to do, but in this moment with the guy who I loved standing before me, heart beating, his body warm and alive beside me, I didn't think I could go through with it.

"Hey." He tugged at my hair, retaining my attention. "Can't you follow an order for once? The world kind of needs you now."

"But *I* need *you*."

His lips turned into a cocky smile. "Let's be honest, all you ever really wanted me for was my body and my peanut butter. Probably together. And don't deny most of the time you did want to kill me."

I tilted my head against his hand as I glowered at him

"Too soon?" He leaned in closer, that damn arrogant grin tugged his lip even higher.

"Yeah."

"Well..."

"Just shut up, Dragen," I mumbled, cutting him off. I went on my toes. My lips met his with an explosion of emotion. Raw desperation, pain, love, and anger delved deeper as our mouths tried to communicate every feeling. My hands went through his hair, pulling him to me. I didn't want to think this was the last time I was ever going to kiss or hold him. His lips ravaged mine, pulling and tugging with need. The taste of his mouth mixed in with the salt of my tears. We did not hold back. I could not get close enough to him. I wanted to crawl inside him and never come out again. The memory of our "almost" first kiss at the waterfall, and then our first real kiss in the forest infiltrated into my thoughts. We had been through so much together. If I had known then we had such little time together.

I clung to him harder. My tongue searching for his with a need so great it was agony. He held me with a deep desperation that set me on fire. We kissed with the awareness of knowing it would be our last.

He pulled away first, leaning his forehead into mine. "Now go save the world, woman."

I love you. My eyes transferred to his.

His bad-boy grin tugged the side of his mouth. *Love is not a substantial enough word for how I feel about you, Brycin. Never has been.*

My heart tore into small shards. Turning my head, I glanced at the sword. I couldn't look at him without losing it again.

THIRTY-ONE

"This is all so tragically romantic." The Queen's silky voice slithered through the room. I reeled at the sound, grabbing the sword off my back. She stood at the entrance. Bruises and cuts crossed her face, her leather pants and top ripped, her hair springing in wild coils around her shoulders.

Lars. He should be here by now. Where was he? Was he all right?

"I underestimated you, Ember. Actually, both of you. I thought you would choose him in the end. Love is supposed to be blind and selfish, and I hoped you would take after your mother and follow the same path. And I never thought a Dark Dweller would sacrifice himself for love." Tiny bells of laughter came from her throat.

"Funny, but when I think selfish and blind, I immediately think of you." My feet shifted into a fighter's stance, waiting for her to move.

"Blind? You are the one without any powers and still think you can kill me." Her smug smile filled her features. "I can destroy you right here, Ember, with your own magic."

I pressed my lips together and swallowed nervously but kept my gaze steady.

"And really... you already failed. Your King is not coming to save you. At this moment he is leading more of his men into death's hands. The barriers are coming down, and you can't stop it." She edged around us in a semi-circle, heading for the Sword of Light. She carried her own saber at her side. "Why do you continue to try?"

With every step, she blocked the sword from me. She still couldn't touch it, but she could stop me from getting to it. I needed to grab it before she moved in front of it.

Eli must have had the same thought because he leaned into my ear. "Go!" With that, his body shifted, his clothes tearing as his Dark Dweller burst forth. A roar powered from his throat as he leaped for the Queen. He was distracting her for me.

Ignoring the tearing pain in my heart, I sprinted for the sword. I had no time to think or hesitate. Eli could only deter her until I touched it. Then it was all me. I needed to be quick before she could react. I shut down and let the darkness come through. Aneira was the reason Eli would die tonight, the reason I would never lie next to him again or laugh at something he said or did.

He would not die in vain.

My fingers wrapped sturdily around the handle as I pulled it off the stand.

Then everything stopped.

The pain slammed into my hand and traveled up my arm. It felt like someone was pulling my veins out through my skin and then pouring acid into the open wounds. My breath caught in my throat. White light flashed, blinding my vision. A scream echoed off the walls. It sounded like my voice, but I couldn't tell if my mouth was open or not. My head slammed onto the hard floor, which was the only way I knew which way was up. The surface twitched and jolted underneath me, and saliva dribbled out the side of my mouth. I convulsed again, and my heart fluttered. *Too much... too much pain.* My body refused to stay awake. It grabbed my mind on the way, taking it into the deep protective cover of blackness.

When my lashes lifted, I blinked a few times, my brain trying to understand where I was.

"Did I not tell you it would cause pain if you touched the Sword of Light?" The Queen looked down at me. "I made sure the suffering would be so excruciating you would not be able to overcome it."

I did remember her warning, but I thought my anger and determination would push through it like in the movies. The agony crippled me. I still couldn't move; my muscles were locked with trauma.

I wanted to confront her, except my body had a different opinion. Grunting, I rolled into a ball on my side. My gaze hit on an object behind Aneira. Eli's naked, lifeless body sprawled in a heap. My heart squeezed so tightly it burned acid through my stomach, tears filling my eyes. The realization of what I did slammed back into me.

Eli was dead.

There were no words for the anguish I felt. The stubborn, sexy, pain-in-the-ass man was no longer. I might have saved him from a crueler fate at Aneira's hand, but the thought didn't help soothe my heart any. The thought of the world without an Eli Dragen was wrong. Knowing I would be without him caused sorrow so deep it took my breath away.

"It is not a multiple choice. You are doing it. It's an order from your Alpha... now go save the world, woman." His voice came back to me.

I could not let his sacrifice be for nothing.

The iron bracelet in my pocket pressed into my hip reminding me of her flaw. The effect of the metal on Aneira was my last hope. My hand shook and banged against my leg as I tried to reach into my pocket. The closer she was, the better the chance I had to get the bracelet on her.

"Such a silly, stupid girl. You are useless, and you have killed your lover for no reason. He's dead, the barrier between worlds has collapsed, and I am still alive." She sneered. There was wildness in her eyes, as if she had finally fallen over the line of reason. "I want to show you your failure before you die. You have lost everything, Ember." She yanked me to my feet, although my legs could not hold my weight and bowed underneath me. "Stand, you wretched girl." Aneira grabbed me by the back of my neck, a dagger digging into my side. "Walk."

When I didn't move, I could feel a pressure coming around me, controlling my muscles without my command. It was the same magic Lars could do. A Demon trait. She was using powers I had not mastered, even though they had been mine. Of course, Aneira had figured out how to use them for evil.

My legs transported me toward a covered window. She flicked the hand carrying the sword, and a gush of wind blew the shutters open. Colors and light filled the night sky. Rays of purple, blue, red, and orange sizzled through millions of holes in the atmosphere. Magic poured out the spaces, enveloping Earth's realm.

I took in the scene raging on the battlefield beyond the castle. Screams of agony and the crunching of metal echoed into my ears. A whimper rose in my throat and stuck there. I had this dream before I found out what I was. It felt so long ago now, but I remembered every detail of it.

Bodies lumped in piles across the burnt meadow. Ash and smoke hung heavy in the air. Blood soaked into the grass, dyeing it a rich shade of burgundy. The sight of carnage and the smell of charred flesh bore down on my stomach, making me retch. A stabbing pain sank into my heart. I was certain, without knowing why, I was responsible for the destruction in front of me.

Aneira had done it, but with my powers, which made me feel responsible. Torin warned me what those abilities were capable of. He wanted me to stop it from happening. But the dream, even slightly altered, had come true.

"Take a good look, Ember. See your failure." A smile

consumed her face, pride at what she had done. "The worlds are nearly one. Nothing you can do will stop it, and soon it will all be in my control. If the humans even survive, they will be mine, too."

"No," I whispered. It was too late—another disaster I could not stop. Earth was lost, being consumed by the Otherworld's magic. My insides rocked with the catastrophe I had allowed to happen. How did I ever think I could beat Aneira? A powerful Seelie Queen against a newly found Dae with no powers. I was a fool. We all had been. But Lars believed in me—everyone had faith in me. I had to keep fighting until my last breath. For them.

Aneira's knife dug farther into my side. "For too many centuries we have hidden like cowards. Now let the humans fear, let them cower, let them go into hiding."

What would happen to the world now? We had all lost so much today. I could not take back what was already done, but I could try to stop Aneira from ruling the new world.

My fingers had quieted, and I slipped them into my pocket. They wrapped around the cool metal. My teeth gritted in familiar anticipation of the pain of the iron. Of course it did not come.

"I knew Lars would try to make his way here. However, he has been detained. You have no one coming to rescue you." Aneira pinched the back of my neck and twisted my head to look to the far left. "I made sure he was kept busy while I dealt with you."

The sharp, familiar wails of Strighoul poured from the forest. I could not see faces, but I knew their movements and unmistakable shrilling cry. Hundreds of patchy bald heads swarmed in like ants, covering the field with thousands of deadly daggered teeth.

It would be a bloodbath, and the more they killed, the more power they would possess. They would be invincible. With dread, I watched the Strighoul move in on Lars's troops. My heart and breath froze in my chest as the groups collided.

"Mercenaries." Aneira clicked her tongue. "They do not have a side. Money is their true leader. Quite helpful in this case. As soon as the war is over, I will obliterate them all."

Then, something strange happened. The Strighoul stopped. Each one flipped around, standing next to the Dark Fae fighters, facing the Queen's men.

Neither of us needed to say a thing. The defiant act was enough. Vek and his men gave a big middle finger to the Queen, telling her where she could stuff her deal. I knew the Strighoul well enough to know they weren't suddenly being honorable or actually on the Dark Fae side. They were switching sides for themselves. They hated Aneira's control and wanted her dead.

Aneira's shoulders hunched as she watched the transgression take place, her eyes narrowing into glinting slits. A low vibrating snarl came from her throat. She looked down, her fists clenched; then she relaxed her hand. When her head lifted, there was an amused smile on her face. "As if I would trust a bunch of bottom feeders. They were merely a perk, but not anything I counted on." She held up her hand. "Discharge the Carrog."

Magic thumped over my skin as it whirled past me, heading for the forest. The thick haze of air rushed through the trees and up the mountain. A second after it disappeared over the hill, deep, booming roars reverberated off the cliffs.

What the hell?

In the far distance, clusters of trees fractured as dozens of huge creatures came down the mountain. I let out a gasp. The beings were so large they towered over the forest trees. They were as thick and tall as a city skyscraper. The heads looked like a cross between a man and bear. Their hairy bodies were more humanoid, but the legs and feet were pure beast. Three of their massive clawed toes faced front, while the other one was more to the side, like a bear's would be. Hair hung heavy off the back of their heads and down their backs in dreadlocks, which matched their long, knotted beards. The tops of their heads were bald. The creatures had large mouths with teeth like blocks. Good for crunching on hard objects, like trees and rocks—and bone. It reminded me of what humans described as giants or another version of trolls.

Hundreds of humongous beasts of varying heights and shades of brown tore paths through the forest heading for the field, for my friends and family. For Lars.

The Strighoul took off running, abandoning their battle against the Queen. Whatever was coming was not worth the fight to them. Honor and integrity were not something they cared about. The hyenas would wait for the others to kill and then come back for the leftovers.

"What are they?" My mouth fumbled with the words as it tried to work again.

"Those are Carrogs. Dumb as rocks, but they will do anything I tell them. Young versions not knowing any better have been seen by humans in different areas around the world. I think they have called them Giants or Bigfoot. I don't truly care. All I care is they are hard to kill, love to fight, and will destroy anyone in front of them."

"Even your own people?"

"War is sacrifice." She pressed her symbol of determination harder into my neck. "All the people you love will die today. Look on the field; look behind you. Most of them are already deceased. And those who have not run off yet will be dead shortly."

I tried to pull out of Aneira's hold but to no avail. Was total defeat how the story was supposed to end? You wished good would prevail and beat the bad. Except here there actually wasn't good or bad, and things certainly weren't fair.

As we continued to stand there, roots were ripped from the earth as the Carrogs tossed trees into the air, crushing bodies in their path. The Carrogs moved slowly, but every step rocked the ground. They held axes and sledgehammers, using them as clubs and baseball bats. A few looked like they were enjoying a round of golf, but instead of balls, they were driving bodies. Screams of death and anguish vibrated into my bones.

Had we lost? The world was destroyed, and soon I would join Eli on the floor. My lashes fluttered as I looked back at him. Numbness blanketed me. Everyone I loved was dead or soon would be, probably horrifically tortured before they gratefully let death take them. I started to envy Eli's quick demise. He would never see what became of the world or experience the torment Aneira would have inflicted on him.

Flapping at the window drew my gaze away from the battlefield and the magic bolting across the sky. "I am here, my lady." Simmons dove through the window, zooming past Aneira.

"Simmons, what are you doing? Get out of here."

"I am your faithful soldier. I will never leave you, my lady."

"Simmons, I order you!"

"Sorry, my lady. Sir Torin has requested my presence here no matter what your objections are."

"Torin?" I couldn't stop the question from coming out. The small bit of hope circled my chest and wanted to land.

"Alive, my lady. Calvin and he both send their apologies since they cannot attend the fight."

He meant they survived but were probably badly hurt. It was still a small bit of happiness. At least they lived. Hope crashed into me, giving me the will to fight. My legs took on more of my weight as I stood taller.

"This is all greatly amusing." Aneira let out a bell of laughter. "A pixie who thinks he can help you. So sweet."

Simmons pulled out his little sword, his eyes lowering in a glower.

"I've learned never to doubt what six inches can do," I said and threw myself back out of her grasp, landing hard on my behind.

Simmons dive-bombed Aneira, diverting her attention

while I pulled the bracelet out of my pocket and scrambled to my feet. Aneira swatted at the pixie, but he kept going at her, circling her head. This would probably be the only opportunity I had. I leaped for her. My legs, not ready for the sudden movement, collapsed under me. I went face first on the rigid floor; the goblin iron flew out of my hand and skated across the floor.

"Simmons!" I yelled and nodded toward the bracelet. He followed my line of sight and dove for the object. Aneira tried to snatch it but pulled back when she noticed what it was. Simmons grabbed it and went airborne.

"How's your iron immunity going, Aneira? How's the Dark Dweller trait helping you?" I pushed myself up. She had to be aware she still couldn't fight the metal. She didn't have any of the Dark Dweller in her. I did, and I could feel it coming to the surface. The sharpening of my vision told me my eyes had turned vertical. "The Dark Dweller never left me because it was given to me through blood. Something you can never have."

"I did wonder. I tried over and over thinking I only needed to work through it." A cruel smile twisted at her mouth. "I should have known the characteristics that slaughtered your mother would stay with you. You ungrateful, little wretch. Still bedding your mother's killer? She would love the respect you have shown her."

"You killed her, Aneira. The Dark Dwellers were only the instruments. You were the one who assassinated my mother. Your own sister."

The bulbs of fire in the room burst, flames flicking with her anger. "Shut up. She would not be dead if it were not for you," she screeched.

I could feel the air becoming denser. She would soon lose it, and I knew all too well what she was capable of if she did. "Simmons, now!"

Cole had told me the goblin word to lock the bracelet on her wrist. I needed to do it fast. Simmons threw me the band,

and he plunged for her eyes. I sprang for her wrists, the Dark Dweller in me giving me the energy and desire to tear her apart.

"No!" Aneira screamed, her hand aiming toward me. My body slammed into the wall, and my head cracked back, causing my vision to go fuzzy. I fell and slumped over. Blood trickled into my eyes, pooling on the floor.

Simmons yelled something and attacked her. She snatched him from the air. "Sub-fae should stick to what they are good at. Being extinct." The Queen threw Simmons to the floor and slammed her shoe on him, twisting the heel of her boot hard onto his tiny body. His wings tore in bits, trailing in arch away from his twisted body.

A scream bounded off the walls—mine. I clawed the stone floor trying to go to him, but I couldn't move my body.

"You're next." Aneira sauntered to where I lay and peered at me. She kicked at my hand, sending the iron skittering from my grasp. She stood watching me. "Your lying there is actually quite paradoxical." She leaned down, getting closer to my face. "I found my sister in the same position and watched her die as well."

I knew Aneira had planned Aisling's murder, but for her to have watched with pleasure showed me exactly how truly cold she was. Anger burned in my chest, and my lids narrowed on Aneira.

"Yes, she gave me the same look before she died. She thought she had outsmarted me, and she had won, even if it was got you out of the Otherworld before I could kill you. Well, Aisling, do you hear me? Your bastard daughter is following you to the dark pits of the underworld. You will finally have some time together." Her eyes scanned around wildly and seemed to be actually waiting for her sister to reply.

Aneira stared down, her eyes widened as she watched me. I felt she no longer saw me, but a ghost. "Aisling?" She jerked back, then shook her head, trying to clear out the haunting memories. She rocked back and forth on the balls of her feet.

Words I could not decipher rushed out of her mouth in garbled mumble. She looked like she had snapped.

Lars told me too much magic could turn someone insane, especially one with Dae powers. She had hers and mine. It was not natural for her body or mind to hold so much. A pure Fay could not handle a Dae's power for long. No other species could. We were designed to handle it better. But we even struggled with containing our magic, some Daes still went insane.

Aneira screamed at me. "Aisling, I know you can hear me. I won, little sister. You did well at trying to best me, but I prevailed. Daddy always said you were the smarter, stronger, more magic-filled one. It looks like he was wrong. I survived you all. And I even won against a prophecy. It was me at the end who outsmarted everyone."

A wave of dizziness enveloped me. My head felt thick and groggy. The blood loss pulled me toward unconsciousness. It seemed I was seeing Aneira through my mother's eyes. Aisling had expected her sister's betrayal. My heart felt heavy with sadness. "I loved you, Aneira. Even when you made it impossible." The words came out of my mouth, but I didn't remember thinking them.

What the hell?

Aneira stopped, and her huge eyes bore into me. "You betrayed me! You left me. You did not love me. You loved those Demons more," she ranted.

Whatever had come over me was gone and left behind a slight tingling in my back. Energy twitched through my tattoo. Heat ignited the curly ink marks, burning through my back, giving me strength. In my fuzzy brain, I knew beyond a doubt my mom had come to me. Aisling was the one who spoke. The strength came from her. My tattoo was her calling card, the thing she sent me in a dreamscape to protect myself. She wanted me to survive. To fight my enemy and get out safely.

Thank you, Mom.

I tried to lift my head, but an involuntary grunt fell from my lips.

Aneira shook her head, her violet-blue eyes sharpening on me. Her confusion was gone. She did not see my mother anymore; she saw me. Her grip tightened around the handle of her sword.

"I have been waiting for this day. It should have been you who died, not my sister," Aneira sneered. "I cannot believe she would betray me for a Demon and a bastard child. A DAE!"

I tried to lift my head again. It stayed long enough to get a better view of the room. The Sword of Light rested on the floor behind Aneira, near Eli's body. With every fiber or ounce of my energy, I would get to the sword. It was my fate, and I could not fail. But power slammed into my chest, knocking my head back. All my muscles locked under the Demon magic, holding me unmovable against the cold stones.

"You will not be leaving here. Alive anyway," she howled.

One single tear leaked from my eye. It angered me. I would not die crying like a baby.

Eli's words came back to haunt me. *We are in this together. No matter the outcome.* Yes, both of us would die in here. Very *Romeo and Juliet* of us to perish together.

I always hated that play.

"Now it is your turn to join your mother and father. Aisling gave her own life to save you... all for nothing." Aneira drew her sword. "You failed, Ember. Even the prophesied one could not kill me."

I shut my eyes, feeling a burst of air hit my face as she swung the sword toward my neck. *I am sorry,* was all I could think, to all the people who still lived and to my loved ones.

A shrill scream echoed through the room. My lids burst open. Only inches from my neck, the sword fell from Aneira's hands. Her mouth opened in a frozen scream. A glowing metal point stuck out of her stomach, blood seeping into the fabric of her clothes. Aneira went limp and collapsed. Her flesh tore as the sword slid out of her body.

THIRTY-TWO

My brain grappled to understand the scene in front of me.

"Daes weren't the only ones whose bloodlines were repressed." Kennedy stood over the Queen's body, the Sword of Light in her hand. It illuminated a warm glow, filling the room with its brilliant radiance. It had come alive for Kennedy. It never had for me... because... I wasn't the one it was meant for. Ever.

By one of the Light, Darkness will take its revenge.
A bloodline that cannot be repressed will rise to power.
A descendant will take the throne.
Blood will seek to kill you.
She who possesses the Sword of Light will have the power.

Holy shit!

The prophecy was talking about two different people, not one. It never said a Dae would take the throne, but she who possesses the sword. It had been meant for Kennedy all along.

My body was released from Aneira's Demon hold on me, and I pushed myself up.

"Ember!" Kennedy's attention finally broke from Aneira. Kennedy dropped the sword at her feet and came to my side to aid me. Her arms shook as she helped get me on my feet. I swayed and almost fell again, but she gripped harder. "Are you okay?"

I nodded. "I think so."

A groan came from the body at our feet. A yelp rose from Kennedy as she jumped back. I went back to my knees and turned Aneira's face to me.

"She's still alive." I looked at Kennedy. Leave it me to state the obvious. Kennedy's face turned white, her eyes looking at me with hope. I shook my head. "Kennedy, it has to be you. It glowed for you. It's you who was prophesized, not me. You are the one meant to kill her. And as long as Aneira lives, the curse is still on me. I cannot touch the sword."

I could taste my desire for Aneira's blood. I wanted to avenge all she had done: the deaths of my friends and family, the annihilation of innocent people. I wanted to destroy her, but I now realized it wasn't my fate to kill Aneira and become Queen. It was Kennedy's.

Kennedy was not a violent person by any means. The only reason she could stab Aneira was because she was about to slice off my head. The idea of stabbing Aneira again made Kennedy look like she wanted to vomit.

"And you have to chop off her head. It's the only way to kill her."

"What?" Kennedy screeched. "I-I can't chop off her head!"

Aneira coughed, blood leaking from her mouth.

I stood. "You have to. It must be you. You were meant to be Queen." My voice sounded strong and sure with the realization I was right.

An eerie chuckle came from the body at our feet. "You both are pathetic. Even the all-powerful Dae and Druid can't kill me." Another spasm of coughs made her sentence trail off.

I grabbed Kennedy's hands, forcing her to look at me. "Kennedy, you and you alone have to fulfill the vision. Remember all she has taken from you: your human family, Ryan, and Jared. Your whole clan died because she wanted to break the spell on the sword. This sword was always meant for you to avenge your family."

Kennedy gulped.

Suddenly, Aneira rolled over and reached for her own personal sword. Kennedy's instinct took over. She seized Nuada's Sword. It burned bright at her touch. Aneira's body leaped up, and with a strangled cry she turned to me. Anger and hatred twisted her features.

Kennedy dove in front of me, swinging. With a bone chilling slash of flesh and bone, the sword cut through Aneira's neck. Blood sprayed across us as Aneira's body fell, becoming a lump on the floor. Her head flew across the room and rolled underneath a bench. Symbolic really. From below her ruling seat—where she would never reign again, the Queen's dead eyes were wide with horror, staring at us with disbelief.

In that moment, Aneira's curse on me broke. I went on my knees with a deep gasp. Magic surged into my body and dumped power through me like water from a broken dam. It was almost too much. I clung to the surface, breathing in sharply. Then the flood stopped. My magic coiled contentedly inside me. The emptiness I had never gotten used to gurgled with happiness. It was glad to be home. My chest opened, feeling the power exude through me. I felt whole again. My arms wrapped around my stomach cradling the core of my energy.

The room stood silent. Only Kennedy's heavy breathing and my own could be heard. Blood which was not mine dripped down my face.

"Holy crap." My stomach clenched as more of Aneira's blood trickled to the corners of my mouth. I would not throw up. "Are you all right?" I turned to Kennedy.

She stood frozen.

"Kennedy? Are you okay?"

She nodded. The sword clanged to the old rock floor as it fell from her hands. A cry broke from her lips.

I rushed to her, wrapping my arms around her. I held her tightly as she sobbed. "Shhhh, it's okay." There was nothing else I could say. No words would make the memory of her slicing off a woman's head go away. No matter how evil the person was, Kennedy didn't work like me. I felt nothing for Aneira's death. At least right then I was numb to it. She had to die.

"She's dead." Kennedy hiccupped in my ear. She turned her head on my shoulder, her tears soaking my shirt.

"You did it." I squeezed her tighter to my body. "That took a lot of balls, girl. I am so proud of you."

Kennedy pulled free from my arms, stepping back. Her legs buckled, and I reached out clutching her elbow in my grip, keeping her from falling. She turned her puffy, blotchy face to mine, and her soft brown eyes stared back at me with sadness and doubt. "*We* did it."

Liquid rimmed at the corners of my lids, and a small pained smile spread over my mouth. "Yeah. We did it. *Together*." Like the prophecy had always foreseen. But no one else had predicted, with the help of a Dae, it would be a Druid who would rule.

The prophecy may not have been accomplished in the way most expected, but it had been fulfilled. We were all heroes in this story.

My fate and strength were not tied to a prophecy or even to my own powers. I learned I was the same person with or without them. Who I was and what I wanted for my life came from me. I dictated it. My powers would always be a part of me, but it wasn't until I lost them did I realize they didn't define me. I loved, lived, fought, messed up, and fell on my face—a lot. But I was me, and I was proud of that.

I'm Ember Aisling Devlin Brycin... and proud of all that my name represents.

EPILOGUE

I stood on a cliff looking down on San Francisco Bay. The famous Golden Gate Bridge lay submerged deep beneath the chilly waters of the Pacific. It hadn't withstood the infiltration of magic which saturated Earth when the barrier between the worlds collapsed. Structurally not much did, not in North America anyway. I had seen for myself Europe had survived better, not counting London, of course, since it got hit twice. Overall it seemed the older the structure, the better it performed against magic.

Technology completely died. Not a lot could withstand the energy storm of Otherworld. Fae weren't completely tech un-savvy. They had their own versions of the necessary equipment. Strangely enough, only the Unseelie King and his men had these tools at their disposal. Thankfully, I was one of those people. The contraption hanging off my belt loop worked like a long-distant walkie-talkie. For my job I had to have it.

Travel was not easy anymore. Planes, cars, and trains had been abandoned and considered useless. The old "doors" to the Otherworld were mostly gone since the worlds now joined as one. Pockets of magic still survived if you knew how to find them. It took me awhile and a lot of wrong entrances, but I was beginning to learn how to get to places I needed to go. I felt bad for the unsuspecting human who walked through one and ended in another state or country. When it happened, it had to be traumatic.

The beach below, which normally swarmed with tourists and locals, stood empty. The sparkling, blue water rolled onto the sand precisely like it always had. But the world was no longer what it used to be. It had been four months since Samhain, when life and the world changed completely. Suddenly, humans could see the monsters they thought existed only in books. They could see the trolls who were their math teachers and the goblins who drove the local bus. Chaos was an understatement. Humans lost their bearings and realities, and life became a free-for-all.

Of course, a lot of Fae took advantage of the disorder, the Strighoul being some of the worst offenders. They were growing in strength and numbers. I knew it was only a matter of time before we would have to deal with them. The more time we took to get our world back on its feet, the larger and bolder the Strighoul grew. The day would come when we could no longer ignore them. Thankfully, today was not that day.

The Unseelie King and the newly appointed Seelie Queen were trying their best to restore order. You'd think a Demon would love bedlam and the extremely heightened emotions and debauchery. Man at his worst. But it had gotten way out of control. Lars favored organized chaos, which he could regulate and govern.

Kennedy had taken to her role as Queen with a strength and determination which made me feel honored to know her. It was as if she were meant to be Queen. If you believed in prophesies, she had been. I had always felt deep down I never was. Being Seelie ruler wasn't me and not something I wanted. I preferred what I did now.

She wrestled with her new title. It was not easy going from high school student to ruler of a kingdom. Kennedy also struggled privately. Jared's death changed her. She desperately mourned his loss. She never talked about it much. Besides Ryan, I was the only one she let see her true emotions. Even then, I could feel she held back.

Kennedy's transition had not been easy for the Fae either. Many of them revolted against her, saying she was not of Fae blood and should not be their Queen. With the help of Torin and Thara, she was beginning to establish a new royal court and building a ruling government.

When she sent me out to find her family, her adoptive parents and sister, I learned they all perished in the aftermath of the war—in the wrong place at the wrong time. The day I revealed the news to her had been horrible. Kennedy cried on my shoulder until one of her men needed her for something. She wiped her face, held her head up, and went back to work. "People need me. I must be strong for them," she said to me before leaving the room. None of her personal tragedy was shown to the outside world. She threw herself into her duties. She was compassionate, regal, and fair.

Many humans were unable to cope with the new world, but Kennedy did her best to provide help for both humans and Fae. She erected shelters for those who were not mentally able to handle the change. The accommodations were basically a new version of a mental hospital.

I learned from Lars about someone I knew who was now in one of the asylums. Sheriff Weiss. A man who only saw a black and white world. After the fall, when the whole world turned gray and monsters and myths were no longer bedtime stories, he fell apart. He could not handle the new reality. He and those like him were put in a place where they couldn't hurt themselves or others. It should have felt satisfying and something like justice to know Weiss was locked up in the exact place where he always wanted to place me. I actually felt bad for him. His mind was not strong enough to accept his unyielding truth had been the lie.

My gaze wandered over the isolated scenery around me. The Otherworld changed Earth's atmosphere. The air was thick and heavy with magic. The sun was setting in the distance, casting an electric purple haze which weaved and rolled with density. My skin tingled from the sensation, causing my hair to stand on end. My powers were teeming with the constant stream of energy.

I felt more content with my abilities restored, but it would be a constant struggle for me to keep them controlled and not let them take over. Daes were not supposed to exist, and many went crazy because of their excess magic. The need to let go and allow myself to fall into the power was sometimes overpowering, especially right after I got my abilities back. Aneira had heightened their need to be used, like an addict pining for the next hit. It wasn't something I would ever overcome, but I hoped I would get to the point I could handle the constant desire. I would not let them dictate me. I ruled myself.

The moment my powers had returned, so had my bond with Torin. It wasn't nearly as strong, but I could feel him again. Our connection would never fully go away. It was another thing I would live with. After the war, I learned Torin had barely made it out of the castle alive. I hoped his experiences would give him a new outlook on life. So far I had not seen a big change, although I felt the darkness beginning to ebb inside him. Even with the returned link between us, we never shared dreamscapes or talked to each other in our minds, and I knew we never would again. We no longer shared the intimacy of those types of "connections."

Torin stood faithfully by his new Queen. Once again he became the First Knight, without the negative implications attached to the title. Maybe having one aspect of his life restored gave him part of his soul back. He stood at Kennedy's side and did his job ceaselessly. Through our bond, I could feel his soul, which had once been so bright and happy, only lighten now when Kennedy entered. She had given him his place back. Some kind of peace. Torin's gratitude to her was evident, although he was all duty and little of anything else.

It would always twist my gut knowing I had a lot to do with his darkness, but I no longer blamed myself. Torin had chosen to deal with what happened as he did. He could have seen there was another destiny in store for him. Like someone told me once: sometimes you choose destiny and sometimes it chooses you. I would never stop caring about Torin. He deserved so much, if he'd only let happiness in.

Thara stood devotedly by his side. She would never give up on him either. He might never see her the way she wanted, but she remained loyal and would always be there for him. I hoped one day he would notice her as a beautiful, strong woman, not only a faithful soldier.

I pulled my leather jacket around me tighter, the wind blowing my hair around my face. The chill crept into my bones.

"Ember?" A crackled voice came from my hip. "You there?"

I unclipped my walkie-talkie and brought it to my mouth. "Hey, Cole. What's up?"

"Actually, I was only checking in. Hadn't heard from you in a while. I planned to send Cooper to track you down soon."

A soft smile came to my lips. Cole had become a lot more "parental" since the war. Losing so many members of his family in combat made him hold on tighter to the ones he still had. Funny, I had grown up till I was six with only one parent. Now I had too many to count. Cole and Lars were sometimes worse than my mother and father combined.

"Is hunting for me actually what you should be assigning your Second to do?" I teased. "Think you guys have more important things to take care of."

"He requested it, especially if you were naked."

They were still the same bad biker boys, the same Riders of Darkness, but they worked with Lars now, exporting and importing items for the King. They were insanely busy. Lars was trying to get the world back on its feet—or onto *new* feet—starting with Seattle. Since the barrier had come down, things were a lot different, especially with testing new technology and structures able to withstand both Earth and Otherworld elements. The RODs were in demand more than they could handle. Cooper was now the Second and doing an exceptional job of it.

A laugh propelled out of my chest. "Tell him if he can actually find me, I'll get naked."

"Challenge accepted!" I heard Cooper holler from the background.

"Think I'll be getting in on that bet as well, darlin'. West's voice spoke behind Cooper's. West had healed on the outside, yet I heard he still had violent nightmares. It would take time, but I hoped he would eventually be all right.

I shook my head, giggling harder. I missed them all so much. Even Gabby. After the horrific losses in our family, she and I came to an understanding. Dare I say, we even liked each other, though neither one of us would admit it out loud. She was someone who grew on you, got under your skin like a burr. Irritated like one, too. Still, I loved her. She was my sister for better or worse. I asked her once if anything happened with her and Alki, and she told me to mind my own business. Okay, it was more like "fuck off." Anyway, I got the gist.

I still didn't know for sure what was going on between them, but it seemed awfully peculiar when Gabby left on a job for Lars, Alki went with them, acting as a liaison. I also noticed when Alki disappeared, doing his Demon thing, Gabby departed on some "personal" outing. It gave me warm fuzzies they found each other in the middle of such sadness.

"We miss ya, darlin'," West spoke into the walkie-talkie. My heart ached hearing their voices. I needed to see them soon and to visit my mom and dad and my Demon family. My mouth constantly watered at the thought of Marguerite's cooking.

I will take one more assignment and head back there for a bit. I said the same thing to myself every time they called. I never did. It was difficult. The ranch felt different. Quiet. I had avoided going back for months.

Lorcan and Dax hadn't returned to the ranch to live but didn't disappear like I thought. Cooper told me Lorcan visited Cole at least twice a week. A lot of tension remained between them, but the brother-pull was stronger. My feelings for Lorcan were mixed. He fought by our side, and an odd truce formed between us. It had been a while since I wished for his death, but it didn't make us best buddies. He was another complex person who somehow worked his way into my life.

Samantha's death did not create any satisfaction. It did not bring Ian back. The only thing making me happy was I didn't have to worry about her coming after me. Ever again.

The loss of Josh was also hard to think about. At least he learned the truth before he died and knew he was loved. The sorrow of his demise was another matter I pushed deep down, locking the pain away for another day.

The losses didn't end there. We also lost Koke and Maya. I had never been close to either, but their deaths still affected us—more vacancies, less family, at the dinner table. Nic lost an eye in the war, but he assured me the whole pirate-thing worked even better for him. He would never change, and there was something comforting in that. He was in heaven in the new realm. When the world falls apart people need more ways to escape, and they don't want to be alone. Nic was booked solid with lonely, scared women and men from sundown to sunup.

Rez was even busier with Lars's new affairs, managing and keeping everything running like a well-oiled machine. Lars could never do without her or Marguerite, at least professionally.

Lars was now sole proprietor of the Sword of Nuada, the Sword of Light, like I had sworn. He told me he put it somewhere safe, where no one could find it. Although he never promised, he said I should not fear for Kennedy. He would never use it on her or to control her. I did love the man, but I've learned never to completely trust a Demon.

The walkie-talkie crackled again, bringing my attention to the present. "Mark has been working nonstop in Owen's lab. He's fascinated by the Otherworld plants and their healing properties. He wants to see if he can create a tea or medicine to help people."

"Oh, jeez, do we have another Dr. Frankenstein on our hands?"

Since the worlds were now meshed, Ryan and Mark were free. Lily and Mark settled back in Olympia on a piece of property which abutted the Dark Dweller's ranch. Mark grew to respect Cole, and they became close friends. Mom would never be totally comfortable around the Dark Dwellers, but they were becoming used to each other's presence. Mom treated them like family members you only tolerate because they're family. They probably felt the same about her fox skulk which visited from Canada frequently.

Mom and I talked on the walkie-talkie almost every other day. We would never be what we were before, but we also weren't the same people. I had been a twelve-year-old human girl when she left. Now I was a powerful Dae who could live thousands of years. We were getting to know each other anew and redefining our relationship. Aisling was my biological mother, but Lily was my true mom. I would never forget what each one sacrificed to let me live. My moms were remarkable women.

There was not one moment I doubted Aisling had come to me the day in the castle. Deep down, I somehow knew she would never come to me again, but she had been there for me when I needed her the most. I felt honored to be her daughter. She remained with me: in my personality, my looks, and even my tattoo.

Ryan and Castien also moved to a cabin on my parent's property. Ryan grew closer to Mark, and I think Ryan felt better knowing he was only a few steps away. For reasons of his own, Ryan never visited his family. He asked me to be sure they were all right, but he did not want to see them. I discovered they now lived in Texas near his father's sister. I think being back with them meant Ryan would have to be the same boy who had disappeared. He thought his father would reject him again because he was even more one of "them"—a true fairy. He also would have to acknowledge the painful truth that Ian was truly dead. Ryan never talked about him and shut me down when I brought him up. Ryan's pain remained too deep and raw when it came to his cousin. Ryan was secure in knowing his parents were safe, and he was happy in the life he chose. My parents became his parents.

My gaze drifted around the vista in front of me. Ryan had always wanted to come to San Francisco, but it was no longer the city he had imagined. I grew up not too far away, in Monterey, another place Aneira destroyed. London and New York didn't have a chance to recover before the full magic hit. With Lars's and Kennedy's help, Seattle now occupied the seat as the hub-city in the U.S.

Standing there watching the water, loneliness enfolded me. I shivered and wrapped my arms around myself. Cole spoke, bringing me out of my thoughts. "Yeah. Well, not many humans have taken the magic well. So many are dying or losing their minds. He wants to find a cure."

"He worked in forestry. He's not a doctor."

"You tell him. He's as stubborn as his daughter." Cole chuckled and then cleared his throat. "He asked if I had talked to you today. Are you going to come home soon? He misses you."

I bit down on my lip, hesitating before I replied. "Soon. I promise."

Cole sighed. I could hear the frustration in his voice. Cole, Mark, and my mom had been trying to get me back there for months. Lars even tried "the Unseelie King demands your presence." It didn't work. Each time I answered the same. *Soon. I promise.* I hadn't. "Okay. Be safe. We *all* miss you."

"You, too." I clicked off the walkie-talkie, getting my

words out fast before emotion cracked them into little pieces. This time I might actually keep my promise. Still, my job took precedence.

Aneira was gone, but she still managed to get her wish. The worlds were one and everything was in havoc. Most humans were not accepting the Fae, and many were trying to kill them. Most Fae still believed humans were beneath them and felt they should either be eradicated or used as slaves. Narrow mindedness was definitely not solely a human quality. It was interesting how many people who hadn't wanted a person to be in government because of his skin color, religion, or gender decided those things no longer mattered. Many bigoted people united with their old adversaries. The discrimination was no longer between humans but between the Human and Fae races. There was a strong *Us* versus *Them* mentality on both sides. It would take a long time for the world to find any sense of normalcy—if it ever did.

The ocean crashed against the rocks below. I took in a deep breath, feeling the magic trickle down my throat. A small popping sound came from behind.

"Fuck!" a voice exclaimed, layered with two other tiny voices.

"I told you!"

"Like *he* would listen to reason, Calvin."

I kept my focus straight ahead, a faint smile curving my lips. "Get lost again?"

A grunt entered my ear as arms encircled my waist.

"You could actually listen to the pixies, you know? They seem to understand the new door system."

"Thank you, my lady." Simmons zipped around to face me. My heart still faltered when I recalled Simmons crushed into the stone beneath Aneira's heavy foot. His nose healed but would be permanently crooked. His wings had been torn from his body and damaged beyond repair. His new mechanical wings hummed quietly behind him. The delicate, beautiful wings were goblin-made and extremely cool. He still struggled with landing, which had nothing to do with his new wings.

"He's actually more bullheaded than you, girlie." Cal flew to my shoulder.

My smile widened. "Don't I know it."

Eli snorted, his chin coming down on my other shoulder. "You are all full of shit. Those stupid things have no rhyme or reason to them."

"Because you are too ornery to see the pattern... or listen to anyone else."

Familiar hands grabbed my waist and whipped me around. Cal went sailing off, mumbling something under his breath. My boys, even though they liked each other, would never acknowledge it. We had become a strange dysfunctional family. And I loved it.

"This coming from the authority of listening and obeying others?" Eli's eyebrows arched.

I lifted my hand and traced the new scar cutting through his skin. The law of the Dark Dwellers: if one were to become Second while the Second still lived, there must be a fight for power. Cooper didn't have to kill Eli, but he had to win fair and square for the authority of a Second to be transferred. Eli fought, but I could tell he held back. He would purposely step into a hit instead of away. It had been brutal to watch.

But I could take anything after almost losing him again. Getting his ass purposely kicked was nothing compared to seeing his corpse on the castle's floor. The moment Aneira died, so had her magic, breaking all curses she put on me, including the one linked to Eli through me.

When I went to his side, after Kennedy decapitated her, I heard his heart beating. It thudded slowly and was almost nonexistent, but enough for me to pour everything I had of my life source into him. The powers Aneira stole were fully charged and ready to be let out. They gave all they could to bring Eli back.

And his response after filling him with everything I had? "What did I tell you, Brycin, about how I wanna go out?" he whispered hoarsely.

I leaned into him with a grin dancing on my lips. "Think we would be venturing into Necrophilia territory."

"You like it kinky."

"I also like them with a little more fight in 'em."

"Good thing." His lips devoured mine.

After his "death" there had been no question we would ever be separated. Where one of us went, the other followed. We sometimes had to "divide and conquer" for a job, but we tried not to go more than a couple of days without seeing each other. The Dark Dweller in me hated when my "partner" was too far away. So much togetherness was something new for me to deal with. I'd always been extremely independent, still was, but when we hit more than four days, a physical pain twitched my muscles and skin, forcing me to go find him. The connection had been quietly there for a while, but the moment he came back to life, and we looked at each other, every cell in us laid claim to the other. In Dark Dweller terms, we had officially claimed "mate" on the other. I still hated the word, my independent streak being too strong. Eli was the only one in the world who could have so much of me.

The ranch unsettled him, too. I was having a hard time going back, but Eli avoided it at all costs. One day he would have to reconcile with the empty spots Owen and Jared left. But till then, like me, he focused on the work.

We were now bounty hunters. Our mission was to keep the problems of the new world as controlled as possible, to keep human and Fae rebels from inciting a revolution.

With the world so topsy-turvy, I needed to be there for Kennedy in any way I could. It felt as if my destiny linked itself to helping the Queen and thankfully not being one. I wanted to help create our new world and be in the middle of it all. Hands on and getting dirty. The person who could sympathize and protect both humans and Fae. My fate had always been about bringing the different worlds and people together. Now the work was on a much larger scale. I was always supposed to lead and protect but *not* by being the Seelie Queen.

We were more like sheriffs in the new Wild West. We needed to gain some kind of order in a crazy world by enforcing laws. Eli and I were the ones to bring in anyone not wanting to follow these new regulations. Believe me... the irony of us being the ones to bring in rebels was not lost on either of us.

When Eli wanted to leave the RODs, Lars suggested Eli and me would be good bounty hunters, pursuing the Fae and humans who were killing each other or trying to start a revolt. We had tracked down many who were using the destruction to their advantage, both Fae and human.

Right now, Faes seemed to be our main bread and butter. We had caught over ninety outlaws in four months. Sadly, the total didn't even create a dent in how many were out there. The number was infinite. And our biggest threats, the Strighoul, were like the mafia. We knew they were there, but we couldn't get to them. They moved in large packs and used the powers of the Fae they consumed to gain more power and slaves to work for them. We would eventually go after them, but right now we hunted the smaller groups before they got out of control.

My hands dropped to Eli's jaw, his facial hair bristling under my fingertips. "So did you get the new assignment from Kennedy?" I asked.

He focused on my mouth as he nodded. "A lich."

"A what?"

He shook his head and grinned. "I forget how little you still know. A lich. It's basically a scary looking skeleton thing with the power to raise the dead."

"Like a necromancer?"

"Kind of. Unlike a necromancer, a lich is 'dead' already and can only work at night. Our new target is trying to form a little gang for himself by utilizing some of his dead buddies from the graveyard. Then he's having them attack humans." He moved closer, his attention still on my lips.

"Where?" I breathed in, leaning into him.

"Portugal."

I quickly estimated the time difference in my head. "It's several hours before their night."

"Plenty of time." He picked me up, and my legs wrapped around his waist. "And look. No one's around."

"We are here." Simmons's artificial wings buzzed near my ear.

"Do you hear anything?" Eli grinned, his lips moving against mine.

"Buzzing from a flying fan?" I smiled.

"Oh, nice." Simmons threw up his hands, which only made Eli and me chuckle. "What did Sir West call them, Cal? Nerfos?

"Nym-com-poops." Cal overlapped his arms with a huff.

I exhaled choppily, trying not to laugh. "The word is nymphos."

"And, Barbies, if you don't leave soon, you are going to see an example of what that means. And another preview of my bare ass." Eli nuzzled into my ear.

"Noooo! The trauma I had to endure last time." Cal hid his face in the crook of his elbow.

"If you guys head to Portugal first and stake out the lich, I will guarantee our tub will be filled with juniper juice." My eyes never left Eli's as I spoke.

"*Auf wiedersehen!*" Cal waved, already heading for the pocket of magic. "Come on, Simmons."

"That's German," I called out over Eli's shoulder.

"Then, *au revoir!*" Cal saluted me before disappearing through the door.

"That's..." I sighed. "French."

"I will be sure he gets to the right country, my lady." Simmons gave me a quick bow and headed after Cal.

"Thank you, Simmons."

"Let's hope this time when *we* are using the bathtub, Cal

will notice we're in it." Eli pretended to shiver. "Having three naked bodies in a bathtub will never have the same appeal to me."

"Cal didn't seem to mind."

"Neither did you." Eli grabbed my butt more firmly, shifting me closer in.

"You told me to never underestimate what six inches can do," I whispered huskily in his ear.

Eli's eyes glinted. "I think you might have to double that."

"We live in Fae-land not imaginary land."

"Shut up, Brycin." Eli moved us to a soft spot of grass.

"Why don't you make me, Dragen? You are all talk and little action."

My back was on the ground, his body between my legs in a split second. "I've missed you." His lips met mine with a heavy desire.

"Is thirty hours, twenty minutes, and forty-five seconds too long for you?"

He smirked. "Yup." His fingers unbuttoned my jeans and moved underneath my underwear, running through my wet folds.

I moaned softy as he tugged off my pants, never losing contact with me, slipping in deeper.

"I can tell you didn't miss me at all." He smiled as he made me gasp louder.

"Not really." I forced my voice to stay even. "I missed Cal and Simmons, though."

He grinned while shoving his jeans down his hips. "We'll see whose name you scream out."

He didn't give me a chance to respond before he positioned himself, plunging into me, my cry blending in with the crash of waves.

The world was in pieces, but there was nowhere else I wanted to be. I finally found my place in this crazy world. Yeah, and that included being next to one tall, cocky, pain-the-ass Dark Dweller.

Eli and I would always be complicated. Things would never be easy for us, but he was my home. He got me on a level no one else ever would. Beyond blood, beyond darkness or light we were connected. We would fight for the new world together. And we would fight for each other.

Always.

I probably should seek therapy for that.

Thank you to all my readers. Your opinion really matters to me and helps others decide if they want to purchase my book. If you enjoyed this book, please consider leaving an honest review on the site where you purchased it. Thank you.

Want to find out about my next release? Sign up on my website and keep updated on the latest news.
www.staceymariebrown.com

The Darkness series isn't over!
Read West's story next!

WEST (Darkness Series #5)

Sexy, alluring, ruthless, and oh so complicated.

West Moseley is known as the "charming" Dark Dweller. With his cheeky grin and southern drawl, he can charm anyone, especially women. And does.

But after being held prisoner and tortured by the cruel Seelie Queen, West's past comes back to haunt him. His memories of a tragic event and the truth of what happened on the Light side goes deeper than anyone realizes. Things he wants no one to know about.

Struggling with his own demons, he battles the very essence of what he is—a Dark Dweller—a terrifying beast from the Otherworld designed to hunt and kill.

When the Unseelie King sends him to Ireland to uncover a dangerous artifact, West's entire world takes a dangerous turn.

When a treasure lands in his hands, one he never suspected, nor wanted, he learns one crucial thing: you don't steal from the Demon King… not if you want to live.

Book Available Now!

Acknowledgements

I can't believe *Blood Beyond Darkness* is the end of the Darkness series! The first book, *Darkness of Light*, started as a little idea, a glimpse of characters who came to me when I was trying to sleep. They slowly melted onto the page when they wouldn't leave me alone. Little did I know those characters would change my life forever. They were leading me to where I am supposed to be. I will forever be grateful to Eli and Ember, for coming to me so loud and strong I could no longer ignore my destiny.

To my readers: You are the reason those characters came to life, live so brightly on the pages, and were able to continue telling their story. They kept me up at night so it's only fair they kept you up, too! Thank you for supporting me (or at least Eli!) so completely. Even though the series is over, Eli and Em will never be, and I hope the next series will be one you love just as much.

To my mom: These books probably would not have made it out to the public if not for you. You are my critic, sounding board, and support. I don't know what I would do without you. Thank you.

To Judi Thank you! You have made the stress of getting my books out on time so much easier.

To my Jay Aheer for your beautiful covers!

To all the bloggers who have supported me: My gratitude is for all you do and how much you help indie authors out of the pure love of reading. I bow down. You all are amazing!

To all the indie/hybrid authors out there who inspire, challenge, support, and push me to be better. I love you!

Glossary

A ghra: Gaelic for "my love."
Ar meisce: Irish for "drunk" or "intoxicated."
Bitseach: Gaelic for "bitch."
Brownies: Small, hardworking Faeries who inhabit houses and barns. They are rarely seen and would do cleaning and housework at night.
Carrogs: Massive creatures. Part human, part beast. They are hard to kill, love to fight, and will destroy anyone in front of them."
Ciach ort: Irish for "dammit" or "damn you."
Cinaed/Cionaodh: Irish meaning "born of fire."
Dae: Beings having both pure Fairy and Demon blood. Their powers and physical features represent both parentages. The offspring of Fairies and Demons are extremely powerful. They are feared and considered abominations, being killed at birth for centuries by the Seelie Queen.
Damnú air: Irish for "damn it."
Damnú ort: Irish for "damn you."
Damnú ort bean dhubh: Irish for damn you black-haired woman
Dark Dweller: Free-lance mercenaries of the Otherworld. The only group in the Otherworld that is neither under the Seelie Queen nor the Unseelie King command. They were exiled to Earth by the Queen.
Demon: A broad term for a group of powerful and usually malevolent beings. They live off human life forces, gained by sex, debauchery, corruption, greed, dreams, energy, and death. They live on earth taking on animal or human form, their shell being the best weapon to seduce or gain their prey.
Draoidh: Another term for "Druid."

Draoidhean: Plural for Draoidh.
Dreamscape: Dreamscaping is pulling someone into a dream, usually only another Fay. But because of the blood they share, Ember can bring Eli into hers. She can fully interact with the person. It feels as real as when you're awake.
Dreamwalk: Dreamwalking is the ability to put yourself in a place that is happening in real life and actual time. But you cannot be seen or interact with people while dreamwalking. You are a ghost to them.
Drochrath air: Gaelic for "Damn it" or "Damn you."
Druid: Important figures in ancient Celtic Ireland. They held positions of advisors, judges, and teachers. They can be both male and female and are magicians and seers who have the power to manipulate time, space, and matter. They are the only humans able to live in the Otherworld and can live for centuries.
Fae: A broad group of magical beings who originated in the Earth Realm and migrated to the Otherworld when human wars started to take their land. They can be both sweet and playful or scary and dangerous. All Fae possess the gifts of glamour (power of illusion), and some have the ability to shape shift.
Fairy (Fay): A selective and elite group of Fae. The noble pureblooded Fairies who stand as the ruling court known as the Seelie of Tuatha de Danann. They are of human stature and can be confused for human if it wasn't for their unnatural beauty. One weakness is iron as it is poisonous to the Fay/Fae and may kill them if there is too much in their system. Also see "Fae" above.
Feliz que esté en casa segura: Spanish for "Happy to be safe in the house."
Gabh suas ort fhéin: Gaelic slang for "Go f*ck yourself."
Glamour: Illusion cast by the Fae to camouflage, divert, or change appearance.
Gnome: Small humanlike creatures that live underground.

Blood Beyond Darkness

Gnomes consist of a number of different types: Forest Gnomes, Garden Gnomes, and House Gnomes. They are territorial and mischievous and don't particularly like humans.

Goblins: Short, ugly creatures. They can be very ill-tempered and grumpy. They are greedy and are attracted to coins and shiny objects. Will take whatever you set down.

Incubus: Male. Seduces humans, absorbing their life force through sex.

Incantation: An incantation or enchantment is a charm or spell created using words.

Kelpie: A water spirit of Scottish folklore, typically taking the form of a horse, reputed to delight in the drowning of travelers.

Lamprog: Oversized ladybug with electric wings which glow every time it starts to fly. Once a year on the full moon before Samhain, thousands gather to mate. They get violent and aggressive and can be very dangerous.

Mac an donais: Gaelic, for "damn it," literally meaning "son of the downturn"

Mo chroi: Gaelic for "my love."

Mo chuisle/Mo chuisle mo chroi: Gaelic for "my pulse."/Irish phrase of endearment meaning "pulse of my heart." Can also mean "my love" or "my darling."

Mo shiorghra: Gaelic for my "eternal love."

Ni ceart go cur le cheile: Gaelic for "There is no strength without unity."

Ninjuitsu, pankration, or bataireacht: Forms of martial arts. Bataireacht is Irish stick fighting.

Otherworld: Another realm outside of the Earth realm where the Fae inhabit.

Páiste gréine: Gaelic for "child born out of wedlock."

Pixies: These six-inched Fairies are mischievous creatures that enjoy playing practical jokes. They are fierce and loyal and have a high "allergy" to juniper juice.

Pooka/Phooka/Phouka: Irish for goblin. They are shape changers that usually take on the appearance of a goat.
Pyrokinesis: The ability to set objects or people on fire through the concentration of psychic power.
Raicleach: Irish for vixen; "easy" woman.
'S magadh fúm atá tú: Celtic for "You're kidding me."
Samhain: Celtic lore describes it as a magical interval when laws of time and space are temporarily suspended, and the thin veil between the worlds is lifted. It is generally celebrated on October 31st.
Seelie: The "Light" court of the Tuatha De Danaan meaning "blessed." This court consists of all the noble (pure) Fairies and Fae. They have powers that can be used for good or bad, but are thought of as more principled as the Unseelie. However, "light" does not necessarily mean "good."
Shefro: A type of male Fairy.
Shuriken: Traditional Japanese, concealed, hand-held weapons that are generally used for throwing.
Sidhe: Another name for the Fae folk of Tuatha De Danann.
Sin payasadas en la cocina: Spanish for "No antics in the kitchen."
Sionnach: Gaelic for "fox."
Striapach: Gaelic for "whore."
Strighoul: "Cannibal" of the Fae world. They consume the flesh of other Fae to gain their powers. Will eat humans, but prefer Fae.
Technokinesis: The ability to move an object with the power of one's thoughts.
Téigh trasna ort féin: A Gaelic swear word with the approximate meaning of "Go screw yourself."
Telekinetic: The power to move something by thinking about it without the application of physical force.
Tuatha Dé Danann (or Danaan): A race of people in Irish mythology. They are the earliest Fae/Fairies.
Unseelie: The "Dark" Fae of the Tuatha De Danaan. These are

considered the un-pure or rebels of the Otherworld and do not follow the Seelie ways. Nocturnal and have powers thought to be more immoral. They can also use their shell to seduce or gain their prey; however, "dark" does not necessarily mean "bad."

Wards: A powerful, magical spell primarily used to defend an area and is supposed to stop enemies from passing through.

Wolpertinger: A kind of squirrel with wings, antlers, tail, and fangs.

About The Author

USA TODAY Bestselling author Stacey Marie Brown is both a PNR and Contemporary Romance writer of hot cocky bad boys and sarcastic heroines who kick ass. Sexy, cheeky, and always up to no good. She also enjoys reading, exploring, binging TV shows, tacos, hiking, writing, design, and her fur baby Cooper. Loves to travel and she's been lucky enough to live and travel all over the world.

She grew up in Northern Califorinia, where she ran around on her family's farm, raising animals, riding horses, playing flashlight tag, and turning hay bales into cool forts. She volunteers helping animals and is Eco-friendly. She feels all animals, people, and environment should be treated kindly.

To learn more about Stacey or her books, visit her at:

Author website & Newsletter: www.staceymariebrown.com

Facebook Author page: www.facebook.com/SMBauthorpage

Pinterest: www.pinterest.com/s.mariebrown

Instagram: www.instagram.com/staceymariebrown/

TikTok: @authorstaceymariebrown

Amazon page: www.amazon.com/Stacey-Marie-Brown/e/B00BFWHB9U

Goodreads:
www.goodreads.com/author/show/6938728.Stacey_Marie_Brown

Her Facebook group:
www.facebook.com/groups/1648368945376239/

Bookbub: www.bookbub.com/authors/stacey-marie-brown

Made in the USA
Monee, IL
06 September 2024

1d04a366-0147-4c1c-bd19-8b074ca57749R01